MW01153732

Joyce Stewart

To Lynette,

you are a lovely wonderful woman

Joyce Stewart

The BBQ

FIREWORKS SPARK

ISBN-10: 1478176865
ISBN-13: 978-1478176862

DEDICATION

I want to dedicate this book to my five grandchildren:
Alexis Mercier, Christian Mercier, Alyssa Mercier, Brandon Stewart and Tatyana Watson.

This is also devoted to every woman and man around the globe seeking to meet Mr. and Mrs. Right.

Table of Contents

THE BBQ

ACKNOWLEDGMENTS

First and Foremost, Jesus my Savior and deliverer for creating me, the Holy Spirit for stirring up the gifts and helping me to stay on the path.

I want to humbly thank all those who were instrumental to the writing, progression and finishing of this book.

Those who prayed, prophesied and labored in love to read, proofread and gave encouraging words as well as good spirited critique(s):

Prophetess Angela, Prophetess Susan, Lisa & Lawrence Griffith, Taffy Myers, Jacita & Michael Martinez (book cover artist), April Walthour Hampton & Renee Walthour, Pastor Nicole Pena, Natasha Gee and Keysha Benedetto.

Without the support of others "my faith" could have withered away. I love you and will never forget the seeds that were sown into my life. God Bless you all!

CHAPTER 1 - THE INTRO

Monica stood in the kitchen while her mentor, Leslie, talked on the phone to Pastor Richard (Monica's Godfather). Leslie's husband, Charles was in the living room glued to the television's marathon of Law and Order: Special Victims Unit. Monica lived about fifteen minutes away from Leslie and stopped by her house to drop off her birthday gift. The perfume was her favorite, White Linen by Estee Lauder. By their conversation, it was obvious that Leslie and Richard had discussed things that God showed them about her life.

Now ending her phone call, Leslie turned toward Monica.

"Pastor Richard says that he expects to see you today, so please don't disappoint him." Though Monica felt like a kid dragging her feet, she hugged Leslie and yelled "Goodbye" to Charles and then began her trip to Pastor Richard's house.

July 4th Independence Day

Monica sat in traffic impatiently waiting to merge onto the Palisades Parkway. Monica despised any driving that was more than twenty minutes travel, but for the sake of her mentor and Godfather she agreed to go to the Barbeque. July 4th's well recognized, Grand Finale of all Barbeques of the summer, but to Monica it may well end up being just another religious function. Cars were literally at a standstill and she just took a long sigh. Even her favorite music couldn't suppress Monica's inward road rage from asserting itself into her otherwise peaceful personality. Monica swerved her car around a disrespectful man driving a Jeep Cherokee. She saw him coming on her right hand side trying to cut her off to merge onto the Palisades parkway. Monica blocked him and continued on her merry little way. She dialed Leslie.

"Hi, just wanted to let you know that I'm only a few minutes away from crossing into New Jersey, but the traffic is overwhelming." Monica wished she could just turn back.

"Well dear, sometimes when you're very close to receiving a breakthrough - you have to do things you don't always feel comfortable with. You are in an important season in your life Monica," Leslie said. Leslie felt that Monica needed to remember "the promise". She was completely aware that Leslie was gifted with wisdom, but at the moment she wasn't feeling very 'spiritual'. Monica was petite; 5' 3 with an hour glass shape. Her face was attractive with defined cheekbones brown eyes, naturally arched eyebrows and a pronounced nose resembling a Native American woman. Her long hair was worn straight or curly depending on her mood. She debated with herself on what to wear for nearly a week and even today she struggled. Knowing that church folk and strangers would be checking her from head to toe, she had to look her best. 'It's funny how men didn't have that pressure', she thought 'They could wear overalls and beat up sneakers—no one would care less.' However, women had to shine like a peacock. She had a few choices: A halter top denim jean jumpsuit, a beautiful floral ankle length sundress or Baby Phat: leggings with a cute powder blue v-neck mini dress. She decided on the jean jumpsuit since it was cool and sexy combined with 3" cork-heel denim sandals.

Monica's navigation system in her 2011 Chevrolet Malibu viewed her three minutes away. The directions were great and she was turning onto the street. The final destination is 409 Llewellyn Circle, Englewood, New Jersey and she just passed 405. Seeing the cars lined up, she hoped there wouldn't be a long walk. "Great!!! Someone's moving out of a space - perfect!" Monica thought out loud. This was her first time visiting Pastor Richard's ranch-style home. It was huge and definitely suitable for large gatherings. The small shrubs on the land swayed with the light breeze on the 85 degree day. Monica sat in front of the windshield mirror to do her last application of chocolate lip liner and peachy toned lip-gloss, then she checked her thin black eye liner and hand combed her soft waves of curled hair; now satisfied that she looked presentable enough. Monica thought if nothing else the food would be a highlight. After all, who could resist southern barbeque cooking? Coming out of the vehicle, she eyed a few dark menacing clouds that lingered above. Monica rang the doorbell and waited for an answer.

"Hi Sis, come on in, the party is in the back." Shelton smiled as he led her through the house to the sliding doors. Shelton was a very handsome guy from her church. She followed him and observed the details of the shiny waxed hardwood floors and every room that she passed had a minimalist homey feel to it. The house had a rustic with country style blend of taupe, green and reddish browns in the furnishings and décor. True to most old school black homes, a rusty-brown toned lazy boy sat in the living area along with an L-shaped taupe sectional couch. Scanning the huge yard she assessed a crowd of about 45 members of Pastor Richard's family, friends and church folk. As usual, she felt that same feeling most women must get on arrival of an event like this one. There were some who looked because someone new just walked into the room and then there were others, women and men alike sizing her up. A smile of relief arose as Monica recognized a familiar face.

"Hey Girly Girl," Monica exhaled and embraced Regina's warmth.

"Hey Monie." "Come let me show you where the food and stuff is." The ladies fellowshipped at her church and were intercessors for the pastor's wife. Her Godfather was near the grill and she went to greet him and his wife. She reviewed the surrounding area and a peculiar feeling came over her and she felt like butterflies had entered her belly.

"Hey YOU!!!" Pastor Richard reaches to embrace Monica. He was a big man; 5' 10, about 295lbs. Monica is sucked in by his bear hug and waves at his wife, Colleen. She quickly goes to embrace her as well. Colleen was maybe 5' 6" and thick, as some would call it. Still not certain of where this strange unexplained feeling was coming from, Monica just smiles and looks for Regina. She saw her speaking to a tall gentleman wearing a blue short-sleeve shirt and dark jeans. Monica stood stationary, not wanting to interrupt. Monica could determine by his persona that he was a man of class. Regina's back was slightly turned away from Monica and the tall gent seemed to want to break away from their conversation. Monica walked towards the table filled with 4th of July favorites while contemplating where she should sit. Monica could feel someone behind her. A hand slid across her shoulder.

"Monica, I want you to join me over there when you're done, okay?" Regina said. She pointed at a table that had four chairs where Shelton was seated.

"Sure, sure…I'm just going to get a few things and I'll be right there." It was plain to see that the Richard's spared no cost for this barbeque. The spread included: Richard's famous barbeque ribs, Colleen's mouthwatering potato salad, corn bread, corn on the cob, T-bone steaks, macaroni and cheese, fried chicken, baked beans, wild rice, hot dogs, hamburgers and desserts galore. Monica took a minuscule portion of Mac and cheese, corn bread, potato salad and fried chicken. Looking towards Gina's table she moved in their direction. Monica was still curious about the guy that Regina was speaking with moments ago but she wouldn't dare turn to see which way he went. She tried to keep focus and put her plate on the table and sat opposite of Shelton. Regina was engaged in a conversation with Shelton making jokes as usual. Realizing that she forgot to get a drink, she was about to get up, but before she could. She saw the shadow of someone sitting next to her on her left hand side. Wow!!!! That brother is absolutely gorgeous! Oooo we! Monica felt like the sun, moon and stars had just sat down beside her. She needed that cold drink now!!!

"Hello, my name is Shawn." The tall gent spoke.

"Hello," Monica answered trying to sound normal.

"Nice to meet you…" he waited for her name.

"Monica, she filled in."

"Monica, he repeated in a confirming tone." Shawn was about 6' 3", caramel complexion and light brown eyes that seemed to smile at her. He sported a bald head accented with a well-manicured goatee. Monica took in the details of him and felt those butterflies again. Shawn noticed that she was postured to get up.

"Leaving already? He asked." He placed his food and drink to the side, focusing directly on her. Dumbfounded for a brief second, and she then remembered her chair was pushed back.

"Oh, yes. I forgot to get my drink, so I... Shawn interrupted."

"What would you like to drink? Shawn asked." Monica was stunned again. She watched as Shawn stood up waiting patiently for her order.

"I'll have ginger ale or whatever you choose would be fine. She smiled in a gratuitous manner." Shawn searched the bucket filled with ice and started pulling out soda cans - searching for the ginger ale. Monica watched as his exposed muscles flexed each time he moved the cans around to look for the right one. Monica had a more up close view of his physique and style. He was wearing a blue jersey crew neck shirt, Selvedge straight fit jeans with a pair of black Cole Haan sandals. This brother was well put together. Shawn was on his way back to the table and Monica's appetite seemed to vanish. When he sat the soda down in front of her - his cologne danced around Monica's nose. Monica was taking it all in - observing that Shawn hadn't started eating.

"Not hungry?" Monica asked eyes focused on him.

"It's a bit warm right now, just trying to cool off. Shawn's glare was almost blinding." She wondered if he purposed to stare a hole straight through her? Shawn examined everything: her lovely face, fingers; her petite legs and long curly tresses. He appreciated her refined look; the halter denim jumpsuit featured a belt around the waist and had a boot cut bottom. To his great satisfaction, her toes were exquisitely adorned with pale pink French nails peeking out of her 3" cork sandals. Shawn was a 'feet' man among other things and boy she was working those babies. She was without a doubt attractive, but now he had to find a way to get her into a much quieter environment where he could talk to her privately.

"Would you excuse me for a moment?" Shawn asked.

"Of course," Monica responded. Monica watched as Shawn walked toward her Godfather's table, she dared to look onward as they conversed. This guy was like right off of GQ's top picks list. Shawn came back, sat down and took a sip from his drink.

"Would you mind accompanying me to the store? There are a few things that Pastor Richard needs?" Shawn was serious and looked at Monica as if to see her reaction to his inquiry. Monica was a bit hesitant as she had never met Shawn before. She looking past Shawn, caught Regina giving her thumbs up discreetly and Monica relaxed.

"I don't mind," Monica said. This guy knew Pastor Richard and Gina gave her approval.

Shawn led but he waited for her to be his equal before continuing to walk. He pressed his alarm from the keys to unlock the midnight blue colored BMW that was parked on the street in front of her vehicle. After opening the passenger side for Monica to slide in, he went to the driver's side, sat and away they went. Monica was never a big name brand girl - but she had to admit that this vehicle drove like a limo - it was supreme luxury and she loved it. On their way to Shoprite, Monica and Shawn talked briefly about the weather, the neighborhood and other trivialities. Shawn parked and exited his side quickly and went to the passenger side to assist Monica. Monica thought,' Is this guy for real? Who does this chivalry stuff anymore?' Oh well, she imagined first meeting and he was on his P's and Qs. Shawn slid his hand slightly on the small of Monica's back to encourage her to go in front of him through the automatic door first. Monica felt the warmth of his hand on her back and was thinking how gentle he was but also how assertive guy; was he was putting his hands there. Monica was baffled about this he this confidant or really arrogant? Shawn was elated and wanted to spend as much time as he could with this beautiful lady. He felt his "soul" leap inside of his being when he saw her. He sees so many pretty and gorgeous women in his business and even on his downtime but this was sooooooo different. She had a way about her that was undeniable; she was humble, yet self-assured as well. Shawn had to hold back from grabbing her hand and treating her as his date. He pointed them to the aisle of sodas/snacks.

"You like ginger ale, right?" Shawn asked.

"Yes, I do." She was starting to feel sort of comfortable with him, like she had known him for a while. Monica was impressed by his character. Shawn grabbed two bottles of Canada Dry Ginger Ale. Then he picked out other flavors and put them in the shopping cart.

"Help me pick out some snacks," Shawn said. He was acting as if they were shopping for themselves. Monica picked up the cheese puffs, white cheese popcorn, plain chips and cool ranch Doritos and put them in the cart.

"Is this enough?" she questioned Shawn.

"Did you get everything you liked?" Shawn looked into her eyes to see her response.

"Well, I tried to get some things that I felt most people would like…"

"Did you get what you wanted?" Shawn cut in. He wanted her to realize that he was interested in her at the moment. Monica's face was a little blushed and her stomach was doing somersaults. She couldn't imagine that she just met this man and he was being so sweet and attentive. Monica picked up another bag of cheese puffs as this was her favorite of the group. Shawn smiled inwardly as he enjoyed cheese puffs as well. He was watching Monica's every move. Just then he motioned for them to go towards the checkout counter. Monica walked in front of Shawn anticipating that he would be right behind her. The cashier rang up the items but she was unaware that Shawn was reaching for some mints off the rack behind him. Now Monica was standing outside in front of the exit doors waiting for Shawn. She notices someone coming up on her right hand side and turned slightly to see who it was. The sun blocked her vision as she leaned to view him.

"Hello Young Lady," he said. Monica could now see his entire frame and face. He stood at 5'11", light toned complexion and slim muscular build. Monica felt a bit awkward with this "beautiful stranger" being so close to her.

"Hi, Monica replied." Not wanting to be rude, but not too friendly either. It was like she could feel Shawn's presence coming near her.

"Do you live around here?" the stranger asked. Monica was now getting annoyed and looked beyond this guy to see if Shawn was on his way. She saw a few people coming and wasn't able to see if Shawn was behind those coming towards the exit.

"To be honest, I'm here with someone and I don't want to be rude but I have to go now." Whew, she said it. Monica was sure this would get this guy on his way.

"I don't want to take up too much of your time, but I find you very attractive and would love to get to know you perhaps on a date. Here, take my card and if you have a moment, please call me." At this point, Shawn was just a few feet away from them - and this man just stood there with his business card sticking out for Monica to take it.

"Though, I appreciate your offer, I must decline. Please have a wonderful evening." Monica looked at Shawn as spoke to him.

"Ready Honey," she asked.

"Yes," Shawn said simply. As they rode back to the party, Shawn was a bit silent almost contemplative. Monica wasn't sure how to interpret his mood change and did not disturb the silence. Once they were parked, Shawn told her to wait so that he could open her car door. Monica was relieved a bit to see that he still wanted to be attentive or maybe he was just being polite. They both walked towards the backyard and Monica stopped by the table that they had been seated at, but Shelton and Regina moved and others had taken the seats. She saw Shawn having a few words with her Pastor Richard and he even looked towards her direction as they talked. Monica looked fervently for a new seat and felt very uncomfortable - not knowing if Shawn would return or if he had spent enough time with her. Monica's eyes fell on a single seat. She quickly moved to get it before Shawn could see if she was waiting for him. After all, she did not want to be overly anxious or seem desperate for his attention. Monica was almost there and that's when she heard his voice.

"Slow down, Lady. Boy you are moving a bit fast. I just have one question," Shawn asked. Monica turned in his direction. They were inches away from the seats available.

"What's your question?" Monica was curious to find out what was on his mind.

"Did I offend you or did you want your space?" Shawn asked with such a boyish but sober tone in his voice. Monica gave him a half smile and saw that his facial expression softened.

"Of course you did not offend me, I noticed the seats we had prior were taken and I wasn't sure if you may want to greet others."

"Trust me if I wanted to be elsewhere, I would make it clear." Before they could get to the seats, the weather changed suddenly. It began to rain softly and then the sky just opened up. Shawn quickly grabbed Monica's hand and escorted her inside. They went into the sunken den. Pastor and his wife led the party down to the finished basement. Shawn motioned for Monica to sit while he went out to help the Pastor and Colleen with the organization of the food, drinks, etc. to the downstairs. The den had a fireplace, television, stereo system and comfortable seating. Shawn came back after a while with a nice jogging outfit. They both sat down on the loveseat and Shawn rested his long arms on the edge of the sofa and turned towards Monica. Monica sat with her back straight and tried to get comfortable, but that was not to be as she waited for their conversation to start.

"Why are you nervous?" Shawn inquired. He was told that he had that effect on some women, but he wanted her to be at ease.

"I look nervous to you?" Monica threw him a look of assuredness, looking perfectly into his eyes. Shawn peered into her face leaving her almost breathless.

"From what I see, you are cool on the outside but on the inward parts…" his voice just tapered off as if he was waiting for the perfect time to speak again.

"Well Prophet, tell me what else do you see?" Monica stated and they both broke out into laughter as it was like the ideal come back from an intense moment.

"I have to admit that was a great response." Shawn was drawn to her like a deer to water.

"I like you," Shawn stated, as if a question had been asked. Monica wanted to just burst from excitement. Here she had not known this man for more than a few hours and already he had her full attention and she didn't want to leave his presence.

"I like you too Shawn," Monica responded. Her face was intent. Shawn chose his words carefully. "When I say that I like you, what I mean is that I would like another opportunity to see you again, if that is something that you would consider." Monica knew that Shawn must be in his own business or the Wall Street type because he made his proposition with such flair. From his body language she could perceive that Shawn was a man used to getting what he wanted and she wondered about what he really wanted from her.

"Sure," she stated simply. Shawn reached for his cell phone.

"Here, take my phone number," Shawn said.

"Why don't you call me on my cell; that way you'll have my number and I'll have yours?"

"Even better," Shawn listened as Monica recited her number, and then saved it to his contacts.

"Do you live in New Jersey?" Shawn asked.

"No I live in Connecticut," Monica responded.

"Oh, I see."

"Do you live here in NJ?"

"Yes, but our distance is not an issue for me, what about you?" Shawn watched for her answer.

"No, not at all," Monica stated.

"Would it be ok to see you this Friday evening?" He inquired. Monica hoped that Shawn could not read her mind as she became extremely excited inwardly. She paused to ponder as if she was mentally checking her itinerary.

"That sounds like a good day, what time about?"

"I was thinking about 8:00 pm, perhaps dinner," he answered.

"Yes, that sounds like a good time," Monica answered.

"Why don't you pick a restaurant local to you, and I'll pick you up at your place," Shawn suggested.

"I can do that, no problem," Monica said. She wanted to sound interested but not over the top. Just then Regina stood in the entrance to the room. They both turned in her direction as she spoke.

"There you guys are, I've been looking for you," she stated.

"I didn't know we were missing," Shawn said sarcastically. Monica looked at Shawn and Regina's face had an "As a matter of fact" look now.

"Well, I wasn't looking for me alone. Pastor Richard asked for you and Monica. He wanted to see if you were interested in taking some food home."

"I guess the party's over," Monica said as she smiled. Shawn did not budge, but Monica sat tentatively as if she would get up at any moment. Regina stood with her hand on her hip, being sassy as usual.

"When I'm done, I'll speak to the Pastor. If you're going in his direction, please let him know," Shawn spoke and turned his attention back toward Monica. Regina didn't respond one way or the other saying ok, as she waved her hand in the air - in a "whatever" manner. Monica stared at Shawn since he was not moved in any way at what just transpired.

"As we were saying, will you be staying for the fireworks?" Shawn's eyebrow raised now.

"Actually, I had intended on being home long before the grueling traffic jams begin," Monica stated. In the rear of them she heard Pastor Richard coming through the house.

"Hey daughter, are you staying for the fireworks?" Richard was so jovial and fatherly. He was the person you never wanted to disappoint.

"Well, as I was telling Shawn, I would love to get back to Connecticut before the traffic gets too heavy," Monica said.

"Awwww, don't be a party pooper. Hang with us for a bit, plus wifey's about to spring her red velvet muffins on us." Pastor Richard looked at Monica with those hush puppy eyes. Monica could not say no.

"Alright, I'll stay for a bit." Monica wanted to see more of Shawn, but she didn't want him to know it. Richard hugged her and left them.

Fireworks

Shawn and Monica were able to go back outside after an hour or so to view the fireworks. The men worked to wipe down the chairs and the heat dried up the other surfaces. Everyone grouped together with loved ones, friends, etc. Shawn had taken Monica out of the crowd and encamped in what looked like a secluded place under a tree in the huge back yard.

"Are you okay? Comfortable?" Shawn inquired.

"Yes, thank you for the blanket; I really appreciate your hospitality." Monica asserted. Their attention quickly changed to the lit up skies. People' Oooo'ed and aaahed'ed at the 4th of July spectaculars beautiful and colorful combinations. At times Shawn would turn his attention to see Monica's reactions to the fireworks show. Forgetting momentarily that Shawn was still a stranger; in her excitement, she grabbed his arm.

"I'm so sorry, Shawn. I didn't mean to…" Monica was embarrassed.

"It's fine. I don't mind." Shawn looked down at her petite frame. Shawn seemed ten feet tall to her at that moment. Shyly, she turned her focus back to the show. Towards the finale, he wished the night would continue until dawn.

"Wow that was so amazing. I guess I never grow tired of seeing the 4th of July show." Monica's face was lit up like a little girl.

"Neither do I." Shawn looked over at Monica; there was something other than the fireworks on his mind.

"I believe we have a date on next Friday, Stamford CT at a restaurant of your choosing 8:00pm, correct." Shawn stated as if confirming a reservation.

"Correct," Monica said softly. Shawn winked - finalizing the deal.

CHAPTER 1 ½ - FRIDAY FIRST DATE

Monica was floating through the day at work and others seemed to notice her joyous behavior. Monica did not speak to Shawn after they left the barbeque, although he texted her to make sure she got home safely. They agreed to speak sometime on Friday to let her know that he was on his way to pick her up. Monica made sure that she did a thorough job of vacuuming the entire condo. She wanted the crisp fragrance of the linen freshener to be in the atmosphere. Monica also put out a fresh bouquet of green and pinkish flowers on her kitchen table. All week Monica battled with the perfect 1st date outfit to wear and it seemed that every day she changed it to something else. Finally, she managed to settle on a fig colored matte jersey dress that was knee length and so ultra-feminine. It had a double strapped one - shoulder style that was form fitting, adding a delicate touch to accentuate Monica's physique. Her zebra printed shoes with matching jewelry accessories gave a great contrast. She also carried her black and white short jacket. Monica wore her hair in lengthy wavy curls and it framed her heart shaped. She chose a memorable scent; Chanel Coco Mademoiselle. She was nervous considering the time was drawing close. Shawn said he should be picking her up about 7:30 for the 8:00 reservations she made. Monica heard her cell phone ring and she tried to wait for it to ring at least two times before answering.

Shawn works in a marketing firm that develops ideas for billboards, posters and various advertising schemes. Some of the ads that his company featured included: Audi, Geico, Liberty Mutual, Lexus, Target, JetBlue, Barnes & Nobles, etc. Shawn has been in this company since he graduated from college 17 ½ yrs. ago. He had worked in various facets of this multi-million mega dollar company. This dynasty was being run by a third generation whiz kid and things were growing in leaps and bounds for all who had come into the company. It started to become a force to be reckoned with in the last 8 years. Shawn's salary went from $55,000 to $150,000.00. Shawn had pretty much everything he wanted and life was prosperous from a financial standpoint. Shawn's GPS system reminded him that he was merely two minutes away from Monica's house. Shawn had been cruising on auto-pilot while thoughts of his past to present led him right to his destination.

"Hello," Monica answered her cell.

"Hi, I just parked in your lot and wanted to let you know that I'm here." Monica buzzed Shawn in moments later. Shawn prayed that she was ready, as one of his serious pet peeves was waiting especially when he was on a first date. He felt it was rude and presumptuous if any female thought it was cute or proper to keep a man waiting just for kicks or to test him. He would use that to rate whether there would even be another date. On the plus side Monica lived in a community of condos, similar to the coveted "Avalon Luxury Apartments".

Monica checked her makeup one more time and moisturized her hands with a travel size of the Chanel she was wearing. She was looking from head to toe to see if she was suitable, then she heard the doorbell ring. Checking the peep hole to make sure it was him, she opened her door.

"Hi, Shawn," Monica tried to appear casual and noticed that Shawn was immaculately dressed. He wore a nice silver necklace with a pendant, buttoned down periwinkle blue cotton shirt with gray slated jeans. As Shawn stepped inside the apartment he was pleasantly surprised. He took in the aroma of subtleties of fragrance not only from the condo, but Monica smelled simply beautiful. His first glimpse of Monica was stunning. Monica had flawless, but natural makeup; her outfit accented every part of her body. He wished he could view the whole apartment to see just what lies ahead. His visual from the entrance showed a kitchen to his left, the dining area right before him, the living space to his slight right and a hallway led to the remainder of her space. She had a nice little sunken den in the far right hand area beyond the immediate living space. When Monica grabbed her jacket, he couldn't help but admire her from head to toe. She looked up at Shawn as if to signal him that she was ready to go. Monica stood as a kid in front of Shawn. Shawn peered down at Monica and their eyes searched one another's for a few moments that seemed timeless.

"Ready?" She could barely get the words off her lips.

"Yea," that's all Shawn would say since his thought was how he wanted to climb into Monica's deep brown mysterious eyes. He watched as Monica went to the door, opened it and he stood there as she locked her door. Shawn had prepared his 6-cd changer to play songs randomly with a purposeful variety of songs that were specifically for their riding music. He had Fred Hammond, Brian Courtney, Marcus Cole, Cece Winans, Virtue and Yolanda Adams. Since he had met Monica only once - he was curious to hear if she recognized and enjoyed similar music. Shawn was the ultimate romantic and almost everything he did was with a desired end effect. Shawn opened the car door for Monica and then slid into the driver's side. Monica felt like she was a teenager again, going out for her first date with a guy that she truly admired and had a real attraction to. As she waited for Shawn to initiate the conversation, she felt right at home when she heard her favorite gospel artist, Fred Hammond, "More of You" played after Shawn turned the ignition.

"So, how was your day?" Shawn asked.

"It went fairly fast, and yours?" Monica asked.

"Honestly, I was looking forward to spending the evening with you," Shawn stated looking in her direction.

Monica felt flushed and she could feel a warm feeling come upon her in a good way. Shawn was very to-the-point and hoped that he was not pouring it on too thick, but the truth was that he could not get Monica out of his head since their initial meeting. This was very unusual for him and he prayed to God about this woman. He felt like the Holy Spirit was being coy, if possible - like he was being set up - for what only God knew. Still, he spoke to Monica's Godfather, Pastor

Richard to verify if she was a true Woman of God. One thing that was of utmost importance was that he didn't want to waste his time or energy with a fake, carnal minded believer or typical hypocritical church goer. As Monica contemplated on what Shawn spoke, he pulled up to the restaurant and she saw that it was fairly crowded. Monica had not visited many restaurants in the area but this one was on the port, near the water. This place was obviously French with the name "L'Escale". Shawn escorted her to the elegant entrance. The corridor was very pleasing to the eye and was stylishly romantic as a dining experience. The tables were dressed with white table cloths, white candles set in marbled stands. Sophistication permeated the atmosphere. Though it was full, the noise level was bearable. Shawn broke away, letting Monica know silently to wait until he secured the reserved seats. She watched him communicate with the hostess and was so impressed by his social demeanor and charisma. You could derive from his mannerisms that he was definitely used to fine dining and upscale experiences. Shawn came back to Monica's side and glided his hand around her waist to nudge her toward their table.

Monica felt like she was on a prom night, everything was so surreal and then it happened; déjà vu…

"Are you okay?" Shawn spoke in almost a whisper. Gathering herself quickly, Monica responded. Monica felt as if she had been in this same restaurant with Shawn like a flashback that she couldn't understand. The scene of the restaurant changed and it had an all-white atmosphere just like a real prom or dance.

"Oh, I'm fine." Monica was flustered, not knowing if Shawn could tell by her behavior that she was in a daze. Sure she had been on plenty dinner dates, but there was clearly something unique happening.

"So, have you ever dined here before?" Shawn was hoping that she had made a wise choice. He was starting to feel that he would have to carry the conversation and that he was not willing to do. Had he made a misjudgment in thinking that Monica was as interesting as he had initially supposed; or was she just not that into him and wanted a free meal and something to do on a Friday night? After all, he had done most of the talking, even when he texted her the day they met - things went well, but he had hoped to hear from her between the time of their date but she seemed illusive.

"I've never been here before and I must say that it not only has a lovely décor, but I love its warm atmosphere." Monica found it on the internet, but wouldn't share that part with him. Shawn's face softened.

"Hopefully, you'll be even more delighted by the service and the food."

"I'm sure that your company alone will suffice." Monica smiled as she looked Shawn directly in his eyes making that statement. Finally, Shawn heard something that sounded like a compliment.

"Wow, thank you. I was beginning to think that you were just not that into me." When he said that - they both laughed together heartily. They both recalled the movie entitled, "He's just not that into you". Recalling certain scenes, they conversed briefly. Just then the waitress came and stood in front of them.

"Good Evening, my name is Kelley; I'm here to serve you tonight. Would you like to order any beverages or have you made your selection for appetizer or entrée(s)?" Shawn looks at Monica while picking up his menu. "What would you like to drink?"

"I'll have another glass of water with lime for now." Monica was still nervous and wanted to make a good impression on a gentleman that appeared to be flawless. Shawn looked at the menu briefly and glanced at Monica.

"How hungry are you?" His eyes waited for Monica.

"I'm fairly famished," Monica said, with a kiddish smile.

"Please pick out an appetizer for us." Shawn wanted to put Monica to a test.

"Alright," Monica picked the menu up for the second time. "We'll have the "Sweetbread in Provencal Style" for starters."

Kelley the waitress duly noted her appetizer, "Any type of wine or drink?" Monica quickly scanned Shawn's face not sure of how to respond. To her surprise - Shawn gave her a strange but peculiar "I dare you" expression.

"I'll wait to order our beverage after our entrees have been decided," Monica stated.

"I'll put in your order for the appetizer and bring more water." Kelley dashed off. Shawn was intrigued. He had thought that Monica would have opted to say no thank you or would have thrown the ball back in his court. Instead she made a more clever decision by seeming to see what the meals would consist of - so as not to clash with our food choices. Hmmm, he thought to himself.

"So, Mr. what is your last name by the way? What are you thinking about?"

"My last name is Edwards. I was thinking of whether you are a "sipping saint" or if you are opposed to Christians drinking." Shawn was adamant to find out some real core things about this young lady before the night was over. After all, no sense in wasting time or energy on someone who clearly is not suited for you. Shawn enjoyed a cocktail once in a while, after work.

"I'm definitely not opposed to drinking. As a Christian, I believe that things can be done in moderation." Monica knew where Shawn was going and she was ready for whatever he was about to throw in her direction.

"What do you like to do in your spare time?" Shawn asked.

"I love to draw, cook and make things beautiful," Monica responded. Shawn thought, what about shopping, every woman loves that? He turned slightly as Kelley came back with their appetizer and put more water on the table.

"Are you ready to order your entrees?" Kelley stood ready to take their selections.

"You first," Shawn motioned.

"I'll have the "crusted sea bass with crab mousse," Monica said confidently.

"I'll have the roasted lamb loin napoleon. Please make sure that it is medium well," Shawn stated.

"Also, I will have the beautiful woman across from me order the drinks for us." Shawn threw the ball back in Monica's court.

"We'll have the "Pinotage" wine." Monica hoped that she had chosen the right one. She knew that the Pinotage was a red champagne and it was heavier suited for both meals. Shawn was indeed impressed and wanted to elaborate on it but wanted to just get into the mind of this absolutely irresistible "brown sugar" of a woman.

"So, how did I do?" Monica had to hold in her desire to snicker at the wine choice. She tried to look as sincere and innocent as possible. She wouldn't let Shawn off the hook that easy.

"It was definitely an interesting choice and I am very curious about you young lady". Shawn spoke in a semi serious tone.

"What would you like to know?" Monica inquired, as she took a piece of sweet bread and sipped on her lime water.

"I would like to know what your passions are and why you are single." Shawn took a small piece of the bread.

"My passions are very simple: God, family and career. I'm single because I have not met the person God has for me and I don't mind waiting." Monica spoke with such conviction and kept eye contact as she conversed; then remembered she never mentioned she was single. Shawn nodded in a manner proving he understood. Meanwhile, Kelley came over and began to setup their table with the entrees, wine and cleared away the rubbish.

"This looks delicious," Monica said. Shawn had to contain himself in regards to how she looked - he didn't want to offend or scare her off. He was enjoying her company and couldn't wait to get beyond all this first date interview talk. He wanted to get into who she really was. This surface stuff for now would have to do, as he understood that 1st dates were merely formalities more than anything. After the meal was done, they skipped dessert and Shawn was still not ready to end the date. They walked through the exit; "Come." Shawn slid his right hand into Monica's left hand and led her to the picturesque view of the port which was on the side of the restaurant. It was refreshing and cool in the area that they decided to sit and look upon the water.

"You look at home here." Monica faced him as she spoke to him gently. Shawn turned completely to look at Monica.

"I waited the whole evening for this," Shawn said with such tenderness.

"Waited for?" Monica was surprised by his comment.

"I was waiting for the young woman that I met last week at the barbeque to show up," Shawn stated. Suddenly, Monica felt an ease come to her and she smiled as her shoulders shifted.

"Wow, I didn't realize that I was being someone different." Monica almost had regret in her voice.

"No, don't misunderstand me, I just wanted you to relax, let go and enjoy yourself," Shawn said.

"There were moments where I was not sure if you were even having a good time tonight, but just now I saw a glimpse of that natural spirited woman that I met before and I looked for her all evening."

"Well, here I am." A glimmer of her womanly appeal seeped out. Shawn wanted so much to take her, hold her and just kiss those luscious lips.

"Looking absolutely gorgeous, I might add." Shawn finally said what he had been holding all night.

"Wow, thank you Shawn. You look handsome as well." Monica felt her face blush.

"So Mr. Edwards, what are your passions?" Monica threw him for a loop this time. Though Shawn had deep dimples in both cheeks but only one was exposed on his right cheek. It was so adorable and sexy in Monica's eyes and she hoped to see it frequently.

"My passions are to love my God with my whole being, live life to the fullest and share myself with my loved ones, which include my two little girls and those that love with the same intensity that I do. And thank you for your compliment." Shawn felt a little nervous momentarily. This was very foreign to him.

"That's beautiful," Monica said. For a few moments Monica and Shawn just peered into one another's eyes. Of course, Monica was the first to look away. "So, how old are your little ones?"

"My girls are twins and they are six years old. Do you have any children, Monica? Shawn inquired.

"No, not yet." Monica spoke.

"Wow, that's very unique." Shawn took a second look at Monica and was taken back that a woman in his age category was single, no kids. "Have you ever been married?"

"No, I've never been married either." Monica hoped that Shawn wouldn't think she was an alien, she realized that it was uncommon for a woman at her age to have no children, never married and single.

"What do you see?" Monica inquired. Monica sensed his prophetic gift.

"Prophetically, you mean," Shawn asked and they both smiled.

"I see a woman full of compassion, fire, love and disappointment," Shawn said. Monica was definitely not prepared for that response and was unsure of what to say next, but somehow managed to speak.

"Disappointment?" she questioned Shawn.

"Yes, I don't want to go there unless you're ready to get deep."

Shawn said it in a way that was sort of a warning. Shawn knew that if he started going beneath the surface, this date may end up being more about him ministering to her through God's eyes instead of getting to know her through his eyes.

"Hmmmm, I see." Monica didn't know whether to pursue this or to change the subject.

"I tell you what," Shawn said, "I'm very straight-forward and some people love it or despise me for it. Nevertheless, I like being honest and expect the same in return. I can see you are getting a bit chilly and I don't want you to be uncomfortable. Are you ready to go home?" Monica was far from wanting to go home and she was more than curious to find out what Shawn saw and meant about the "word of knowledge" that God showed him. She put her jacket on.

"I'm more ready to find out what lies behind your eyes," Monica said, while boring into Shawn's gaze for the third time that evening. Shawn felt something begin to stir again in him and he was not about to let Monica go home anytime soon. He felt that she had just challenged him -to what - he was soon to find out.

"Let's take a ride," Shawn said. They both jumped into the vehicle and left the restaurant. This time Shawn switched the music to something more imaginative, more ethereal. He put on a combination of classical sounds, piano landscapes, saxophone solos and melodious nature reflections. Monica felt nervous, but there was still calmness about being around Shawn. It was like being with someone that you met in another time and space. The music reminded her of what she listened to when she was being creative. Monica managed to break the silence.

"Where are we going?" She turned slight left to view his face.

"I had hoped to surprise you," Shawn stated and looked over at Monica's face - as if to assure her that his intentions were honorable. The scenery was lovely and it reminded you of a foreign place and all of its characteristics; manicured cut bushes, flower beds and lights that were placed to encircle the grounds. Monica saw the signs that said Norwalk and the neighborhood was of mini estates. Shawn appeared to be taking her to a semi-gated community with an eye appealing
lakefront landscape that was quite serene and had a true God-like quality in the atmosphere.

"I brought you here because I wanted to answer you in a more vivid manner." Shawn paused. "I'm pretty familiar with Connecticut as I spent some summers here with relatives when I was a young boy." At this point - Shawn stepped out of the vehicle, knowing that Monica would wait for him to open her car door and help her out of the car. Taking her hand he spoke again.

"What lies behind my eyes is the symbolic nature of what you see here." Shawn watched Monica as she perused the scope of the locale and seemed to mentally record the area. The locale, to her symbolized a lifestyle, a certain expected environment - but more importantly, a dimension where God would speak.

"So Prophetess," Shawn was more sober - "what do you see?" Shawn had walked Monica to a well-lit area and stood there in front of a bench looking intently into her soul. Monica's face was like a little girl who just found out that Heaven is a real place and Angels were not Fairies. Wow, Monica thought. She knew, Pastor Richard must have told him that she flowed in the Prophetic gift. Shawn patiently waited, which was a miracle in itself as he was so impatient to hear what Monica would say.

"What I see is a Man after God's own Heart - A Dreamer, Intuitive, Passionate, but more than that Vulnerable." Shawn cringed on the inside, but would not dare to look affected by Monica's words. He felt a slight lump in his throat and cleared it, before speaking again.

"You saw all of that." Shawn was certainly nothing short of shocked. He stalled, thinking of how to respond to the words that Monica stated. On one hand, he knew he was not that transparent to other people especially women. Now he considered whether Monica was truly seeing prophetically, or was she seeing right through him, because he allowed himself to be that vulnerable in the 2nd day that he has known her?!??! Either way, he was definitely not comfortable.

"Did I offend you?" Monica asked. Monica felt the shift and it was clear that Shawn was looking for a different response and she only spoke what she saw. Truly she had felt somewhat special that he allowed himself to be so vulnerable so soon after meeting each other. Shawn knew he had to gather himself and not appear so touched.

"No, I was not offended. To the contrary, I'm just taking everything in with the time that we have together." Shawn needed to take the focus off of him.

"It sounds like you're wrapping things up?" Monica tried to keep a semi smile but she did not want this night to end - even though it was inevitable.

"Only if you're bored or tired, "Shawn said.

"Can I ask you a question?" Monica disregarded the suggestion Shawn threw in.

"Of course." Shawn welcomed anything Monica wanted to know and the moonlight was perfectly cast in such a way he could see what was necessary.

"What did you ask my Godfather the day we met and why?" Monica changed positions slightly for more comfort and anticipated Shawn's response. Shawn exposed that dimple again and Monica wanted to put her arms around his neck and kiss his whole face including that dimple.

"I asked Pastor Richard who you were and if you were single," Shawn said. Shawn's eyes were absolutely the most engaging that Monica had ever known. His eyes were a light brown, but they had a depth that was at times intimidating to look at.

"Was there something he revealed that caused you to want to know me?" Monica began to see the shade in his eyes deepen. Shawn knew exactly where Monica was going.

"I won't tell you all that Pastor Richard said to me, but I will say that he let me know that you were single and he advised that I should be very careful with you and I guess you could say that's all I needed to know." Shawn was waiting for the next question that was sure to come. Monica didn't want to sound like a teenage girl who needed to be liked or validated but wanted to ask the following question without being that typical woman. Shawn saw the struggle that Monica was having and decided to intervene.

"Come here," Shawn motioned her to come closer to him. Now Shawn and Monica were seated on a sort of wrought iron bench together. Facing one another - Shawn's head was looking slightly downward toward Monica's eyes and he held her attention while speaking with her.

"I want to share something with you, because most women want to know even if they don't ask. I've been to plenty of gatherings at Pastor Richard's house and I've met dozens of women, even the day that we met. What actually drew me to you was the "light" that you emanated. That may sound strange to you but that's the truth." Shawn could tell by Monica's eyes that she was totally amazed at his disclosure.

"Thank you Shawn," she responded.

"For?" Shawn already knew the answer, but wanted to hear Monica say it.

"For being transparent, it is definitely a "lost art" with Men and Women in our times. Wouldn't you say?" Monica had such an intense and fiery look in her eyes now. That wasn't quite the answer that Shawn had expected.

"You're absolutely correct," still looking down, but across at Monica.

"I hope that we can restore this lost art," Shawn said. Being face to face with Monica, there was a sort of heat between them.

"I'm looking forward to that." Monica tilted her face as if she was positioning herself to receive something. Shawn couldn't articulate his emotions or the pull he felt, but one thing he did know was that it was happening way too fast and he was not going to allow anything to take him by surprise. He couldn't deny the seemingly intense vibe that he had with Monica. He stared at her long enough to know that she was unusual, provocative and she had such a gentleness of Spirit. He was so attracted to her and not just physically, but wait - this was just their first date. Monica watched Shawn's every move and could feel his resistance to something. He was on the cusp of expressing a side that she knew he wanted to keep hidden at least for the moment.

"What is it?" Monica inquired.

"I'm just..."Shawn paused. "Just pondering, something(s)," he answered.

"Oh." Monica would not push or elaborate.

"I see, maybe you will share them with me one day," Monica said in a childlike manner. Shawn realized that his thoughts had wondered off and needed to get Monica home. It was getting late, especially for a 1st date.

"It sounds like you are willing to see me again?" Shawn asked.

Monica smiled. "Yes," was her only response.

Shawn and Monica drove back to her condo and they were walking from the elevator to her 3rd floor apartment. Shawn waited for Monica to open her door. Monica turned to say goodnight to Shawn. His eyes were looking directly into hers.

"Thank you for a special night." Monica looked up at Shawn's face.

"I pray that this is just one of many." Shawn took Monica's right hand and placed a tender kiss from his lips on it. Monica was thoroughly undone. She waited for the release of her hand.

"Will you call me from your car, to let me know that you are safe?" Monica asked.

"Yes, I can," Shawn said.

"I will wait for your call," Monica said. Shawn was minutes from his New Jersey home. His gated community in West Hills was very elegant and it was his hideaway. He drove in a state of visual rewind. Taking every part of his 1st date with Monica and dissecting it. He decided to call Monica as he promised to let her know that he was safe. Monica closed the door and waited as she could view Shawn from her bedroom window getting into his vehicle. When he pulled off she just bounced backwards onto her bed and laid there recapping her time spent with a beautiful man from the inside out. Next she heard her phone ring...Wow he's calling me already.

"Hello," Monica answered.

"So how did it go?" Monica looked at her phone sure that it would have been Shawn on the other end. It was her mentor Leslie.

"It went really well. I'm just here waiting to hear from Shawn as he promised to call me when he arrives home."

"Well, what do you think? Is he "the one?" Leslie loved putting Monica on the spot. In other words, what did God show you?

"I'm not sure. I just know that there is an overwhelming attraction physically and he's seems like such a nice guy." Just then - Monica heard her other line beep in.

"Oh, Prophetess L - that's him. I'll call you later, ok?"

"Alright, you can call me later or tomorrow. Enjoy your night," Leslie said as she hung up.

"Hello." Monica was a little anxious to hear this man's voice again.

"Hey. I'm parking into my driveway and wanted to let you know that I'm here and safe," Shawn said.

"I'm glad you made it there safely," Monica said.

"So Ms. Monica, I hope you enjoyed your evening as much as I did."

"Yes, thoroughly." Monica was filled with excitement.

"Are you available tomorrow? I would like to see you if you're not busy." Shawn didn't want to waste any time.

"What did you have in mind?" Monica was curious as to why Shawn wanted to see her so soon; it wasn't that she didn't want to see him, but she just thought it to be odd. Shawn chuckled to himself, understanding why she asked a question rather than just say yes.

"I thought maybe I could plan something a little more interesting than just a dinner and movie." Shawn didn't want to reveal his cards just yet.

"Hmmmm, as long as you tell me how to dress - it sounds tempting," Monica said.

"Great, so I'll call you later today with the details, because as you can see its 1:38 am," Shawn stated.

"Oh yea, it is." Monica couldn't care less about the time. "So, I'll speak to you later today, ok?"

"Yes. Lady, get some rest and I'll call you." They both hung up.

CHAPTER 2 - THE DREADED FRIEND ZONE

Monica was awakened at 8:30 am by her phone vibrating. A text message that read: Please pack fine dining wear and dress casually as our first stop will be brunch. Monica was up earlier that morning - praying and fell back asleep. She wondered why Shawn texted her versus calling her? She responded to Shawn's text. What happened to my phone call? Next her phone started to ring.

"Hello," Monica said.

"Good Morning, how are you?" Shawn asked.

"I'm wonderful, and yourself?" Monica said in her squeaky morning voice.

"I just finished doing some research. I've been up since 7:00 am, but I didn't want to disturb you too early, so I decided to text you and then I would know when you would be available."

"So where will we be going?" Monica inquired.

"That, my Dear, is a surprise, but I would suggest for you to be comfortable, bring a small bag to change into evening wear." Monica thought to herself how bold this guy was to assume she was available for the entire day. However, she appreciated his confidence.

"Uh Hmmm," Monica commented.

"Do these plans work for you?" He wanted to be sure that Monica wanted to spend the day with him.

"Yes, it works," she said.

"Great, what time can you be ready?" Shawn was anticipating seeing Monica again.

"I can be ready between 10:00 and 11:00," Monica suggested.

"How about 10:30?" He needed to be precise.

"That's agreeable," Monica said.

"By the way, Monica; what is your last name?" Shawn inquired.

"It's Phillips," Monica said. Shawn planned an all-day affair with Monica for two reasons. His attraction to her physically and mentally was without a doubt; but he had to know if this was just a fluke. He had never taken such a gamble by spending date number two on an all-day venture. He hoped to find out if this was just a fleeting infatuation; or if there is authenticity to what he sensed it truly could be. That was the first thing; secondly, he had dated in the last six months three ladies all of which were all physical beauties and fairly smart, but inwardly selfish, superficial and more religious than spiritual. He spent approximately two months with each of them and the more time he spent with them the more he grew disinterested.

Monica rolled off her bed in delight. After tidying her bed she walked over to her walk in closet. The organization that she put in this space was perfect. Everything was conveniently compartmentalized. On the left side of her closet were all her accessories: shoes, belts, purses and etc. On the right, she had her dresses closest to front, skirts, blouses, tee shirts, slacks and then jeans. At the middle section were her suits, special occasion and evening wear. She wanted to look her best as she knew Shawn to be a very elegant and stylish man. She showered while her clothes rested on her bed. Her casual outfit consisted of a violet colored bandeau jumpsuit that had a sash tie belt knotted on the side of her waist. The genie styled legs was buttoned at the ankle. She chose rhinestone designed thong sandals with a 1 ½" heel. Monica didn't want to be uncomfortable and still needed a bit of height for a man of Shawn's stature. She hoped that her choice evening wear would complement his outfit, as she put on her matching rhinestone earrings and bracelets. All she needed was face powder, eyeliner and lip-gloss. Her fragrance choices: she decided to wear Lovely by Sarah Jessica Parker for the day and save Touch of Pink for the evening. Just then she heard her buzzer downstairs. Gosh, Shawn is right on time again - it was 10:30 exactly. She buzzed him in and quickly went back to her bedroom for her stuff. Shawn again, purposely showed up to see how long he would have to wait. Monica grabbed her purse and changing bag and walked through her hallway to the door. After looking in the peephole, she opened the door.

"Hi," she greeted Shawn with a pleasant smile. Shawn looked at her with those awesome light brown eyes.

"Hey you." Shawn's teeth were perfect. He stood there with a short sleeved chocolate jersey and matching slacks. He wore traditional loafers, but you could tell they were expensive. Shawn's taste was impeccable right down to his manicured nails.

"Ready?" Shawn asked. He once again wanted to see what lies beyond the corridor of the hall that they were in, but he restrained himself.

"Yes, Monica said." Shawn reached to carry her bag with her change of clothes. On their way to the city, Shawn and Monica shared mutual songs, books and movies that they enjoyed. Still, unaware of their date plans, Monica hoped that she was dressed appropriately and more so for the evening. It was about 11:15 and the temperature was a wonderful 83 degrees without any humidity. Shawn pulled up to the building's parking lot; he retrieved the ticket from the automated box and the lever rose so that they could drive through. Monica was happy that she would be going to a place that she had never been. She was tempted to open her own car door from her excitement to start this delightful date.

"Oh no, stay right there," Shawn teasingly commanded her.

"Never do that, that's my job." Shawn was serious, but playfully advised Monica. Monica waited and then they both walked to the entrance of the Museum of Modern Art. Shawn handed his tickets to the clerk in the booth as Monica stood by. She liked that they did not have to wait in line as he most likely bought them online. Walking and talking through the exhibits and the art galleries was like being with an old friend. It was getting so comfortable that soon Monica let down her guard a bit by laughing more and taking more initiative in conversing.

Shawn was having such a good time that he forgot that they did not eat yet. It was now 11:45.

"Are you hungry yet?" Shawn asked.

"Yes, I'm a bit hungry," Monica said. Shawn walked them in the direction of the directory where the map of the museum showed everything.

"So, we have three choices: Café 2, The Modern and Terrace 5 restaurant." Shawn pointed them out. Monica could derive from the three restaurants that each was a scale higher of one than the other. The café 2 was more casual and was arranged in a traditional cafeteria fashion, but definitely an elegant café. The Modern restaurant was a step higher in the menu; you would sit and they would have a waiter serve you. But, alas Terrace 5 was without a doubt the most upscale choice with fine dining. You could tell by the images given that a lunch from this superior style restaurant with its amazing views and great right-ups by food critics that it was definitely going to be the most extravagant experience. Shawn waited as Monica looked at each restaurant's model and brief description of the style and atmospheric concept. I believe I would love to try the "Café 2" restaurant. Shawn's jaw almost fell to the ground. As many times as he has taken any woman out to lunch or dinner - given a choice - they always chose the most expensive place. He was flabbergasted, but he attempted to keep a cool demeanor.

"Ok, Honey, let's go." Shawn held his arm out for Monica to grab hold of him. Gosh, the sizes of his arms were almost the size of her thighs and so defined. Monica and Shawn quickly were able to attain a seat and they ordered the foods that they desired. This restaurant reminded Monica of Panera Bread, but an upscale version. The foods were scrumptiously prepared and they had a wide variety of soups, sandwiches, desserts, specialty coffees and a slew of other selections. Shawn and Monica finally sat with their desserts as they ate until they were content. Monica and Shawn both had a cappuccino.

"So, Monica I have to ask," pausing for a second.

"What's that?" Monica looked up.

"What made you choose this restaurant versus the others?" Shawn's curiosity was driving him nuts.

"Well, I know that we have a full day- and we'll also be doing dinner later on tonight…So why not just grab something simple." Shawn was still confused even though she answered him. He felt that most women weren't practical especially when their money wasn't involved. This made him more and more intrigued with this woman. Looking at his watch, Shawn saw that it was just about 12:20.

"What's next?" Monica was almost anxious but her face looked like a kid in a candy store to Shawn. He loved that there was such a purity about her and he truly hoped that he was seeing the real her.

"How would you like to see a movie?" Shawn spoke.

"Sure," Monica said. She was a movie fanatic and waited to see their choices. Shawn and Monica headed for the enclosed parking lot and he pressed the alarm for his BMW. The sleek navy blue 2011 luxury edition was so incredible. The only thing it didn't do was drive for him. Shawn used his console to view the internet. He searched for theatres in the area which were showing the movie "Jumping the Broom". Shawn set his navigation for the Regal Cinema. Shawn was fully aware that the theater was close to the area where they would dine later. The movie was scheduled to start at 2:00 pm and they had 15 minutes to get good seating. Monica only wanted medium popcorn and caramel circles with the white powder in the middle. They were able to get seating right in the center at the last row of the front row seating. It was ideal as it wasn't too close or too far from the screening. Once seated, Shawn ran to the concession stand and brought Monica back what she desired. After that, they were on a roller coaster of laughs and were like teenagers. Monica wondered why, not once did Shawn attempt to get close to her and though his arm was on the back of her chair -he never put it directly on her shoulders. Shawn appeared to be having a good time but in a more buddy friendly way. After the movie, it was 4:00 pm and now Monica wondered where they were going next. Shawn and Monica headed for the exit and he led her to a park that was close by. The sun began to set and they found a place to sit near a fountain and steps.

"I have a place for us to dine and I know that you'll want to change outfits." Shawn appeared to be setting the conversation up for something. Monica looked at his body posture, noticed the change and became concerned and nervous.

"I have made arrangements for you to have access to a private lounge area close to the restaurant's restroom. A staff member will escort you to change your garments. If you choose not to change, then you are actually dressed well enough now to fit with the atmosphere." Shawn was sounding as if he wanted to skip this part of the date. Monica feared something she couldn't quite grasp about him.

"Wow! Shawn you look so spent. Would you prefer to skip this portion of our date?" Monica's heart was beating so fast that it hurt.

"Oh no, no. I'm fine, unless you are ready to go?" Shawn looked at Monica and she shook her head no. Shawn could tell that Monica used her discernment gift off and on and he had to be careful not to reveal too much to her. Shawn was encountering something he just couldn't put his fingers on. Monica was intelligent, attractive and an independent women. But more than the physical and mental - there was this uncanny spiritual depth and inner beauty that kept him wanting more. He decided to fall back a bit emotionally.

"Well then." He stood and waited for her hand to touch his. They had only a few blocks to walk and there it stood, the "Blue Water Grill" Restaurant-a classic restaurant and well known to NYC for its seafood, jazz and beauty. Shawn had gone to the car earlier for their change of clothes.

"I'm going to change clothes and wait for you in the lobby." He looked at Monica and she nodded. Monica was wowed on so many levels and she could hardly believe that this guy was number one, spending so much time with her after meeting so briefly. Number two, the money that he dished out was staggering. The museum and movies alone must have cost anywhere from $80 - $100 minimum. Now this restaurant would cost another $100 plus. Monica was overwhelmed and wondered what was up with this guy. Is there something desperate or wrong that he has invested so much on a woman he barely knows? She began to feel a sick feeling in her stomach. Now she was fully clothed in a head turning knee length, lacy v-neck short sleeved dress. The smoky grey dress had intricate tiny beads embedded into the sheer design and lined with a slip that gave a smooth contoured hug feature. Her earrings were three glittery stars ranging smallest to biggest. Her bracelet was delicate with light and dark shades of silver and grey tones. Monica wore her hair blown straight and the layers created a romantic hue surrounding her delicate face. Monica changed lipstick to a bolder shade of pink that was toned nicely with a brown toned liner on her lips. She made her eyes smoky charcoal and boldly highlighted to give the image every woman wants - sensual. Monica transformed herself into a whole new creature. Thankfully her silver BCBG 2 ½ heels that tied around her ankles accented her shapely, petite legs. She felt taller and more confident. Shawn sat patiently as he saw their reservation was for 6:00 pm and it was 5:50 pm. Shawn saw Monica or he believed it might be her, but she was barely recognizable.

"Wow, you look simply beautiful." Shawn's face brightened.

"Thank you," Monica said. Shawn walked Monica towards the dining area as people were being seated. Monica waited to the side while Shawn secured their seats.

"Right this way Mr. Edwards, the host stated." Shawn reached back for Monica's hand and she quickly caught up to him. The seating had a nice view, as they were close enough to hear the live music being played on the piano. A waiter came by and took their orders for drinks.

"So how do you like this place, so far?" Shawn asked.

"It's wonderful, beautiful atmosphere, tasteful music and the menu looks enticing." Monica still questioned Shawn's motive and there still seemed to be a standoffish presence. Throughout the evening Shawn was a complete gentleman and they even danced. On their way back to Monica's house she was quiet as she felt the unanswered question nagging her.

"What's on your mind?" Shawn asked.

"Just going over the day in my mind," Monica said.

"Did you have a good time?" Shawn was not sure, based on Monica's solemn demeanor.

"I enjoyed every moment and I appreciate you planning such an elaborate day for us," Monica said. Shawn felt a "but" lingering there.

"I did it, because I wanted to spend as much time with you as I could before the weekend is up." Shawn said, now parking the car in her parking lot.

"Oh, I see," Monica said.

"Let me walk you to your door." Monica still felt uneasy and prayed inwardly about what it is she was feeling. She thought to herself God if this guy is real and you approve of him, please let my cell phone ring or his. Monica opened her door and turned to Shawn not comfortable to invite him in just yet.

"I had such a supreme day and I hope that you did too," Monica said. Seeing that she was apparently nervous to let him into her apartment, Shawn moved off a bit.

"I enjoyed your company and hope that we can see each other again." Shawn felt almost saddened that the date was coming to an end. Just then Monica's cell phone rang - it was her Mentor calling her.

"Hi, Les." She was never so happy to hear her phone ring. "Ok, just hold on one minute, okay."

"Would you like to come in for a minute?" Monica asked Shawn.

Ecstatic now. "Sure!" As he stepped into the apartment he could smell the freshness and a sweet fragrance. Monica loved fresh flowers and made it a point to buy them weekly. This time she had blue hydrangeas, white carnations, white roses, spice mums and poms in a silver and black mosaic glass vase. It was placed in the center of her octagonal glass table. Her table was decorated with black and white plates with pink cloth napkins, various stemmed glasses and accessories tying the color scheme together. Monica motioned for Shawn to follow her into the living space. Shawn took in every image and tried to take photo shots in his mind. It was like she had a designer come in and decorate it. He recalled she had told him on their first date that she enjoys making things beautiful and this was the evidence. There were two seating areas. The sunken den had an L-shaped sofa set in a neutral beige color and a glass table in front of it. On the wall directly across from it was a wall mounted 26-28' flat screen television. There was one small round coffee table on the right side of the sectional. Prior to this area was a fireplace that stood from the ceiling to the floor in a limestone slate ivory tone and freckles of grey accentuated it. This was the focal point of the room and surrounding it was more casual seating, as it had wicker style seats with fabric cushions in the brown tones. There were sculptures, paintings detailing her love of butterflies, nature and she had many displays of candles. This area seemed to be for those who just stopped by for a short visit - as it focused on artwork, a beautiful bookcase and plants. Shawn was thrilled at her showcase of beauty. While Monica finished boiling water for tea or coffee, she was comforted by the voice of her mentor Leslie.

"Shawn, she yelled, would you like coffee or tea?"

"I'll have whatever you are having." Shawn replied. Monica was going to make her special coffee blend and now she was just about ready to serve it.

"Okay, Leslie I have to go now, I have Shawn waiting for me in the other room, so I'll finish filling you in later - alright Momma."

"Yes, Dear - just remember to get him out of there before 12am, ok," Leslie said.

"Alright." Leslie was so motherly but she knew she spoke from her heart. It was 10:45 and she wanted things to remain respectful. After all, this was still their 2nd date and she had only known Shawn for approximately, eight days. Wow, she thought. Carrying out her wooden serving tray, Monica brought two coffee cups filled with a blend that she made almost as good as Starbucks.

"Looks delicious," Shawn commented. The coffee was a mixture of white chocolate, unsweetened cocoa, instant coffee, evaporated milk with whipped cream on top and caramel swirls around the cream.
Shawn took one of the coffee cups and sipped.

"Whoa, this is really, really good. This lets me know that you have another talent."

Monica's face lit up. "Thank you Shawn. You are so gracious."

"No, I mean it Girl. You really make a great cup of specialty coffee."

"I must also say that your home is exquisite, inviting -just like you."

"Thanks again." Monica was feeling again like there was comfort in being with Shawn, but the essence of romance was a bit lacking. He was so good looking, charming, intelligent - yet he seemed a bit aloof.

"So, Shawn, what do you like to do in your spare time?"

"Boxing, tennis, swimming and scrabble."

"Oh, that's interesting." That's where the muscles and defined chest came from.

"So, what do you like to do - other than make things beautiful?" He asked.

"I enjoy drawing, cooking, movies, select TV shows and music. I also enjoy praying for others, sharing the Gospel and learning as well."

"I see," Shawn stated. "I saw your talent to decorate, but I haven't had the privilege of viewing your drawings."

"You did see some of my work in this living area," Monica replied. Shawn looked around wondered which framed works were hers.

"Perhaps, I can share them with you at another time." Monica sipped on her coffee with her eyes tilted up at Shawn's reaction.

"I see you're pretty well rounded. What are some of your favorite TV shows?" Shawn was confident that Monica wanted to see him again because of her last comment.

"I like HGTV, the Food Network, Law and Order, Thrillers, Comedy, and the list can go on and on….,"Monica said.

"I actually love Law and Order -SVU and Criminal Intent," Shawn added.

"Me too!!!" Monica shared. "Actually, they were having a marathon on July 4th and I recorded them. I really didn't get the chance to view them." Monica's voice almost retreated in silence. Shawn looked at Monica wishing he could say something.

"If you want, I could get going so you can watch some of your recorded programs." Shawn was like a boy just rejected on a prom invite.

"Well, in actuality I can watch them anytime unless you wanted to watch an episode before you go. I don't want to infringe on your night but you are welcome." Monica's eyes searched Shawn intently hoping that she wasn't crossing the line.

"If that was an invitation, yes," Shawn spoke. Monica stood up and motioned him to follow her over to the sectional sofa and Shawn sat on the left side near the wall (which was exposed brick). Monica grabbed the remote as she sat to his right. On the glass coffee table were dinner mints in a covered tin container. They were the type that you would buy for the holidays in assorted flavors, but butter mints were her favorite. Monica offered Shawn some and of course he reached for her favorites. Shawn struggled seated so close to Monica as she smelled so good and he wanted to be closer to her. Monica normally would be interested in this episode but Shawn was unforgettably handsome and boy did he smell magnificent.

"Come here." Shawn spoke.

"Huh?" Monica was startled that out of nowhere Shawn requested her to come near to him. Without too much thought Monica did just as Shawn asked. Shawn's arm was spread over the top of the couch and Monica's head fit just beneath his shoulder. Shawn was comfortable and put his arm over Monica's shoulder. Monica reached for another mint in nervousness-not sure what else to do. She reached instead for two instead of one and offered it to Shawn -unaware of the intimate suggestion.

"Would you like another one?" She asked Shawn.

Shawn nodded. "Give it to me."

Monica was like what in the world am I doing feeding this man with my fingers!!!!!! As Shawn's mouth opened to retrieve the mint, he kissed Monica's fingers. Next he took her hand and placed a small kiss on it. Watching Shawn as he came even closer, Monica observed him pulling her close to his chest. He leaned in and kissed her softly on her lips. His lips opened slightly and Monica felt his moist lips suck her small lips into his. Monica was thinking how long she could kiss him without breathing. Shawn came up from the kiss and kept his eyes looking into Monica's.

"Can I have some water?" Shawn asked.

"Sure." Monica was glad to get up and take a breather. She had not kissed a man in about three years and it felt like a dream. She could tell that Shawn was a good kisser. He did not rush, and he didn't overdo it. She could hear Shawn stand up and Monica looked over at the clock and noticed that it was 11:48. Monica carried the ice water to Shawn.

"Thank you," Shawn said and looked at Monica with seriousness in his eyes.

"I'm going to get ready to go, but I had a wonderful evening."

"So did I," Monica walked Shawn to the door. She reached for the door knob but Shawn grabbed her hand, looking at her intensely.

"I want to see you again, if that's okay with you."

Monica nodded as she didn't even have words to speak. Shawn peered down to Monica's 5' 3 frame (5' 5 ½ with her heels). He put his lips on top of Monica's and taking a more passionate kiss as her hand cradled his face. Shawn pulled himself up regrettably.

"I'll call you, okay?" Shawn said soberly.

"Alright," Monica responded. She opened the door and let Shawn out. For a few moments, Monica leaned with her back against the front door. Thinking about that Man, that Kiss. Whatta Man, Whatta Mighty Good Man…she thought to herself.

Shawn sat at the red light contemplating how little time he has known Monica, but she has really captured his thoughts, his energy and he wondered how he could get infatuated so soon. This couldn't be happening!!!!!

CHAPTER 3 - BACK TO THE OLE BALL AND CHAIN

Shawn studied the new advertising project and knew that they needed a fresh face to pull off this ad. The industry of sports cars was dominated by men and they wanted a GQ face that spoke elegance, charm and undeniable sexy. This was for the 2013 Cadillac Series called the Alien Edition. It was sleek, large interior, more gadgets with the promise of luxury with a sports look. Now the man that would be affiliated with this would be the new IT guy.

Just as he pondered this, His boss, Selena came into his office. Selena was about 5' 8 with a model's body: long shapely legs, light skin, long dark hair, and dark chestnut eyes and a walk that defied gravity. Selena was part Jamaican (dad) and Latino (mother). Her voice was defined by her distinctive accent.

"Good Morning, Mr. Edwards. How's our prospective "Alien Ed" guy going?" Selena inquired.

"I've looked at these portfolios over and over and I don't see any fresh faces. I want a guy that jumps out and pulls our clients in," Shawn stated.

"Sounds like you're speaking of yourself, Mr. Edwards." Selena loved to tease Shawn. Shawn became uncomfortable and thought of a way to change the attention from him.

"While your taste is complimentary, I'll leave this search for professional models." Shawn had heard about Selena's seductive tactics, as a colleague warned him 3 months ago when she was transferred to his division. His friend, Jalek advised him that she liked to collect things: men, money and material things were her objects of affection - just in that order.

"Ms. Selena. You have a call on line 2, its Mr. Levitt from Success Industries." Renee, Selena's secretary, popped her head in just in time.

"We'll finish this conversation later," Selena said as she strutted away.

Monica Prepared for Work

Monica was almost late to work when she woke up. She completed her daily devotions and read a scripture for the day: Jeremiah 1:5-10. This scripture that God led her to was the confirmation she did not want to hear. She knew God was leading her to give a word to someone in a Manager's position. She tried to convince God that he wouldn't listen to her and probably it would be better if he sent someone more spiritually mature. Still, the words were engraved in her mind: "Before I formed you in the womb I knew you; before you were born I sanctified you; I ordained you a prophet to the nations." I guess you couldn't get much clearer than that. The director Roy Clemons of Human Resources was a man in his mid-60s and you could tell by looking at him that he was ready to retire. His hair was salt n pepper and he was slim; 5' 9 1/2" weighing about 150lbs with a beer pot belly to boot. He was dealing with legal issues in regards to hiring/promoting people within the company. Recently, there had been a lot of controversy over the hiring tactics and the lack of fairness in promotions within the structure of the business. There was a petition written and signed by many employees expressing their dissatisfaction and what they felt was unmerited favoritism and a lack of integrity within management. This petition promised the Human Resource department the repercussions if reasonable or satisfactory response was not provided. First, the media would be notified and if that was not sufficient, then a class action lawsuit would be filed. The company's legal counsel advised that this was not something to be overly concerned about. Still, Roy was not comforted and felt a more menacing fear to prepare for the worse. Monica was new to the department and God had performed a miraculous wonder by promoting her from a salary of $39,000 to $60,000. Her position as quality assurance to paralegal was one of her greatest testimonies yet. The miracle actually was not only done in her eyes, but even in the history of her company. Monica had not even obtained an associate's degree and only had a paralegal certificate, which was nearly 10 yrs. prior. She had only worked in the paralegal field for 1 ½ yrs. -which made her entry level at best!!!

"Monica, can you run these documents to Roy Clemons office as he is waiting for them?" Carolyn, Monica's current supervisor was a great person to work for and she had the patience of a saint.

"Sure, Monica reached out to accept the brown interoffice folder that held the documents." Monica knew without a shadow of a doubt that God wanted to use her to speak to Roy Clemons. Her dream showed God's word of wisdom. Now, God's timing was surely coming upon Monica as she had to give Mr. Clemons what God had entrusted to her. Monica's heart beat uncontrollably and as she came closer to Roy's office, she could hear that he was on the phone. Monica stood a little distance from his doorway - visible but not intrusive. Roy waved Monica into his office, while he continued his phone conversation. Monica pointed to his desk as an inquiry as to whether she could leave the documents there. Roy nodded in agreement. Now feeling a slight relief that she would be able to leave his office without having to say a word, Monica proceeded to leave Mr. Clemons to his phone call.

"Uh, young lady," Roy called out to Monica.

"I need you to drop something off to Carolyn." Roy dismissed his phone call as he shuffled various documents on his busy desk. Roy mumbled under his breath about this insidious plot for his demise on his last few months to retirement.

"You know," Roy began to speak "I have 8 more months to retire and this whole shenanigan brewing is trying to kill me; but you know, my grandma used to always say: "The Good Lord, never put more on you that you couldn't bear." Roy had a strained smile on his face as he completed that thought.

"Hear it is!" He finally found the file that he was fervently seeking, under the massive papers scattered on his desk. Monica knew that was her queue and she had to be obedient to God.

"I see that you are a man of faith and like you, I do believe that there are no accidents in life just incidents for God to be God. I actually had a dream recently that was startling and also enlightening regarding this incident and you as well."

Roy's face went blank and he didn't know if he should stop her in her tracks or let her voice whatever her thoughts were. After all, if he was dealing with a religious fanatic, he needed to be aware of how to handle such an employee. Monica saw that Roy crossed his arms and she felt a tingle of nervousness rise up in her belly. Just then Mr. Clemons phone rang.

"I don't mean to take up your time and if I've overstepped my boundaries, I do apologize." Monica was painfully aware that this was a very fragile subject and she wanted to be obedient to God, but remain professional if that was possible.

"No my Dear, finish what you began." Roy now decided that whatever comments this young gal had - he was curious to hear it.

After Monica divulged her dream, she left no details out. Now feeling a huge weight off, but at the same time feeling concerned whether he would dismiss her out rightly…Roy pondered all that Monica said. He thought that what she shared was either pathologically diluted or insanely genius. Roy was a just man and never made decisions without a fair assessment. That was part of the reason that he was elevated to his current position five years ago. Roy was not as eloquent in speech as most of his counterparts, but his wisdom and ability to listen and reason made him the best man as the director of the "Human Resources Division." Monica felt like biting her nails, even though that was not a practice she ever partook of. She didn't know whether to wait to hear Mr. Clemons opinion or to make a quick departure. One thing was for certain, nothing from this point on would ever be the same.

"Well Ms. Phillips, I will take all what you said into consideration and I have more than enough work to sort through. Please be sure to give Carolyn the paperwork, as I need her to contact me regarding it."

"Yes, Mr. Clemons I will be sure to do just that." Monica was floored and she felt like a dog that left with his tail between his legs. The utter shame was tormenting to her and she could do nothing but pray that he doesn't share what she told him or worse get rid of her. Monica finished preparing a standard legal agreement with a new client who wrote a series of tutorials on how to train parents to discover their children's gifts at an early age. Monica worked for a book publishing company named "Readme Now" and they specialized in EBooks, teaching manuals/software and computerized games as tools for learning. Readme Now also produced their own lines of encyclopedias, history books, religious reference books, etc. Monica noticed that it was 4:20, she had not heard from Shawn and she wanted to talk to him. She thought to herself how silly it was waiting for him to make the first move - again. So she decided to call him. Anticipating Shawn's voice, Monica listened to the phone ring.

"Hello," Shawn answered with his relaxed steady tone. "Hi Shawn," it's Monica.

"I recognize your lovely voice." Monica blushed all over herself hearing his words.

"I was just thinking about you, so I thought I'd call to see how your day is going."

"My day is hectic and I wish I could see you. I have stacks and stacks of work; but I want to see you tomorrow, if you are available?"

"That sounds perfect," Monica said.

"Cool, I was thinking perhaps we could go bowling or something like that." Shawn wanted to spend as much time as possible with Monica.

"I would like that" Monica answered.

"Alright, sounds like a plan. What I'm going to do is call you later on tonight if you're up, okay?"

"Sure, no problem. I'll talk to you soon," Monica said. Shawn and Monica hung up. Monica gathered her purse, cell phone and her car keys. As she walked past Carolyn's office, she noticed that she was still working feverishly.

"Goodnight Carolyn," Monica spoke out. Carolyn just waved her hand as she was apparently preoccupied with the conference call that she was on. Her phone was on speaker and Monica knew she was not thrilled to be working long hours. Monica hit her alarm to unlock her car door and felt her cell phone vibrate.

"Hello," Monica answered.

"Who is he?" The voice demanded.

"What do you mean?" Monica was bewildered

"I repeat, who is he and when am I going to meet him?"

Monica couldn't restrain herself anymore and she just burst out in laughter.

"Ok, okay he's a nice guy that I met at a barbeque."

"Well, when were you going to tell me?" Keiki, Monica's best friend was happy to bust her chops.

"C'mon Girl, you just came back into town last night and already, you're on my case." Monica was now in her car trying to cool off her 90 degree interior.

"So, what are you about to do now?" Keiki asked.

"I'm leaving work why, you want to do something?"

"Yea, let's get something to eat. Damien is with his dad or dad's mother more than likely; so I thought we could hang for a little bit and you could tell me the low-down."

"Alright, that sounds good. I can meet you at the mall and we could do that Mexican place, Green Cactus." Monica was hooked on their fish tacos.

"I'll be leaving in a few minutes," Keiki said and then hung up. Monica met Keiki at a barbeque that one of her ex-boyfriends took her to. Heartbroken, that things didn't last, still Keiki and her survived a lasting friendship for over 10 years. Keiki was a beautiful woman with Hawaiian roots. Keiki was married to a thuggish guy and they were recently divorced. Monica always thought them to be an odd couple, not because he was African American and she Hawaiian, but because their backgrounds were so different. Keiki always dated black guys and she preferred them, mainly because they always were wowed by her physical beauty. Keiki was 5' even and her hair was long with a straight pattern, which she liked to perm periodically for waves and curls. Her hour glass shaped body broke plenty of necks and Keiki enjoyed the attention. Keiki had a seven year old son from her former husband Damien. Monica parked near the Nordstrom's entrance and figured she would browse through the store until she could locate Keiki. Monica's phone vibrated.

"Where are you, Keiki asked?"

"I'm walking through Nordstrom."

"I'm waiting for you upstairs. Do you want me to order for you?"

"Yes, get me four fish tacos and a medium drink," Monica said. She knew their fish tacos were very small and she wanted to be sure she could enjoy every bite. Monica saw Keiki putting the food in place as she was coming off of the escalator. The food court wasn't as busy as usual, probably because it was forecasted to rain.

"Hey you." Monica greeted Keiki with a smile. As the conversation, went on. Monica filled Keiki in on almost every detail, with the exception she was scared that she would fall for this guy too quick.

"Sounds like a cool guy, so does he have any kids?" Keiki asked.

"Actually, yes he has twin girls age six," Monica stated.

"Whoa, that's serious Man." Keiki eyes got wider.

"Yea, I know but we're not rushing into anything - at least I'm not. I'm not making any moves without Jesus' approval. So, I'm just enjoying my time with him and keeping my options open," Monica said.

"I see," Keiki said, but she knew Monica better than that. This she would have to see. A man with all that going for him was a catch for any woman. After all, she was still looking for her Prince Charming. Monica and Keiki watched how the sky turned dark within the twenty minutes that they sat staring out the huge windows of the second floor in the mall.

"Girl, looks like we better get outta here before it starts pouring," Monica warned. Monica and Keiki took their garbage to the trash area and quickly went for the parking lot. They hugged on their way out and made a dash for their prospective cars. Monica was almost to her numbered parking spot and then the heaven released itself like a river. It was raining so much that in just the two minutes that it took for her to get to her building's entrance, she was drenched. Monica was soaking wet and as she entered her condo, she took off her shoes and stripped down to her undies to keep from tracking water everywhere. Monica headed to her bedroom and took a quick shower to get rid of her gritty feeling. Monica put on some worship music, as she wanted to spend some quality time with her Heavenly Father tonight. After taking a quick shower, she wrapped her hair and put a scarf around it. If it didn't turn out well tomorrow, she would just wear a ponytail. Monica had a youthful appearance for a 40+ woman and she kept herself in shape by running. Shawn never asked her age and she didn't ask his as she liked keeping that a secret. Monica wore her black slip dress that she lounged in when she was alone. Monica began to sing love songs to Jesus and praise him -then she prayed for her friends, family and co-workers. She made a special prayer that God would continue to reveal Shawn's heart and intentions. Before long it was 8:30. Monica decided to call her mentor, Leslie.

"Oh, you remembered me," Leslie playfully teased. Leslie was a stern, old fashioned Jamaican Woman. She gave you the truth whether you wanted to hear it or not. Leslie had a ministry to women of all ages and she had a gift to build, groom and train others for intercessory prayer, marriage and career. Monica appreciated Leslie's advice and her deep caring heart beneath all her tough exterior. Leslie only recently got married (six months ago) and Monica tortured her about how she would finally have to submit to someone other than the "Holy Spirit's" authority.

"Of course Les, I wanted to check up on you and see how your hubby is doing," Monica said.

"Oh, Charles is in the garage organizing his precious tools." They both snickered as her husband was like "Tim the Tool Man".

"So my Dear, how is everything with your new position and this guy, whatcha say his name?" Leslie could see what God was up to as clear as day.

"Well, I followed the "Holy Spirit" today and told our director what God showed me."

"What did he say?" Leslie was anxious to hear.

"He actually didn't say anything, seems like he disregarded it." Monica said.

"Well don't feel anyways about it- just watch God, you hear what I say. Before it's all said and done God is going to move. Remember I told you that," Leslie stated with confidence.

"So what's going on with this guy you're seeing? God is showing me something," Leslie said.

"We went out again and I had a great time. We spoke today and I'll see him tomorrow, hopefully."

"I see that this young man is serious you know, he wants a wife. Be careful with him, don't take him lightly. He's very focused."

"So, is God showing you if he is the one.

"God wants you to use your gift and spirit of discernment. In time he will let you know this man's role and you will see for yourself." Just know that he has some scars concerning women in relationships and he will not play games or allow games to be played." Leslie cautioned her. I can tell you that God is giving you a choice but be careful that you don't operate in your flesh concerning the choices, okay?"

Monica heard a beep with a second call coming through. One second, Prophetess. Monica could see that it was Shawn on the other line.

"Prophetess, could I call you tomorrow that's him?"

"Sure, sure Dear. Call me later and don't forget what I told you." Leslie hung up and Monica clicked over.

"Hello, she answered."

"Hey, I have a question for you?" Shawn asked.

"Okay." Monica's guard went up.

"Would it be too late for me to see you tonight?" Shawn asked. Monica drew a blank as she did not expect that type of question. She looked at her clock in the living room and it read 9:06 pm.

"Depends on what time, you could be here." Monica thought about not being overly anxious or the appearance of it. Just then Monica's doorbell rang.

"Could you hold on Shawn?" Monica walked to her door and looked out the peephole to see one of the maintenance guys named Joe standing there. She was like 'Why is he here this late? I didn't request for anything to be looked at recently'. Monica put her robe on and opened the door slowly.

"Hey Ms. Phillips, I'm sorry to bother you so late, but I was asked to deliver these to your door." To Monica's astonishment Joe was holding a dozen lavender roses.

"Who gave you these?" Monica was totally shocked. Joe stood there smiling and said, "I don't know, but he's a good tipper."

"Wow, thanks for the message Joe." Joe said goodnight and left. Monica was amazed and knew this was a setup. "Mr. Edwards, where are you?" Monica asked in an authoritative yet sweet voice.

"I'm on my way up to see you," Shawn said in a tone that nearly shook her.

"Let me go get decent," Monica said casually. Monica hung up and knew that she only had minutes to do her hair and find something suitable to wear. That guy is soooo sneaky she thought - but in a good way. Monica felt like a teenager again and she couldn't help wanting to see him more and more. Monica pulled her hair back into a ponytail and quickly grabbed a maxi tee shirt dress. Coincidently, it was the same color tone as the roses. She had to hurry, as she heard her doorbell ring again, grabbing the roses as they were sprawled across the table in haste. Monica was glad she had just showered.

"I'll be right there," she called out. Monica took one of her glass vases and put the roses in it and then went to open the door. Monica opened the door and there he was - just as fine as Monica recalled.
Shawn reached down and put a kiss on Monica's cheek. Monica blushed and walked towards the table and started to run water to put in the vase for the roses.

"These are so pretty, thank you," Monica said

"Not prettier than you." Shawn was definitely a captivating man. Monica reached up to embrace Shawn to thank him properly for the flowers.

"Please sit," she motioned for Shawn to get comfortable.

"Do you mind if we sit on the sofa?" Shawn wanted to make sure he could stretch his long legs.

"Of course."

"I wanted to come over, even though I asked to go out tomorrow, for a reason." Shawn cleared his voice. Shawn could barely concentrate smelling Monica's sweet scent. Monica sat up waiting to hear what Shawn had to say.

"I really like you. I enjoy spending time with you and would like to see you exclusively." Shawn waited, watching Monica's reaction. Monica was speechless and truly didn't know what to say.

"I'm not asking you to be my woman, as I think that it may be too soon for that type of decision to be made, but I'm asking for the opportunity to see you one-on-one." Shawn hoped he wasn't pushing Monica away from him.

"So let me see if I understand what you're saying. You want to date me one-on-one without a true commitment?" Monica paused, as if thinking about his proposal. Monica was like is he serious. Shawn wanted to ask her if she had been to law school, but didn't think this was the right time to make jokes. Shawn felt frustrated as that was not what he meant.

"Look, to be honest with you, I don't want our distance or work schedules to hinder me being able to see you. It may sound selfish and maybe it is selfish, but I don't want to share your attention with anyone else. If it makes you to understand how serious I am, then I'm willing to ask you to be my lady. I just didn't want you to feel that I'm moving too fast." Shawn didn't know how else to convey to Monica that he was deeply infatuated with her and he just wanted to be in her presence. Monica heard what he was saying but she was scared and felt like he was moving very fast.

"I'll tell you what, let's just pray about it," Monica said so naturally. It was the first thing that came to mind. Shawn was so undone, that all he could do was agree with Monica. Monica stood up and slid her hands into Shawn's until he stood up to join her. Monica said a simple prayer:

"God here we are bringing you our hearts, minds and intentions. We come humbly before your presence and ask for you to lead and direct our paths in the newness of our relationship. Shawn and I need your guidance, wisdom and understanding. We need your knowledge and protection. We ask that you would be in the midst of this friendship, and that you would be the head of this relationship that we are embarking upon. So, Holy Spirit, we ask you to show us the way we should go and make everything plain. We pray that you would remove all baggage from past relationships, hurts and memories that would be stumbling blocks to our future outcome. And Lord, we pray for your counsel in every decision we make, in Jesus name we pray, Amen."

Shawn was more than impressed and words would not do justice to express what was going on in his heart and mind. Monica went to let go of his hands and Shawn squeezed her hand, letting her know, that he was not finished with her.

"Father God, you are our refuge and the center of our worlds. We Bless your name and we thank you for the Honor to come boldly to the Throne of your Grace. We ask for your blessings to be upon our lives independently, as well as together. We know that many are the plans of Man, but it is only your plans that shall stand. So we request that this relationship be governed and watched over by your Angels. We ask for you to bless our comings and goings. We ask that nothing breaks the three braided cord that you fashion between us and you. We thank you that you give us sensitivity towards one another and create balance in each other's life to build a foundation that is firm and rooted and grounded in "Our Lord, Jesus the Christ". Father we will promise to give you the lead role in this relationship in Jesus Mighty name we pray, Amen." Shawn took both of Monica's hands and kissed them.

"Baby, I have to get up early tomorrow - I have a lot of things on my plate for the next 2 to 3 weeks but I will see you tomorrow, okay?" Shawn said.

"Of course, honey." Monica could see that Shawn's eyes grew a deeper shade of brown, but there was a golden hue surrounding his light colored eyes. Monica walked Shawn to the door and they hugged for a moment and Shawn kissed Monica and left. Shawn was so emotionally turned on and he wished he could express what he felt, but he knew it wasn't the right time. It was like wow, this woman keeps surprising him. Shawn dated women that were beautiful, highly intelligent, gold diggers, ministers - you name it and he could tell it all; but somehow Monica was like a precious gem and he wondered why she didn't have anyone. The fact that she wanted to pray about the future of their relationship was mindboggling. I mean Shawn was used to other women praying, but the content of her prayer was what blew him away. Typically, Shawn would initiate prayer with a woman and she would silently pray or not pray at all and say amen at end. Or even worse, some women would compete with him during prayer - instant turn-off for him. Shawn knew that he didn't want to get in the habit of hanging in the house too much as the physical heat between them would get very intense. Shawn also saw from a prophetic standpoint that Monica was a firecracker and he knew from past experience if you play with fire you get burnt. Monica lay in her bed and thought about Shawn until she felt drowsy. She wondered why he rushed out of her apartment. Monica felt confident that God wanted her to use wisdom and follow the leading of the "Holy Spirit" and everything would go well with her.

CHAPTER 4 - BOWLING NIGHT/FRIGHT NIGHT

Monica made sure that she pulled out an additional outfit for bowling as she decided her work wear. The traffic was exceptionally challenging today on her commute; so Monica did all she could to avoid road rage. Every lane that she changed to had a different pest who would drive ultra slow or ride their brakes. She managed to put on her favorite gospel singer, Fred Hammond and praise her way until she reached work. Actually, her 25 minutes turned into 40 minutes and she saw that Norwalk's traffic wasn't as congested as Stamford's today. Monica found a great little parking spot not too far from her supervisor Carolyn's 2011 red Maxima. Monica strolled, still singing "more of you," giving her greetings of good morning as she passed by co-workers. She stopped by to converse with Sabrina, the receptionist and they discussed the story of the month (co-workers potential lawsuit).

"Actually, coming from that department myself, it gives me certain sensitivity to their concerns, but my mindset is always by "prayer and supplication that I carry my concerns to my Savior and Lord, Jesus." Monica made no bones about her faith and confessions.

"I hear you Sweetie," Sabrina shook her head as she answered her phones. Hanging up from the call, Sabrina spoke, "I wish I had that type of conviction that you convey," Sabrina said with a tender look.

"It's all so simple, my dear. I know that when you make the choice to just surrender, you will see how very easy it is to choose obedience rather than sacrifice." Monica knew that it was only a matter of time before God would grip Sabrina's heart. Knowing that God is married to the backslider - Monica just continued to drop seeds of love, certain that, in time that God would reap the harvest. Monica sat down at her desk and pulled up her software applications. Brrrrrrgggg...Her desk phone rang so loud that Monica jumped.

"Hello," Monica answered.

"Hi," Sabrina whispered. "Carolyn and Mr. Clemons are waiting for you in the conference room."

"Really," Monica said. Monica hung up with Sabrina and she could tell that Sabrina was having a busy day on the switchboard, so she quickly let her go. Monica immediately tried to figure out why her supervisor and the director were waiting for her. Unless, she thought, Mr. Clemons was upset by what she said and he brought it to the attention of Carolyn. Monica took her pen and pad to the bathroom and had a conference with the Holy Spirit prior to going into this unscheduled meeting. Nervously, Monica turned the door knob of the quiet filled room. Monica slowly opened the door and Carolyn was facing her near the windows and the Director, Clemons, was at the head of the rectangular table facing her.

"Please come in and close the door." Carolyn said. Monica noticed a folder with small papers peeking out. She wondered what was on those papers. Wow, did what she say warrant a write-up. Surely, a verbal talk should have been sufficient. Monica sat down and watched as Roy Clemons opened the folder. Taking one page out, he passed one to Carolyn and then one to Monica. Monica was afraid to look at the document in front of her, but she reluctantly looked down…Interrupted by Mr. Clemons, "What you have in front of you are some of the things that were discussed during our conversation that your supervisor, Carolyn was not privy to."

Monica felt her stomach twisting and turning from fear. Monica glanced at Carolyn as Mr. Clemons spoke her name. She saw that Carolyn's face was very stern and borderline impatience was lingering.

"Carolyn you've heard my thoughts on what's written here and I believe in documenting things as you already know." Carolyn answered "yes," in agreement with a small voice.

"I'll now let Carolyn explain what is about to occur." Roy crossed his hands as if to give her, Carolyn, the floor.

"Basically, Monica - The conversation that propelled this document into action - which by the way, I was very surprised that you had the boldness to speak so freely - but nevertheless…" As Monica listened to Carolyn, she wished she could just evaporate into the air. She thought was this was the cross that she would have to bear for the word that she obediently relayed. Carolyn continued saying…"Mr. Clemons felt that it was in the best interest of the company and this department…"

"Oh my God, they are about to fire ME!!!!" Monica was fit to be tied.

"We both agreed that this is the best proposal for the employees, as well as the managing staff. While your approach was a bit unorthodox in presentation, Roy understands your inexperience to the usual format and structure to a "Human Resource/Legal" environment."

"Also, because of the "sensitive nature" of your introduction to the idea and concept that developed this proposal, we, Roy and I, would prefer you to use discretion regarding this new procedure." Monica couldn't believe her ears! Could it possibly be that they agreed on the plan that God had allowed her to share with them?

"So, Monica, Roy and I would like to include you in the "roll out" meetings that will be actually set up for today at 1:00 - 2:00."

"Do you have any questions, so far?" Monica's brain was filled with question marks, but she was more relieved of the stress that she carried into the conference room than anything.

"No, I am just elated that you have looked beyond the methodology of how I presented the concept and are open-minded enough to consider the idea." Monica had confidence in her voice again.

Roy spoke again, "Every employee will have a package that includes instructions and reading materials that will guide them accordingly. So Ladies, I have some other things to attend to and will be meeting you here at 1:00 pm sharply." Roy advised. Carolyn stood up and Monica followed. Monica walked back to her desk with the document in her hand. Carolyn told her that the packets would need to be prepared for 30 employees and three supervisors. The information was on a template that was already saved to the main drive (F), ready to be downloaded. Monica was truly amazed how these things transpired overnight. Monica looked at God's miraculous hands and couldn't wait to share this news with her mentor and best friend. Monica had a timeline of about three hours to get things ready.

Shawn browsed through his emails as he turned off his pop up feature. He had wanted to catch up on a few ads that he had been working on. His company "Make Me Over" just transitioned from doing just billboards and posters to media, which included television and internet commercials. This company specializes in giving his clients a fresh face to their perspective industries. Recently, they celebrated recognition that benefited a client, named "Empire" that manufactures tires. The advertisement-commercial featured an animated tire race. At the starting line they had a tire named called satire, one named retire and the star of tires was called "empire". As they began the race; satire had patches and a headband wrapped around it and rolled out making wise cracks. While "retire" looked worn and you could see the steel coming through the ridges showing its age, it wobbled along the stretch of the race; but "empire" had a crown upon its head and rolled straight into victory. As a robe was placed around his ribbed shoulders; someone from the stand shouted: "Long lives the ring." Then the crowd roared in agreement. Shawn loved his job, with the exception of his extended hours and inappropriate supervisor. He was just promoted as the top "Advertising Manager" and given the assignment of handling the new range of clients for media: internet and television. Shawn had two clients that he was looking to market with. One was a credit repair company named "Born Again". The other company is named "Men's N Things," which is a new retailer that meets the needs of men who like gadgets and non-traditional items. Shawn already wrote his proposal for the Born Again commercial and today he would do his presentation. Once Shawn finished editing the information that he would be printing, he scrolled through his unread emails. There he found the one that his friend Jalek sent him. Jalek wanted to have lunch with him at their favorite restaurant, a local sports bar that was about 8 minutes away from their offices. Shawn replied to his email and told him that at 1:30 he would be free for lunch. It was now 1:05 and Shawn headed to his go-to-team. Shawn's new position gave him a raise in salary (from $150,000.00 to $175,000.00). Shawn also had the responsibility of managing two interns and two veterans in the business. His staff consisted of Ralph a 50 year old that was average at best, but not a self-starter. Ricky was an overly aggressive Italian, whose "know it all" approach turned many of his coworkers off. Then there is 22 yr. old Malcolm, an intern almost complete with his 6 month apprenticeship. Lastly, was Travis 23 years old and a bit withdrawn, strong work ethic but needed more coaching than the others. Yep, this was Shawn's "dream team" as he described them to Jalek. Jalek had taken Shawn under his wing when he started with the company some 10 years or so ago. He's been his constant confidant and mentor, but more importantly his prayer partner. Shawn gave each member of his staff the vision and they took a portion to bring everything into complete fruition by the end of the day. Jalek sat on the bar stool watching the news of upcoming games. He spoke to Jake, the bartender, as he was waiting for Shawn.

"So, Jalek, where's your buddy?" Jake poured Jalek's seltzer water with lime. As he began to speak, Shawn walked up and gave him the pound (fist to fist). Jalek got up and they sat at a table so that they could talk privately.

"So, what's up with you man?" Jalek was so pleased with Shawn's progress over the years. He watched him flourish and become one of the elite men of the business. He used to wonder what his secret to success was. One day during one of their lunches at the sports bar, Shawn revealed that he was a man of God and from that point on, Jalek was even more perplexed with him. Jalek came from a Baptist background and never pursued an intimate walk with God, until he attended a revival service with Shawn. That's when he was introduced to the third part of the trinity. That night Jalek was filled with the Holy Spirit and spoke with tongues. Ever since then, the two of them became Covenant Brothers like David and Nathan.

"Man, things are going great. We miss you on the 3rd floor, but I'm so blessed that you decided to accept the partnership." Shawn said with such vibrancy in his voice as well as on his face.

"Ah man, that's a blessing to hear; but for real, you look different your face is just shining…like a glow," then Jalek stopped.

"Wait a minute, are you seeing anybody?" Jalek flowed in the prophetic and he started to focus in at that moment.

"C'mon dude, don't give me that prophetic eye. Yea, I'm seeing someone, but it's yet in its very early stages." Shawn tried to downplay the way he felt.

"Well, I don't know I'm sensing something more than that. Come clean - you know you can trust me." Jalek was far from slow.

"Ok, alright. I met this "Beautiful Sista" and we've been dating for about …" just then Shawn realized he's only known Monica for a mere nine days…" We met on the 4th of July…" Shawn stated.

"Hold on, not even two weeks and she's made that type of impression on you? Wow!" Jalek was sharp and he was a bit concerned about what he was sensing.

"Look Man, I'm digging her true," Shawn was reaching for the right words, "but I have enough experience to know that things are a bit soon and I'm trying to just let the Holy Spirit guide me." Jalek listened and knew what he was hearing and decided to just "be easy".

"I hear what you're saying bro, but I also know you and I'll be praying for you, you've had some major disappointments over the last year or so. Just looking out for your best interest; But hey, you're no slouch and your prophetic gift is usually on point," Jalek said.

"I know you want the best for me and so do I." Shawn and Jalek chuckled a bit on that comment.

Jalek and Shawn discussed some of the new projects that were being headed up and they finished their lunch. On their way to the inside of the office building, the automatic doors opened.

"Alright Man, I'll check on you later on this week," Jalek stated.

"Yea, I'mma check with you later." Shawn and Jalek did their usual brotherly upward hand and arm high five. Shawn walked through the office and saw that his team was preoccupied on their perspective picks and he sat down to check his emails and voice messages. Shawn saw that a document was forwarded by Ricky, Travis and Malcolm. They each gave a draft of their creative skit for a commercial concerning "credit repair" issues. Shawn also found an email that Ralph sent regarding him leaving early and taking some sick time. The thing that bothered Shawn about Ralph is that number one, he never once made any mention that he wasn't feeling well; number two he didn't even start on his assignment given prior to leaving work. Shawn viewed the time of the email sent-which was ten minutes prior to him getting back from lunch. This, in his estimation, would have allowed Ralph at least 45 minutes to gather some ideas by which to start working on a skit. Shawn knew that something had to be done and he felt it unfair that his teammates had to carry the weight of a so-called veteran in his field. Shawn looked at his watch and figured he'd leave early today. He'd accomplished what he needed to and now wanted to prepare for his evening with Monica. There were certain advantages to working a salary paid position versus hourly and this was one of them. He could leave early, but then when the crunch was on for deadlines, he had to sacrifice fun or meeting up with friends/family. Shawn's weekend for spending time with his girls was coming up and he wanted to spend quality time with them as they were always first in his life - outside of God. Shawn had not talked much to Monica about his twin girls Sharde and Shantell. They just turned six on June 26 and he joined their mother who took them to a neighborhood splish splash park and they thoroughly enjoyed it. Their mom, Lydia, was physically beautiful and intellectually enjoyable, but she lacked a certain emotional stimuli that Shawn desired. She was adventurous and career driven. Their relationship suffered from a lack of quality time and cultural differences. When Shawn gave his life fully to God, all hell broke loose. Lydia was raised in a catholic environment and she was vehemently opposed to the charismatic-prophetic flow that Shawn wanted to expose her and the twins to. This, of course, caused conflict and eventually Shawn knew that this would be a deal-breaker for him. He maintained a cordial and cool relationship with Lydia and usually did not have any drama with her concerning his girls. Lydia's only concern was that her girls would not be exposed to any females that he was not serious about. Last year, Lydia married a doctor, which made sense, since the two began working together just prior to their separation a year ago. Lydia was a pediatrician and her new husband Rick was an ear, nose and throat doctor. They started their own practice together and seemed to be very content with one another. Monica reached her parking lot and grabbing her purse, rushed out of her vehicle. The FedEx guy was coming out of the building and upon recognizing Monica, he smiled.

"Just in time Ms. Phillips," the FedEx guy stated. Aaron was an attractive Latino fellow with a personality that could brighten any cloudy day.

"Do you have anything for me today? Monica asked.

"I always have something for you," Aaron responded with a daring smile.

"I mean any deliveries," Monica stated. Monica and Aaron had an ongoing "thing" between them. Recently Monica tried to share her faith with him and an amazing thing happened. Aaron's face turned flush and his dark brown eyes became almost teary. Monica didn't know what to say or do at the sudden change in his mood; so she grabbed his right hand gently and asked if she could pray for him and he agreed.

From that time forward he was still playfully flirty, but he would go out of his way to make his last deliveries near the time she normally came home just to see her.

"As a matter of fact, I have it right here." Aaron pulled out a medium sized box and it was a little bulky. "I'll take it up for you," he offered. Monica opened her door and Aaron passed her the package and he left. Monica knew what was in the box. She tore it open and left it on her dresser with the flaps pushed away. She was satisfied, studying its content. She promised herself that she would put it in her closet later. Monica remembered that Shawn would be picking her up by 6:00 and it was already 5:25. Monica put on a pair of black acid washed rhinestone boot cut jeans. Since they were low rise jeans, she put on a skinny silver-grey toned belt and sported a v-neck cut silvery blue colored tee shirt with ribbed details on the waist. The outfit accentuated her youthful body and when she put on her 3" peep toe Nine West pumps- she looked every bit as urban as any 25 year old. Monica had just finished putting a white liner that played up her small but curious looking eyes. Then she saw her cell phone light up; Shawn's name populated on her phone.

"Hello," Monica answered.

"Can you open the door, please?" Shawn asked.

"Sure." Monica hung up and wondered why he didn't ring the doorbell, but she grabbed her jean jacket and off she went. Opening the door, she saw that Shawn had a small bag in his hand. She hugged Shawn and he handed her the bag instructing her not to open it until later when he wasn't there. Monica took the bag and put it on the living room table.

"You look exceptional," Shawn told Monica.

"You don't look so bad yourself," Monica smiled. She admired Shawn's attention to detail. He had dark grey washed jeans and a navy blue jersey shirt with a mock neck. Shawn's neck was thick like an athlete's. She remembered that he said he played sports growing up, but he looked like he worked out frequently. Monica knew they were going to bowl, but she wasn't sure where. Shawn wanted to go somewhere not too far, but not too local. He'd heard they opened a new "Dave & Busters" only twenty minutes away; they arrived at 6:32 pm. Shawn as usual opened Monica's car door and they walked hand and hand into the restaurant.

"Are you hungry?" Shawn asked her as they stood at the entrance.

"No, not yet." I can wait. Monica responded.

"Alright". Shawn walked over to one of the empty lanes and claimed an area for both of them. As they waited for the bowling shoes, Shawn couldn't resist sizing Monica up from head to toe. What a good looking woman. Her body was so attractive and he laughed inwardly that even on a bowling date, she wore her heels; which by the way, were so provocative. The rhinestones on the bow of her black pumps complimented the rhinestones on the back pockets of her jeans. Monica caught Shawn studying her rear side and couldn't help but laugh to herself.

"Ahhhh, can I help you?" she asked with a smirk on her face, letting Shawn know that she was aware of his deeds.

"I was just paying attention to your flair for fashion, anything wrong with that?" Shawn now showing his beautiful teeth and loving the moment they were having. Monica continued and changed into the bowling shoes. After playing for nearly thirty minutes, Shawn won the first game and Monica was winning the second one.

"I'm getting hungry," she said as she leaned into Shawn's chest.

"You want to quit now?" Shawn smiled down looking into her lovely face.

"Tell you what-we can come back, right?"

"Yea, we can, so let's go," Shawn said.

"One thing, I have to use the ladies room."

"I'll get us a table in the meantime and wait for you okay, beautiful?"

"No problem." Monica changed back into her cute slide-in pumps and looked at the signs. She saw that the bathrooms were just beyond the pool area. Shawn was so mesmerized by her jeans, but he asked God to forgive him. Monica was happy that the bathroom wasn't dirty. She reapplied her pinkish lip gloss and put lotion on her hands. Satisfied, she walked out toward the dining area.

"Monica." Hearing her name she turned in that direction.

"Hey….wow." The voice spoke again. Monica was stopped in her tracks as she thought her eyes were deceiving her. "How on earth could this be?" She hadn't seen him in three years…stuttering.

"Hi"…that's all she could muster.

"Well can I at least get a hug?" Before she could say anything, he wrapped his long arms around her body. This 6' 2 tanned complexion hottie had a lean body perfect in stature. His hair was close cut, naturally textured hair and he wore a thin mustache. He kind of reminded you of "Will Smith" but much better looking.

"You look fine as ever Baby." Brian unashamedly, looked her up and down. Still in shock Monica barely whispered a thank you.

"Are you here alone?" he asked.

Monica remembering - glanced back and saw that Shawn had a clear view of them. She cringed.

"No, I'm not alone and I have to go now." Monica left that hunk of a man standing there in the dust. Brian thought he would never see her again but now that he did, it was only the beginning.

CHAPTER 5 - TRUST IS EVERYTHING

Monica was still shaken a bit and hoped that Shawn didn't see too much. Shawn was getting the drinks as Monica walked up to him and touched his solid muscular arm.

"Where are we sitting honey?" Shawn nodded and pointed at the table about four seats away. He began to walk towards the seat without saying a word. Monica was desperate to hear Shawn talk - wanting to be sure that everything was okay. Shawn sat and Monica followed trying to appear unmoved. Monica looked intently into Shawn's piercing gaze. Shawn's expression was unreadable.

"Do you want to finish our bowling match?" Monica reached for a French fry as she spoke.

"Nah, I was thinking we could play a game of pool," Shawn said to her. Monica felt her heart skip a beat, because she knew that Shawn had witnessed more than she desired. The atmosphere surrounding them became a bit thick…Out of the corner of Monica's eye she couldn't believe it…

"Hey, I'm sorry to interrupt you guys…I'm Brian, an old friend of Monica's and I'd like to invite you to a game of pool. That is if you're up to it." Brian thought he'd check out his competition. Shawn was feeling this guy out from the moment he sensed his eyes on him. This guy looked like a player and Shawn would never turn down a chance to win anything.

"Sure, I'm Shawn and I was just telling Monica that we should come over and play some pool, right babes?" Shawn knew that Monica was uncomfortable but this was man to man stuff. Shawn stood up and shook Brian's hand, with the "Black Man's" handshake. Monica was too through with Brian; and this was right up Shawn's alley, it seemed. With her face turned slightly sideways, Monica just stared briefly. Shawn was ecstatic and he had a sarcastic glare to his confident smile.

Brian looked like he couldn't wait to show his stuff since he played pool every chance he got. Some would say he was a pool shark.

"You mind, Babes?" Shawn inquired but his mind was already made up.

"Whatever, it looks like you guys would enjoy it."

"Great, I'll meet you in a few after you finish your meal." Brian content, walked towards the pool room. Monica was not happy and Shawn picked up on it.

"What's wrong, honey?" Shawn asked. If she didn't know better, she'd swear that he was having the time of his life making her night extremely uncomfortable.

"Why did you interrupt our date to play pool with him?" Monica was getting perturbed.

"He did say he was your friend. I didn't think you would mind and I did ask." Shawn knew exactly what he was doing.

Taking the last bite of her turkey burger with cheese, Monica wiped her mouth and took a sip of her drink. Monica reapplied her lipgloss.

"I'm ready when you are," Monica stated with an attitude. Monica was determined that if these guys wanted to flex their ego driven muscles, then so be it. Monica would just sit by and watch the stupid show. She just hoped that Shawn had good game, because Brian was no slouch. Shawn stood up and waited for Monica to come out from their table and he followed her to the pool room. Brian was there, he along with a few other guys that he frequently played with. They were watching a replay of a basketball game on the widescreen TV.

"Hey, we were waiting for you guys." Brian looked excited. Brian introduced the guys to Shawn and they commenced to playing the game.

"Don't worry sweetheart, I won't keep you from your date for too long. Just going to be a friendly 9 ball game we'll be done in no time," Brian said. Monica rolled her eyes. She was annoyed by Brian's arrogance and usual charming personality. She just leaned against the wall watching play by play. Brian started the game and he was able to put 5 balls around the table in the first 8 minutes. The sixth ball came close to the pocket, but was short one strand of a hair. Shawn stood patiently until it was his turn. Methodically, he called out every shot until he was down to his 5th ball. The solid blue ball went right to the mouth of the corner pocket and stayed there. Shawn stared at it and in 5 seconds if fell. Brian was obviously shocked and you could tell that his boys all paid more attention and no one moved as Shawn continued to be the sharp shooter. On his last ball, Shawn rubbed the chalk on the tip of his cue stick and studied this long shot. The ball was in a catty-corner position - one of those shots that you had to angle the stick awkwardly. You could see that Brian was almost biting his lip with the hope that he would miss. Shawn broke the silence when he came down on the cue ball with a short and quick hit. The ball made a loud thump as it hit the inner pool hole.

"Wow Man," Brian was impressed. "You play a mean game of pool." They both slapped each other in a respectful brotherly manner.

"Well, till we meet again," Brian said. "You got this round."

"Always good to meet a formidable player," Shawn said. Shawn looked over and reached out to Monica for her to take his hand. He knew that she was ready to go 20 minutes ago. Monica looked at the time and it was 9:33 pm.

"Are you ready to go, or do you want to play more bowling?" Shawn asked.

"I'm ready to go." Monica did not elaborate. Shawn led her to the car and as usual he waited for her to be seated. As he drove back to Monica's condo, she was very quiet. Shawn parked and walked Monica to her front door.

"I didn't mean to make you upset, Monica." Shawn was so humble in his words. Monica looked and saw the sincerity in Shawn's face.

"I know you didn't," Monica replied. Monica turned to open her door.

"Can I use your bathroom?" Shawn asked.

"Sure, why not." Monica's voice expressed her displeasure as she pointed him in the direction. Shawn was happy that he was able to have a chance to hopefully make up for his poor decision earlier. He hoped Monica would give him a moment. Shawn washed his hands and used the Shea butter hand lotion displayed in Monica's girly bathroom. Monica took the bag that Shawn had given her earlier and was tempted to view what was inside, but she put it down upon hearing his footsteps.

"You are going to open that later, right? Shawn suggested.

"I can wait - no rush." Monica's voice wasn't cold but neither was it warm as normal." Shawn grabbed hold of Monica and pulled her into his arms. He looked in her eyes and Monica's body nearly melted against his chest. Shawn reached down and used his right hand to cup her head to meet him as he placed his thick lips upon hers. He began to explore her rhythm as he kissed her deeper and their mouths were moist from each other's affections. Monica had to come up for air.

"I'm sorry, but I couldn't resist," Shawn said.

"Resist?" Monica was tipsy from the intensity of Shawn's magnetic pull.

"I felt I needed to take your ex-boyfriend's challenge. I did it for a reason that maybe you'll understand later."

"Oh, I see." Monica thought he meant their breathless kiss.

"I also wanted to feel the passion of your touch, your kiss." Shawn now held Monica's hand inside both of his. Monica smiled with relief and sighed simultaneously.

"I need to go Baby, Shawn said."

"Alright," Monica said, as Shawn kissed her hand and grabbed the other one, kissing it too. In his car, Shawn put on some of his eclectic jazz wanting to meditate. He put on one of his favorite groups, "Pat Methany". Shawn knew that he was going against the grain of his rational mind; it was telling him to put on his brakes and monitor his speed in this relationship. He thought about how he barely knew her, haven't met any of her friends or family members. Now he just met her ex-boyfriend, but other than that, what else did he know? Only what Pastor Richard revealed. Shawn couldn't deny that he was truly smitten by her and he knew the next stage. Shawn decided he would try to find out as much as he could about Monica before getting caught out there. Shawn normally did his homework before letting his guard down. That's it he thought, I have to be smarter Monica ran her fingers lightly across her lips in memory of Shawn's irresistible kisses. Shawn had such a gentle way with her, but he was definitely a man not afraid of taking charge. He was vulnerable, but straight forward at the same time. Monica grabbed the small bag that Shawn gave her and took it into the bedroom with her. Monica reached her hand in the bag and pulled out a white rectangular box with a red ribbon tied in a bow surrounding it. Monica wondered what could it be and she took the ribbon off and opened the box. It had a noted folded up on top of the gold sachet covering the gift. Monica read the note written in bold navy blue letters.

Monica, I hope you value the time that we spend together as much as I do. Please accept this as a symbol of my appreciation towards you. Shawn.

The box contained a black and white sterling silver tennis bracelet. Monica immediately took it out of the box and put it on her wrist. Monica was overwhelmed in her emotions and did not like how she felt so comfortable, even though they have not even dated anywhere close to a month. Monica spent an hour talking to God in prayer and fell asleep like a child into her daddy's arm.

CHAPTER 5 ½ - PROMOTION AND DEMOTION

Shawn was awakened by a neighbor's dog barking while its owner came into contact with another dog. He wiped his eyes as sleep was constricting his vision. He saw that it was later than he had supposed. Now at 8:30, he knew it would take 25 minutes in traffic and he jumped up and took his shower. Shawn strolled through the office at 9:30 and his supervisor, Selena, passed by him on her way to her office. Greeting everyone, he went to his office, turned on his computer and looked at his current projects. Shawn's line 1 was ringing.

"Good Morning, again," Shawn said in a mellow tone.

"Yes, I need to see you in my office." Selena was obviously annoyed by something or someone. Shawn gathered his faithful pad and pen as was normal whenever he met with anyone. Although he had a photographic memory, he never relied solely on this unique ability. Shawn greeted his team players just before he walked into Selena's office.

"Please close the door, behind you," she said. Shawn knew something of a serious nature was about to happen.

"I looked at your weekly report and I'm very concerned with one of your team players, Ralph," Selena stated. Shawn already knew where this was going and quickly calculated his words before speaking.

"I understand your concerns, Selena. I have not spoken with Ralph yet, but I too am disappointed in the quality of his work for the last 3 assignments," Shawn noted.

"What do you propose to do about this?" Selena sat back in her sleek black leather office chair; positioning her body as a psychiatrist would upon reading her patient.

"I am going to speak with him and put him on probation for thirty days. If things do not change, I will afford him the chance to retire early." Shawn wanted to be diplomatic as Ralph was here when he first started and was a top advertiser for 20 years until his wife passed away last year.

"That sounds like a good plan. I agree that we don't want the man to keel over since his wife died just a year ago." Selena could be quite cold at times.

"Absolutely, that's why I'm going to use some discretion with him". Selena was now content that Shawn had things under control in that area. She studied Shawn from his magnetic eyes to the dimples in his face, to his well-defined physique. She knew that Shawn was 12 years his junior, she being 50. He was the prize that just kept slipping through her fingers; her body temperature rose in his presence and she did nothing to hide her attraction to him. Shawn began to feel uncomfortable under the gaze of Selena. Even though she was significantly older than him, she was gorgeous. Shawn in his worldly years prior to getting, "born again", would have surely taken advantage of the quest of "Cat and Mouse" with her. He knew the type of woman she was and he would have done all that was necessary to tame this tigress woman. Selena stood at about 5' 7, had a redbone skin tone, eyes shaped like almond slits, full lips and a slender build. Her hair was layered and the longest of her tresses was to the middle of her back. Selena was hard to resist in any man's flesh, but alas he wasn't just any man. Shawn wanted to get back to his desk as soon as possible.

"On another subject, I want you to start working with the other clients that we have taken on and I want to see some progress next Thursday, as we scheduled some meetings to give them some feedback," Selena said looking at her calendar.

"I'll get right on it".

"When will you be finished with the "Alien ED" project?"

"I will finalize the concepts today and present them in the a.m."

"Perfect." Selena's phone buzzes with her assistant. "Line two, your brother is on the line." Selena turned slightly in her chair to take the call. Shawn was relieved that he could go on with his day. He closed the door behind and Selena gave him coy eyes as he dismissed himself. Shawn relayed the situation to Ralph and the poor man's face became so pain filled. Ralph shook his head knowing that all that was being discussed was true and he went back to his desk and worked. Shawn pulled out the other clients' files and began to brainstorm on marketing ads. Shawn knew his days and nights would be long, as he had to get these projects out and ready to present to the new clients as well as his current ones. Shawn was used to working 10 to 12 hours a day, but he wondered how this would affect his new relationship with Monica. He looked at his cell phone and realized Monica had sent him a text message: "Please call me at your earliest convenience."

Monica's work day was very busy and her supervisor and manager put off the meeting from the other day until today. Monica printed out stacks of documents and had them collaged into booklets easy to present to the QA's staff. Monica's stomach felt queasy thinking of facing all her old co-workers and being now in a promoted position. Monica had her share of haters in that department and they were shocked that she was able to be chosen for a position that on paper was impossible to even be considered for. They obviously did not know her God! Monica felt victorious that God used her in such a mighty way and she was able to not only see the prophetic word come to pass, but she was intricately involved. Monica read the proposal that her old coworkers were about to receive. Now it was 12:45 and Carolyn (her supervisor) told her to bring the stacks of documents to the conference room. Monica brought one box and the receptionist helped her carry the other box with all the paperwork. Roy Clemons walked in with his bottle of water and nodded with an inquiry in his expressive wrinkled face. His eyes were swollen with worry and lack of sleep. In came Monica's old supervisors and the trail of workers followed. Bench like seating was on the far right hand side of the room near where Roy would begin his presentation. Carolyn and Monica were prompted to sit there to assist if necessary.

"Good Afternoon Everyone, I thank you for your patience and today we are going to present to you a concept that I hope you will find suitable for all persons concerned." Mr. Clemons had a tough audience and he could tell that they were only there because they had to be.

"Our Human Resources department is here to serve you and the company's needs as they both benefit one to the other."

"I recently sat with my colleague, Carolyn Ruthfield. You all should know her as she is the one most people contact when there are complaints or misunderstandings."

"We both met and agreed to the packets that you see all around the conference table and will soon be able to examine as this meeting goes forth. To be completely honest with you, our new team player and "firecracker", Monica, is the whiz that came up with this proposal." The whole room turned their focus on Monica in utter shock. Monica was completely flabbergasted, as she did not feel comfortable being the focus of the meeting.

"As a matter of fact, I want Monica to come and join me in presenting this "out of the box" concept." Monica looked at Carolyn and her supervisor motioned for her to go up to the front next to Mr. Clemons. Regrettably, Monica walked over and stood near Roy.

"Ok, what we are going to do is explain the format and structure of how this applies to your work day and then we will open the floor for any questions you all may have," Roy said. Roy whispered to Monica that he wanted her to read the introductory statement. Monica cleared her throat and gathered her thoughts, asking God to speak through her (in her silent prayer).

"Good Afternoon. If you will follow along by each taking a packet and I will go in the order of the documents as they are organized."
Monica started reading:

"The recent promotions that led to misunderstandings and mistrust between supervisors/managers and most employees in the Quality

Control division have caused the management to take a more discerning approach to the needs of its employees."

"If you take a look at page 1, you will see a questionnaire of 20 entries, an essay and a section "your last 3 - 5 positions held." The next page gives you a list of job descriptions for upcoming positions. The last page is optional, it applies to hobbies, short term/long term goals and various other personal data".

"This package was developed to provide a more talent or skill-based approach to job placement. Although, everyone will not have the ability to be promoted, the primary goal in this concept is to put the best suited persons in positions that they would feel a sense of importance and recognition in."

"The rule of thumb with the guidelines shown here would be as follows: All applications will be reviewed by the Human Resources department. Once the information has been examined, interviews will be scheduled. Within the time frame of two weeks, decisions will be made to determine who will be placed where. Everyone will have the chance to obtain a work schedule and job that they have applied for. There will only be three choices that any person can apply for. These positions will not have a pay increase until six months have expired; the main agenda is to give an opportunity to each individual to have a fair selection of job choices." Monica was finally finished and quite relieved. All of the staff, including their supervisors, skimmed through their packets and conversed with one another and you heard chatter. Some were delighted and you could feel hope rise up in a way that Monica had never seen in this department before. Even her haters gathered in a positive manner amongst themselves. Yet Monica noticed that their demeanor had not changed towards her, but their envy increased. Still, Monica knew she had accomplished what God asked of her. Mr. Clemons gave the final instructions and told the supervisors that they would meet after all the applications had been received. Everyone was dismissed and Monica proceeded to her desk. The time on her phone showed 2:30. Monica looked at her cell phone and didn't see any response to the text message that she had left from the morning. She tried to call Shawn on her way to work, but it went straight to voice mail. Carolyn came towards Monica's desk.

"Roy wants to speak with you." Carolyn was acting a little weird. Monica didn't understand why Carolyn who normally had a very sunny position, seemed to have a dark cloud surrounding her. Grabbing her silver writing pad and matching pen, she walked into Mr. Clemons office and he told her to sit.

"I observed you today young lady and I was very impressed with your presentation. You definitely have a gift of speaking and I'm glad we have you on board with us."

"Thank you so much, I appreciate your feedback." Monica was taken back.

"Now, I advised Carolyn that we will have you go over the applications and cross reference the positions that they apply for and see who would be the best candidates. Carolyn then will take the optional pages to make the final decisions. How does that sound?" Roy asked.

"I can't wait to get started, Mr. Clemons." Monica's heart was smiling.

"Good. I also looked at your starting salary and made an increase as your responsibilities here are going to change. I believe that you are more than a coordinator and I told Carolyn to look into having you attend some of our training courses to sharpen the skills that I saw you display." Mr. Clemons gave Monica a wink of the eye as an uncle would to his favorite niece.

"I can't thank you enough for your confidence in me," Monica stated soberly.

"Alright, one thing before you leave - its Roy not Mr. Clemons, you're making me feel my age," He said as he picked up his phone and began dialing. Monica knew their meeting was done and she left feeling totally amazed. She had just been promoted and had only been in the department for less than a month. She couldn't wait to tell Keiki. Monica was almost back at her desk and saw she just missed a call from Shawn. She dialed him from her desk phone.

"Hello, I saw that you called."

"How are you, is everything alright?" Shawn asked.

"I'm doing wonderful, and how are you?"

"I'm glad you're having a good day. I'm swamped over here. I wanted to hear your voice and let you know that I was thinking about you."

"Well, I'll be leaving in about half hour." Monica was hoping they could get together.

"Awww baby, I'll be here for who knows what time. For the next few days, I'll probably be working extended hours," He admitted.

"Does that mean I won't see you this weekend?" Monica hoped this wasn't a sign.

"You mean Saturday?" Shawn inquired.

"No, Friday, I was hoping you would help me celebrate my Birthday, and I wanted to properly thank you for my special gift."

"Your Birthday?!?!" Shawn was perplexed.

"You're just now telling me? You deserve a spanking for that one."

"Maybe that's not the worst thing that could happen," Monica stated. She knew she was treading the line of being flirtatious, but she figured she had it like that with Shawn.

"Wow, Girl. Don't tempt me." Shawn's face lit up and he felt his adrenaline climbing. "Still I would love to help you celebrate your birthday. Where do you want to go?"

"Actually, my best friend and I previously planned to go to a restaurant called the "View" in Manhattan and I hope you will come and then I could introduce you." Monica had a sinking feeling that perhaps it was too soon for him to want to meet her people(s).

"Sure, I would love to, just text me the details and I'll definitely be there." Shawn promised. Monica and Shawn hung up and Monica saw that it was now 3:30. Carolyn left early and told Monica that she could leave after her meeting with Roy if she desired.

CHAPTER 6 - BIRTHDAY GIRL

The last few days seemed to creep by as Monica had not seen Shawn due to his lengthy work hours. Shawn would call Monica on his way home approximately 9:45 nightly. Today was her birthday and she was excited that she would see him for dinner. Monica pulled out a dress that she had never worn. It was a classy tiger print cocktail dress with an empire waistline. It was just above the knee and had a v-neck shape front and back. Monica chose peep-toe metallic pump shoes. She also wore her new black & white tennis bracelet with loop earrings and necklace to match. Monica had planned an all day excursion with Keiki, as she took her birthday off as a vacation. Keiki and Monica decided to stay in a hotel with a day spa until her evening dinner. They treated themselves to a body mask, facial, hair appointment and manicure/pedicure. From head to toe they felt like movie stars when they were done. They decided to go to see a movie at about 5:00 and dinner was reserved for 8:30. Monica and Keiki were like teenagers, they laughed through the entire film, called "The Dilemma". Although the movie was a comedy it dealt with some serious moral issues. Now her watch showed 7:15 and they went back to the hotel to get dressed. The restaurant was about two and half blocks away and they strutted through the beauty of the city. Manhattan was such a gorgeous place, especially at night. The lights were divine and she couldn't wait to see her date. After being seated, Monica checked her phone. She saw that Shawn had left her a text message - apologizing that he would be a little late - approximately 20 to 30 minute delay.

"What's up, Keiki asked?" She noticed her change of expression.

"Shawn will be a little late," Monica wanted to sound nonchalant.

"So tell me more about this guy. You say you met him at a party?" Monica described their first date to Keiki, as she had only spoken of her initial meeting the last time they talked. They decided to order appetizers while waiting for Shawn to order their entrees. Monica's face became more relaxed as she saw Shawn being directed towards their table. He looked absolutely fine as any brother could possibly look. He wore a two-button gray blazer with an ice blue button down shirt. You could tell that his pants and suit were tailored to fit his body. When he saw their table, Monica could see a glimmer of spark in his eyes. He of course was carrying a dozen of blood red roses.

"Hey you." Monica stood as he came to greet her.

"Happy Birthday." Shawn embraced her and kissed her cheek. Monica held and sniffed her flowers. The host came with a vase and placed the roses on their table.

"I apologize for my tardiness." Shawn stood holding Monica's hand as Monica began to introduce Keiki.

"Shawn this is Keiki and Keiki this is Shawn." Shawn turned his body slightly to shake her hand. Keiki responded politely. They all sat and looked at the menus.

"I hope I didn't keep you too long ladies," Shawn spoke.

"No, we had just finished our appetizers," Monica answered. Keiki lifted her head slowly. "It's cool; we were just having our girl time." The waiter came to the table to remove the dishes.

"Are you ready to order yet?" The waiter was a white male of about 25 years in age, wearing a tattoo that ran from his forearm all the way to his index finger. The drawings were of various snakes climbing on a tree that ran from his hand to his shoulder. In complete opposition, he had a studded cross that he wore and a silver ring that had an onyx stone. This young guy had a type of biker bad boy look and you could tell that he worked out, by his chest and well defined arms.

"Ladies." Shawn looked at the women. "Are we ready?" He addressed Monica. Monica looked at Keiki.

"I'm ready, how about you?" she asked Keiki.

"Definitely," Keiki responded. Everyone ordered their entree and continued to have light conversation. Shawn was more reserved and he spoke about things more in a general fashion.

"So Ladies, what did you do all day here in Manhattan?"

"Oh you know the typical, spa, movies - girl stuff." Keiki responded.

Shawn nodded with a slight smile acknowledging Keiki. Monica was happy that everyone was getting along and felt comfortable.

Keiki studied Monica and Shawn trying to see the mutual attraction that joined them. Keiki exerted her great sense of humor throughout their dinner.

"Is anyone going to order dessert?" Monica looked from left to right to see if there was an interest in either Shawn or Keiki.

"I'm going to pass on this one," Shawn said.

"Why don't we order something we can share?" Keiki advised. The waiter came by just in time and was very attentive throughout the night.

"We would like to order the "red velvet slice with vanilla ice cream" on the side," Monica stated.

Shawn excused himself to go to the men's room. He was happy to be spending time with Monica, but he actually wished that they were alone tonight. If only he had known Monica's birthday was today, he could have scheduled something for them separate instead of dividing her attention. With his work schedule this week it would be nearly impossible for him to plan something and this weekend he would be seeing his girls. Shawn stopped by to ask the waiter a question. Shawn recognized a lot of the symbolism in the tattoo and the jewelry. He made mention of his tats and gave him more of a brotherly handshake. Shawn was interested in getting guys like him opportunities that would lead them to a better future. He told him his name was Frank Ispolito and he gave him a card to come workout with him one day and they could discuss a career opportunity. Yet Shawn was more interested in this man's soul. The restaurant wasn't overly noisy so the singing entourage of a few members of the staff bringing a small red velvet cake (instead of a slice) to their table had heads turning.

"Happy Birthday to you, Happy Birthday to you, Happy Birthday, Dear Monica, Happy Birthday to you!" Monica was overwhelmed and almost embarrassed. She knew that Keiki had not planned this and she was so speechless.

"Oh, Shawn, I know you had something to do with this." She smiled and almost was teary. She looked at the smiling faces of the staff and they went off about their business. She looked over at Keiki and she was just as much surprised as Monica.

"That really looks delicious," Keiki spoke up. "I

hope you like it," Shawn said.

"Like it, it's my favorite." Monica couldn't wait to blow out her candle and they all took a piece - including Shawn. Shawn noticed that Monica was wearing the bracelet that he had purchased. "I see you are wearing the bracelet."

"Oh Sweetheart, I'm so sorry. It is so beautiful and I absolutely love it." Monica was smiling from ear to ear at Shawn. Monica wanted to properly thank him, but she didn't want to alienate Keiki by being overly affectionate. Shawn whispered in Monica's ear asking if she had driven there. She noted that Keiki had driven them there and she would be riding back with her. Monica knew what Shawn was getting at and she waited for him to "go there".

"I'll be right back; do you want to go to the ladies room?" Keiki asked.

"Yes," stammering. Shawn was close to her ear and neck and she could feel his breath dancing on her skin. "I'm right behind you," Monica answered.

"Do you think that Keiki would mind if you rode back with me?" Shawn asked.

"Of course she would, Baby." I don't want to make her feel like I'm kicking her to the curb.

"Alright, alright, just thought I'd try. You're right," Shawn said with a kiddish grin. Monica gave Shawn a quick kiss on his cheek and told him she'd be right back. Shawn thought Monica looked so good in her dress that he couldn't imagine not spending some time with her tonight, but this was planned before they met.

"It's wonderful to be in such a beautiful and clean bathroom, right girl," Monica said upon entering the restroom.

"True. So what are you planning to do later?" Keiki inquired. "Go home, why?" Monica was curious now.

"Well, I figured that you and Shawn would want to hang out or something." Keiki was feeling more like a third wheel and was getting uncomfortable.

"Shawn knew that these plans were made before we even met, so he can see me later." Monica wanted to hang with him, but didn't see that as being fair to her best friend.

"Oh, ok." Keiki smiled showing her pretty smile and straight teeth. Keiki was such an attractive woman with a natural tan. Monica hugged Shawn and they all got into their vehicles ready to head home.

"Very nice guy, Girl. It looks like you got yourself a winner this time," Keiki said.

"Not me, Honey. That could only come from God or...the other one." Monica and Keiki both broke out into laughter.

Keiki and Monica rode together and Monica updated her about her new promotion.

"Girl, you need to get me a job," Keiki joked, but was partly serious.

"You don't need to get a J.O.B. when you have a promising career ahead of you," Monica advised.

"Look, you just finished your Bachelor's in Finances and Marketing, maybe Shawn knows of any available positions. After all, he works in that field," Monica said.

"Well Girlfriend, if he knows somebody maybe he can hook me up."

"I'll check that out the next time we get together," Monica said. Keiki pulled up to Monica's condo building and they said their goodbyes. Monica had a memorable birthday - with the exception - that she didn't get her birthday kiss or gift for that matter. I guess she figured Shawn paid for dinner, flowers - just no tantalizing kiss. She grabbed a different Asian inspired vase with gold, green and reddish orange hues she put her roses into it with water. She lay in her bed and contemplated calling Shawn. Instead she decided to pray and spend time with God in his Holy Scriptures.

CHAPTER 6 ½ - IT'S ALL IN HOW YOU SAY IT...

Thank God, Damien (Keiki's son) was spending his weekend with his dad. Keiki rolled out the bed and looked outside to get a sense of the weather. Nothing could ever compare to her beautiful native land, Hawaii, where she was born and raised until her parents moved to Greenwich, CT. Her dad had a great job opportunity here and she was totally culture shocked into "another world". Meeting Monica had brought her slightly out of her introverted shell. Monica was outgoing, friendly and talkative. This helped Keiki to develop a trust knowing that her friend was always there for her and not that far away. Ten years later she had a failed marriage, but finished her bachelor's degree in marketing/finances while raising her highly intelligent, mischievous son. With no plans on the horizon, she decided to get up and go grocery shopping and pick up a few things. Keiki drove to her local supermarket, Shop and Stop. Keiki grabbed some fruits, vegetables, pork chops, jasmine rice, eggs, juice, chicken and various condiments. In the checkout aisle, Keiki did like most shoppers and scanned through the magazines and scrolled through one, while waiting as customer four behind in her lane.

"Hey Girl," a voice spoke to her. Keiki looked up and wondered where he came from.

"Hi, Brian?" She was surprised to see him. In three yrs. she had only seen him once, since he and Monica broke up.

"What's good with you?" Brian asked.

"Everything's good." Keiki always thought that Brian was a good-looking guy: Tall, Carmel tanned skin, sexy smile and he always took good care of his body. He had olive colored sweats, but still managed to be GQ anyways. Brian thought this must have been fate, him meeting with Keiki in this way. Brian never missed out on an opportunity.

"So I was thinking that perhaps I could invite you and Monica to a barbeque at my boy's house tomorrow?" Brian said.

"I don't know about that Brian, why don't you ask her yourself?" After Keiki was introduced to Shawn, she knew that Brian would be hard pressed to get Monica interested. There was no comparison in terms of quality. Shawn was, from what she could see, very hot, smart and seemed to be a decent guy. But you never know when things appear too good to be true - they normally are. Brian waved his arm to a brotha a few feet away. Keiki was shocked when she saw her cousin, Randy, come up to Brian.

"Randy, I want to introduce you to an old friend, Keiki."

"No need dude that's my long lost Cuzin...What's up Girl, where you been?" Randy asked. Randy hugged Keiki and smiled with joy in her heart.

"So you think Monica would come with you, Keiki?" Brian was anxious now and he knew the odds were greater with Randy and his family throwing this party.

"I mean, I don't know. She's kinda busy these days." Keiki didn't want to crush his ego.

"Yea, I know she's seeing somebody, but still we will always be cool and besides I have to talk to her anyway." Brian was relentless. Keiki's turn came up and Brian continued stating his cause and even saying how he wanted a second shot at Monica. He was very convincing and if she was Monica, she would have been compelled to at least hear him out. Keiki's cousin pulled her to the side and told her how Brian has changed his lifestyle and his career has picked up. Randy went on to tell her that Brian was actually listening to gospel music and considering joining his church. Brian and Randy walked Keiki to her car. They helped her put her grocery bags into her 2011 Subaru Forester.

"I like that platinum finish on this Subaru, plus it has all the bells and whistle upgrades." Randy loved cars.

"Thanks, guys." Keiki was now in the driver's seat.

"So you coming cuz, we haven't seen you in eons?" Randy pleaded. Keiki looked at their faces and she felt sorry for them.

"I'll come, but I make no promises that Monica will come."

"Alright, you got my number, right," Brian verified.

"Yeah, I got both of your numbers, later." Keiki pulled off. Brian watched Keiki's vehicle as it drove away. Now all he could do was pray, he thought to himself. Keiki thought of how Brian looked like he had turned over a new leaf. No signs of the seedy guy that he used to be. Keiki thought about how their relationship was so nice in the

beginning. Brian introduced Monica to Keiki and her ex-husband at a barbeque, coincidently. Although, Shawn appeared to be a decent guy, she wasn't convinced that he was the right guy for Monica - he was just too perfect.

CHAPTER 7 - SATURDAY'S THE NEW MONDAY

Shawn normally worked one Saturday in a month when deadlines needed to be met. He planned on working about four to five hours to get the presentations ready for Monday. His Boss Lady, Selena, changed the meeting from Friday to Monday which meant that he had to have everything completed, edited and ready for viewing. On paper, everything was genius, but on video he needed his media crew to finalize it. Shawn understood that nobody liked coming to work on Saturdays, so he went the extra mile for breakfast and lunch. Since he was just about done, he sent his staff home.

"Hello, Shawn." Selena came through the office with red polka dot shirt and white shorts. Shawn couldn't believe how her cleavage was literally spilling over her top, her shorts were mid-thigh, and she wore white heels that had a leather strap wrapped around her ankles. Shawn had to freeze to keep himself from doing a double take.

"Hi," was all he could muster without being obvious of his stupor. Selena could tell she finally had Shawn's full attention and he would be hook, line and sinker very soon.

"I just dropped by to see how things were going. Did the guys leave already?" she said coyly.

"Ah, yeah. I sent them home; they did an awesome job today." Shawn felt that someone turned off the air conditioner.

Selena was fully aware that they left early. She called fifteen minutes ago and spoke to Harvey the media guy. He advised that they were finishing lunch and everything was being packed up to go. Selena lives close to the area and decided to wait in the parking lot, knowing that Shawn was an overachiever and couldn't resist viewing the work again.

"So let me get a peek at what the final version looks like." Selena noticed Shawn was playing it cool, but no man could resist her wiles.

"Sure, let me just set things up and you can see the finished product." Shawn prompted the media player and grabbed the first DVD and stuck it in the player.

Monica spent her morning cleaning and watched a couple of her recorded programs of "Changing World - Creflo Dollar", "Property Virgin and Undercover Boss". She decided that she wanted to get out before the day was spent. Monica already took her shower and decided to do something spontaneous. Monica missed hearing Shawn's voice and knew that he was working so many hours. She packed a hungry man's lunch and hoped that he was still hungry. Pulling into his company's parking lot - she quickly recognized his BMW shining like it came straight out of the showroom. Monica starting getting quite nervous as she had never done an unannounced visit to Shawn. She figured this would be safer, as he would just be working on a casual day. Shawn told her he would be working from 10:00 until 4:00 approximately. It was 3:15 last time she looked at the time in her car. She hoped she could get a quick date with him since he would be spending this weekend with his twin girls. Monica looked at the directory for Shawn's name and division to locate his office. There it was: Shawn Edwards - Marketing Director, Main Floor, and Section D. Monica felt like the pit of her stomach was tied in notches, the closer she got. She could hear a television playing as she came to the glass see-through doors.

Shawn played two of the three introductory videos that they worked on. From what he could see, Selena was pleased.

"So, what do you think of what we were able to accomplish?" Shawn asked. By now Shawn stood up gathering the DVDs and putting them away in their cases. He picked up his cell phone and moved towards the doorway of the conference room.

"I had all the confidence in you Shawn since I took over this position. "You are a remarkable man. On top of all your many accomplishments, you are strikingly handsome and nearly irresistible."

Selena had to strike as this was the perfect moment and perfect timing with nobody there to interrupt or distract him from her devilish charms. Selena had managed to push Shawn, using her body, towards the wall leading to the main area of their offices.

"Wow, I don't even know how to respond to that, Selena. I really appreciate your belief in me and I thank you for being so painfully honest in regards to my (looking at himself) physique, but I want you to know that I..." Before he could finish his thought, Selena had his body up against the wall with her face buried into his neck with her hands outstretched around his waist touching the wall behind him. Shawn was in a panicked state. On one hand he didn't know how to maneuver himself from her grip without using force and secondly she was putting her lips around his ears...He knew he had to think quickly!!

"Selena! he screamed. "This can't happen!" Selena lifted her face and looked into his smoldering eyes. As she gave him the tiniest room, Shawn took that liberty and moved as fast as he could. As he turned to his right looking at the glass entry doors he saw a woman standing there, with a yellow, halter top. She seemed to be staring at him. As he looked again he thought .... NO!!!! Monica was fixated-frozen as she witnessed Shawn standing there letting some woman (dressed up like a Hollywood bimbo) grope and chew on his ear.

"Oh, that must be your little girlfriend," Selena said as the sarcasm slid from her tongue. Shawn wasted no time responding to Selena, but he ran towards Monica who had already begun speed walking towards the exit.

"Monica, wait!" Shawn called her loudly. Monica ignored Shawn and commenced to using her alarm system to unlock her car. By then Shawn caught up to her and reached for her arm.

"Wait, Monica. Don't leave please." Shawn pleaded. Monica could see that his eyes were like fire and he had such a magnetic hold on her and she knew she had to be strong.

"Why?" Monica said. "Why shouldn't I?"

"Because I need to talk to you, this looks bad - I know but don't just run away." Shawn had to convince her. Monica thought to herself - "Girl run -run for your life." Shawn took the basket of food from her left hand and put it on the roof of her car. He looked at Monica, grabbed her, hugging her without letting her go.

"Let's get out of here Baby." Shawn looked into Monica's eyes hoping that his eyes would convey his truest feelings for her.

"I never said I would go anywhere with you or talk to you for that matter." Monica was not making this easy for him. Shawn saw Selena come out the building with her shades on looking like a California girl and he shook his head.

"Can you really picture me with her? Shawn asked Monica.

"Yes, I just did and she's modelisque," Monique said.

"No, don't misunderstand me, she's easy on the eyes, but she's not my type. Go into the realm of the Spirit Monica." Shawn said.

Did he just go there? Monica thought to herself. He was really asking her to pray right now?

"Shawn, I don't want to make more out of something then it is. We are fairly new in getting to know one another and maybe it's foolish of me to think that we are an item, a couple of any sort. So I'm just going to let it go and be on my way." Monica decided she wasn't going to let Shawn draw her in.

Shawn leaned his head back slightly as if to say - Lord, give me strength. "I understand, but I want to show you something before you go," Shawn suggested.

"What's that?" Monica was curious.

"It's at my house and before you say no, please - hear me out first. I bought you something for your birthday, but I wanted to give it to you when we had some alone time; so I kept it at my place and I want you to have it, alright." Monica knew it was more to the gift thing than he was owning up to, but she wanted to believe Shawn. Shawn knew he had her thinking, so he had to do something fast.

"Come I want to show you a part that goes with your gift," Shawn said, pulling her hand. Monica followed reluctantly to his vehicle. Shawn unlocked his car and picked out a cd and put it in the player. As the music started, with its sultry piano, Monica's heart dropped. She couldn't believe what she was hearing. Shawn watched Monica's expression soften.

"That's unbelievable...what gift could compliment that?" Monica asked. She realized the song was "Forever Forever" by one of her favorite jazz pianist. This man was a class act.

"You have to come and see." Shawn's vulnerable side was showing. "Don't worry, I won't kidnap you. Come go with me." Shawn was almost begging now.

"Why should I?" What could convince her she mused? Shawn smiled from the inside of his heart. He knew Monica wanted to go, but she didn't want to be too easy. He admired her confidence. Shawn couldn't divulge his growing attachment to her presence, but he focused his eyes on hers wishing she could read his thoughts.

"What I have for you is more than my words can express. Don't deprive me of this last request. Just follow me please, it's about twenty minutes," Shawn said. Monica went to her car and put the basket on the back seat. After getting into the driver's side and putting on some cool jazz, she heard her cell ringing. She saw that it was Shawn and she answered.

"Yes."

"I want you to be careful, as the police patrol here is very strict. I don't speed as I've had my share of tickets. Stay close to me okay."

"No problem."

"If you want some company, you can call me back." Shawn looked into his rear mirror and she could view his dimples and awesome eyes.

"Ok." Monica hung up. Monica contemplated where Shawn lived and if he kept his place as tidy as his person. Nobody's perfect, as her mother always used to say. Still, Monica marveled at Shawn as there weren't too many flaws that she could see. With the exception that he found this woman wrapped around his neck. Monica wondered how he would explain that. Their ride was smooth and before she knew it, Shawn had made a few turns and they were in a picturesque neighborhood. She could tell that these homes were in the range of $400,000 - $600,000. Shawn pulled into a gated community and it was breathtaking. It was an end unit surrounded by nature's best, a lovely garden bursting with various flowers. Monica's eyes took in its country feel, but it was in a "road less travelled area". It was definitely not what she expected. Shawn motioned for Monica to come in, as he held his front door. Monica joined Shawn at the entrance and she stepped in. Shawn rushed around turning on the central air system and next, he used the remote to turn on his stereo system which was supreme in sound. He apparently enjoyed very similar music genre. Monica took in the color scheme and design of his space. The architectural ceilings were arched and intricately designed with white wood trim with a three tiered chandelier. The rug was an Asian black and gold with cream color as its base. His furnishings were a blend of mix matched separates. The sofa was creamy beige with a few pillows scattered on it. One side chair had a foot rest and pillow for the back colored in a dark taupe. The other chair was brown and taupe. There was a lovely beige fireplace with a few pictures and a nice candle decor featured. But surprisingly, he had a grand ivory piano sitting to the side of the fireplace. Looking from a distance the room had charm, sophistication and an air of Shawn's rustic nature.

"Come in Baby, have a seat, get comfortable." Shawn waved her towards the living area.

"Let me make you something to drink," Shawn said.

"I'll take you on a tour momentarily." Shawn left to get the drinks. He yelled out from the kitchen to her, "Did you bring the basket of food in?"

"No," Monica said while taking in more details to the room. Noticing the bookcase and peeking through the titles - she had an idea of what literature influenced him. She had no intention of making herself at home; she only wanted to see this mystery gift that he needed her to view.

"Give me your key and I'll grab the lunch you made." Shawn had put their drinks on the coffee table. Monica handed over her keys.

"Feel free to visit any part of my home, the bathroom is to the right. I'll meet you back here when you're done." Shawn took the keys and left. Monica did as he suggested and went towards the bathroom and could see from the hallway that there were three bedrooms. The first two were closed but the main master suite was open. Monica tipped through the house like she was a burglar. She saw the master suite had French doors and she swung them open. The room had light carpeting and the walls were mute as well. The bed had a chocolate padded headboard with a hug cheetah printed pillow and velour like comforter. He had a seat at the end of the bed with books and the night stand had modern lamps. Overall it had a bachelor's feel or a hotel suite. It was neutral, but extremely neat and he had plants large and small throughout his home. One thing that stood out was a huge painting of an African American couple intertwined in a loving pose and the bold red, gold and brown details were exquisite. It was centered over the bed perfectly. Monica heard him come back into the house and quickly went into the hallway and entered the bathroom. She wanted to freshen up and make sure everything was in place. Ready to reenter the living area, she came in seeing Shawn seated on the couch with his back to her and the drinks and food were displayed on the table. There was a tall frame standing between the couch and the wall next to him.

"Ready for your gift?" Shawn said in a manner like a dad that wants Christmas to be special.

"Of course." Shawn picked up the frame and ripped off the brown paper that covered the picture.

Monica gasped. "Oh my goodness, Shawn Are you serious?" Monica examined the artwork and recognized the famous artist's work and loved the painting. It was a scene of a black pianist playing to a woman, as she lay sideways facing him and the background was almost a replica of the jazz restaurant that he took her to. She thought this was a very extravagant gift and she could hear the jazz music that he played in his car in the background. Shawn knew that she was stunned by this gift. It was an original.

"What made you get something like this?" Monica knew that this present was expensive and very thoughtful.

"Monica, I think you are an extraordinary woman and I wanted to give you a gift that represented your style and could compliment your home. You said that you like beauty and enjoyed drawing. Looking at your place, I knew you could appreciate something of this nature." Monica sat staring at Shawn while he paused before speaking again.

"Now, I guess I have a few things to explain. I want to start by thanking you for coming here and trusting me and not your eyes (they both smiled); but here it is in a nutshell" - He took a deep breath.

"Recently, our company went through a lot of internal changes, some people retired and some were transferred and others were promoted. I was promoted, my long time boss retired and as a result I received a new manager. Selena, the lady you saw today, took over our division. Unbeknownst to me- she is a 'black widow' of sorts. I found out that she collects men and some go to better positions, others get fired and the rest-let's just say they leave the company. For the last few weeks it's been merely innuendos and I've managed to keep my distance; but today, she crossed the line and now I've got to find a way to keep my job without compromising my Christian image." Monica listened intently. Either Shawn was a pathological liar, or he was telling the truth. One thing that she couldn't deny was that Shawn never looked back or acknowledged that Lady as she left.

"I hear you Shawn," was all Monica could say.

"No dear, I don't want you to just hear me; I want you to believe me." Shawn took the picture from Monica and he pulled her close to him and their lips locked for some time. Monica's mind wandered thinking of taking her lips to his neck, instead she just used her hands to stroke his face, neck and back. Shawn's mouth began to sweep across Monica's face and then to her jaw bone, reaching her throat and he could feel her pulse racing. Looking at her sweet smelling neck, he ran his fingers gently down its grooves and ridges. He stopped and returned to her face where her eyes were closed. He put a final kiss on her forehead. Monica's eyes opened slowly and they were filled with passion. Shawn's phone vibrated and he looked down to see the caller ID.

"Be right back," he said at almost a whisper. Shawn was filled with a sensual quality that only movies seemed to capture. Monica sat there knowing that soon she would have to leave. It was getting dark and the clouds were threatening to do more than drizzle and she didn't want to get lost. Picking up her cell phone the time read: 6:45 pm. Shawn came back in the room with a strange look.

"Is everything okay?" Monica was concerned.

"Yea, it's cool." Shawn didn't want Monica to know how he truly felt.

"My girls had a surprise visitor come into town today. Their grandmother from Puerto Rico is here. So, they will be coming next weekend instead of this one." Monica could see the disappointment and its heart wrenching to see a big strapping man head so low.

"I'm sorry that they won't be here today. I wish there was something that I could do to make you feel better; but nothing can replace the space of your sweet little girls." Monica looked at his fireplace mantel and he had four photos of his girls ranging from infant to about five yrs. old.

"You're right that nothing and no one could replace the time that I view as precious with my little girls; but if you really want to cheer me up, you would stay with me tonight." Shawn knew he was treading on thin ice. Monica's neck almost broke as she turned her head looking more intently at Shawn as he sat on the couch next to her.

"You're joking right?" Monica could tell that he was not playing with the look that he gave her.

"Before you jump to conclusions, I'm a gentleman and I will sleep in the den. You would have complete privacy in the master suite. I just want to be with you, I'm not trying to do anything that God doesn't want me to, understand?" Shawn was pitching the best that he could.

Monica thought, this brother had a serious "Rap Appeal". I mean he could convince the Devil to repent, Monica thought.

"Shawn, I just don't see that as being appropriate. The bible says in Romans 14:16 "Let not then your good, be evil spoken of."

"You're right my dear, but in Titus 1:15, 16 it also says 'To the Pure all things are Pure.' Let me put it another way, I understand that you're concerned about your reputation - so am I. I live on the end house. This is a dead end street and I'm surrounded by nothing but trees, nature and an elaborate garden. I chose this home for more than its square footage, because I'm a private man. Trust me I don't invite people here that often and I also make a mean breakfast." Shawn smiled. His face had such an angelic quality at times and you could tell he never gave up, just wasn't in his genes.

"If I decided to stay, just if, I have nothing to wear, no personal feminine items, plus what would we do for the entire evening?" Monica was smart enough to know that they couldn't just sit around making out all evening. Things were already hot enough - they needed balance.

"Tell you what, there's a shopping center 8 minutes away, let's go get you some things right now." Shawn stood up now that Monica had nothing else to debate him about.

Monica had a solace look on her face as she stood up and faced Shawn. "You haven't answered my question about what will we do with the entire night?"

CHAPTER 8
SLEEPOVERS ARE FOR KIDS AND WOMEN

Monica had a pouty look and her eyes were truly like a little girl. She was so adorable to Shawn.

"I'm going to prove to you that we can have a night together without doing anything wrong. We are going to have fun, okay." He had to reassure her. If it took all night, he was determined to make her trust him. There was a strip mall that had a WalMart, PathMark, TJ Maxx, Barnes & Noble's, Sports Authority, Wells Fargo Bank and a Wendy's Restaurant there. Shawn pulled his BMW near to the TJ Maxx store. Monica was thinking he would have taken her to WalMart, but she just shrugged it off and they walked into the store. The first aisle they went to was the sleep wear. Monica quickly found the cutest pajama set: a pink tee shirt that said "Angel" and the pants was black and white striped. The fabric was soft and felt like good quality. It was on sale for $25.00 down from $39.99. Shawn grabbed a cart like a smart partner would do. Monica looked for a good lotion, body wash and found a traveler's case with toothbrush, deodorant and sponge. When she went to shop for the undies she looked at Shawn and he got the message and walked a couple of feet away. Monica picked up two boy cut panties, and looked for an inexpensive yoga pant and top. She found one that was gray/pink with a v necked front. Shawn came up with a pair of cute sneakers and footie socks.

"I wasn't sure what size shoes you wear, your feet look tiny so I brought a size 7 and 7 ½." Shawn looked down at Monica's feet. Monica put the intimates into her cart under the sweat suit.
She was totally undone by this guy's ability to even think of it, let alone go and find something remotely cute.

"Those are so cute," Monica said. "This is going to run me quite a Buck, but I'm digging those." Monica examined the sneakers as they were chocolate with a thick heel and had a pale pink trim inside and on the outer edges. They were totally her style.

"When I said we were going shopping, I didn't mean you were paying," Shawn stated. Shawn left Monica standing there with her mouth ajar and rolled the cart near the check out.

"Since there's normally a line here, why don't you grab anything else that you want and I'll wait for you, okay." Monica agreed and went for a camisole to wear with her sweats. Unbelievably so, the one customer that was in front of Shawn was called to cashier number 3. Monica went and stood next to Shawn and the announcer called for the next customer to go to cashier 1. They stood there and as Monica watched the ringing up, she noticed that the pajamas did not ring with the sale price.

"Excuse me, but that item did not ring with the sale price," Monica stated. The cashier looked like she had not only a rough day, but a rough life. She looked to be in her thirties and she wore all types of piercings in her lip, nose and her hair was stringy like a hippie. Her attitude went from bad to worse.

"I don't think this tag belongs to this outfit," she said with such a nasty tone. Before Monica could respond, Shawn jumped in.

"Does it really matter that someone in your store labeled it incorrectly, the consumer has to get it at the price that it's listed." Shawn stood there to wait for her rebuttal.

"Sir, I'm going to call for my manager." Her manager had just come up one of the aisles and the cashier waved her over. She pulled her manager over and explained what happened.

"Ok Sir, I'm going to do a price check for you and it will just take a moment, alright." The manager seemed to be a sixty something Italian lady, a bit nervous since her hand shook a bit.

"Let me explain something to you, there's no need for you to do a price check as there are no other pajama sets back there; secondly, consumer law states a price listed is a price honored. Now I know your corporate offices would hate to know that one of their stores have unscrupulous practices by ignoring statutes of law." Shawn was getting agitated but still maintained a level head.

"Ok Sir, I don't want to lose a customer over such trivialities. Frances, please finish ringing up these customers." The manager saw that the cashier had walked from ears distance, so she completed the transaction. Shawn didn't speak much as they drove back to his house. Shawn went into the back where the bedrooms were and he came back with a robe, towel and some other items.

"I left a towel and a few other things out for you, if you need anything else, let me know." Shawn looked at the time and it was 7:45.

"I'm a little hungry, would you like me to order something as I didn't take anything out to cook?" Shawn asked.

"What are the choices?" Monica asked.

"We have Chinese dominos, or I could go pick us up something." Shawn really just wanted to spend some time with Monica, instead of all this running around stuff.

"Dominos are cool," Monica said.

"How do you like your pizza?"

"With a thin crust, extra cheese, pepperoni and sausage." She gathered her stuff and went for the bedroom. "I'm taking a shower now."

"Alright." Shawn called in the order and he knew they would be there in twenty minutes. Shawn set up the flat screen TV for a few movies and he wanted to take his shower after Monica was done. Monica contemplated that she was really about to sleep over this guy's house who she knew for less than a month. She couldn't get over how quickly things were happening, even though nothing bad was being done; it was just the thought of how it looked. She was also scared over the idea that she was actually digging this man, to the point where she dreaded being out of his presence. The shower was exactly the way she liked it, hot with strong pressure. A little paranoid, she locked herself in the bathroom, putting on creams, perfume and deodorant. Now she could slide into her pajamas with comfort. Monica came out of the bathroom into the bedroom and put her dress into the TJ Maxx's bag. Her new footie socks felt so soft on her feet and she heard Shawn closing the door. The pizza must have arrived.

"That was quick," Monica stated.

"Yea, I know. I have the den set up with some movie selections that you might like. Can you carry the drinks while I get the rest?" Shawn asked.

"Yes." Monica followed Shawn to the den area, which was like the ultimate entertainment room.

"I am going to go take a quick shower and then we can chill out." Shawn took his robe with him and off he went. Monica sat down and took a small piece of pizza, not wanting to eat too much without Shawn. Shawn took what he would call a "speed shower". He washed his face, brushed his teeth and had the shower running, and then jumped in. He washed his body with attention, but he quickly came out. After he put on deodorant and scents, he put on his black pajama bottoms with a sleeveless tee shirt. He slid his slippers on and walked through the hallway. Monica could hear his footsteps getting closer. Shawn liked how Monica was getting comfortable and put a throw over her legs.

"Whatcha watching?" Shawn looked at the TV.

"Seinfeld reruns," she chuckled.

"Did you see anything of interest in the movies that I put out for you?" Shawn grabbed a slice of pizza and sucked it down in a split second.

Monica looked over the three films on the table: Agora, The Proposal and Prince of Persia.

"Honey, let's watch a movie before we go to sleep."

"Wait, I have a better idea," Shawn replied.

"Ok, what?"

"I'll be right back." Shawn left and came back with a long rectangular box in his hand. Monica smiled as she recognized what it was.

"This is going to be a long night," Monica said.

"Oh don't be like that," Shawn said. Monica remembered that Shawn said he liked scrabble. The pizza was done in ten minutes and the cheesy bread sticks were left over. They played two games that lasted about an hour. Monica yawned and Shawn took that to mean she wanted to rest.

"Tired?" Shawn inquired.

"A little," Monica said.

"I'm going to let you rest, Baby," Shawn said as he put the letters and board away.

"We had two good games, you won the first and I won the last." Monica's smirked.

"Hmmm. Well, this isn't over and neither are we." Shawn gave Monica a passionate look. Shawn reached in and began kissing Monica. Monica grew fearful that he would go overboard.

Shawn sensed her hesitation. "What's the matter?" Shawn stopped.

"Nothing, I just don't want us to get too caught up."

"Don't you mean swept up?" Shawn stated, now challenging Monica on her feelings towards him.

"Wow, you're pretty confident," Monica said sarcastically.

"It's not that I'm being cocky, Monica. I'm just stating the obvious connection that we have. Do you deny what's going on?" Shawn said. Monica was not comfortable expressing what she was feeling- not just yet. Still she saw that Shawn was not about to let her it go.

"I'm not denying the chemistry between us. I'm only saying we are fairly new at getting to know one another. That's all." She tried at all costs to avoid her real feelings.

"I'm going to let you off the hook tonight, Monica. You are avoiding the issue," Shawn said in a irritated tone. The television theme song for Law and Order SVU came on right in the midst of their conversation.

"Would you like to watch this or are you ready to retire?" Shawn asked. Monica was happy that he changed subjects.

"Sure we can watch this," Monica said. As the show played, Shawn pulled Monica close to him. Monica lay on his chest as they sprawled out on the sofa, in a cuddled position. As the credits rolled, they had both dozed off. Monica was awakened by the loudness of the commercial on the television. Still asleep, she didn't want to disturb Shawn. Monica tried to move as softly as possible; but to no avail, Shawn moved and woke up.

"I'm sorry Baby, I fell asleep on you." Shawn's eyes could barely focus.

"It's okay Sweetie, go back to sleep. I'm going to lie down in the bedroom." Monica got up and made sure Shawn's head was on the pillow. She covered him up like a little baby. She put a small kiss on his forehead and stood up to leave. "Good Night," she whispered.

"I love you," Shawn said with his eyes shut. Monica stopped in her tracks, but realized Shawn was fast to sleep. She got into Shawn's luxurious bed, it felt nicer than hers. My God, she knew that her sleep would be pleasant. Now if she could only get those words out of her head - "I love you?"

CHAPTER 9 -
THE PAST ALWAYS WRESTLES WITH THE FUTURE

Monica was awakened by the smell of bacon and something sweet. She picked up her cell and the time showed 10:00. She decided to shower, as she did not want to overstay her welcome. Monica couldn't help recalling what Shawn's last words were the night before. She wasn't sure whether he was talking in his sleep, or if he knew what he was saying. Monica put on her deodorant and always carried a travel size bottle of perfume. The one she had in her purse was "Daisy" and she put only small drops on her, because it was a strong fragrance. The jogging suit fit perfectly and her sneakers were very comfortable.

"Good Morning Sleepyhead," Shawn said to her as he saw her pas the couch. The kitchen faced the living area.

"Good Morning, how long have you been awake?" Monica was curious.

"I woke up about an hour ago, slept like a baby and now I'm about to serve you breakfast." Shawn was definitely a morning person.

"Smells good," Monica said.

"Come over and have a taste," Shawn said. Shawn had hot water for tea and coffee. He made French toast, scrambled eggs, bacon, turkey sausage and grits.

"I'm impressed, it all looks delightful." Monica smiled at Shawn. Shawn blushed and his dimples were more defined.

"Thank you," he said simply. They sat down as the food was prepared in a buffet style arrangement. Once they were finished, Monica held her stomach.

"This was so good, I can't imagine why any woman would let you go," and she said laughing.

"Well Monica, none of us are perfect and I guess God has the right person put to the side for all of us," he said profoundly. Monica was jilted into a more serious mode. She realized she struck a chord in him.

"I agree with you Shawn," She became a bit uncomfortable. As she helped Shawn clean up and was almost anxious. She had to get her things together and didn't want to take up any more of Shawn's space.

"Well Darling, I thoroughly enjoyed my evening and morning with you. I'm going to run along, and get some things together and I'll be speaking to you soon okay."

"Yes, Baby. I want to hear from you soon." Monica went out to put everything in her car, including her birthday gift. She left the front door open so that she could go back in the house and say good bye to Shawn. Monica walked over to Shawn and slipped her arms around his waist and got on her tippy toes to kiss his lips. Shawn pulled her up and sat her on his counter top. He held her face and kissed her passionately. Monica received the weight of his fire and was almost disintegrated. When Shawn released her face, his face was very sober. He picked her up again and allowed her feet to stabilize her.

"Call me, okay," Shawn said.

"Alright, Sweetie, enjoy your day." Monica left without looking back. She felt something that she didn't know how to articulate. Monica didn't want to leave, but it was in the best interest of both of them that she did. The heat between them was getting unbearable. Monica had not dated anyone since she became a born again believer. Her last encounter 4 years ago was with a man that caused her so much pain that it took her about a year to heal. In her backslidden state she went against her own values and had lowered her standards. Now she had a firm foundation in her Lord and Savior Jesus Christ and nothing and no one could convince her to stumble or fall. Her Spiritual antennas were up and she did not want to fall prey to her emotions or intellect. Monica missed Sunday Service, but she knew she could go to a mid-week service to have corporate worship and fellowship. Monica heard her ring tone (More of you by Fred Hammond) playing. She picked up her cell from the console and answered.

"Hello."

"Hey Girl, what's up?" Keiki asked.

"Just on my way home, what's up with you?"

"Where are you coming from?" Keiki wondered.

"I had breakfast with Shawn." Monica tried to trivialize it.

"Oh, I see. I thought you said he lived in Jersey?" Keiki inquired. Monica knew where this was going and she tried to make it as simple as possible. Monica gave her a mini version of how she went to see him and the misunderstanding that transpired.

"So you slept over?" Keiki was surprised.

"Yea, but of course nothing happened. He gave me his bedroom and he stayed in the den. It was kinda cool - actually." Monica struggled to make this sound innocent.

"Well, I'm just thinking - you said his boss is trying to seduce him and you walk in and see what you saw with your own eyes. I just think you might like him so much that you're not being realistic. Then he invites you to stay with him almost like to suck you in even more. You don't see anything wrong with that?" Keiki was getting annoyed at Monica's gullibility. Monica felt stupid and knew that no matter what she said, Keiki had already made a judgment not only on Shawn, but on her as well. Monica felt defenseless and wished she'd never shared this with Keiki.

"I can see how you would feel that way. It didn't look good, but I did pray about it and I will continue to ask God to show me the motives of his heart. It's not like we're in love or anything," Monica said.

"I just hope you will slow down at least. That's my opinion. You're my girl, so I'm just looking out for you; but anyway. I wanted to know if you would go with me to a barbeque today," Keiki asked.

"Who's barbeque?" Monica was glad that other conversation was over and would be more careful in the future of mentioning Shawn.

"I have a cousin who I haven't seen in years invite me. It's actually not that far from you, so no excuses!!!" Keiki laughingly spoke.

"What time is it going to be?" Monica was pulling up into her usual spot in front of her condo.

"It starts at 2:00 until." Keiki just noticed it was 12:05pm.

"I guess I can find something to wear and get myself ready. Why don't you text me the directions and I will meet you there?" Monica said.

"I'll pick you up. I have to come in that direction anyway. I can be there around say...2:00. The directions show they're just 13 minutes from you." Keiki said.

"Sounds good - call me when you are on your way." As they hung up from one another, Monica knew that 2pm meant more like 2:30ish. Monica did some light cleaning and laundry. As she searched her walk-in closet, she found a cute pair of denim Capri's. She paired it with a rainbow striped shirt. The shoes were raspberry in color, matching her blouse. Monica decided to pull her hair back in a pony style hairdo with lots of dropped curls that fell into a wide spread of wave patterns. Time was moving quickly and Monica saw that it was now 2:03pm. Her cell phone lit up and she answered before it could ring.

"Hello," Monica responded.

"I'm on my way. I'm about 10 minutes from you," Keiki advised.

"Ok, I'll see you when you get here." Monica continued to get dressed and putting on her final touches of lip-gloss, she decided to peek outside to see if she could see Keiki's car. Perfect, Monica thought. Gathering her purse and key, Monica went out to meet Keiki. Keiki and Monica were in front of her family's home in no time. Keiki admitted to Monica that her old flame, Brian might be at the barbeque.

"I can't believe you didn't mention anything to me about Brian before, when you told me about the barbeque." Monica was so irritated.

"I didn't think it would be a big deal, seeing that you guys haven't dated in like 5 years. Besides, you've moved on and seem to be digging on this other guy, right?" Keiki challenged Monica. While Monica was clearly over Brian, thank God! She still didn't want to be in his space and she didn't appreciate Keiki concealing this information, up until now. She wished she could just go back home.

"Whatever." Monica removed her seat belt. Keiki wore T-shirt dress above the knee. The dress was a pastel green and complimented her olive undertones in her complexion. Her makeup was flawless as usual and her shoes were gold thongs with a 2 inch heel. Keiki had a wonderful reunion with her aunts, uncles and cousins. She went about introducing Monica as her close friend and they grabbed food and sat to eat. After a few hours went by and Monica started to feel comfortable that Brian was not there, she just mingled with Keiki's family. She took a special liking to Keiki's Aunt Suza. They talked for at least an hour and Suza explained some of their native dishes and how some were Americanized.

Brian was very annoyed that Randy decided to take a detour to pick up a couple of his cousins. Had he known that they weren't going directly to pick up ice and some other stuff, he would have taken his car. Brian left his 2011 Chevy Corvette parked about a block away from the barbeque in Randy's driveway. Now that they were just minutes away from their destination, Brian tried to adjust his mood swing. Brian quickly departed the vehicle that Randy and his two cousins: Emma and Halima were riding in. After he opened the car door for Emma, he dodged them by telling them he had to use the restroom. As true as this was, his real motive was to see if Keiki managed to convince Monica to come to the barbeque. Brian went into the house and used the restroom quickly. Brian gave his self an overview while washing his hands. Once, he was satisfied that he looked fine, he opened the door and started to scan the yard. Brian's adrenaline was working overtime as he did not see Monica anywhere. Just as he began to feel that sinking feeling (he saw Keiki but no Monica) Brian walked back into the house about to greet Randi's Mom and to his surprise, there was Monica.

"Well, there you are, I've been looking for your beautiful face since I got here." Brian's face lit up. Both, Suza and Monica looked back surprised.

"Hey my long lost son, come hug your second Mommy." Suza held her chunky arms out wide for Brian to meet her. As Brian held Suza and kissed her on her fat cheeks, he winked at Monica in a sheepish manner. Suza let go of Brian and he stood off for a second.

"So what's going on in here, you teaching the women some cooking tips?" Brian said, now staring at Monica like she was his next meal.

"Oh, this pretty young thing is definitely an apprentice in the making." Suza smiled, but then took notice that there was unsaidness between the two.

"Oh, you know, I need to get Randy to bring in the ice, where is he dear?" Suza made an excuse to leave the room.

"He's outside, Momma Suza," Brian affectionately called her. Suza patted Monica as she moved out of the way of the two.

"I'll be right back, play nice." Suza left. Monica could see the setup, but had no power to do anything about it.

"So, we meet again," Brian said teasingly.

"It would seem so," Monica said sarcastically.

"I know this might be awkward for you, but I am glad to see you. I mean while we're here, there's no reason we can't at least be cordial to one another."

"I thought that's what we were doing." Monica knew that she couldn't let her guard down for one second dealing with Brian. He was like a bull and he was used to intimidating his way into any situation.

"Maybe I deserve that, but I know you're tired of just standing here. Why don't we just sit outside in a nice shaded area and just enjoy the weather, good food and so-so music." They both laughed as he summed it up right. Brian led Monica out into the yard area which was really spacious and quiet tropical looking, since they had a pool and the seating reminded her of one of HGTV backyard makeovers. The food spread was unlike anything that she'd ever seen. The buffet style setup contained everything from Chicken Satsu, Loco Moco (hamburger patties), macaroni salad; Mahi Mahi garden salad, various desserts and other American dishes were spread out.

"So Monica, how are you, really?" Brian asked.

"I'm doing quite well and you?" Monica asked.

"I'm doing great and you look good if I might add." Brian stared into Monica's eyes looking for a glimmer of hope.

"Thank you," She said begrudgingly.

"Look, Monica, you know I'm not one for small talk, so I'll just make myself plain if that's okay with you?" Monica nodded rolling her eyes.

"I have had a lot of time between the last time that we saw each other to think about how things went. I would like to ask for your forgiveness for all I've done, said, or neglected to do, that hurt you or caused damage to our friendship. Because at the end of the day, if we never had anything else, I pray that we would always be friends," Brian confessed.

"Wow Brian, that actually sounds like a speech of reconciliation from some support group." Monica was not impressed with this new and improved Brian.

"Man you really know how to hit a Brotha where it hurts. Yes, you are right, I've completed my 12-step program with AA and it is important that I reconcile with those in my life past or present that I wronged during those drug/alcohol filled days." Brian's face was now flushed. Monica felt compassion and wondered if she had gone too far with that comment. But she wanted Brian to understand that she was a different woman and none of his sly charm could permeate her armor of protection.

"I'm glad that you stuck it out and I pray that you will continue to press towards the mark. You have the potential to do so much and this will be my prayer for you." Monica had a sober look.

"Thank you," Brian said simply. Monica glanced around and noticed that Keiki was quite comfortable. Monica longed to check her phone to see if Shawn had called. Monica was ready to go and she wondered how much longer she would be there. They had been there a few hours and she was ready. Brian could see that Monica was preoccupied and knew that if he had the right setting - he would be able to tackle this wall that Monica had built. He understood that it would take time, effort and he was willing to give it his all.

"You look like you want to venture out, so I won't hold you back," He observed solemnly. Monica could see Keiki and a guy headed to their table.

"Hey Girl, this is my cousin, Randy."

"Good to meet you, Monica." Randy held her hand in his briefly.

"Nice to meet you as well."

"Are you enjoying yourself?" Keiki noticed a bit of stress on Monica's face.

"I'm okay, just getting a bit tired. I had a long evening last night." Monica gave Keiki a look. "What time do you think we'll be heading out?" Looking at her watch, Keiki knew she was not ready to go - not for at least a couple more hours.

"Well, if you want, I could have Randy drop you off?" Keiki offered. Monica had just met the guy and that would never do.

"I'll take you," Brian volunteered. Great, Monica thought-what a set-up, but what were her choices- a man she just met or her old flame.

"That's very nice of you, Brian."

"Let me go get the car, I'll be back in five minutes," Brian said. Monica said her goodbyes to Keiki's family and she took Suza's phone number to keep in touch. Keiki walked Monica to the front of the house and they saw Brian pull up. Brian jumped out of his fiery red corvette and opened the passenger side for Monica. Monica sat in the vehicle and put her seat belt on. Monica gave her address to Brian and he put it in his navigation system.

"Nice car," Monica commented. It matches your persona," she said.

"Thank you, if that's a compliment," Brian stated. Monica wondered how he kept the soft leather white interior so immaculate. While thinking, Brian opened the sunroof top and she felt the sweet breeze as they traveled. Brian didn't speak much, as it was a fairly short trip. He wasn't interested in looking or sounding desperate as he wasn't. Brian wanted Monica to be interested, because he struck a chord in her. He just needed to find that connection they once had, but maybe he was too late. Monica was glad that they were just about pulling into the parking area of her building.

"Safe and sound, you're here," Brian said.

"Much appreciated," Monica said. Brian reached over and removed Monica's seatbelt. Monica was taken by surprise and her face was in direct proximity to Brian's face. Monica could smell the aroma of his cologne sweep across her nose and she unintentionally breathed deeper.

"I hope we will see one another again soon. I enjoyed your presence and here's my card, it has my contact information listed," Brian said. Monica took the card and put it in her purse. She opened the car door and started up the walkway leading to the entrance. Brian watched her walk into her building and suddenly received a surge of energy. He thought about how he could just let her walk away - he had no phone number and she had not volunteered her phone number either. Brian jolted out of his car.

"Monica!" He called out. Monica's hand was on the door and she turned to look in Brian's direction. She let the door close and stood waiting as Brian came towards her.

"I hate to be a nuisance but would you mind me using your bathroom?" Brian asked. The ole bathroom trick, again - Monica was thinking. How could she say no? Brian followed Monica to her condo and couldn't wait to get inside; at least now he knew the floor and condo number.

"The bathroom is through the hallway on the left hand side." She pointed to the main bathroom. Brian's brain was still spinning on how he could get Monica's phone number. He quickly rinsed his hands and opened the door. Monica stood close to the door, as she did not want Brian to get comfortable.

"Hey, I'd like to invite you to a fashion show that I'll be featured on next Saturday. Your support would mean so much to me," Brian suggested.

"I'll think about it," Monica said.

"Can I get your contact information so I can give you the details?

"I'll tell you what, I have yours - so I will check with you prior to Saturday, if that works for you," Monica said.

"Alright, I look forward to seeing you soon." Brian gave Monica a kiss on the cheek and left. Monica had to give it to him he was soooooooooo persistent.

CHAPTER 9 ½ - A FIERCE TUG OF WAR

Brian knew he needed to step up his game, if he was to regain Monica's trust. So she didn't want to give her phone number, but he had access to her condo and also her best friend. Brian was not turned off by the challenges set before him, but on the contrary he was turned on. Brian was a fierce competitor in anything he put his hands to. Brian decided to skip going back to the barbeque- as he wanted to get some much needed rest. His new venture and career depended mostly on looks and his competitive edge. Brian spoke to his agent and had a scheduled interview for his next gig. He would go home, shower and listen to some new gospel songs that a female friend gave him on a mixed compilation cd. One way or the other, Brian was moving steadily and tenaciously towards Monica.

Monica checked her phone messages and to her dismay, no calls from her new interest, Shawn. She wanted to hear his voice, but she was concerned about being too available to him. She hoped spending the night with him did not take the fire out of his pursuit of her. Now she felt like she was in limbo. Hearing her cell ring, her heart was delighted.

"Hello."

"Hey Girl," what's up? Keiki asked. Monica was disappointed that it was not Shawn on the other end, but she tried not to convey that to Keiki.

"Hey Sis, whatcha doing? Great barbeque by the way," Monica replied.

"Yea, it was really cool. I haven't seen that side of my family in like eons," Keiki said.

"So how was the ride home?" Keiki asked.

"It was alright. It's just you know, I feel that Brian was trying to rehash something that's dead. I think he sees that I'm not really into him like I was in the past."

"Well, you never know. I mean I spoke with my cousin, Randy and he had some really good things to say about your ex. I'm not rallying for him or anything."

"I'm happy for him. Cleaning up his act was the best choice that he could have made. I wish all of the best for him."

"So what's going on with Shawn?" Keiki switched quickly.

"I haven't spoken to him yet, but I'm sure I'll probably speak to him by tomorrow," Monica stated.

"That's weird. I thought you guys would have talked by now after spending the night together," Keiki said.

"I don't see it as a big deal. He has kids, so I give him his space to be a dad and all." Monica really didn't want to get into this conversation too deep.

"Just surprised, I guess. I just want you to keep your options open, keep a safe pace. You don't want to crash and burn, babes - you know. You deserve the best." Keiki felt Monica needed to wake up.

"I hear ya. I'll do just that." Monica just wanted to escape this subject.

"So did you see any guys at the barbeque of interest, I know they weren't all relatives?" Monica wanted to turn the focus away from her.

"Child you already know the type of men I like, dark chocolates". They both broke out in laughter for a few minutes.

"Alright Lady, I have to get ready for work tomorrow. How's the job search?" Monica asked.

"Funny that you ask, I have a temp to perm assignment through my agency tomorrow. So pray for me," Keiki stated.

"Okay Girlie, I'll send up some timber. You get some rest for your new gig. Love ya," Monica said. Monica layed in her bed and thought about what Keiki said. Her heart was telling her one thing and her head another. Monica said her prayers and left all cares with her Heavenly Father.

Monday Morning

Monica's morning was a blur, she had to process the information and sort through all the applications. The data that was provided on the forms that was given out previously from the prior meeting needed to be put on a excel spreadsheet. It was now 12:00 noon and Monica was working fervently. Her supervisor, Carolyn, was in and out of her office all morning. Carolyn was usually a happy-go-lucky type of person, but recently it seems that she is uptight. Monica was concerned that she was perhaps over worked or experiencing some personal issues. Monica's thoughts were sporadic and she wondered why she hadn't heard anything from Shawn and hoped everything was okay with him. She decided she would call him after she had completed most of her projects at work.

Shawn woke up with what felt like a golf ball lump in his throat. The night before it was like a minor sore throat. He wanted to speak to Monica, but since he wasn't feeling he decided to call her later. He gargled and drank tea with lemon. Now he wasn't sure what was going on. He called his primary care provider and was advised to come in. Shawn's voice was faint and his doctor, Larry Douglas did not even recognize him on the phone. Shawn spoke to Selena's assistant to let her know that he may be coming in late, after his doctor's appointment. Shawn's doctor's office was about twenty minutes away from his home, so it actually wasn't very far from his office. Shawn studied the parking lot of his physicians building. It seemed to be always packed, mainly because the three story building was like a one stop medical facility. The offices were all under the "Douglas Foundation" a genius prodigy that other doctors and private practices were taking notice of. Larry Douglas's father coached a group of college buddies, who studied medicine, science and technology, into collaborating their talents into a foundation initially for the community. Now they have branched out centers for various neighbors. Inside their offices are labs, sliding scale fee-based clinics, students, professors for all the major medical specialties, even a pharmacy. The only thing they lacked was an overnight hospital facility which was on the horizon as their next goal! Shawn saw that the office actually was empty! Shawn approached Sara the check in receptionist. She was an older lady in her sixties with short pixie styled platinum blonde hair. She had been with Dr. Douglas for ten years and he would probably have to shut down his practice if she ever retired.

"Good Morning Sara, where is everyone?"

"Hello! Dr. Douglas was actually scheduled for a half day and a few of his appointments were cancelled, which means you are a lucky man today!" She smiled. Sara's presence was like the sun.

"Sara, you know I don't believe in luck, only Jesus." Shawn smiled at Sara with a wink as she understood what he meant. Shawn filled out the sign in sheet, noting one other name written in prior to his. Their sign in time was only ten minutes before his. He sat down and browsed through the magazines. A story caught his eye from Oprah O's magazine. Shawn sat back and delved into the story.

Normally, Selena would be very upset that her number one guy, Shawn, was not in yet, but she was a bit distracted by her current timeline. She also knew she had to play it cool, since the last time they saw each other things got a little hot and heavy. Not in the way that she had wanted, but nevertheless she would get what she wanted. Selena set up a few interviews for some needed help and had already hired a temporary assistant through one of her trusted recruiters for an elite hiring agency called "Quality Works". Selena and a few other execs would meet for another group interview of three men. This consultation was so important, because whoever was chosen would be the face of their new marketing video.

"Dang, that Shawn!" She spoke in a low voice, "of all the days to get sick." She wanted Shawn to do this interview, as he had an eye - more like an intuition when it came to what sells and what people were willing to buy into, but she was determined not to be crippled by his absence. Selena walked by the receptionist, Heather.

"Ms. Campbell, they're waiting for you in the conference room."

"I'm aware," Selena said in a matter of fact manner. Selena slithered down the hallway towards the conference room. She peeked in through the small upside rectangular glass window. She saw three men seated, along with one other executive named Bob Stanley. She stepped into the room and all eyes fell on her. Selena was all business and she had a sort of witchy attitude, as she made her way to the last seat at the head of the table. Looking at Bob she became a bit perturbed.

"Where is Leon?" She asked annoyed.

"Leon was scheduled for another meeting that conflicted with this one?" Bob saw that Selena was in a no nonsense mood. Selena breathed in then glanced over her papers that she brought for the interview, pressing the button on the phone.

"Heather can you send me Ricky from Shawn's team."

"Good Morning Gentlemen, my name is Selena Campbell and I'm sure my colleague, Bob Stanley, has already introduced himself. I apologize for my delay, as one of my top Marketing guys is out of the office for the moment. Once we have Ricky from his division join us, we will be able to start this interview process."

Ricky was elated that he, obviously, was being called into an important meeting. By the tone of Heather's voice it was urgent. Ricky quickly grabbed his writing pad and two pens -on the chance that something happened to one.

"Great," Selena stated as she watched Ricky close the door behind him and sit beside Bob.

"Now, I've reviewed all of the resumes here. I would like each of you gentlemen to introduce yourselves, starting from left to right."

"My name is Kevin West."

"I'm Paul Walker."

"Brian Jones."

Selena looked over each one as they spoke their name. Kevin had more of an urban edge to him; had a silky chocolate tone to his skin and his eyes showed a street grittiness to them. Paul had a California beach boy image, with his piercing blues eyes and dirty blonde locks. Brian was like a mixture of caramel and cream; his dark brown eyes were captivating and his stature was not only athletic (like a basketball, player) but the image of a born model.

"Alright, why don't we break up into groups to make things go easy and quickly? Bob, I want you to meet with Kevin. Ricky, you can sit with Paul and I'll interview Mr. Jones, is it?" She looked directly at Brian and motioned him towards her area at the far end of the room. He was dressed in casual wear (as were the interview instructions); he donned a dark brown hat, with an ivory one button jacket and a light salmon tee shirt underneath with dark blue jeans. His shoes were a dark stone with specks of brown throughout it. All in all Selena liked his look.

"You certainly look the part Mr. Jones." Selena looked at Brian with her face tilted.

"Thank you," was all Brian said.

"Unfortunately, viewing your resume it appears that you fall short." Selena sat back in her chair, waiting to see if Mr. Jones was all looks. Hoping there was a brain behind all that beauty.

Brian chuckled inwardly as he's never been called short, or been measured in such a term before.

"If your measuring tool is merely a piece of paper, then perhaps you might have a point. However, there is more to me then a piece of paper or the clothes that I'm wearing. Correct me if I'm mistaken, but the job description was for a masculine male that every man could identify with and at the same time want to emulate. This man should have an ease in front of the camera and exude confidence in any setting with or without in audience. I believe I fit the description that your company is looking for," Brian said. Certainly not what Selena expected to hear.

"You certainly make a valid presentation for yourself Mr. Jones, but that doesn't make up for the fact that there is no background work to justify me hiring you." Selena liked Brian, but she would not compromise.

"Why don't you validate me? It seems that you are the boss here. So whatever you say is accepted. You have me here 'live and up close'. "Aren't interviews supposed to help you determine what resumes can't articulate or uncover? Why don't you put me to the test?" Brian's look was sober and yet intense. Brian saw if he didn't have her attention before - she was all ears now. Selena was actually turned on - not just physically. This man had her entire attention. She was not just curious about his outer man, but intrigued by his inner man. Selena sat up in her seat... dialing her secretary.

"I need you to set up a quick run with Harvey the media guy. Yes, right now." Selena hung up and looked at Brian directly in his eyes.

"I hope that you can perform as well as you can talk, Mr. Jones." Selena stated.

"Gentleman, Mr. Jones and I will step out indefinitely, so when you are done with the interview(s), please check back with me." Selena led Brian to the media room where it was a studio setup. Harvey was there waiting for them and Selena introduced them and left them to work. Selena was anxious to see whether Brian was all talk. Time would tell, she thought walking towards her office. Selena was checking her voice messages when her email pop up showed an email from Harvey, the media guy. Selena hung up and opened the email.

The subject read: Brian's take 2 of Men's N Things. Selena watched the three minute video stream and was utterly amazed. Brian's charisma on camera was greater than in person. Harvey wrote in the email: "He's definitely a natural." Selena office phone rang with Harvey's extension.

"I just watched the video," Selena said.

"It was a pleasure to work with Brian. I have him looking at the two takes that we did and I showed him some areas of improvement stalling for time. I didn't know what you wanted me to do with him, as normally we work with people on staff." Harvey was scratching his head.

"You can send him to my office. Just have one of the guys over there direct him to me. Thank you for taking him on such short notice." Selena had great respect for Harvey. He never let the company down and never complained. Selena could see hear one of her employees directing Brian to her office. Soon Brian tapped lightly on her slightly ajar door. His frame was long and appealing.

"Please come in Mr. Jones, have a seat." Selena waited for Brian to sit.

"Impressive. I'm pleasantly surprised." Selena looked at him in a curious.

"I'm glad I was able to perform up to your standards." Brian was careful to keep things as professional as possible, even though Selena was fine. Her long curly tresses were falling randomly as she moved naturally and seemed to pose when she paused between words. She was modelisque in every way. He wanted to ask her, but knew this wasn't the right time or place.

"I would like to offer you the assignment." Selena sat back now, and her body language shifted to her "business as usual" mode.

"Wow, Brian smiled slightly, I wasn't expecting that." Brian was caught off guard thinking she would drag this process a little.

"Well, Mr. Jones, when I want something - I just reach out and grab it. I don't play to lose, I play to win. So if you are interested in the position, it's yours." Selena was playing with her pen and threw it down as she made the last comment.

"I accept your offer," Brian stated calmly.

"Great! Welcome aboard! Though I'm sure you've read the stipulations and are aware that you are a free agent here, tomorrow you can come in at 9:00 and we'll have your badge and locker information ready. Any questions?" Selena stood as she was ending the meeting.

"I believe you've given me all that I need for today, thank you." Brian was amazed at how quickly things went.

"So, I'll see you in the A.M." Selena stuck her hand out to shake Brian's hand. Brian obliged her and reached out to shake her hand. When her hand reached his - Selena felt a surge of fire - an unusual heat. Not wanting to appear nervous she withdrew slowly. Brian could feel Selena's energy and his eyes held hers while she took her hand back.

"Thank you for the opportunity, Ms. Campbell. Have a wonderful day." As Brian walked out of the office he felt the impression that was left behind. Selena was a bit stunned by what just transpired. She wasn't sure of what occurred. She shrugged it off and thought of herself being silly. Her thoughts went to Shawn. She hadn't heard from him since earlier this morning. She hoped that their last meeting hadn't scared him off. She didn't hear of anything from human resource and knew that would have been the first notification. She knew she had to play it cool for now, Shawn was different; finally, one that wouldn't compromise.

Doctor's Office

Shawn had all his vitals taken, and he waited for the swab results of his throat. Dr. Douglas noticed his glands were swollen and he knew that antibiotics would be prescribed.

"Alright Son, you definitely have laryngitis and a bronchial infection and your sinuses are irritated." I'm putting you on this asthma vaporizer machine to clear up some of the wheezing I hear in your chest. Meanwhile, I'll have Sara call in your prescription(s). I want you to relax and take it easy this week, understood?" Dr. Douglas was like an uncle to Shawn and he has been taking care of him since he was in college.

"No problem doc." The doctor's assistant Sherrelle put the mask on him and he laid back and tried to be comfortable. Shawn was not going to go home, as he had too much work to catch up on. He just received a flashback of Selena and their last encounter. He hoped that Selena came to her senses before things got ugly. Shawn didn't want to rock the boat, but his career was on the line and he would do whatever it took to protect himself. Shawn picked up his prescriptions and decided to follow his doctor's instructions and take the rest of the day off. Dr. Douglas prescribed pain medicine for his throat and he advised that it would make him drowsy. However, tomorrow he would not rest - as he needed to make sure that things were in order. He reached for his cell and activated his hands-off to dial his office. Barely able to speak, he just hung up and decided to send an email. Monica flashed before him and he was conflicted he wanted to call, but he knew she wouldn't be able to hear him clear or understand him. Once he got home, he would take his meds and text Monica.

Monica's day was stressful and hard, but it went quickly due to her work load. She was still feeling strange about not communicating with Shawn. She had just spent an awesome night with him and thought that everything was going well. It was close to 4:30, so she began rapping everything up. Monica sent her excel sheet to her supervisor, Carolyn and the Director Roy Clemons. Monica worked very close to her job and would be home in less than 15 minutes. Monica reached the traffic light and stopped for the red light. She heard her cell phone as a new text came in. She picked it up, although, she knew there may not be enough time to read it before traffic would start again. Still her curious nature wouldn't let her wait. Monica went to her messages and was surprised to see a text from Shawn. The light turned green and Monica placed her phone in the console. Monica became agitated that

Shawn would send her a text instead of calling her. She drove into the complex and headed for her parking area. Monica gathered everything and closed her car door. Entering her building, she was adamant to wait until she got herself settled before she would read her text. She was nervous to even look at the text message, as she didn't know what to expect. She sat on her bed and scrolled through her cell for his message. Shawn's Text: Hi, Monica. I'm sorry I wasn't able to speak to you or call. I just got home a little while ago from my doctor's office. I have laryngitis, a bronchial infection and my voice is at a whisper. He advised me to take it easy for a few days, but today will be the only day I rest. I pray that we will talk tomorrow, if my voice allows. Miss you.

Later Monica leaned on her canopy post from her bed. She didn't know how to respond to this text. It seemed too unreal. Could Shawn be avoiding her? Perhaps he is just a player and he needed his space for the moment. All sorts of thoughts flooded Monica's mind. At any rate, this was just too convenient. A few days ago - he didn't even have a cold. Monica was frantic and knew there was only one way to handle Shawn. She texted him back.

Monica's text: Hope you feel better, my prayers are with you. Shawn lay in his bed with his pajama bottom. He tried to watch TV, but the TV ended up watching him. He heard his cell phone vibrate with Monica's response. Shawn read what she wrote. He thought to himself she sounded a bit impersonal, but his medicine was beginning to take its toll and he really did need to rest. Monica checked her phone frequently over the next few hours. Her emotions ran rampant and she settled herself with the knowledge that she hardly knew Shawn and it was just silly to have put so much trust in him. Normally, when it seems too good to be true "it is". Unable to stand the landslide of her own thoughts, Monica took a break. Dialing a familiar friend she waited for an answer.

"Hello," Keiki answered.

"Hey, what's up?" Monica tried to sound normal.

"Nothing just watching a movie, what's up?" Keiki asked.

"Just got home from work and relaxing, that's all." Monica felt that she would break into tears.

"You sound funny, is everything alright?" Keiki asked.

"I'm just, you know tired that's all." Monica hated telling a partial truth.

"Oh, ok. So how's your new beau, what's his name - Shawn?" Keiki thought it strange Monica didn't mention him.

"He's sick, but other than that, I guess he's good." Monica wished she didn't have to bring him up.

"Sick? What like a cold?" Keiki started getting suspicious.

"No, he has laryngitis and an infection. He told me his doctor gave him a few prescriptions." Monica wanted to end the call now.

"Girl, do you really believe he just all of a sudden got sick? When did you talk to him?" Keiki was annoyed.

"How could I talk to him if he has laryngitis? He sent me a text." Monica knew what Keiki was thinking, as all those thoughts already crossed her mind. She just wanted to bury them.

"Look, he texted you telling you all that crap! It sounds just a little convenient that he hasn't been able to speak to you and now he has laryngitis. I mean you can believe him if you want, but Girl-that just sounds like a bunch of concocted mess. I know you like this guy, but he seems like he's trying to play you." Keiki was done at this point.

"Don't you think I've already thought about all those things you're saying? I just really don't know. All I can do is just step back, pray and God will show me which way to go." Monica's face was wet with tears. Keiki could tell that Monica was very upset, crying now.

"I just don't want to see my best friend get hurt, that's all. Maybe you should just keep your distance, you know. Listen, I saw Brian the other day and all he could talk about was you. I was kinda skeptical about him, but he could really have changed. When he gave you a ride, he gave you his number, right?" Keiki asked.

"Yea, he did." Monica calmed herself down.

"So call him. There's no harm in just talking and at least you know what he's about and find out what's going on with him. Nobody's saying you have to make any commitments or anything. Just enjoy yourself and don't get your heart set on anyone for the moment." Keiki advised.

Monica knew there was some truth to what Keiki was saying, but she was feeling hurt and a little confused as to what to do.

"We'll see what happens. I'm just going to pray right now and I'll call you back later, alright?" Monica needed time to think.

"Alright, Girl. Don't let these men stress you out. "Too Blessed to be Stressed", that's what you taught me, remember?" Keiki tried to make light of the situation.

"Yep, absolutely."

"Talk to you later."

"Later," Monica hung up. Monica laid there contemplating her conversation with Keiki. She talked to God in her mind. She decided that she would watch some TV. Monica flicked the channels and channel surfed, but nothing could keep her interest. She picked up the phone and dialed the number. She decided that it was better to know, than to guess what was in her head.

"Hello, the voice on the other end cleared his voice."

"Hi, I hope that I didn't disturb you?" Monica stated.

"Actually, I am surprised to hear from you" he said.

"I wanted to see how you were feeling, so I called." Monica had goose bumps and hoped she made the best decision calling him.

"I'm doing better, now that I hear your sweet voice," he said.

"Good, so how was your weekend?" Monica asked.

"Why don't we do this, let's just skip the small talk. I want to see you. Can I see you tonight?" He asked.

"Wow, um. What did you have in mind?" Monica asked.

"If you haven't eaten dinner, why don't I pick you up and we can eat?"

"What time?" Monica asked.

"About 30 minutes."

"That's doable." Monica agreed and they hung up. Monica went to her closet to find something unique to wear. She knew it would be a casual, local dining as it was short notice. She found her black halter jumpsuit. The mid section was black lace, so she grabbed her wide cinch belt to accent the sheer part. Monica jumped in the shower as she knew that 30 minutes was short. Monica put skin-so-soft oil on after she came out the shower and began spraying her perfume on to take advantage of every minute. Looking at the clock, she saw that twenty minutes had passed. Quickly, she put on deodorant and slid her jumpsuit on and began combing her hair. She decided to put her hair in a ponytail and let her loose curls dangle naturally. Putting just a bit of eyeliner on and pink tinted lip-gloss, Monica heard her buzzer ring. She grabbed her cell, purse and keys.

"I'll be right down." Monica said. Feeling a bit unsure as to all that had transpired this weekend, she tried to tell herself that she wasn't being desperate.

As she reached for the handle on the exit door, she saw him leaning on his vehicle waiting to open her car door. His smile was dynamic and he was definitely "eye candy".

"Hey, you are looking foxy," he said.

"Thank you, you look nice too." Monica was being modest as Brian always looked like he stepped off of a magazine cover. He was wearing slate grey stone washed jeans and a light turquoise crew neck tee shirt. He had white sneakers with specks of turquoise in them. He opened the car door and waited as she got comfortable. He sat down and looked behind before reversing his corvette and he drove off. Turning back and forth to view Monica, he spoke: "I hope you don't mind the casual attire, I just got home, showered and was going to go play some pool, but then you called," Brian said.

"Oh, I didn't know you had other plans." Monica's looked like a guilty kid.

"Nah, trust me this is much better than pool," Brian stated. "By the way, I know that there is a whole strip of restaurants, but I'm not sure which you would prefer?"

"Olive Garden or Hooligan would be fine." Brian parked in Hooligan's lot and stepped out of the car. He retrieved Monica and pressed his alarm system off, prior to walking. It seemed like a fairly quiet night and that worked in Brian's favor, as he wanted to just talk to Monica without too much disruption. The hostess seated them and the waiter came shortly after that. They ordered their food and waited for the drinks. Monica sat back and looked at Brian while he ordered his food. His nose was well suited for his face, as it had a high bridge and ended like a button shape. His lips were framed with a lovely mustache. Monica was always attracted to a man who had great grooming and manners. It was like a trademark of good looks to her.

"So, Monica, you still look fabulous. What's new in your life?" Brian had taken mental photo shots of Monica in that chic black jumpsuit. It really measured her attributes quite nicely and he wished he could pull her to his side of the table.

"I was just recently promoted on my job and I'm enjoying the new role." Monica smiled with a bit of nerves.

"How about you, how's your world? Monica remembered their breakup was filled with drama. She hoped that Brian had really changed. The waiter brought their food and drinks simultaneously. They both ordered appetizers, as they were not terribly hungry. Brian sat back as if he was prepared to fully engage Monica.

"Firstly, I would like to thank you for even calling me. I didn't know if I would see you anytime soon. My life has taken such a turn for the best. I'm modeling and trying to get my feet into doing various projects like, commercials, videos and whatever my talents will allow. My ultimate goal is to be a role model for others that were bound by drugs and alcohol. If I can do it, then I know that it's possible for anybody. Besides, I believe someone prayed for me." Brian's face grew warm and his eyes sent her a message that she could understand. Monica knew that Brian had a serious "gift for gab"; but he definitely could still make her feel things that she did not want to feel.

"I'm happy to hear that you are rooted and grounded. I pray that God will have his perfect way with you," Monica said as she took a bite of a chicken egg roll.

"I pray that God will grant me the desires of my heart, as he says in his word." Brian could not afford to waste one moment, he wanted Monica back and would do whatever it took.

"Are you a practicing Christian now Brian?" Monica knew that Brian knew the way, but she wanted to see if this was just a facade.

"I'm not going to tell you that I'm walking the straight and narrow, but truly I want to." Brian couldn't lie when it came to God. That's where he drew the line. Monica nodded her head.

"Tell me, what happened to the guy I saw you with at Dave and Busters?" Brian asked. Monica forgot about that, she was hoping she could limit her conversation to just them.

"Actually, we just recently met and he seems like a really cool person." Monica did not feel the need to say any more than that.

"Hmmm. I'll leave that for now." Brian knew better, he perceived that things must have shifted if he's here with Monica and the other guy is not. Monica was like "whew". She appreciated Brian leaving that sore subject alone.

"How did you like the food?" Brian asked.

"It is delicious; would you like to try one of my egg rolls?" Brian shook his head no.

"Nah Babes, I'm full now." The waiter stopped by to check on them and Brian had him bring the bill. He handed the waiter the money and left him a tip.

"Would you like a dessert?" Brian asked.

"No, I'm fine," Monica replied.

"Yes that you are." Brian stood up and Monica picked up her purse and they were off to the car. Brian put on some smooth jazz and they rode away. At the point that they reached Monica's building, Brian sighed.

"Are you okay?" Monica asked?

Parking, Brian sat back in a sort of moody way.

"I just really wish I had more time with you. Believe it or not, I feel comfortable with you and no one has ever made me feel that type of security." Brian turned and looked at Monica. Monica didn't know how to respond at first. She didn't want to be cool, because he appeared to be genuine. At the same time, she didn't want to egg him on.

"I'm sure that our history makes it easy to just allow feelings to be triggered," Monica commented.

"Do you not have any feelings toward me, Monica?" Brian wanted to invoke something in her.

"Of course, I have feelings. I just deal with them differently." "I see. You ignore them?"

"No, that's not what I mean. I just"... Brian interrupted; taking her face he placed a soft kiss on her lips as light as a flower. Monica's eyes widened. She was in shock. When Brian released her, he waited for her to recoup.

"If you weren't feeling me, I'm sorry. I needed to feel you and I couldn't resist it any longer." Brian watched Monica for any response.

"I have to go now, Monica said simply." She did not wait for Brian to open her car door. She got out quickly and heard Brian calling her, but continued toward her entrance. She could hear Brian's footsteps right behind her and she pulled the door and it closed just as Brian come close to her. She turned looking through the glass partition: "Thanks for dinner." She waved and walked away. Brian watched Monica until he could view her no more. He wondered if he had come on too strong. Maybe she was a different woman, or perhaps she no longer loved him; but she didn't resist his kiss. Her running away was a statement by itself. Monica couldn't wait to get into her bedroom. She took off her shoes. Next she grabbed her kneeling pillow. Monica prayed to Jesus. She asked for his guidance and wisdom. She prayed that he would show her what to do and what was his perfect will for her. She needed to know whether Shawn was the imposter or Brian. Or worse, neither one was who God sent. Monica stayed in that position for about forty minutes. Now, it was 10:00 pm and she put her nightgown on and crawled in her bed. Monica was emotionally drained; she fell asleep in less than ten minutes.

CHAPTER 10 - SPARKS FLY

Over the course of the following three days, Monica had not had any phone talk contact with Shawn. Tuesday she received another text message and Wednesday he called while she was in a meeting at work. Monica tried to return the call, but they appeared to be playing phone tag. Now it was Thursday and that morning she woke up to another text. This time it was about seeing her that night. Meanwhile, Brian had not missed a night in calling Monica; he even sent her red and yellow roses to her condo. Monica stopped wondering about what Shawn was really about. She even ignored Shawn's call that Thursday afternoon, while she was sitting at her desk at work.

At the office of "Make Me Over"

Shawn was having one heck of a week. He comes into work on Tuesday. He knocks on Selena's office door and she calls him in. "Good Morning, I hope you are feeling better today," Selena said.

"I'm here." Shawn's voice was barely audible.

"Oh my Lord, you really have no voice at all." Selena threw her hands up in a sigh.

"I wanted to discuss with you what's going on. I hired a couple of people and I wanted to introduce you to them. Now, because of your voice, what we'll have to do is work around this," Selena said.

Shawn had a pad and pen and began writing in response, since he could not strain himself to speak louder. Shawn wrote on his pad ripped it out and gave it to Selena. Selena read it and picked up her phone, nodding towards Shawn.

"Yes, can you please send in the new guy and stop in my office so I can introduce you." Selena wanted to catch Shawn up to speed. Selena was glad for the additional workload. She did not want Shawn to feel that her aggressive come on would by any means change or disrupt their business relationship. Selena was cunning and focused when it came to her role in the company. Shawn sat waiting to meet the new hires and chuckled inwardly at how cold Selena was. One minute she wanted to rip his clothes of and the next she was icy as it pertained to business. Truly she was dangerous and unpredictable. She reminded him of his last ex. Selena was wearing a bold red suit with white and black accessories. Her blouse was an off-white rounded neckline, nine west shoes were also off-white trimmed in black. Her hair was spiral curls layering from her jaw line, to her mid back. She wore bangs cut, fairing a china doll. Shawn sat to the left of the door to Selena's office and could tell by Selena's expression that someone was about to enter the office. Shawn this is my new assistant, Keiki Thompson. Shawn stood up to shake her hand and was surprised to see Keiki. Keiki was shocked and stood there stiffly.

"Hello, Shawn". Keiki finally was able to blurt out.

"I'm sorry Keiki - Shawn is unable to speak much, he has laryngitis." Selena advised her. Keiki felt totally ridiculous, now realizing, Shawn was really sick.

Shawn wanted to find out how she had managed to come to know about the opening for the position. It was just as well that he couldn't speak, as he couldn't think of anything to say. Selena could tell reading their eye contact, that there was more than meets the eye.

"Do you two know one another? Selena asked. Shawn turned his attention to Selena wishing he could verbalize what he wanted to say.

"Yes, through a mutual friend." Keiki volunteered. Shawn nodded his head in agreement.

"Well, enough of the small talk, I want you to prepare the conference room for the viewing of the latest commercial with the new guy." Selena said in an impatient manner. Keiki looked at Selena with a disdained expression as she left the office. Shawn was still standing and caught a glance of the image of a male figure coming towards the doorway. Not a chance he thought, as he quickly saw him in entirety coming into view. Shawn was more flabbergasted then anything. He thought maybe "he was being punked." Brian walked into the office dressed in "fatigues". Selena took in the view of him and she was more than pleased.

"Good Morning Mr. Jones, this is my "right-hand" guy Mr. Shawn"-and before she could finish...

"Awww, I believe we've met before," Brian stated as he held out his hand to shake Shawn's." By now Shawn was truly bewildered.

"Sorry, Shawn may not be able to reciprocate your enthusiasm as he has a case of laryngitis." Selena advised.

"Still, I wanted you to meet, as we will be going over some of your work today. How was it working with Hank and the others in the media department?"

"I am very comfortable with your staff, as they are very knowledgeable and professional. Hopefully, that will come across in the videos that we worked on today." Brian commented.

"I'm sure that based on the feedback I received today, everything went well," Selena stated.

"Great, well unless you need me, I'm going to head out and will see you tomorrow," Brian stated. Selena walked closer towards Brian and her body spoke louder than the words that came out of her mouth.

"I'll walk you out then," Selena said.

"Walk you out?" Shawn perplexed. "What just happened?!" One day out of the office and if seems that all mayhem broke out. Not only was his lady's best friend working in his office, but her ex as well?!?! This seemed too coincidental. Not only did this Brian guy seem to have captured Selena's interest (new meat), which actually works in Shawn's favor, still...something seemed altogether wrong; and, incidentally, Monica appeared to be distant lately. He wondered what was happening?

Wednesday flew by like a blur. Shawn had worked 12 hour shifts since Tuesday trying to catch up with last week's work. Although he had the bulk of his assignments completed, he still had to help edit the videos and fine tune the other projects. He knew Thursday would be the latest that he would have to do his one-on-one reviews for his team. He wasn't looking forward to this, as one of his veteran guys was about to go on a verbal warning. Now Thursday, he was kind of relieved when he found out that Ralph called in sick; but after he found out that he was in the hospital, he felt bad. Shawn knew that the standard policy was to send a card and flowers depending on the length of stay, but Shawn always took the scriptures literally when it came to visiting the sick. Shawn made a call to Monica, as his voice was good enough to have a conversation. Shawn left a brief message as it went to voice mail. Selena came by Shawn's desk just when he finished leaving the voice message.

"Are you busy, Selena asked?"

"No, I was just about to check on the latest edition of the "Men's N Things" commercial."

"Great, I was headed over there myself and wanted you to join me, so that I could get your views." Selena led the way in her usual fashion. The video was already queued for viewing. Selena pressed play. The footage was a scene that Brian was sporting the fatigues. The camera zoomed on Brian among a typical day of shopping amongst other men shopping in a men warehouse. There were rows and rows of suits, walls of ties, and the camera gave a wide view of shoes and sports related products. As it appeared that Brian was lost in a maze of a man's never never land, a retail clerk came out of nowhere. The retail clerk was wearing a MacGyver type uniform. "I can help you, the clerk stated." At that point in the commercial, Brian looks into the camera and says "Of course you can - cause "You're the Man."

Selena and Shawn watched about 4 videos for the "Men's N Things" project and the time was close to 5:00pm. Selena saw Shawn eyeing his watch.

"Do you have a prior engagement, Shawn?"

"Actually, I need to take care of some things."

"Well, I guess you had better get going," Selena stated while catching a glimpse of Brian. She moved on to see if she could get his attention. Shawn gathered his keys and cell. He noticed that there was no response from Monica and he was a bit surprised. Shawn now entering his BMW, turned the engine on and proceeded to use his headset to dial Monica.

Monica had just washed her hair and was air drying it while she prepared her dinner. Brian had invited her to see a show tonight, so she wanted to make sure her hair would be nice and freshly done. She could hear her cell ringing in the living room and caught it on the last ring.

"Hello." Monica was almost out of breath.

"Hello Stranger," Shawn said.

"Hello," Monica said simply.

"Just hello, hmmm." Shawn was not sure how to read her coolness.

"Well, it's been a few, but I'm glad you seem to feel better," Monica said.

"I did try to text you while my voice was healing, other than that; I thought that you would understand that talking on the phone was a mute issue-literally." Shawn felt himself getting agitated as he thought Monica was being a bit petty, if she couldn't understand that he was sick; she was just immature and selfish.

"True, you did reach out to me," Monica said. At this juncture, Shawn sensed almost boredom in Monica's general attitude and her responses.

"Listen, did I catch you at a bad time?" Shawn asked straight on.

"No, not really, just took a shower," Monica stated.

"I was actually wondering if we could see each other, tonight?" Shawn asked.

"I'm really tired and I just washed my hair," Monica responded.

"I see, is there something that you want to share with me- other than you are tired tonight? I'm a "Big boy" and I can handle whatever is on your mind, since apparently it's not me." Shawn was now upset, as he had been looking forward to seeing Monica.

"Shawn, I just think that we are moving way to fast and I don't think we are giving each other time to really get to know one another."

"It sounds like you are letting me down gently." He felt sick to his stomach.

"I'm at a loss for words." A tear dropped from one of Monica's eyes.

"You don't have to say anything. I get it. Enjoy your evening, Monica." Shawn was exasperated.

"Goodbye, Shawn." Monica said solemnly. Shawn hung up more confused than he was, when he saw Monica's ex and best friend working at his job. Truly, he did not have a clue as to what just transpired. Monica wanted to shrug her empty feelings. She decided to make a phone call.

"Hello."

"Hey Girl," Monica said.

"Oh, guess what?!!??" Keiki asked.

"What?" Monica said.

"I'm working with that guy, Shawn that you're seeing," Keiki stated.

"Really, that's weird. How did that happen?" Monica was curious.

"Well, I'm working with a temp agency, I interviewed and got the position of admin assistant to his boss," Keiki said.

"I see, well I'm not seeing him anymore - we just broke things off." Monica's eyes were runny with tears.

"Wow, what brought that on, I thought things were cool." Keiki was actually surprised, but glad. Thinking he still was too good to be true.

"I just realized that things were moving fast and I need some space, you know? Don't want to repeat my past mistakes," Monica said.

"Oh, ok. That's smart. I noticed something while I was in my boss' office, which is his boss too - and it was weird, because there was like a vibe - like more than just business was between them." Keiki said.

"Doesn't matter one way or the other, I'm free of any drama and I got out before I could get hurt...so I'm good." Monica was saying the words, but she wasn't feeling them. She kept her emotions bottled up.

"I hear you. I have another call; I'll speak to you tomorrow, alright?" Keiki said.

"Ok, talk to you later," Monica agreed. Monica started to cry softly and wished that she could understand why she was being so sensitive. Part of her was embarrassed that she let another man play her. The other part was she really enjoyed his company and felt that something special was beginning, but now everything was over.

Shawn sat in his car for ten minutes staring at his house before he exited the vehicle. He was literally stunned. He couldn't understand what just happened and was totally confused. It was like he was speaking to another woman, not the sweet, warm lady that he met. She was distant, unresponsive and almost repelled by him. He tried to recall what brought things to this point in only a few days that he was sick. Unless, he thought - she was seeing someone else. That was it. That was the only reasonable conclusion that he could make. Wow, he pondered, another waste of time, but at least she didn't drag it out like the others did. Shawn felt like someone took the wind out of his sails and as he sat down on his leather couch, he put his hands on his head and leaned back to think. Even though their relationship was short, it still left him with so many unanswered questions. It's simple, his mind rationalized-she's fickle and that's the end of it. Somehow his heart wouldn't let him rest, he had no peace. Shawn decided to talk to his Heavenly Father - he needed wisdom, knowledge and understanding.

CHAPTER 11
WILL THE REAL BOAZ PLEASE STAND UP!

Monica spent her Friday morning recalling the events of Thursday night. Monica spent a really nice evening with Brian after she broke the news to Shawn. Monica had decided to just move on and make room for whoever God wanted for her. Brian and Monica had plenty of history together and she believed that Brian had changed so drastically from their last encounter. Her and Brian kept things simple and went to the movies to see an action packed film called "The Real Deal". The movie was about a woman and man who were married, then separated due to his constant deploys for his army commitments. They lived different lives, but never were officially divorced. Now Julie was a fitness guru, hired by the military to train some of their special ops team. Her husband, Tom, soon met up under less than loving terms and found that they were set up by secret organizations that wanted them both dead for information they stumbled upon in documents and delicate data that they were privy to. As the movie unfolds, they have to stick together to stay alive. Monica enjoyed the movie with Brian and the movie let out about 9:45.

"Did you enjoy yourself?" Brian asked, looking intently into Monica's eyes.

"Yes, it was an awesome movie." Monica smiled and was picking up her purse from the floor of his vehicle.

"Well, if you're not too tired, I was hoping we could spend a little more time together." Brian wanted to keep the momentum.

"Sure, I can hang out for a bit longer," Monica said. Monica opened her condo door and walked through with Brian's tall figure right behind her.

"Have a seat; I'm going to the ladies room." Monica went into her bedroom suite and freshened up. Monica could faintly hear a sound. Then she realized it was music. Monica walked into the living room and found Brian scanning her cd collection.

"Oh, there you are," Brian said. "I hope you don't mind me finding something for us to relax with."

"No, it's ok, but I'm curious, what made you choose that artist?"

"I've never heard of this artist-Keiko Matsui and was curious as to what you listen to in your pastime."

"I see," Monica said as she walked past Brian to sit down.

Brian joined Monica on the sofa and looked around at the decor in admiration.

"You've done very well for yourself, Monica."

"Thank you." Monica now stroked her hair, as it was relaxing to her to feel a pull on her tresses.

"I missed you." Brian looked into Monica's deep brown eyes. His beautiful face was shadowing Monica's as he drew in close to her.

"Really, a guy like you? You must appeal to hundreds of women,"

"Doesn't matter about all those others, you never left my memory and I'm sorry that I wasted so much time not appreciating all that you have to offer. I hope that you will not hold my mistakes against me." Brian was now holding Monica's right hand and peering into her face.

"I don't hold grudges, Brian. I just try to apply life's lesson and not duplicate the same mistakes." Monica could feel Brian's warmth and knew that she had to keep things into perspective. Brian kissed Monica's hand and came in close to hold her. He slid his left arm behind her back to pull her closer to him. He put his face into her neck and slid his right arm around her head to massage her scalp gently. Brian knew that's what relaxed Monica. Brian leaned up looking into Monica's face; he used his left hand to caress her cheek and placed a soft kiss on her face. Brian moved his lips strategically towards Monica's mouth. Monica had to keep her emotions intact. Brian's kisses were familiar and she fixed her mind to keep from getting caught up. Brian could feel that Monica was not yielding totally to him. He only pecked her lips and decided to visit her naked neck and put tiny kisses from the top to the bottom. Her scent was driving him crazy. Monica knew she had to put an end to this or else she would be sorry.

"Brian," Monica interrupted. Brian stopped hesitantly and sat up in a position to look directly at Monica.

"What's the matter?"

"I'm just trying to keep things slow and gradual. I want us to really spend time learning one another. Yes, we have a real history, but we also have a lot that we don't know of one another."

"Is that all it is, Monica? Because I'm feeling your resistance and I want to know if you still care about me." Brian felt disturbed.

"Well, I am also concerned that our lifestyles have some conflicts. Me being a born-again Christian, I'm concerned that things may get too hot to handle physically." Monica looked into Brian's face intensely to see his response.

"Oh, you're concerned that I will make you stumble," Brian said. "I can't promise you that being together is going to be easy, but I don't want you to feel that I will pressure you either. I would like to get to the same place that you are Monica. Just don't know how. Will you show me?" Brian asked.

One thing about Brian was that he could give the sweetest and most innocent puppy eyes ever, making him so lovable.

"I would like to help you Brian, but I can only assist you as much as you're willing to want God's help," Monica stated.

"Thank you," Brian said. "I guess I should go now, it's getting late." Monica walked Brian to the door and they hugged before she let him out. Monica was torn in her emotions, she felt a certain comfort of familiarity with Brian, but she also felt something different with Shawn.

One thing that was a stain in her brain was something(s) that Brian said. He told her that he was comfortable, he felt secure and that he missed her. Not once did he say that he loved her. This was the unsaid words that left her muddled. She knew that Brian cared but how much? Choices, choices. She recalled that God said she had choices.

She knew what she had to do to get some answers. Monica called her mentor, Leslie. Monica waited while the phone dialed.

"Are you married yet?" Leslie joked.

"Not quite, how are you and hubby, Charles?" Monica asked.

"I'm good; we just came off of a three-day fast. I'm making some spaghetti for tomorrow's dinner," Leslie said.

"Just you and hubby?" Monica asked.

"Well, I'm just having my daughter and grandson, but what's going on with you and the handsome fellow you're seeing?"

"Actually, we're not seeing each other anymore."

"Oh, really." Leslie got quiet.

"Things just didn't feel right and we ended it."

"He ended it or you?"

"We both agreed."

"I know you both agreed, but again who initiated it?" Leslie reiterated the question. She knew that Monica was evading the issue.

"I did," Monica said finally.

"Why?" Leslie asked. Monica explained in detail how things went without mentioning her overnight stay with Shawn.

"What I see is that Shawn did not want to break things off. What God is also showing me is you need to seek him about your relationships. It's true that Shawn has an agenda and so does another one...Hmmm, who is this other one, Monica?

There she goes, Monica felt naked under her prophetic vision. "He's my ex. She ashamedly admitted.

"God will reveal them to you, as only he can." Leslie encouraged. "I don't know if that's good or bad."

"God is your Heavenly Father - he says lean not on your own understanding."

"Thank you, Woman of God. You sound tired."

"Yes, I'm finished cooking and I'm going to put everything away and go to bed. Call me and let me know how things transpire, alright?"

"Alright, Good Night." Monica hung up. She dropped to her knees and prayed until she fell asleep.

CHAPTER 11 ½ - GOD ANSWERS PRAYERS

Shawn spent most of Thursday evening on his knees. He replayed every word that Monica said to him and could not believe how things flipped within a matter of a few days. Shawn felt now that her ex-boyfriend Brian may be a key factor and that Monica wasn't ready for the level of commitment that he was willing to give. Ultimately, he decided to "Let go and Let God". The funny thing was he really believed there was such a strong connection to Monica. It was real magical, if one could say it that way. Like a pair of leather gloves that were new, but weren't stiff or too tight-they just fit and moved naturally. After Shawn meditated on all the different scenarios of possibilities, he prayed. God gave Shawn a scripture just before he passed out. Shawn woke up Friday at 6:30AM and had what he felt was a pain in his heart. How? He knew that he wasn't in..... he couldn't even say that four letter word out loud. Shawn had not verbalized the L-Word since he said it to his kid's mother-Lydia. Shawn had driven on auto pilot to work and now sat at his desk reviewing the new commercial drafts that Harvey emailed to him for editing. Shawn had to admit that "Brian" had that star like quality- the camera loved him and He in turn loved the camera. While viewing all of Brian's work, he knew immediately that Brian was just the guy that he was looking for. Shawn jumped out of his black leather office chair determined to shift his energy into his work, to block out his emotions. Shawn walked over to Selena's office, wanting to update her on some of his concepts for the new client. He could hear Selena speaking to someone in her office, but the door was closed. He knocked on her door.

"Come in," Selena said.

"Oh, great I have the two of you." Shawn was surprised to see Brian seated across from Selena's desk, but it was just as well.

"I'm glad to see that you are 100% now. Have a seat. I was just expressing to Brian how well his work was and I was about to get your take on things," Selena stated.

"Yes, it's really amazing. Especially, when you consider that Brian's resume had no prior experience?" Shawn looked towards Brian, while he took the other seat.

"I've done a lot of modeling and some fashion shows. I know that they may not count as experience, but I'm comfortable in front of an audience and I enjoy the creative adventure that this type of genre brings. I'm hoping to continue to grow in this business," Brian affirmed.

"I'll tell you what, I would like to see you in another project that we have on the horizon with a new client, Cadillac. What do you think, Selena? He has the presence and all we have to do is give him a wardrobe change." Shawn looked at Selena for her answer. Brian was a bit taken back that He was so open and willing to help him stay on for another gig. Really, he had thought that he would have an attitude. Or maybe, as Monica said, they only recently met and they weren't really an item.

"Send me the DVD draft and I'll sign off, Shawn." So, guys, I need to get some other things done, so shoo..." Selena grabbed her phone. Shawn stopped Brian to give him the next phase.

"Ok, so here's the plan, I sent Harvey the criteria for the next few Cadillac commercials. Harvey will tell you what to do."

"Great Man - By the way I want to thank you for being such an upstanding brother and helping me get closer to my goal." Brian was amazed at Shawn.

"It's all business and when you've got what it takes, nobody can take it away from you. God gave you a gift, use it for Him." Shawn said brotherly. They both went in opposite directions. Shawn decided to go the lower level in the building where they had a gym, cafe, and cleaners for the employees. They even had a movie theatre on that level. Shawn went to pick up a few shirts from the cleaners and get a bottle of water from the cafe. Shawn stood with his back to the cafe, waiting in line for his pressed shirts.

"Well, hello Mr. Shawn." Shawn turned to see where the small voice came from.

"Hello." Shawn recognized Keiki.

"This is a really great building to work in; all the comforts right here,"

"Yep." He wasn't sure if he wanted to talk to his ex-girlfriend's friend.

"Alright, well I'm not going to take up your time; just hoping to keep things cordial, since we'll be working together from time to time."

"I'm just waiting for my turn," Shawn said with an added interest in his voice. He thought if anyone would know the truth about what happened Keiki would. He figured he would take a shot.

"I'll tell you what; I'll be just a minute while the guy retrieves my things. I'll meet you at the table that you were seated at for a minute." Shawn could tell that Keiki was like the canary that swallowed a secret.

"Oh, ok. No problem." Keiki walked over to her table that had her lunch waiting for her. Now, just the fries were left. She ate a few while waiting for Shawn. She had to face it ..... That brotha was toooo fine! It was no wonder why Monica was getting so wrapped up in him. That's the type of eye-candy that she always dreamed about, but never had. Keiki watched Shawn walk over to her table and even his walk was gangsta, like Denzel Washington sexy. Shawn pulled out the only chair across from Keiki and sat.

"I'm glad I caught Ricardo before he left. I know he usually leaves by this time." It was 6:00 p.m. "So Keiki, I'm sure your Girl told you that we split up." Shawn put on his "Prophetic Eye," now.

"Yea, she did," Keiki said.

"I guess she couldn't get pass me having two young kids. It's a shame too, because it's so difficult to find a "real woman" who can accept me and my girls," Shawn said.

"That's what she said?" Keiki was surprised.

"She claimed that things were moving too quickly, but I read between the lines," Shawn said.

"Well, I don't think she's that shallow, Shawn." Keiki could tell that Shawn really did like Monica after all. His eyes shined a kind of sorrow.

"At any rate, I'll have to start all over again. Good women are not easy to come by," Shawn said.

"Well I would imagine that any Girl would be lucky to have you." Keiki didn't mean to blurt that out.

"Yea, but where?" Shawn looked into Keiki's eyes peering into her soul. Keiki felt like evaporating. This man seemed to be able to read her like a book. Her face turned a shade of red.

"All I could do is pray for you." Keiki was nervous now. She may have bit off more than she could chew.

"I feel like an idiot, I believe her ex- boyfriend got to her." Shawn examined Keiki's body language as he waited for her response.

"How do you know about him?" Keiki asked.

"Let's just say he is a persistent guy," Shawn said.

"Oh, yea well. He definitely is that." Keiki nodded in agreement.

"I guess the better man won," Shawn said as he put his hand behind his head.

"I wouldn't put it that way Shawn. I don't see it that way. If God put them together, then God has someone else for you." Keiki wished for a moment it could be her. She felt that she may have misjudged Shawn entirely. Just then Shawn and Keiki turned their heads and glared out at the parking lot as they had a clear view through the glass wall. They both saw Selena and Brian flirting with one another. Brian appeared to be showing off his bright red corvette to Selena. They watched as Selena leaned on Brian's driver side of the car. Selena was obviously teasing Brian. It was also clear that Brian took her on. Brian overshadowed Selena's frame and whispered something in her ears. At that point, he took her by her waist and spoke to her close. Selena stood in a pose as to walk. She walked as Brian followed her closely and opened the passenger side of the vehicle for her to climb in. Next he jumped into the vehicle and they left the almost empty parking lot. It was 6:30 and almost all of the staff was gone.

"That Brotha moves fast, I can say that much about him," Shawn said with a sigh in his voice. Looking at Keiki, he knew that what he was seeing in the Spirit was true.

"So Keiki, I hope that your Girl is not going to get hurt by this dude." Shawn said while watching her reaction.

"Me too, I have to go," Keiki said, as she gathered her things and threw the remainders in the garbage.

"I'm sorry, Shawn." You're such a special person. Here's my number if you ever just want to talk." Keiki left her card on the table and walked outside to the parking lot. Keiki was sick to her stomach, knowing that she played a small role in getting Monica back with that jerk. Well, she thought - no turning back, as Shawn was not likely to take her back. She hoped he would keep in touch with her. She wanted, if nothing else, but to have a friendship with such a nice (fine) guy. Nothing wrong with that she hoped.

Shawn held his emotions down pretty good in front of Keiki. He was boiling on the inside and knew that he had to do something with this anger. Just then his cell phone rang. He took a breath and answered.

"Hello."

"Hi, I have the girls here with me, but I hope you won't get upset." Lydia prefaced before speaking. Shawn bit his lip hoping that he was not about to get any more bad news.

"Why would I get upset?" Shawn was fuming already.

"I took the kids upstate for the day and now we're having a storm up here. I don't think it would be safe to get to you tonight." Lydia waited to hear Shawn vent. Shawn was so full that he thought he would explode.

"Alright," was all he could muster to say. He leaned his head back and held it with his hand.

"Do you want to speak to the girls?" Lydia asked.

"I'm still at work. I'll call them later, ok?" Shawn wanted to just go.

"Alright, if I don't hear from you, I will call you tomorrow." They hung up and Lydia just stared at her cell phone. The man she just spoke with was not her ex. He never gave up the chance to speak to his girls. He must have been under some serious stress. Shawn headed for the gym and changed quickly. This was a full gym including: punching bag, sauna, pool, a staff and security. They would be closing in an hour, so he did some weights and worked out on the punching bag. He had been working out on the punching bag for about 15 minutes, while sweat poured from his face. He didn't realize that he was treating the bag like his enemy.

"Whoa Dude, who are your envisioning? I would hate to be that bag, right now." Shawn glanced over his shoulder, stopping to view Jalek. Shawn stopped and the adrenaline that was pumping through him suddenly manifested itself through his eyes.

"Hey Man." Shawn greeted him with their normal hand movements. Jalek handed Shawn a towel to wipe his face. Shawn wiped his head, neck and hands.

"Let me talk to you Man." Jalek motioned Shawn to a quiet area. They stood in the locker area.

"What's eating at you?" Jalek asked.

"I had a tough day, that's all." Shawn truly didn't want to divulge what really happened. After all, Jalek did warn him and he couldn't bear the embarrassment - at least, not right now.

"Man, check this out. I understand what you're going through. Let me pray for you." Jalek didn't wait for Shawn's response.

"Heavenly Father, You are the Master of our Universe and the Lord over our lives. Please come Holy Spirit and touch and saturate my brother and your son Shawn. Please give him peace and strength to handle all the fiery darts that the dark one has shot. We ask that you renew his Heart and raise him up like David. Make him soar like the Warrior that he already is. Show him the plots, plans and devices of the enemy. God reward your servant with the blessings that you promised. Angels, we stand in agreement with Jehovah and by faith we send legions out to retrieve blessings and fight on our behalf. God, we thank you for already answering us - even as you did with Daniel. By the Blood of the Lamb we are over comers. We seal this prayer in Jesus name. Amen."

Shawn's sweat turned into tears and he was not ashamed to allow Jalek to see them. Jalek embraced Shawn briefly.

"God is with you Shawn. All is not lost. Don't allow anything to deter you from what God is speaking in your Spirit. God Bless you Brotha." Jalek left Shawn to collect himself. Shawn showered and prayed inwardly.

CHAPTER 12 - FLIGHT OR FIGHT

Monica had a fairly busy day at work. She went over all the applicant's documents with Carolyn and her supervisor seemed to be back to her sunny self. Monica was still in shock over the meeting that she had between herself, Carolyn and Roy. They offered her corporate trip to Chicago. The company had another branch there. As she was advised, she was to train the other paralegal to implement the same concept for their offices. This would take about a couple of weeks. The only catch was the short notice. They wanted her to fly out Tuesday, which was in four days. Monica agreed.

"Oh by the way Monica, Roy wanted me to give you this "Belated Birthday" gift," Carolyn said as she handed her the small wrapped box.

"Awwww, that was so thoughtful." Monica took the box and packed it in her oversized Sienna Ricchi handbag. Monica rode home thinking how it was just a few months ago that she was promoted and given a pay raise. Then God gave her another pay raise and now this? She thought to herself now she understood the scriptures in Malachi, when God promised to open up the heavens and pour out blessings that you would not have room to receive. Monica's bosom was becoming full. She had to pack tonight, because she had plans for the entire weekend with Brian. Although she was glad to be with him, she still had lingering feelings for Shawn. Monica packed and packed. She started to feel like she was moving, as putting together a wardrobe for two weeks or more was not easy. She left space for shopping, as she was sure that would fill in some of her outfits. She heard her cell ring and figured it must be Brian.

"Hello." Monica was out of breath.

"Hey Girl," Keiki spoke.

"What's up?" Monica couldn't wait to share her news with Keiki. "I hope you're sitting down," Keiki said with regret.

"Why?" Monica was not sure what Keiki meant.

“What I have to say is not nice or pretty.” Keiki wanted Monica to be ready. Monica released her suitcase zipper and sat on her couch in the living room area.

“I’m not sure if Brian told you, but he was hired as a temp employee at the same company that myself and Shawn are working.”

“What? He never mentioned anything to me.” Monica’s temperature shot up.

“Well, I saw Brian leaving work today. He left with my boss, Selena,” Keiki said.

“Ok, so, what does that mean? Were they kissing? Tell me.” Monica’s stomach muscles tightened.

“Although they weren’t kissing, they were flirting with one another and their body language pretty much said it all.” Keiki was glad to get that off her chest. Monica was speechless and tears immediately filled her eyes. He did it again she thought. This man played her and worst of all - she was now out with two guys at once.

“I can’t believe you are telling me that Brian, knowing that you would be able to see him, brazenly left with a lady he just met and now works for?!? Explain what you mean by body language, Keiki.” Monica was furious.

“Jesus, Monica! Brian was holding Selena by her waist and basically treating her like someone he wanted to be with. I really have nothing more that I can tell you,” Keiki said.

“I wasted my time, energy and emotions again on two losers, what does that say about me?!?!” Monica was crying profusely now.

“Monica, don’t do this to yourself, they’re the ones that are losers and you have to just accept what God is revealing to you. Better now, then months or years down the road,” Keiki said. Keiki left out the portion that she spoke to Shawn.

“I have to go, Keiki. I have too many important things to do. I’ll speak to you later,” Monica said.

"Alright, call me if you need me," Keiki said. They both hung up. Monica was flooded with emotions and determined that she would close her heart. It just wasn't worth the pain. She cried bitterly. Monica fell asleep on the couch in a puddle of tears. She was awakened by her doorbell ringing. She went to the door and saw her FedEx guy. She looked terrible and didn't want him to see her in this state.

"Who is it?" Monica was stalling for time.

"It's Aaron, your favorite FedEx guy," he said.

Occasionally, Aaron would deliver a package directly to her condo when he missed her outside; even though he could leave it with the 24 hr. security guy in the main lobby. Monica took off her pony tail holder from her hair and finger combed her hair to camouflage her tear streamed face and put some lip-gloss on as she went to the door. Opening the door...

"Hi Aaron, you have a delivery for me?" Monica asked.

"Yes, I do, in the form of a person." Aaron said.

"What person?" Monica looked and saw the form of a man to his left and at once recognized him.

"I told him that although, I believed his outlandish story, I would still wait to see if you were safe and wanted a visitor." Aaron stated. Aaron was Latino and he was not afraid of a fight. She knew secondhand, through rumors from the security staff.

"It's ok, Aaron," Monica said. She beckoned Shawn to come into her apartment and thanked Aaron as he continued his rounds. Monica closed the door as Shawn stepped inside.

"I'm very curious how you could convince Aaron to escort you to my condo, but first I need to know. Why are you here?"

"I'm here because I wanted to talk to you face to face." Shawn had a no nonsense face on.

"I want you to tell me the real reason that you blew me off." Shawn was going to get all the answers he needed before he left Monica's presence tonight.

"You are so arrogant to question me, Shawn. You have the nerve to come into my home and interrogate me. When you played me like a fiddle!?!?!" Monica was livid and had no more patience. Shawn began to study Monica and was actually turned on by this side of her. She really had a spicy element to her underneath it all.

"I never played you, Monica. I was always honest with you; which is more than I can say about you, Lady." Shawn's body shifted.

"What do you mean by that?!" Monica put her tiny hands on her hips now.

"I mean you had me believing it was all about me, but in reality it wasn't all about me. There was another person in the mix, right?" Shawn accused her. Dang, how did he know? Monica's thoughts were racing.

"I never hid anything from you Shawn," Monica said defensively.

"So, Brian was never a factor? Don't lie to me, Monica!" Seething now, Shawn was so angry that his voice carried a thunderous echo.

Monica was startled and stood still for a moment, as she took in the hurt in his eyes. His body was tense and by the conviction in his voice, she wished to God that she had not been so quick to judge him. Monica spoke with humility as she answered him.

"Yes, Brian was the ex-factor and he stepped up to initiate himself back into my world." Monica held her tear filled eyes with sheer honesty.

"Why did you make me think I did something wrong, huh Monica?" Shawn bit his lip waiting for her response. Even in his anger, he could feel another emotion struggling to break through.

"I believed you were playing games, and then I became afraid," Monica said softly. She realized that she had made a huge mistake and tears streamed down her face. Shawn walked towards the door with his hand gripping his neck.

"Will you forgive me, Shawn?" Monica tried to redeem herself as best as possible. Shawn stood with his back facing her, contemplating her words. Then he turned to face her, he spoke.

"Where are you going?" Shawn inquired. Monica realizing her travel bags was standing against the wall.

"I have to go out of town on business," Monica spoke softly. Shawn looked around and saw the red and yellow roses in a vase that appeared to be a few days old. He felt a prick inside, but he chuckled to himself that he was acting like a foolish teenager.

"I have to go," Shawn said with finality. Monica winced, realizing that Shawn saw the roses.

"Please don't leave yet?" Monica needed to recompense.

"Why should I stay, Monica?" Shawn was bleeding on the inside and a part of him wanted to be done with her, the other part of him wanted her to make him whole again. Meanwhile he wondered if her girlfriend, Keiki was at least honest to tell her what she witnessed.

"I want to share something with you," Monica said. Monica moved closer to Shawn and he peered down at her. She reached for his hand slowly; looking up into his eyes lovingly, and began to tug him gently to persuade him. Shawn made himself numb and followed her lead.

Monica took Shawn into her master suite.

"This may sound insignificant but I have never felt comfortable enough to invite anyone into this bedroom for as long as I have lived here. This is where I meet the Holy Spirit and where I feel safe. I brought you here hoping that you, as a Man of God, could understand and discern my heartbeat. I pray that you can not only forgive me, but give us another chance." Shawn took advantage of being in her space by touring her bedroom and bathroom. He took mental shots of the uniqueness and tidiness of her bedroom. Monica even opened her two walk in closets for Shawn to view. Inside he saw a medium sized box with the label marked as "art" and there were various frames and canvases alongside, surrounding it.

"What are these?" Shawn was curious.

"Oh, this is some of my drawings that I like to play around with; one of my hobbies."

"Can I see one?"

Hesitantly she responded, "Sure." Shawn pulled out the largest canvas and was shocked at what he was envisioning. The 40X40 painting was exquisite with bold colors. The picture was of an ivory desert scene that opens up to a man and woman who just discovered an island. The sun had just begun to descend in its fiery burnt orange delight, the water was aqua blue and the grass was jewel green. The muddy earth covered their feet. The man and woman clothes were tattered, but still intact as they welcomed the new treasure of God's glorious nature. The man swung the woman around celebrating the miracle that God had granted them. Shawn felt his defenses shattering. Still he needed to protect himself from any further disappointments, but he also wanted to believe Monica since there was something so pure and real about her; despite her shortcomings.

"Thank you for sharing this with me," he said.

"Will you stay for a little while?" Monica pleaded. Shawn was silent. Monica was so irresistible to Shawn. She took his hand gently again and led him back into the den area, where the seating was more comfortable. Once he sat, Monica put her arms around his neck and began to kiss him with all manner of kisses. Monica kissed his face, his mouth, his eyes, his nose, his jaw line and when she went for his neck...she heard him sigh. Monica knew she had reached a place where she needed to be careful. Shawn held her waist, while she planted delightful pieces of the aroma of her affection. He didn't know how much more he could take, but she stopped before he was about to boil over in his desire for her.

"I missed you so much," Monica admitted. "I missed you too." Shawn spoke.

"I don't know about you, but I need something to drink." Monica got up and walked towards the kitchen. Shawn followed, but stopped near the bar side of the kitchen. Monica passed him a drink of homemade lemonade from across the bar on her side. She then walked over next to Shawn, while they both took huge swallows to quench their thirst. They drank about a third of the glass and then set it down on the kitchen portion of the bar. Shawn decided to pick Monica up and put her on the bar to face him.

"That's the second time that you've deserved a spanking from me," Shawn stated.

"I have one more strike, right?" Monica stated with her beautiful smile shining through. Shawn grabbed her face softly.

"I hope I never have to let you go again," he stated.

"Just kiss me, Shawn."

CHAPTER 13 - THE TWINS INTERVENE

Monica was awakened by her cell phone vibrating. Monica picked up her phone to see if there was a text waiting.

Text Message: Hey, whatcha doing today. Let's hang out. Keiki.

Monica hesitated to respond, as she did not know what today would hold for her. She had fallen asleep on the coach late last night, after sending Shawn to her bedroom to rest. She tried to be as quiet as possible, as she wanted to prepare breakfast for him before he was on his way out. It was now 7:30 am. Monica perused her refrigerator and cabinets looking for ingredients to cook with. Monica took out her eggs, sausage, turkey bacon, and preheated her oven to make sure her biscuits had ample time to bake.

Shawn lay in Monica's bed soaking up her fragrance that remained on the pillows, sheets and even in the atmosphere. He couldn't seem to get enough of her, her energy, time, attention and that shook him at times. Monica was not only a beauty to the eyes, but even in her soul. The painting that she created should be displayed and he didn't understand why she considered it just a hobby. He could hear the light movements coming from the kitchen. No doubt Monica was cooking up something in there. He pondered what he would do since he had not prepared to stay with Monica last night; therefore, he had no toothbrush, extra clothes, etc. At least, he thought to himself, he could wash his face and rinse his mouth with mouthwash (if she had some). Shawn went into her ultra feminine bathroom and was shocked. He saw hanging on a coat rack a brand new Hugo Boss sweat suit (gray with white accents); on the counter near the mirror was a tee shirt, boxers and a traveler's compact for men (carrying all the necessities). Also, a large beach style towel and black sandals to boot. He wondered where all this new stuff came from, but he just jumped into the shower and blessed his God. Monica was just about done; just finishing her table settings. Monica threw out the roses that Brian had brought her and put a lovely hibiscus pink/red leaved plant from her kitchen window as the center piece on the circular table. She drew her window curtains and the sun bounced off her walls. Monica used white, red, yellow, gold and black as her decor for the table. On her table were her off-white plates, featuring tiny red flowers on the edges, flatware that was two-toned silver with gold stems, a tall, slender glass that was opaque with clear flowers, a gold stem wine goblet and a white mug trimmed in black and gold. The table cloth was black trimmed in white. As she had finished putting all the food on the table, she could her Shawn's' footsteps coming through the hallway.

"My Goodness, what a lovely sight!!! Good Morning Baby." Shawn embraced Monica and then took a seat. Shawn's eyes were smiling as he took an overview and saw how the food was delightful. The spread included: Pancakes, Turkey Sausage, Home Fries, Biscuits, and Eggs made two ways; Grits, homemade orange juice, tea, and water with a twist of lemon.

"Baby, I feel like I just walked into a Waldorf Hotel dining area. "Let's pray." Grabbing Monica's hands he lifted his voice:

"Heavenly Father, I come to you with Praise and Thanksgiving; appreciating another day that you breathe life through us. I pray that others should be so blessed as to have a meal and the ability to call on your Glorious name. I also thank you for your precious Daughter that prepared this meal and make it nutritious to our bodies. Amen!" Shawn did not waste any time making his plate from the containers of dishes prepared. Monica watched as he first went for pancakes, then the
sausages, homes fries and eggs. His second serving was turkey bacon, grits, more eggs, and two biscuits. Although there were a variety of things to eat, Monica made portions suitable for tasting.

"So, how does everything fit?" Monica asked?

"Oh yeah, I forgot to ask you, where did these clothes come from?"

"I bought them," Monica said looking down to put another piece of pancake in her mouth.

"Where and when did you have a chance to do that?" Shawn's face was perplexed.

"I went to the WalMart that stays open to 1:00 am. You fell asleep at 11:45 and I walked you to the room, took your shoes off and you did the rest. Don't you remember?"

"Oh I see you took advantage of me in my tired state." They both roared in laughter. Monica and Shawn finished their meal and he sent Monica to get dressed, while he washed the dishes. She went into her closet and pulled out a pair of skinny jeans and a cheetah printed fitted tee shirt. Monica put her intimates in her bathroom and jumped into the shower. Shawn turned on the TV and caught a glimpse of Creflo Dollar; he was ministering about relationships and divine connections. Shawn's thoughts trailed off and he meditated on Monica. What a woman, what more could a man want in a partner, lover and friend?

Monica put on her platform heels and gave herself a once over. She flat ironed her hair and gave it a flip and parted her hair on the side. Her face had a natural island girl look, with medium sized hoop earrings. Her lip-gloss had shimmers of pink throughout it. She used a light colored eyeliner on the top of her lid and a black for the bottom. Satisfied that she looked presentable, she walked towards the living room. Shawn looked up and saw Monica and stood up.

"Wow, come here." He pulled Monica close. I know I can't really kiss you now, since you have your lips glossed up but..." Shawn put a kiss on her forehead.

"You know you're fine!" Shawn gave Monica a look like he wanted to devour her. Just then his cell phone rang. He looked down and accepted the call.

"Hello". Shawn held Monica's hand while talking.

"Yea, what time will you be here? I'll speak to them simultaneously."

"How are my favorite Girls? Daddy missed you and I can't wait to see you. I have a surprise date for you, so put your mother back on the phone and I'll see you soon."

"Ok, so I'll meet you there later." Shawn hung up. He turned his attention back to Monica. Monica felt certain sadness come upon her as she would have to let Shawn go. Shawn could sense the shift.

"So, Baby as you heard, those were my "Girls" and I will be seeing them tonight."

"Truly they are blessed to have such a wonderful Daddy." Monica smiled, trying to hide her feelings. She would call Keiki after Shawn leaves to plan her day.

"Thank you, but I was wondering if you would hang out with me and meet the twins today?" Shawn felt apprehensive, but he had to see if Monica was really the whole package or not? Monica felt honored and uncertain for a moment, but managed to speak.

"Wow Shawn, I'm surprised that you would invite me to meet your Babies," Monica said.

"I'm surprised too, but you didn't answer my question." Shawn's stomach had butterflies waiting for her reply.

"Sure, I would love to meet your "little ladies." How am I dressed? Monica wanted to be sure that she was appropriate.

"You look like a young, vibrant woman, just my type." Shawn had so much expression dancing in his eyes. Shawn drove to New Jersey, parked in front of his house and turned down the mixed cd they were listening to.

"They should be here any minute. I planned to take the girls to the amusement park, so I hope that you will be ok in those shoes for the rest of the day," Shawn said.

"Oh Sweetie, I normally carry an extra pair of shoes anytime I wear heels. I'm fine."

"Yep, that you are." Shawn said. Lydia's car pulled up in front of his vehicle.

"I'll be right back. I have to prepare the little ones." Shawn winked as he opened the car door. Monica felt a bit awkward and hoped that this was a good idea. She knew this moment would come eventually, if this relationship was going anywhere. After about five minutes, Shawn took one of his daughters hand and motioned her towards the car. The other one walked on her own to the car door and opened it. She left it open, while her sister climbed in, she sat and her father closed it behind her. You could tell she had a little bit more independence by her demeanor. They were identical twins. They both had hair that reached to their mid back and one wore two pony tails, the other wore three pony tails. They each had a creamy caramel complexion, with pronounced eyes like baby dolls. They were really pretty.

"So ladies, this is Monica, the lady I told you about. She's going to hang out with us today and I want you to say hello and introduce yourself," Shawn said. "Sharde you can go first."

"Hi, I'm Sharde and it's nice to meet you." Shawn motioned for her sister to speak.

"Hi, my name is Shantell." That was all she would say, before bowing her head in shyness.

"It's so wonderful to meet you both and my name is Monica. I must tell you that you both are extremely beautiful..." Monica gave them the biggest smile she could muster.

"So now Girls, we are headed to one of your favorite places. Sit back, make sure your seat belts are secure and we're on our way." Shawn pulled off. Shawn and Monica talked amongst themselves, as the girls had their own conversation going on in the back. They were not far from their destination. Shawn parked the car and retrieved his daughters.

"Your mother told me you guys ate not too long ago, so what ride do you want to get on first?" Shawn waited for them to reply.

Sharde yelled, "race cars"; Shantell then spoke, "merry go round."

"Well, you both picked different rides, so we'll have to take turns." Sharde spoke up first, so we'll do the race cars and then we'll do the merry go round, ok." Shawn spoke directly to Shantell.

"Ok," Shantell was a bit disappointed. Shawn reached to get Shantell's hand and motioned for Monica to come closer to him. Sharde grabbed the free hand of her father. Once they finished on the race cars, they went to the merry go round. Monica watched how happy Shawn was when he attended to his daughters. She knew he was an excellent father and she admired that. What woman would not want Shawn, he was almost flawless. She knew there must be some faults, but up-to-date none were revealed to her. Shawn bought them cotton candy and he won them stuffed animals; and as the day went on he tried to keep Monica included, but it was challenging for him. Monica understood the dynamics of what Shawn was doing and commended him for it.

"Alright Girls, it's getting late and you can get on one last ride, what will it be?" Shawn asked. They both yelled out at the same time. Sharde said bumper cars and Shantell said submarines.

"Alright, you know how this works. We may have to flip a coin to see who can go first," Shawn said. Shantell went up to her Dad and whispered something to him.

"That's a good idea Shantell. Monica, Shantell wants to know if you would go with her to her ride and I can take Sharde to the bumper cars." They all turned to look at Monica. She had been almost a silent observer, not wanting to usurp too much; wanting things to go natural.

"Of course I will." Monica reached out her hand towards Shantell and off they went. Monica and Shantell stood in the line for the submarine shaped ride. The man that assisted the children motioned for two kids at a time to get into the animated vehicles. Many children were able to get on with a friend or relative, but when Shantell's turn came a little Asian girl sat in the submarine as he motioned for her to join her. Shantell was resistant and Monica knew she was gripped by fear.

"What's the matter Shantell?" Monica asked. "I don't know her," she replied.

"I know you don't, but I'm going to be right here watching you and making sure that everything goes well," Monica said with a comforting expression. Shantell still stood motionless. Monica squeezed her hand gently and began walking her towards the sub.

"Take a step up Dear." Monica led her to the tiny vehicle. Shantell took the assistant's hand and got into the sub. He buckled them in and the ride began. As the ride tilted and moved with a wavy motion, the kids were smiling and making faces. The sub made little dips and Monica was careful to cheer Shantell on. Now Shantell and the Asian girl giggled together and they both were having fun. Within four minutes - the ride was over. Shantell was helped off the ramp and Monica grabbed her little hand. They talked as they made their way back to meet her sister and dad. Shantell ran as they grew closer to Shawn.

"Hey you." Shawn grabbed Shantell and held her in his arms. Shantell looked up into her daddy's eyes and spoke everything that happened. Meanwhile, Sharde never let go of her father's other hand. As they walked to the car, Monica took in the substance of the awesomeness of this man and the love he has for his daughters. Monica opened the back door and the girls slid in. Next she sat in the passenger side and put her seat belt on and waited for Shawn to buckle up. During the car ride back to Monica's place, it was still light outside and Shawn let her know that he would call her later after the kids had gone to bed. Shawn pulled up into the parking space directly in front of the complex.

"I really appreciate you spending the day with me and my girls," Shawn said.

"The pleasure was mine."

"I will call you later, ok?" Monica nodded, while Shawn quickly jumped out of the vehicle and opened the door for Monica. He whispered in her ear before she walked away.

"I wish I could feel your lips tonight, but trust me - I will take a rain check." Monica blushed and feeling the warmth of his sweet breath on her neck.

"Good Night, Girls. Thank you for a wonderful day." Monica walked away and the girls replied by waving and saying goodnight simultaneously. Monica made it into her condo and went straight to her bedroom. She thought about changing her bed, but on second thought she left it wanting Shawn's scent to linger for one more day. She pulled out a yellow and white - fit and flare stretch cotton dress for church. It had a belt and pleated skirt. She pulled out her patent leather chunky heels with a metal buckle on the top near the toe. Her white patent leather nine west bag was a perfect match. It was 7:10 now and Monica decided to put on a movie to distract herself from missing Shawn. She smiled as she knew that only God could have turned things around so quickly.

Shawn made his famous spaghetti for his girls. They told him his version was better than mommy's, because he used sour cream on top with sprinkles of shredded cheese. The broccoli wasn't their favorite, but they knew they couldn't get any dessert without eating their veggies.

"Daddy, where did you meet that lady again?" Shantell asked.

"We met at Pastor Richard's house," Shawn replied. "So what did you guys think about her?" Shawn asked.

"I think she's pretty," Shantell said. Shawn looked towards Sharde for her response. "I think she really likes you dad," Sharde stated. Shawn was intrigued, but perplexed by his daughter's answer. He knew that Sharde was a wise Soul, but sometimes she was just too unpredictable.

"How do you know that, Sharde?" He asked

"I could see it in her eyes," Sharde said. Shawn decided to leave well enough alone, as he wanted to get them settled in their room and ready for church in the morning. Shawn left the girls in the kitchen, since they would wash the dishes for him. He ran their bubble bath and then he promised he would read a chapter in the bible before they would go to bed.

"Girls, hurry, so you can take your bath." Shawn heard their little feet scattering down the hallway. Shawn left them in the main bathroom with towel(s) to disrobe and then had their perspective pajamas, and everything else was laid on their individual beds. They shared one of the three bedrooms in his home. He left the other bedroom as a guest room or mostly his office space. Since they were just 6 yrs. old, he felt being in the same room would be sufficient. Their personalities seemed to be as different as night and day. Shantell took on more of Shawn's persona: compassionate, curious and creative. Sharde was more like her mom, Lydia: calculating, confident and competitive. On Shantell's side of the room were: all forms of arts and craft projects, baby dolls and a cd player for all her favorite music. On Sharde's side of the room were a variety of puzzles, activity books and her faithful DS player and collection of video games. Shantell favored colors in the pink family, while Sharde loved yellows and greens. They both enjoyed physical activities such as: swimming, bike riding and skating.

"We're done daddy," he could hear Sharde proclaim. He knew what that meant and he grabbed his bible and waited for them to get settled in their beds.

"Ok Girls, the third chapter of the "Book of Jonah"." Shawn read from the NIV Version. He bought them both the NIV Adventure bibles to read in their own personal reading time. Shawn finished reading chapter three of Jonah and did his usual question and answer to solidify the bible reading. Shawn would ask two or three questions.

"Shantell how many days did the city of Nineveh have to change?"

"The bible says forty." Shantell peeked in her bible making sure she was correct.

"Sharde, what did the Ninevites do to please God?" Sharde had her head reviewing the story just as Shantell did. "They stopped eating." She said.

"Correct, you guys are so quick. I'm going to leave you and take my shower. I don't want you to forget to pray together before you fall asleep. It's now 8:50 and you have until 9:15 before you have to pray before bed, alright."

"Ok Daddy." They said in unison. Shawn jumped in the shower and took inventory of his day. He enjoyed his time with the girls, but wasn't sure of Monica's take on everything. She was quiet and he didn't know if it was in reflection or she was uncomfortable. At any rate, he knew that God didn't lead him to go after her for nothing.

Monica enjoyed the movie, "A family that preys" by Tyler Perry. She didn't watch many movies, since a lot of her time had been devoted to studying the word and spiritual mentorship. It was 9:05 and Monica went to make a phone call.

"Hello." Leslie answered.

"Hi, how are you?" Monica inquired. "I

was just thinking of you."

"Well Prophetess, here I am."

"Charles asked about you too my dear," she said.

"Oh well, tell him I said hi and don't forget to make my crab legs before the summer ends. I told him before, that I would release you for marriage - only if every summer he would make his special butter sauce with the seafood barbeque feast." They chuckled together.

"Alright, let's just cut to the chase. What's going on in your life?" Leslie inquired.

"Yea. I finally had an opportunity to speak with Shawn and there was a bit of miscommunication between us and we worked it out," Monica said.

"Just a bit Monica? Let me tell you something; don't get people involved too much in your personal business, especially those who have not accomplished success in the area you are trying to move into. Do you understand where I'm going with this?" Leslie was very stern with Monica.

"Yes, I hear you." Monica could sense that Leslie was speaking wisdom and wanted her to hear with her inner ear.

"Use much wisdom - everything is not always the way they appear to be. Please hear me tonight. Don't allow your flesh to lead you astray." Leslie was sending her a warning.

"Yes. I understand," Monica agreed.

"Charles is calling me, but I want you know that God is going to open your eyes and show you some things real plain, ok?" Leslie stated.

"Yes Ma'am," Monica said. They hung up and Monica sat there and mulled over her prophetic utterance. She felt her phone vibrate.

"Hello." Monica said.

"Hey beautiful," he said. Monica looked at her caller ID and responded.

"What's up?" she asked.

"It's you. I've been working my A-off." Brian bleeped the curse part out of respect.

"Really?" Monica was not ready to hear the b-shh.

"Yes, the new gig is really harder than I thought. I just did a fashion show today and I met a lot of contacts. How was your weekend?" Brian asked.

"It was relaxing and…while speaking she saw that Shawn was calling on her other line. Brian, I have an important call to take," Monica said.

"Oh, alright. I'll be up late, so give me a call." Brian said. Monica clicked over without responding to his last request.

"Hello," She responded.

"Hey Sweetheart," Shawn said. Monica could immediately feel her face smiling as he spoke.

"So, how did your girls enjoy their day out with you?" Monica hoped that they didn't see her as an intrusion.

"Oh they loved it, and again thank you for your patience and willingness to share me with them." Shawn knew that it took a lot meeting and entertaining kids that were not of her womb.

"Baby, just the fact that you thought enough of me to tag along with them, was truly special to me," Monica expressed. Shawn felt such an ache in his heart for Monica as she professed those words.

"Wow Lady, you never cease to amaze me. I would like to invite you to my church Labor Day weekend, as we will be having a special function," Shawn said.

"Oh that sounds great," Monica inquired.

"Monica there something that I must tell you that I felt uncomfortable about since you told me. Please receive it." Shawn's tone was serious now.

"What is it?" Monica was clueless as to what Shawn was about to say.

"The trip that your company wants to send you on is a setup, decline it." Shawn hoped that she would take heed.

"Sounds like you are giving me The word of the Lord, Shawn." Monica was taken aback by the force of what he said.

"I don't play with The Things of God Monica and I pray you don't either." Shawn felt the "Fear of the Lord" resting upon him.

"No. I hear you. Would you pray for God's divine protection for me at work?" Monica felt she needed to be covered. Shawn prayed a strong warrior prayer over Monica and after he finished, Sharde knocked on his bedroom door.

"Daddy, Shantell is annoying me," Sharde complained.

"Alright Dear, I have to play referee. Get you some rest and I will call you tomorrow."

CHAPTER 14 - HEADS TURN

Shawn pulled into the parking lot of "Church of the Living Word" under the Pastoralship of Bishop Earl Cunningham. This church had a membership of approximately 200 members. Shawn had done his best to be low keyed in the church, but the pastor did not take long to tell him that his services were required as God had plenty of work for him. He had only been a member for six months and he attended the church four months prior to joining. Initially, he was on the treasury board and then he became an intercessor; now he flowed as the house prophet. His girls were about to cross the entrance of the sanctuary.

"Why, good morning ladies," Mother Henry spoke. She wore one of those white doily things on her head. She was real old school and no matter what you told her, she was convinced that was her covering. Even when Bishop did a series of teachings on the spiritual covering of the Husband and Jesus, Mother Henry was not to be moved.

"Good Morning, Mother Henry." Sharde and Shantell spoke almost simultaneously. They had on adorable plaid dresses but the top part was made as a solid colored mock collared shirt. Sharde's was yellow and Shantell's was fuchsia and they had matching patent leather shoes.

"Sunday school is about to start Girls, so hurry." Mother Phyllis spoke up and took each of their hands as she had just walked by. Shawn waved goodbye and greeted other saints as he walked through. He would be going to the altar to kneel and intercede before worship began.

Monica didn't mind walking with the Pastor's wife. She made sure that she sat close to her and interceded for the pastor. Her church was small having only 100 members. The new branch (Harvest Time Ministries) grew out from the mother church located about 30 minutes away. Pastor Ronald Jones was newly ordained and his wife was eight weeks pregnant. Marilyn, pastor's wife was actually three years Monica's junior, but she looked a bit older for her age. She once prophesied to Monica that she would marry a pastor one day herself. Monica cringed upon hearing that. All she wanted to do was just serve the Lord and that was it. Why couldn't she just marry a man that loves the Lord the way she does?

Shawn peeked in the room where his daughters' children church was being held. He saw that they were practicing for the "labor day's" play and he smiled with pride watching them.

"So Brother Edwards, we're having a barbeque featuring all your favorite dishes. I hope to see you there." Sister Wanda grinned.

Shawn knew better than dealing with any of these off-site dinners or so-called fun filled events. He had heard too much about deacons slipping and sliding with women from the church and a vast amount of people prophe-lying, who operate under the disguise of ministry or church-related affairs.

"Well Sis, I actually spend most of my holidays with my girls and parents. This is one of my iron clad rules. You know, balance is so important to me." Shawn defied anyone who tried to come between God and his family.

"I see, I understand." Sister Wanda has had her eyes on Shawn from the time he hit the door. She recalled the first day back when she was ushering, he came in and "heads turned" all over the sanctuary. Wanda was too far away to seat him, but Sister Barbara was all too happy to oblige him. A lot of the women upon meeting him and watching, have thought of him as being too arrogant or sharp with his tongue for their taste; but there were still quite a few remaining that kept a glimmer of hope. Wanda even had a dream about him a few months ago, that he was in her bedroom and boy, she had to repent later of her imaginative thoughts. Shawn saw his daughters racing to him and he received them.

"Brother Edwards, I see something on the horizon for you, Son." Pastor Cunningham grabbed hold of Shawn and put his arm around his like a father. Shawn just smiled and they both walked, with his girls trailing behind them.

After service Monica met with Regina and the other woman that walked with the Pastor's wife every other Sunday. "So my dear, before next week, I want us to schedule a prayer session together on behalf of Pastor Jones and his wife, as well as Pastor Richard and his wife."
Pastor Richard was the youth pastor in the church.

"Yes, yes Sis. I will definitely make myself available."

"How about Thursday?" Katrina asked.

"That's doable. So I'm going to get out of here, God Bless you and I'll speak to you later this week." They embraced and Monica headed for her car.

While Shawn cleaned the kitchen after having dinner with his daughters, he contemplated the message that his Pastor ministered on: "The Attack comes right after the Prophetic Revelation". The message was from the story of Joseph. He showed how the spirit of jealousy came from his brothers, Pharoah's wife attacked his character, and then he was cast away, soon to be forgotten in a cell; but because Joseph had the right attitude and continued to use his gift, God was able to promote him as he promised. That message quickened in Shawn's Spirit and he knew that the Holy Spirit was charging him with something(s).

Monday morning at Readme Now

Monica was not looking forward to talking to her supervisor and director about her change of heart. She prayed that they didn't now take it the wrong way and think she was ungrateful. Nevertheless, she conceded that God had given her favor and that was that.

"Good Morning," she called out to Carolyn.

"Good Morning," Carolyn replied with a smile on her face.

"I was wondering if I could speak with you for a minute, when you get a moment." Monica wanted to get this off her chest a.s.a.p.

"Sure come into my office, right now." Carolyn motioned her to follow her. Monica gathered her courage and sat down across from Carolyn's desk.

"Carolyn I just want to thank you and Roy again for your faith in me and the awesome opportunity that you have offered me; but, unfortunately, I will have to decline on taking it." Whew, Monica thought. Carolyn's face turned a shade of red orange.

"What, why?" she stammered. Looking confused and waiting for an explanation, Carolyn sat up in her office chair.

"I had time to consider it over the weekend and based on personal reasons, I decided to change my mind." Monica looked at Carolyn thinking, this is not that serious, or is it?

"Well the ticket has been paid for and the hotel arrangements were prepared. If we had known, we could have delegated it differently." Carolyn was noticeably upset. Just then her phone rang.

"Yes. I have Monica here and she just advised that she no longer wants to go to the office in Chicago." Monica listened and she saw Carolyn shift the phone to speaker phone.

"So I hear, you dropped the ball, young lady," Roy stated.

"I apologize, Roy. It's just timing and a lot of personal things going on, that it would not be wise for me to go out of town now." Monica could not reveal the real reason.

"Well, don't worry. We can rearrange something's. Carolyn, this means I need you to take her place. So, I'm going to have my secretary change the name on the reservations and tickets. Check back with me later and I will finalize everything before lunchtime." Roy sounded very casual in comparison to Carolyn. You could tell that Carolyn was fit to be tied. Monica left just before Carolyn hung up. Carolyn took the phone off speaker to try to convey that there was no way she could leave on such short notice. Carolyn left about 12:30, after the secretary delivered her tickets and other important documents. Monica had spent all morning gathering all the forms and details that Carolyn would need to do for the presentation at the Chicago office.

It was 4:00 pm and she heard her cell phone vibrate. Great, just who she wanted to speak to!

"Hey Mom" Monica was excited.

"Hi, how are you," she asked.

"I'm absolutely wonderful," Monica replied.

"It must be man-related." She and Monica laughed briefly.

"Yes and no. I'm doing well in my new promoted positioned that we talked about a few weeks ago; and yes, I met a really nice guy." Monica didn't want to reveal too much, as her mother could be overly critical.

"Well, I was calling to tell you that we want to fly in for Labor Day weekend," her Mother said.

"Oh that sounds perfect. Will you guys be staying with me or a Hotel?" Monica inquired.

"You know better. Jeremiah and I are booking the nearest and best hotel in your area. We just need you to pick us up."

"So send me the details and I will be there."

"Ok Dear, I will be checking back with you in a few days. Love you, Bye." Monica's Mother, Frances, was definitely high maintenance. Monica was about to grab her keys and purse and her phone rang again.

"Hey Darling, I was thinking about you," Monica said.

"Hi, Baby Girl. I wanted to grab some dinner with you," Shawn said.

"Sure, where do you want me to meet you."

"I'll pick you up at your place in 20 minutes. You don't have to change or anything. Just come as you are."

"Ok." She wondered why he appeared to be in a rush. Maybe he was just that hungry. At any rate she had been parked in her car for about two minutes before Shawn pulled into the parking space next to hers. Monica locked her car and waited for Shawn to open her door after a brief hug. Shawn and Monica shared their Sunday service message with one another, as they were on their way to the restaurant. It looked like a quiet night for Hooligans, but Monica felt uncomfortable going to the same restaurant that she had recently gone with Brian. Boy if he saw her with Shawn -he would flip; but funny enough, he had no right to feel any kind of way. The hostess walked them to a booth and there were, maybe, five other couples in the entire restaurant.

"You seemed anxious earlier, when we spoke," Monica observed.

"I wanted to ask you a question and hope that you do not have any plans." Shawn seemed on edge for some reason. Although in Shawn's mind, any other plans would have to be cancelled.

"So ask me," Monica said as the waitress came and interrupted.

"Hello. My name is Linda and I'll be your waitress tonight. Would you be having any appetizers, or do you need a moment to order?" She spoke in a slow southern accent. Shawn looked at Monica as if he wanted her to decide.

"You choose tonight. The ball is in your court," Monica said.

"Alright, that's suits me fine. I'm going to go ahead and order pasta with shrimp and scallops. For now, can we have a glass of water with lime." Shawn wanted as little interruptions as possible.

"Alrighty then. Are you ok Sweetie?" Monica was concerned as his behavior was a bit peculiar.

"I'm fine baby. I just want your full attention." Shawn relaxed a bit.

"I'm right here." Monica assured him. The waitress dropped off the water and left.

"I would love for you to come to my family's yearly Labor Day barbeque, as it is a big family event. It's actually their anniversary too." Shawn was on pins and needles.

"That's huge Shawn. Do you think your parents would be ok with me being at such a large family affair, since I am a stranger to them?"

Monica was impressed and definitely knew that Shawn was really getting serious about her.

"I'm sure my parents would love to meet you; you being the love of my life and all." Shawn said it and he couldn't even believe he leaked it out himself.

"What did you just say?" Monica thought for sure she heard the L-word.

"Yes, I said it." Shawn confessed and both of his dimples surfaced. "I Love You Monica." Shawn had to get that weight off his chest.

Monica took a large breath inwardly and took in the sound of his words.

"Shawn you are so incredible that I can't help but love you. You're irresistible." Monica would not hold back her feelings. Shawn stared at Monica and held her hand until their food came. They talked about the weekend coming up and a flashback came to Monica.

"Oh, no," Monica just remembered.

"What? What's wrong?" Shawn asked.

"My Mother and her husband are flying in this weekend to see me." Monica felt a lump in her stomach.

"That's no problem, they are more than welcome. Let me explain something to you. If I invite someone to one of our affairs, my family will roll out the red carpet, understand?" Shawn encouraged her.

"I believe you." Monica still felt a bit uneasy with just meeting his family by herself. That would be much, now her parents would be there. She thought to herself - "awkward."

"By the way, you can invite Keiki. You know what - No, let me invite her. That way she can feel that I am now becoming a real authentic part of your life, okay. Don't mention it to her, I will do it myself," Shawn offered. Shawn and Monica talked and flirted all night and now he was parking next to her car again. It was just 8:00 pm.

"Well, baby. I enjoyed every bit of your company as usual." Shawn stroked Monica's hair while he talked.

"Will you come up for a bit?" Monica hoped.

"Baby, with all this fire that's shut up in me, it would not benefit either one of us for me to hang out tonight." Shawn always kept it real.

"I understand. Thank you for your honesty," Monica said.

"But I'm still going to cash my 'rain check' that I promised you last time." Shawn leaned over and took Monica into his arms. Passion seemed to envelope them in ways that seemed to make them forget where they were. They kissed and kissed and kissed.

"Baby." Monica couldn't take it anymore. She was breathless and grew weak from his kisses. Shawn wanted more and he knew more would be too much.

"Yes Babes. I know. I have to let you go." Shawn walked Monica to her door, but refused to enter her condo. They hugged goodnight.

Make-me-over needed a Makeover

It seemed that Selena's "Golden Boy", Brian and her were having some disagreements. The entire office could hear their dispute, but no one dared to say a word.

"Look, I'm not one of your little servants around here. I can leave anytime I want. Matter of a fact, let me do just that." Brian glared.

"So you can't handle things when your little ego is deflated." Selena ranted.

Shawn knew something had to be done. He walked over to Selena's office, where Brian was about to leave and she was about to follow him.

"Hey, hey. What's going on?" Brian pushed open the door.

"I'm done here," Brian said.

"Let him go, we can always get another pretty face." Selena shot back.

"Really, Selena. C'mon. Things have got to simmer down. Surely, there's a better way to handle things than this." Shawn said.

"Shawn, are you really trying to tell me how to handle my office." Now her anger was diverted towards him. Brian wanted to leave, but he had to see how Shawn would handle this wild woman. One who needed to be tamed.

"I'm not telling you how to run your office, I'm making a suggestion." Shawn's eyes were fiery and his voice took on a whole other tone.

"Well, I don't need your advice or suggestion." Selena was very rude and even though she was surprised that Shawn had taken a different persona. She would not be punked.

"Selena, Shawn breathed deeply, I'm going to make a suggestion to you for the last time. This is an office environment and I refuse to allow the employees to be put in a position that defies the reputation that plenty of honorable men and women have written policies to protect. So if you want to be defiant, then I will take a stand for them, if you choose to ignore my advice." Shawn spoke like a veteran attorney. Selena now obviously shook, changed her attitude quickly.

"Alright, point well taken." Selena knew when she was beaten, she just hated to lose.

"Brian, I need to get a few things from you before you leave." Shawn dismissed himself at that juncture.

"Your reputation precedes you," she said.

"Meaning? Shawn asked."

"It's all over the office, how you "Tamed the Cat", Keiki spoke.

"Well, an intervention was needed."

"Any plans this weekend, Keiki?" Shawn asked.

"Are you asking me out, Shawn?" Keiki was surprised.

"I'm trying to invite you to a fabulous barbeque that is the hotspot." Shawn showed his magnificent dimples and his teeth were just a shining.

"I'll have to see," Keiki said. She wondered if Monica was privy to this event.

"C'mon Keiki, I promise you won't regret it," Shawn said.

"Alright, I'll come." Keiki felt it couldn't be that bad, if it was a barbeque full of people.

Ten minutes later Brian was closing Selena's office door. Selena called him and seconds later they were walking down the hallway together and whatever went on after he left, proved to change the atmosphere. Throughout the week, it was becoming more and more noticeable that Selena had more than a sexual attraction to Brian. At times, they would be in a meeting together and Selena's eyes would soften as Brian would share some of his creative suggestions. There were also moments that Selena would slip back into her hellion state and Brian would give her a look or a word that would put Selena into check. If he didn't know better, he would say that Selena had met her match.

Every night Shawn and Monica would take turns to call one another and act like teenagers in love. Monica received the flight information and it was on Saturday, September 3 @ 2:00 pm from Orlando, Florida. Monica was excited over her weekend and throughout the entire week; she had not once spoken verbally to Leslie. They had been communicating daily via email. Monica saw that it was time to pack it up, so she grabbed her cell and purse and headed to her vehicle. While in her car, she decided to dial.

"Hey you're going to live a long time." Shawn said.

"Oh really, were you thinking of me?" Monica was being coy. "Of course! I have a great idea, if you agree."

"I'm listening."

"Why don't we put your mom and stepdad in a taxi from the airport? That way you don't have to frustrate yourself with traffic; parking and you can meet your mother after they settle in?" Shawn asked.

"That's an absolutely wonderful idea. I wonder what the cost would be," Monica said.

"Don't worry it's on me. I want you to relax, after all its Labor Day weekend." Monica and Shawn hung up in agreement. Monica needed to update her mom and stepdad about the transportation arrangements. Monica dialed her mother. Phone rang into voicemail.

"Hello, Mom. I'm calling to let you that I've made arrangements to have a taxi service pick you up. The name of the taxi company is: Anytime car and limo service. They will have your name and flight information. If you have any questions, please call me. We can meet for dinner, after you have settled into your hotel. Love you, later." Monica hung up. She suddenly realized that she had not heard from Keiki in a while. She decided to give her a call, since tomorrow she would be too busy getting ready for her mom's arrival. Monica dialed her friend, Keiki. Hmmm she thought voice mail again. She didn't leave a message, she just figured - she'd try back sometime before the barbeque.

Saturday rush hour

Monica went through her condo like a tsunami, making sure that everything was perfect and in place. Her mom and stepdad were neat fanatics and she did not want to leave any rock unturned. She dusted, mopped, swept and washed some walls. The fresh scent that was released by the cleansers was pleasant to the nostrils. Her bathrooms and the kitchen were immaculate and she put out fresh towels and other toiletries. Even though they booked a hotel room, she just wanted her place to be comfortable and inviting. Monica could barely sleep last night, with all these events coming up one after the other. First her mom and stepdad would be here for the entire weekend and then she would meet Shawn's parents; then she would also fellowship in his church. It was like a whirlwind was coming right in her direction. She did manage to pick out what she thought to be the right outfit(s) for each occasion. Now she was about to jump in the shower and get ready for her parents. It was now 1:45 and her mom would soon be calling her to let her know that she landed and then again when she has checked into the hotel.

Keiki had just returned from a birthday party with her son Damien. She saw that she missed a phone call from Monica. She decided to call her. Monica's phone rang into voice mail. Keiki heard Damien calling her and she just hung up. Monica put on a crisp white button down shirt with a black skirt. The blouse's neckline was embroidered with clear stones and had gathers on the side that accentuated her waistline. The set fit her nicely and her earrings were perfectly matched. She wore 1 ½" open-toed black heels. Monica saw the missed call from her mother and dialed her back.

"Hello," Frances said.

"Hey Mom, I see you guys made it. How was your flight?" Monica asked.

"It would have been nice, except Bebe's kids were seated right behind us," Frances said with contempt.

"Well, I'm just glad you are here. What time will you ready for dinner?"

"Actually, we are both famished as you know that airline food is horrible."

"Alright Mom, I'll be there in 10 minutes. Maybe you can obtain a table since I'm so close to you guys," Monica suggested.

"I'll see you when you get here." Frances hung up. Monica drove up to the beautiful Marriot Hotel/Spa and it was gorgeous. She knew that this hotel rated well and was sure that their dining experience would definitely meet their expectations. Monica checked with the hostess and was escorted to her mother and Jeremiah's table. They both stood upon recognizing Monica.

"Hi." Monica hugs and squeezes Frances and Jeremiah before she takes her seat.

"You look well, my dear," Frances stated.

"Thank you Mom. I'm eating better and drinking plenty of water," Monica said.

"Oh, I thought your skin glowing may have something to do with this mystery man that seems to have a permanent smile on your face." Frances' normal tone was laden with sarcasm.

"That probably has some effect true. Did you guys order yet?" Monica directed her question to Jeremiah now.

"I ordered me a steak dinner. I hope this restaurant is a good as the reviews." Jeremiah was very picky.

"Yes, my dear. I ordered the salmon dinner," Frances said. Just then the waiter stopped by.

"I see your guest arrived. My name is John; can I get you something to drink? Or are you ready to order?" The young twenty something man was obviously gay and very over the top with it.

"I'm ready to order. I'll have the liver entree and a glass of water with lemon."

"Great, I'll have the chef add this to come out with the other order." John nodded and left their presence.

"You know in our day, guys like that would never be able to work in this type of establishment. What is this world coming to? Geez, a man ought to know that he's a man!" Jeremiah was "ole school" and his face had such a despicable frown.

"Honey, you know parents these days, just let these kids grow up like weeds and no effort is made. I tell you, God is not even in their vocabulary," Frances stated.

Monica listened as they went back and forth until their food was served. Monica had better things to talk about than the why's of the world when she knew everything was spiritually connected. Her mother and Jeremiah were a bit pious and religious. She did not include her thoughts, as she did not want to declare a religious war.

"So Mom, tomorrow I have a function to attend and wanted you guys to accompany me." Monica held her breath, hoping she could convince them.

"What type of function? I came to visit you; I'm really not interested in going someplace and being uncomfortable," Frances complained. Monica said a silent prayer inwardly, while her mother fussed.

"I guarantee you both will enjoy it. My current partner and I wanted to spend the Labor Day together, so we decided to spend it with each other, his parents and you." Monica knew that wasn't quite the order of how it went, but she repented to God for not telling the whole truth.

"Are you talking about dinner?" Frances asked. You could tell that Frances was ready to refute any possibilities of meeting these people. She was waiting for Monica to say something that she could tear apart.

"Actually, it will be a barbeque/anniversary celebration. It's actually a very elegant affair, because this is an annual event so they really planned it luxuriously," Monica said. She knew her Mom to be a bit snobbish, but if she thought that is was upscale, she would be more motivated to go.

"I don't know, Monica. These people are strangers and we'll be eating what? Where will this event be held?" Frances asked. Why did her Mom have to be so difficult?????

"Honestly Mom, it would mean so much to me for you to meet someone that is very special to me and only God knows if this opportunity will arise again." Monica's voice showed her frustration.

"Ok Frances, it's obvious that Monica has some strong feelings for this young man. Why don't we go for an hour and if we don't like the atmosphere- no harm no foul?" Jeremiah felt sorry for Monica. Frances thought about what Jeremiah said.

"Ok." She sighed. "On one condition Monica, if we want to come home, you will bring us back. Not in a taxi." Frances agreed.

"Great." Monica was thrilled. She just prayed that things would go well with his family meeting hers. That was her only hope. Monica, her Mom and Jeremiah talked about what they would do after church on Sunday and then they departed, since they would get an early breakfast at Monica's house and then head out to the barbeque. Monica had just walked into her condo, when she realized she needed to get the complete address from Shawn for the barbeque. Monica dialed him.

"Hello Beautiful," Shawn said happy to hear from Monica.

"Hey Handsome," Shawn blushed not expecting that response.

"How was your parents' flight in?" Shawn asked.

"It went well and I just left them after having dinner."

"Good, Good. So are you ready for tomorrow?"

"Yes, I just need to get the address."

"Let me know when you are ready, or better yet - I'll text it you."

"Even better. So what town do they live in?"

"They live in Greenwich, CT."

"Really, they live closer to me." Monica was surprised.

"Yes, remember on my first date with you, we took a ride to Norwalk and I showed you an area that I used to frequent. That was an old neighborhood that I grew up in."

"Oh that's right. It was so exquisite and picturesque."

"I take it that your parents agreed to come with you tomorrow."

"Yes, they did." Monica would not elaborate that it was like pulling teeth.

"I'm so excited to meet your mother. I'm sure we will have a night to remember. My parents are looking forward to meeting you," Shawn replied. Monica felt that her emotions were like a rollercoaster. She was happy, but nervous at the same time.

"I pray that we will all have a blessed time tomorrow," Monica said. Monica and Shawn prayed for both families that God would meet them at his mom's home and the Angelic Host would protect their day.

Monica had butterflies in her stomach and somehow managed to drift off to sleep.

Labor Day

Monica packed an extra outfit on the chance that she would spill something on her 1st choice. Monica prepared brunch for her mom and Jeremiah, because they wanted to sleep in. They finished about 1:30 and she took them to a mall in the area, and her mother took advantage of the many Labor Day specials. Jeremiah looked a little bored and he wandered into "Men's N Things". Jeremiah almost got lost in this sporting goods/men's department store.

Looking at the time, Monica was to head back to her house to change into her prepared outfit. They realized Jeremiah was nowhere to be found.

"Now where did he go?" Frances became annoyed.

"Well, why don't you call him on his cell?" Monica suggested.

"That's if he answers it. You know he can hardly hear," Frances retorted, as they both broke out into laughter.

Jeremiah was about to purchase some fishing gear, as he likes to spend time at the lake and relax in nature at times. He felt the vibration of his cell ringing.

"Hello," he answered.

"Where are you?" Frances inquired.

"I was about to buy something. Why, are you ready to go?" Jeremiah wished he'd come alone.

"We have to get ready for the barbeque now. Monica says it started about an hour ago, so we will be fashionably late." Frances' face had a satisfied smile. This was one of the few times that Monica wanted to be late. She didn't want to appear to be too anxious to meet his parents and, also wanted things to already be put together prior to them arriving. It was now 4:30. Monica went into her bedroom and changed. She carried a nice tote bag, large enough to fit one change of clothes in it. She could hear her mom and Jeremiah playfully arguing. Monica proceeded to the living room area, ready to leave.

"Wow, you look lovely," Frances said.

"Thank you Mom." Monica's face lit up and she knew it was a genuine compliment; her mother did not flatter you unless it was true. Monica had the directions and it was just a fifteen minutes' drive. She knew the area that they would be visiting was where most of the estate homes were located. She considered that this house must be nice. The address led her to a gated community and Monica knew her mother would be impressed. The grounds were immaculately kept and she called Shawn to let him know that she had arrived.

"I'll be right there to get you," Shawn promised.

There were a few cars in front of hers and someone was directing the traffic for parking. She could see Shawn coming from the back of the house to greet them. Boy, that was one fine brother, Monica thought to herself. Shawn walked up to Monica's driver side.

"Hi, I'm glad you are here," Shawn said as he kissed Monica lightly on her cheek. Frances and Jeremiah had stepped out of the vehicle now that they were parked. "Shawn this is my mother, Frances and my stepdad Jeremiah." Shawn shook their hands and led them on a tour, prior to taking them to the main area of the party. Shawn was dapperly dressed as usual. He wore dark jeans and an olive green v-neck short sleeve jersey shirt. He wore a very classy gold chain and bracelet to match. His muscle flexed each time he pointed or used his hands to guide them. The aroma of the food was amazing. Monica could see that her mother's whole demeanor had changed. From the time she saw the home she was like a zombie. The house was a light colored brick stone and featured two fireplaces, two-car garage, 8 bedrooms, a completed basement and a chef's kitchen. The decor was professionally done. Now, Shawn took them to the backyard where about fifty people were gathered in various groups.

"I want to introduce you to my mom and dad, before we get you seated," Shawn said. Shawn led them to a table that a light skinned lady, looking elegant with a chic cropped blonde close to her nape, was seated. Her skin was tanned and she reminded you of Dorothy Dandridge. His dad was dark and handsome. Monica noticed that he reminded her of an older Denzel Washington.

"Mom, Dad I want you to meet someone very dear to my heart." She stood as he was talking.

"This is Monica, her mother, Frances and dad Jeremiah." Shawn introduced them. They all shook hands and smiled cordially.

"It's nice to meet you dear," Shawn's mom Patrice said. Shawn's Dad, Kenneth, just smiled as he sat down and observed.

"It's wonderful to meet you both," Monica expressed. Frances and Jeremiah smiled and nodded in politeness.

"Well Mom, I'm going to get them seated. Shawn noted and he led them to a table that he had reserved with balloons and his jacket.

"Please take this table and as you can see, food is in abundance. Feel free to mingle; no one will make you feel like a stranger," Shawn assured. Shawn told Monica he would be back shortly.

"This seems like a nice party" Frances had to admit. "Jeremiah let's get something to eat."

"Ok Mom. I'll hold your seats," Monica said. Monica scanned the party and took notice of the crowd of people and she saw that more people were coming. Her eyes quickly located Shawn and she saw that he was talking to two pretty ladies. Monica felt a tinge of insecurity, as these girls were hanging onto him. Monica refused to let him see that she lacked confidence and put on a face of indifference as he was headed in her direction.

"Hey Baby, these are my sisters: Leah and Rachel." Shawn smiled and his dimples once again captivated her.

"Oh, nice to meet you," Monica greeted.

"As you can see, our parents have a real sense of humor," Leah suggested. I'm the black sheep of the family." Leah retorted. Leah was unmistakably a lesbian. Although she was pretty, she had the overlay of masculinity. She wore tattoos on her forearm, had a nose ring, her jeans were baggy and she sported a man's tee shirt. They both had long hair, but Leah pulled hers back in a ponytail.

"Pay no mind to her girl. That's her way of taking all of the attention as usual," Rachel deflected. She looked like a runaway model, she had a tender, sophisticated style. You could tell that she and her sister were close, the way they looked at each other.

"Ok Barbie, don't you have a mirror to look in or something," Leah edged.

"Ladies, ladies, we have company," Shawn said. Just as they were talking, Monica couldn't believe her eyes.

"Please excuse me. I'll be right back," she told Shawn. Two tables away, Monica was ecstatic. "Hey You!!!" Monica exclaimed.

Keiki did a double take and almost didn't recognize Monica. Her thoughts were miles away. Keiki tried to compose herself before standing up. Monica went over to hug her.

"Why didn't you tell me you were coming?" Monica asked. Keiki was searching her mind for the right words.

"Shawn just said to come and I took Damien to his dad and here I am. I tried to reach you but you didn't call me back."

"I didn't see any missed calls, but I'm glad you made it. I wasn't sure if you'd be here. I have so much to share with you but later."

"Why don't you come to our table, it's just right over there? Bring your chair." Monica walked towards the table where her parents were already eating.

"Hey stranger. Frances sat waiting for Keiki to greet her. Keiki kissed both Frances and Jeremiah, as she said Hi and sat down between Frances and Monica. There was a live band playing jazz, contemporary gospel and some oldies but goodies music. The music was silenced, while Leah, Rachel and Shawn each wished their parents "Happy Anniversary." The vibe of the mixture of people was warm and happy. There were all cultures represented in the vast array of couples and families at the barbeque. When it was time for Shawn to speak, he became very serious and everyone tuned in with all ears.

"I'm very proud to be the son of such loving, God-fearing parents. My whole life, my father preached and preached (laughter), but his words did not fall on deaf ears. They are the reason I pursued academic goals and accomplished what they said was the ultimate mission-to serving Jesus the Christ. Anyway, Congratulations Mom and Dad, I pray for many more happy years for you both. You've paved the way not only for me, but for future generations. I also don't know if you all have met someone who is very precious and dear to my heart. Her name is Monica. She's over there, where the balloons are attached to the chairs." Shawn looked for her in the direction of her table at that point. Monica's face turned red and her heart fell, as everyone turned in her direction. Monica couldn't believe that Shawn put her on the spot like that.

"Why don't you come up here, dear?" Shawn asked with his eyes beaming of love.

"Do I have to?" Monica said and the crowd roared in laughter.

"Don't make me come and get you, because you know I will," Shawn teased her. Monica felt self-conscious, but she stood up and made her way to the stage that the band and Shawn were standing on.

"See that wasn't so hard." Shawn hugged Monica; he could see that she was nervous.

"Isn't she lovely," Shawn said. "Well, I say she's lovely," (people whistled as he spoke). Monica wore a jewel green over the shoulder one piece classy jumpsuit that was elegant and made her look like a princess with her white gold necklace featuring a butterfly pendant in lavender tone. Her earrings were glittery two tones of yellow and white gold. Monica's makeup was a duet of shades of purple, green and highlighted gold complimenting her silvery pink lip glass.

"I wanted to request a song for my mom and dad, but also for the love of my life," Shawn said. The band began to play a song entitled "Love Is" by Brian McKnight and Vanessa Williams. When the band proceeded to play the first few notes, Shawn interrupted them.

"Wait a minute, before we get this going, I want my Mom and Dad, all the couples and married people to come out to the dance area for this song," Shawn asked. Everyone did as Shawn had asked. He turned to Monica to grab her hand to dance. The microphone still in his hand, he turned to Monica.

"Monica, I want the whole world to know that I love you. Will you marry me?" Shawn said. Everyone just froze. Monica's eyes grew very large and tears welled up in them. She was in so much shock, but Shawn was still staring in her eyes.

"Yes" Monica said while crying, Shawn grabbed her and held her. Leah ran on stage, took the microphone and advised the band to play the requested song. The people were cheering them on as they danced on stage. Monica's body shivered and she cried on his shoulder, as he kissed her tears, they danced the whole song till it ended. After the song was over, friends and family members greeted Monica and Shawn, as they made their way through the groups of people and he stopped by the table where Monica's parents were seated.

"Wow that was unexpected." Frances stood and Shawn hugged her.

"I love your daughter and I intend to make her happy," Shawn said.

Jeremiah embraced them and smiled. Keiki was shocked, even though a smile was spread over her face. She hugged Monica and Shawn. Shawn asked them to excuse them as he wanted to stop by his parents.

"Well, well, well," Kenneth, Shawn's Dad, said. "You are full of surprises today."

"We only just met this Young Woman, my dear, but I'm sure you have prayed on this," Patrice said.

"Of course Mother, that's how you trained me," Shawn replied. He hoped his mother didn't feel bothered by his doing this during their anniversary event.

"Come let me hug you, you'll be my daughter soon." Monica embraced her and hugged his dad as well. Leah and Rachel came to their area, waiting for the chance to congratulate them.

"I wanna see the ring," Leah said.

"Yep, he's in Love." Rachel and Leah slapped each and laughed simultaneously. Shawn slipped the engagement ring onto her finger after they slow danced. The ring was an elegant 3.5 carat princess diamond with a platinum setting. Shawn spent the next hours introducing Monica as his fiancé and unbeknownst to her, Monica's parents enjoyed every moment. Around 8:00 PM things started to die down and Monica knew she had to get her parents back to the hotel to prepare for church tomorrow. Keiki had left about 6:30, to pick up her son.

"Ready to go," Monica asked her family.

"Ready when you are," Frances commented. Monica noticed that her mother seemed just a little too happy, and then she realized they had the champagne bottles on their table.

"Ok baby, I guess I have to say goodnight." Monica turned facing Shawn and while hugging him, she peered into his eyes.

"Yea, I know, but I'll see you in church tomorrow," Shawn stated.

"Oh yea, tomorrow; I'm glad you mentioned it, for some reason I thought it was next Sunday." Monica smiled, as Shawn kissed her button nose.

"Nope, it's tomorrow and don't disappoint me." Shawn gave her a more sober look.

"I won't." Monica and Shawn released each other and he walked them to her vehicle.

"Alright you all have a pleasant evening and I will see you in the AM." Monica pulled off and began to drive.

"You met him at your church?" Frances asked.

"No Mom, I was just invited to go to his church tomorrow," Monica said.

"He seems like a fine young man. Meeting his family, you can tell he was raised right, with God and all. Plus they live quite fancy. I pray you guys aren't moving too fast. How long have you been dating? You only recently told me about him," Frances said. Monica could tell this could turn into a lecture.

"Mom, I'm a little overwhelmed right now. Why don't we talk about this tomorrow after church?" Monica said.

"Alright, alright, I get the message." Frances knew she was irritating Monica.

"Have a good night's sleep; I'll be here to pick you up by 8:00." Monica was now in her car alone. She wanted to call Keiki, but she decided to just bask in the moment. Monica threw her keys and purse on the table and headed for her bedroom. She carried her cell with her, as she did not want to miss Shawn in case he called. Monica fell asleep and woke up to her phone vibrating.

"Hello." Her voice was barely audible.

"I just wanted to hear my future wife's voice before I went to sleep," Shawn said.

"Ahhh! You are so sweet."

"I know..." He laughed.

"But seriously, get some rest and I'll see you at church," Shawn stated.

"Alright Baby, love you. Goodnight." Monica and Shawn hung up and Monica went fast to sleep.

Sunday "Labor's Day Play"

Shawn was up at the crack of dawn, 5:00 am, praying to God about the previous days and its events. He knew that Monica was the woman that he had been praying about for the last six to eight months. Shawn had originally wanted to get married out of sheer loneliness and to fulfill his seemingly insatiable fleshly desires. During his season of waiting on God, he had weeks of fasting and praying to bring him to a more intimate place with God. He obtained wisdom and a greater appreciation for his singleness. God had trained him and disciplined him in areas that he never thought possible and now his dream was about to come true. Shawn's only concern regarding marriage was how his daughter's would react. Of course, he raised Sharde and Shantell to be respectful, but in time their true feelings would surface. He wondered how Monica would be as a stepmom; only time will tell. Shawn flooded "Heaven" with his intercessory prayers about his thoughts and concerns. He picked out a suit that he had never worn to church. It was a silver gray Armani suit paired with a mauve shirt and a Victor & Rolf tie, with orange and copper hues. His Stacy Adams, deep chocolate square, toed leather shoes were perfect against his trench coat. Shawn had already advised Monica that he would be sitting on the left side of the sanctuary, as that's where the ministers and prophets were instructed to sit. They were the watchmen on the wall and had to sit in the front row, to see who came into the church and observe others in the congregation. He knew that most likely she would be seated in the middle aisle, depending on what time she came in. Shawn felt a tinge of nervousness knowing that his soon to be wife, mother-in-law and father-in-law would be there. He never knew when God would speak through him. He just prepared himself for whatever the Holy Spirit would do.

Monica was parked in the lot of the hotel waiting for her mom and stepdad to come out, so that they could be on their way to church.

Monica was meticulous in her dress code, more than usual today. Today would be very unique and special, as she would be in a different church and meeting those who Shawn fellowships with. Monica looked down at her new engagement ring and was baffled as to how things played out over the last few days. Monica decided to wear an outfit that still had tags on it. It was a champagne colored, pleated one shoulder sheath dress that had a mock wrap style accentuating the waistline. The shoes she wore were a bone colored pair of Guess, 4 ½" Honda pumps. The stone colored snakeskin Guess purse that she carried, tied in with the tan Neiman Marcus cropped sweater. Her jewelry consisted of a stretchy three layered beaded pearl bracelet, matching ring and earrings that had a white gold base. Monica even wore a new perfume from Chloe with its crème. Monica was fixing her makeup when her parents each reached for the car handle, positioned themselves in the car, securing their seatbelts. Monica's mother sat up in the passenger side in front with her.-

"My God you look unbelievable," Frances commented.

"And she smells nice too," Jeremiah chimed in.

"Good Morning and thank you." Monica was delighted to be greeted in such a positive manner. Monica was used to her mother divulging all of her critique; but I guess she had mercy on her, as they were on their way to church. It was 8:45 and Monica was able to get a really good parking space when they arrived, since someone was pulling out from a spot close to the entrance. Monica and her parents could hear the worship from the lot. She knew service started at 8:30, but she wasn't sure of the location and traffic was monstrous getting there. The church was huge like an auditorium or movie theatre. The usher led them to the middle aisle and he found three seats on the third row to the left end of the aisle. Monica skimmed through the Sunday packet that they received. The program described the order of the service. After worship, announcements quickly followed and Monica felt the dread that she faced anytime she visited a church for the first time.

Renee was an outgoing nineteen year old and she enjoyed doing the church announcements. Her parents served faithfully as a deacon and deaconess. Renee loved to see souls saved and her dream was to become an evangelist.

"If there are any first time visitors, please stand," Renee stated. Monica, Frances and Jeremiah stood up.

"Would you please let us know your name and how you found out about this church?" Renee had such a welcoming smile.

"My name is Jeremiah and this is my wife, Frances and daughter Monica and we were invited by Shawn Edwards," Jeremiah spoke.
Perfect, Monica thought, she didn't even have to speak.

"On behalf of our Pastor Cunningham, his wife and the "Church of the Living Word" we want to welcome you. We hope to see you back again. The choir then broke out into a song that they sang as a welcome anthem. The Bishop stood, as he was introduced to the congregation and came to greet the church.

"Praise the Lord Church. I want to welcome the Holy Spirit to dwell with us today. I won't take up too much of your time, as we have already done our opening prayers. We have a special treat for you today and I won't be preaching until later this evening, because the 'children's church', bless their hearts; have prepared a play for us commemorating Labor Day. So buckle your seats and I'm going to release the service in the hands of our "Youth Group Leader(s), Pamela and Victor, Bless them Lord." Bishop handed the microphone to Victor.

"Hallelujah and welcome Saints of the Most High God. Today we wanted to do something with the children to exemplify the value of labor and the example of God's rest. So please, sit back and watch these 'anointed vessels' that God is raising up in this hour. Lights please," Victor announced. The curtain was drawn and the lights went out.
The entire stage was dark and you could scarcely find light anywhere in the room; it seems that every window and door must have been covered somehow. The stage in this church was very theatrical and the ceilings

were high, as it would accommodate performances comparative to a Broadway event. A voice came through as the narrator:
"In the beginning God Created the Heavens and the Earth.
Narrator: It was 6 days of creation and 1 day of rest."

Day 1 - "Let there be light". The stage was filled with lights streaming from various spotlights and melting into each other.
Narrator: Day 2 - Tonya an eight -year old opened her arms and a blue canvas dropped down from the ceiling, as a blank canvas depicting a clear sky.
Day 3 - A little Maria came out on stage and began picking up cardboard clouds that were lying face down on top of water puddles made of thick plastic/rubber materials, and attached them to the blank canvas, as if creating a picture. You could hear sounds of water splish splashing.
Day 4 -Then Jarron, Henry, Carrie and Tonya moved and separated the created waters into special ponds and rivers, using more special effect sounds of waterfalls and oceans.
Day 5 -Groups of kids came and carried small plants, flowers and miniature trees, creating a colorful garden.
Day 6 -Shantell- She uses her fingers to paint and design the stars, moon and the sun to appear. More images dropped from the ceiling.
After that, Leo removed a curtain that unveiled a huge aquarium with fish, turtles and sea creatures. A cage with a parrot dove and red robin mocking bird appeared. Then Shantell, Sharde and Linda led a cat, dog, and pony onto the stage.
At this point the audience was ecstatic, clapping their hands at each interval until the final climax came:
Teens, Frank and Suzie, came out as Adam and Eve to tend the garden and the animals.
Finally, God/Narrator spoke and gave charge to Adam and Eve and they bowed down hearing the voice of God.

The Narrator came out as the satisfied creator and sat down on a seat made to look like a throne.

The whole church stood and gave them a standing ovation, clapping for about five minutes. Monica recognized the twins, as the entire cast came back to the stage and bowed as their cheers and standing ovation continued. Shawn was feeling all manner of emotions, from one extreme to the next. He was proud of his daughter's performance and excited that his fiancé was seated in the mid-section earlier. Shawn could see his girls still dressed in their white robe-like dresses with gold sashes around their waists. He hugged them and kissed their cheeks. Shawn spoke to his girls last night after the barbeque, along with their mom. They were hanging out with their cousins and other children when he announced his engagement. He told them that he was in love with Monica and she made him very happy. His ex-wife pulled him to the side to express her thoughts.

"I don't understand why you didn't discuss this with the girls prior to just springing it on them like this." Lydia was apparently upset.

"My decision was not based on how my girls felt about Monica, although I want us all to be happy." Shawn was up to whatever Lydia could have thrown at him.

"I'm just very surprised at your approach and more so disappointed that it seems they are an afterthought in the process of the life changing event in not only your life, but theirs as well." Lydia spoke in a manner that almost was demeaning.

"Look, I'm not interested in your analytical breakdown to the matter at hand. My happiness and choice of a mate is my decision and the happiness of my girls is never a backburner issue. I don't owe you or anyone else any explanations concerning my personal affairs. I don't recall us checking with them about our divorce or your remarriage for that matter and up till now I believe they are doing just fine. So do yourself and me a favor - you run your household the way you want and I'll take care of my end accordingly!" Shawn spoke with such an authority and Lydia face turned a pinkish hue.

"I was only looking out for the best interest ..... " Lydia was cut off.

"Don't!" Shawn interjected. "I know what's best for my little girls."

"Fine. I won't utter another word." Lydia knew that she needed to back down.

"That would be for the best," Shawn stated. Shawn cooled down before approaching his daughters again.

"Come Sharde and Shantell. I want to speak with you privately." Shawn escorted his girls into the den, where the traffic was limited.

"I know that this may be a major change in our lives and I hope you understand that some decisions will be left up to your parents primarily. Still, that doesn't mean that your opinions don't matter; it's just that life is not always easy." Shawn said. He looked for words that would be suitable for a child to relate to.

"Daddy, does this mean that Monica is going to move into your house?" Shantell asked with a curious look in her eyes.

"Daddy has not made up his mind about that yet. That's something that Monica and I will talk about," Shawn said.

"Daddy, are you and Monica going to have a new family with a baby?" Sharde asked.

"Sweetie, only God knows that; but for now, I just want you girls to pray for Daddy and Monica. Will you do that?" Shawn said.

"Ok." They both chimed in together. Shawn's thoughts had gotten the better of him and he was brought back to reality, as his daughters pulled on the sleeve of his suit.

"Daddy," Shantell said, "look it's Ms. Monica - right over there." Shawn saw that Monica had gathered her purse on her arm, in preparation to leave as soon as the Pastor would dismiss them. Shawn did not want to miss them, so he kept his eyes on them as he motioned his girls to sit with him while the Pastor spoke.

"Well congregation, I hope you enjoyed this message via the play as much as I did. These young people deserve to be supported and I want to encourage everyone who can to come and bless them with a love offering. This basket here, next to youth leaders, is to sow for the continued costs. God is going to minister through these young people and we want to help with this fabulous production." Row by row, deacons and ushers directed the congregation to come up and they brought their offerings. Monica, her Mom and Stepdad went up together to drop their seed into the basket. As Monica placed her offering into the basket.

"God has his hands upon you young lady." Bishop Cunningham addressed her. Put your hands up and let me get my wife." Bishop looked around and his wife Shirley came up from the left side of the room. I want you to anoint this "virtuous woman of God". Bishop instructed her. Shirley took the oil from one of the deacons and began to anoint her hands and her head. Monica fell back under the power of the Holy Spirit. "Help her up. God's not through with her," Bishop stated. By this time, Shawn was totally enthralled.

"Who did you come here with?" Bishop asked. Monica could hardly speak or stand for that matter.

"I came with my mom and dad." she answered, as she tried to steady herself."

"My God, I see you getting married real soon. Do you have a date yet?" Bishop asked.

"Not yet." Monica was all ears now.

"I tell you what young lady; your husband is going to make you real happy. You see God is rewarding your faithfulness." Bishop was ministering and just then, one of the male deacons came up to whisper in his ear. You could hear a pin drop, since the order of the church was that during the prophetic ministry no one was to move or leave unless they were released to do so.

"Ok, Prophet Edwards please come up and give the word that God is giving to you." Bishop waited for Shawn to come up and prophesy. Shawn came up to the altar area and walked over to Bishop and spoke in his ear.

"Oh, oh I see." Bishop broke out into a jolly laughter and the church was none the wiser and they seemed to have an inside joke. Bishop reminded you of a T.D. Jakes in his demeanor and stature. "Ok, let me see. This is how I want to do this. Church, Prophet Edwards and this beautiful woman are engaged." Bishop had them turn towards the congregation as he announced it. Most of the married couples, youth and elders of the church clapped and broke out into a praise mode. Others were stunned, shocked and some even appalled. Bishop continued in his prophetic presbytery as he was led to do.

"Alright, this is what the Spirit of God is telling me...Seek me now together and apart, seek me with all thy heart. I will do a breaking and shaking in many hearts, as others will show their true intent and others will merely mock. I will use you as an example of what I can do and I will make you into whatever I choose to do. This union is ordained of me and I will make it work. Your vows shall never be broken, because surely I'm in the middle of this and will cut off any enemy that seeks to lurk." Bishop finished the prophetic word without the microphone and they walked to their prospective seats and the offering resumed. After the service, Shawn hurried to meet Monica in the parking lot while his daughters went to change from their costumes into their church
clothes.

"Monica," Shawn called to her. Monica had just pressed her alarm button to unlock the car door. Her parents sat in the vehicle while Shawn came closer. Shawn took in the totality of how she was dressed and was thoroughly pleased.

"Hi Baby. I was hoping that I would catch you before you left." "Hello Frances and Jeremiah. I hope you enjoyed the service." As Shawn popped his head into the window of the driver's side, they both shook their heads with smiles and waved at her. Shawn returned his attention to Monica. She was flooded with emotions some good and not so good.

"Are you okay, Monica?" Shawn now had a frown on his face.

"I'm fine. Just something's on my mind. We'll talk later." Monica wanted to sound as calm as possible.

"Don't do that, talk to me." Shawn toned down his volume.

"Have your parents come in for a minute, they are serving food inside. That way we can talk." Shawn was almost pleading with Monica. Monica was looking behind Shawn and noticed Sharde and Shantell coming towards them.

"Hi Girls, you guys did such a wonderful job today. Can I have a hug from both of you?" Monica asked.

"Wow, you look like a first lady," Sharde said, as she hugged Monica.

Monica giggled. "Why, thank you Sweetie." Shawn went on the other side of the vehicle and began talking to Jeremiah and Frances. Sharde went underneath Monica's arm to allow herself to be hugged. Monica still holding onto the girls and could hear her car doors shut and seeing her parents stepping out of the car, she was confused.

"Ladies, Monica's mom and stepdad have agreed to have dinner with us at the church. Why don't you show them around, you are now their escort?" Shawn said. The girls were used to serving in church and wasted no time showing Frances and Jeremiah around their church. Shantell grabbed Frances hand and Jeremiah looked at Sharde, she broke down and took his hand. The twins felt that they had their hands full. Monica was truly amazed that this man did it again.

"How on earth did you manage to pull that off? Monica couldn't believe it even with her own two eyes.

"All I did was make a suggestion," Shawn stated. "Now back to you, what is bothering you?" Shawn asked. Monica was hoping that she would at least have a moment to be alone with her thoughts. Kind of mull over how things were going, but no, Shawn always had to be in "the knowing".

"I told you that I'm just mulling things over, that's all," Monica sighed.

"Monica, I know you better than you think. Let's not play this game." Shawn was getting short now. Monica bit her lip and turned slightly away from Shawn and tried to form her words.

"Shawn how old are you?" She turned back to face him and peered straight into his eyes. Shawn was taken back, as this was the last thing that he would think she would mention - not at this point at least. He chuckled as in a matter of fact manner.

"What brought that about? Does it really matter?" Shawn asked.

"Can you just answer the question, please?" Monica was eerily serious. Monica turned this time with her back totally to Shawn. She felt the blood rushing to her face and she took her hand and held it to her forehead. She was now recalling the voices of the ladies whispering in the seats behind her about Shawn being a bachelor in his mid thirties now being scooped up. Shawn was more than bewildered and grabbed Monica to turn her towards him. Now getting a bit angry, he could see the tears swelling in her eyes.

"What is the matter with you? How is my age affecting you to this level? Shawn wanted to just shake Monica right here in this parking lot.

"You don't understand." Monica held back her tears.

"I don't understand. Explain it to me." Shawn became a little less aggravated as he could see that she was truly upset.

"I guess in all of the time that we were seeing each other, the subject just never surfaced." Monica was struggling to speak now.

"Say it. What number has you so upset? What is our age difference?" Shawn now was more intrigued than anything. Monica was silent for a moment and Shawn wiped her face with his hands as one tear escaped. He prompted her now with his tenderness.

"I'm.... " she stopped herself.

"Say it..." Shawn said softly.

"I'm 45." Monica closed her eyes and another tear raced down her face. Shawn pulled her close and just held her. He ran his hand down her straight hair that she had parted on the side and continued to rub her head. He then pulled her chin up to face him.

"Listen to me. I don't care if you are 45, 65 or 105. I love you and more importantly this relationship is ordained of God. We are seven years apart. So what!!! Don't allow the world systems to dictate; what God put together no person, circumstance or number can put us asunder. Do you understand me?" Shawn stated. Monica just shook her head and wiped her face. Shawn continued to hold her and kissed the top of her head.

CHAPTER 15
THERE ARE GIANTS IN THE PROMISED LAND

Shawn and Monica talked Monday, the night before her parents left for the airport. Monica prayed that things would remain the same. Although Shawn made it clear that this age thing was not a stumbling block, Monica was still a bit uncomfortable. For the first time Monica's mother expressed her acceptance of her before they left. "I'm so proud of what God is doing in your life; and I must say, you could not have asked for a better husband than Shawn. Every relationship has its challenges dear; it's just how you work out your differences. God knows what he is doing - so let him do it." Those were the last words that Frances spoke prior to her getting on the airplane. On her way back from the airport, Monica smiled at her mother's approval. Monica prepared herself for what her new work week would bring. Monica browsed through her closet and looked to see what she would wear Tuesday. She heard her cell vibrate.

"Hello."

"Hi, just wanted to see how your mother and stepdad made it to the airport."

"I decided to take them. I appreciate you paying for their taxi trip initially."

"It's not a problem Babe; but we need to discuss some things." Shawn stated. Monica was hearing Shawn get real serious again.

"We need to set a date." Shawn did not want to waste any time.

"Oh, yes. You are right. How many people are we looking to have and what budget are we looking at?" Monica asked.

"I guess the question that I should be asking is...what type of wedding would you like? Shawn responded.

"This kind of seems strange to be talking about this over the phone," Monica observed.

"I can be there in 20 minutes," Shawn said and Monica agreed. Monica felt like she was living in a dream. She could have never imagined that she would have met the man of her dreams in such a normal setting as a barbeque and now she was about to plan her future with this exceptionally handsome, Godly brother. He was nothing short of beautiful from the inside out. His tall, athletic build was enhanced by his beautiful eyes and bright white teeth. Shawn had a pronounced African American nose and his baldness -whew! Shawn was so well manicured, that even on a bad day he looked good. Monica did not even have any bridal books or anything that she could draw energy from. She looked for her new journal book that she purchased from Barnes and Noble - it was purple and a pretty rainbow colored butterfly was spread on the cover. Monica labeled the book "Wedding Journal". She looked at her ring finger and admired the way it shone on her hand. Monica looked at the clock and it was 12:15 pm - she thought that she should take a quick shower just to freshen up before Shawn would arrive.

Shawn was waiting at the traffic light about five minutes from Monica's condo. He forgot to ask her if she had eaten yet. Shawn rang Monica's cell. It went into the voice mail. Shawn decided to just go with his instinct and stop by the Shoprite close by, before turning into her complex. Shawn thought to himself he had never even tasted his future wife's food -with the exception of breakfast the night that he stayed over. Hmmmm, he thought I wonder if she can fix dinner on such short notice. Shawn gathered some of his favorite items and put them in his shopping cart. Monica dried off from her shower and quickly looked at her phone to make sure she did not miss Shawn.

"Darn it, I hope he's not downstairs waiting for me," she said to herself. Monica dialed Shawn.

"Hello," He answered.

"Are you here yet?" Monica asked.

"I'm actually at the Shoprite around the corner from you," He waited for her response.

"Oh, what are you getting?" She was curious now.

"I figured we would hang out today and just eat in tonight," Shawn stated. Monica thought that's pretty presumptuous, but she didn't say a word.

"Alright Babes, just buzz me when you get here." Monica hung up and continued to get dressed. Shawn went through the vegetable aisle and asked an older Caucasian lady to assist him in choosing the right items for a good salad. Satisfied that he had all of the items needed, Shawn went to check out at the counter. Monica lit some candles in the bedroom and in the bathrooms. She liked the scent of her place to resonate a welcoming fragrance. The perfume of her choice was Gucci II and a splash from Victoria Secret. Monica put on a violet tank top trimmed with a black lace and a pair of gray yoga stretch pants. She unwrapped her hair and parted it on the side. Monica put on some tinted chap stick, gave herself a once over and her ringer buzzed. Monica buzzed Shawn in and looked for some mood music.

Shawn was glad that the elevator was open, as his hands were filled with 5 grocery bags. Monica left the door cracked and made sure the main bathroom had enough toiletries, as she heard Shawn shuffling around and her front door closed.

"Hey Babes," Monica yelled.

"Hi Honey. It smells wonderful in here and I'm digging the music, you have exquisite taste." Monica walked down the hallway to greet Shawn.

"It's Chris Botti playing," Monica said.

"Uhmmm. You just don't know what you do to me," Shawn said, as he let go of the bags, grabbing her. Monica put her hands around his neck and kissed his lips lightly.

"I know what I'd like to do to you." Monica backed away as her eyes teased him in an innocent way. Shawn breathed out a heavy sigh and bit his lower lip momentarily.

"Don't worry, you'll get your opportunity," Shawn promised. Monica smiled and turned towards her counter top with the grocery bags seated.

"Oh, let's see what you got here." Monica began to empty the bags and she went from oooohhh and ahhhh to breaking out into moments of laughter. You really are serious, huh?" Monica said.

"What, who knows how long it will take us to go through our wedding planning? Shawn had a sheepish look on his face.

"From the looks of these items, I need to start right now to get something ready for later. Did you eat?" Monica asked.

"Nope," Shawn said.

"Oh Boy! Have a seat Honey." Monica began to put her chef hat on. The many hats women wear, she thought inwardly.

Shawn noticed Monica's velvet purple journal on the table. Shawn's grocery list consisted of: lasagna and spaghetti noodles, ground beef, Ragu sauce, cheese, cabbage, a bag of prepared salad, buttermilk ranch dressing, tomatoes, cucumbers, and mixed fruit salad. He bought Hawaiian Punch, ginger ale, Tostitos, salsa dip and various pieces of cheese cake as the dessert. Monica knew that Shawn was testing her cooking skills, but at least he gave her the option of lasagna or spaghetti. Monica seasoned the meat and sautéed some onions, garlic and then began browning the meat. After preheating the oven, she pulled out a rectangular pan for the lasagna and a smaller one for the cornbread that she would be making. Shawn was busy looking through a magazine, while Monica concentrated on getting things prepared for lunch or dinner, she wasn't sure. Monica made an in-the-meantime snack making chicken salad (using chicken breast baked the night before) on rye and a bowl of cheese curls, popcorn, pretzels and Tostitos. She combined the Hawaiian punch, ginger ale, and lemon to make a zesty drink.

Shawn was so appreciative of how Monica could take the smallest details and pour her love and passion into it. "Thank you Baby," Shawn said.

After everything was in the oven twenty minutes later, Monica sat next to Shawn and saw that he was looking at a Bridal book.

"Where'd you get that?" Monica asked.

"At the grocery store," he responded.

"You are too cute, anything good?"

"I guess I was just looking at tuxedos and gowns."
Shawn was sitting in the living room area near the fireplace.

"So, my dear -have you thought about the type of wedding that you would like?" He inquired. Monica was almost stumped as she thought, is this how this is supposed to be. She didn't want to sound ridiculous but she wanted to be honest.

"I would suppose that our budget would dictate what's realistic," Monica responded.

"That's true," Shawn acknowledged, "but that evades the question. I really want you to tell me what you want." Shawn looked deep into Monica's eyes. Monica thought carefully, before she spoke again.
"I want something elegant, unique and spiritual," Monica stated.

"Can you give me some more details regarding the image of your expectations?" Shawn sat back as if taking mental notes. Monica finally realized what Shawn was doing. He was treating Monica like a client. Not in an impersonal manner, but this was his nature. He needed to analyze, reflect and bring order to things. This was his gift and he really was a perfectionist. Monica knew how she needed to relate to him.

"When I think about my wedding day, I get images of a sentimental wedding and whether in the mountains of Colorado, or the sea shores of Hawaii it matters not. It's the essence of love, romance and family that is the real memoir of the affair. I can imagine fine dining and the laughter of kids and waves goodbye, as we begin our honeymoon in a faraway place from our normal excursion of day to day work. I would like the wedding ceremony to be quaint and the reception to be accommodating of our families, churches and co-workers. Is that descriptive enough?" Monica hoped she didn't scare the poor man.

Shawn had his hands behind his head and his eyes were closed as he responded.

"I heard everything you said and I know what it requires." Shawn sat up and opened his eyes as he spoke.

"You painted a wonderful wedding and an alluring honeymoon; but now we need to figure out how we can accomplish this without either of us going into debt," Shawn responded laughingly.

"Last night, I went over my finances and I wrote out a plan for us to live comfortably. I'm going to go over them with you, but first I need for us to be honest about our financial state, which includes: salary, savings and bills or any debt at hand," Shawn said. Monica was thoroughly impressed and she knew that Shawn was no slouch in business or in his personal affairs. Monica told Shawn that her salary was $60,000 a year; she revealed her car, housing expenses and expressed some credit issues that she was currently working on.

"Do you have anything in your savings?" He inquired

"Not really." Monica hated to admit that.

"Ok. Now that's the first thing I want you to work on. As my wife, you will not be living from paycheck to paycheck. So, we'll work on that, is that fair?" Shawn asked.

"Yes, that is fair."

"Alright, so here is the breakdown of what I have, my yearly salary is $175,000, my home was a foreclosure and I paid for it cash. My taxes are about 9,200 a year and my car payments are $650.00 and insurance $155.00, utilities are approximately, $200 monthly. I have joint-custody of the girls, so we split the cost of school, clothes and anything related to their needs. I also have a trust fund for them for college. I have two savings accounts and two checking accounts. I use one checking account for automatic payments for bills; the other is just for my own use. So, here's the scenario breakdown." Shawn now drew Monica in closer to him, as he described from his notebook. Monica was amazed my Shawn's business sense and wisdom that came so effortlessly to him.

"Wedding on shoestring would be a wedding destination consisting of about $10,000 to $15,000, it would allow us to shop around for a nicer home and get new furniture."

"Moderate wedding of $20,000 - $25,000 gives us the option of keeping one of our places to live and to make adjustments."

"Elaborate wedding of $30,000 or more would cause us to sell one of our places, live in the other and make do with what we have with minor updates." Monica browsed over the various choices and felt blessed just to have choices. She knew what the best choice would be and she excused herself to get the food and shut the oven off.

Shawn knew that he had more than enough between their salaries to do whatever she choose. He also knew that his parents would want to give them a generous gift. He never depended on anyone and that's the way his father raised him. He knew that Monica was not good with finances, so he hoped she would allow him to take control of that area.

"Ok, the food is ready when you are," Monica noted. Shawn patted the seat next to him for Monica to sit beside him again.

"I want us to finish most of this decision making process. Talk to me." Shawn loved listening to Monica.

"Alright, I believe my choice is the "moderate wedding," Monica said.

"Ok, that's cool. So do you know how many people, approximately, we will invite to the wedding/reception?" Shawn asked.

"No and I probably won't be able to figure all that out today. Where do you want us to live?" Monica asked him curiously.

"Ok, here's what I think. Obviously, your place is too small. My place is paid for and we can rent out your place and that will give you income to save money….not to spend." Shawn gave Monica a fatherly look. Monica didn't say that she owned it.

"Oh, I see so I will just use the rent to pay the mortgage." Monica shook her head in agreement.

"I have a lot of real estate agents that can help you get more for your bucks, how much is your mortgage? Shawn asked.

"Its $1750.00 and the association fees are $245.00."

"So we'll see what can be done in that area." Any ideas for the colors of the wedding?" Shawn asked.

"I was thinking green for the men and amethyst for the women," Monica said.

"Wow, interesting. Green just happens to be one of my favorite colors besides silver/blue." Shawn smiled. "Let's eat Babes." Shawn and Monica ate and he was completely satisfied with what they discussed. The food was delicious and he could tell that Monica enjoyed cooking. Everything was so right. Shawn helped Monica clean up after dinner and the clock read 5:35pm. Monica took Shawn's hand and led him into the den area and they sat.

"I love you," Monica said softly.

"I love you." Shawn leaned to kiss Monica and they molded themselves into different degrees of passionate kisses, until things became unbearable. Shawn felt such a fire emanating from Monica and she just paused while Shawn continued to kiss her lightly.

"I have to go. We can't keep up this pace," Shawn said as his body began to torment him.

"I know you do." Monica's eyes remained closed and Shawn held her in the same position. "I don't want to let you go," Monica said. Shawn put a tighter grip on Monica, as he understood where she was.

"Soon Baby, I won't have to go," Shawn said. Then Monica's body just quivered under his and he felt her melting down. "Don't cry Baby.

Please." Shawn held her even tighter and her drops of tears slid down his neck. "When do you want to get married?" Shawn asked Monica.

Monica gathered herself as best as she could.

"As soon as we can get our finances and details together," Monica's tear streamed face stared at Shawn.

"Don't worry about the finances. If you can trust me with that, I'll make things happen. What I want you to do is the details of the wedding planning. Make your list - do the homework and I'll handle the rest. Who will be in the wedding party?" Shawn questioned her.

"I would like your sisters to be my bridesmaids, Keiki the maid of honor, the twins as the flower girls and I have a few others that will complete the party," Monica said.

"Alright, that sounds good. My sisters both are gifted in the areas of events and completing what they start. So, good choices," he said.

"I'll tell you what, if you promise to be a good girl we can watch a movie together before I leave," Shawn teased Monica.

Monica went and got a couple of pillows and some blankets. Shawn picked out a thriller suspense movie and they lay together with a pillow between them. They had enough wisdom to realize they were getting to a point where kissing was just not enough.

CHAPTER 16 - LIFE WOULD NEVER BE THE SAME

Monica was excited to show off her engagement ring. Actually, she knew that heads would roll and necks would break to see it. Her supervisor, Carolyn, was back in the office today.

"Good Morning," Monica said, as she walked by Sabrina. Sabrina waved Monica over.

"There's some serious tension in this office. I don't know what happened, but apparently "Ms. Thing", your supervisor, didn't leave a great impression in the Chicago office." Sabrina whispered.

"Wow, that's definitely going to trickle down into this office," Monica said.

"You don't have to worry Lady. Mr. Clemons sees you as his "Golden Child" so you're untouchable."

"Hey, what's that? Let me see your hand." Sabrina's eyes got larger. Monica put her hand on her desk.

"Whoa, that's amazing. I want to meet the man that put that rock on your finger. He's a keeper Girl." Sabrina's expressions were priceless.

"Absolutely, he is a keeper and I intend on doing just that." Monica chuckled.

"Congrats, you deserve it. I'll shoot you an email, if I find out what happened with the Chicago thing." Sabrina's lines started ringing.

Monica walked to her desk and had a view of a very disgusted Carolyn. It looked like someone was in her office, as she paced a bit and her attention was to the chair that was in the corner of her office. Monica turned on her computer and pulled up her apps. Now, she found an email from Roy Clemons, cc'd to the Chicago office and her. It read: "The new policy of hiring and promoting within will be handled by our senior human resource personnel, Monica Phillips. I pray that going forward, any misunderstandings or questions can be handled in a manner that is conducive to what our offices represent in respect to fair and consistent treatment." That was the excerpt that left

Monica bewildered and she wondered what could have transpired during a weekend that caused such a commotion. There was another email from Roy that did not include Carolyn. Monica read the email from Roy and she prepared herself to meet with him as requested. As she stood near his office, she could tell he was wrapping up a personal phone call.

"Come in Ms. Phillips." Roy's face was sober and it was obvious that he was about to unveil something.

"Have a seat, please." Roy was troubled.

"I want to fill you in regards to what transpired in the Chicago office this weekend. Our offices are normally closed on Saturdays, but we made special arrangements to offer the other legal secretaries the updated policies that you were a major part of. As a result, we allowed them an extra day for the holiday weekend off. During the training session, Carolyn who will not be continuing in our offices, made some very belligerent comments about a few staff members who happen to be of a different lifestyle. I am now going to be short-staffed, until we find someone to fill her position. In the meantime, I feel that you are competent to work in some aspects of her position. What I would like to offer you at this time is a raise and a bonus to work under two titles for a season. How do you feel about that? Monica was flabbergasted to say the least.

"I'm really and truly grateful that you have the confidence in me and I would like to assist you in any manner that I can," Monica said.

"The only question I have is how long will I need to work in that capacity?" Monica was sensitive to the wedding planning and under no circumstances could she travel or work weekends.

"We are right now interviewing. I need to know if you are willing to travel and work some Saturdays," Roy asked.

"Honestly, that's definitely out of my range." Monica would not compromise her personal time.

"I see. Well if you can perhaps, work with my crazy schedule and come in early some days or stay later, then that's all I can ask. For your trouble, I have sent a new pay scale to get approved for the next paycheck period. Your new title is "Senior Human Resource Personnel." I need you to take some online courses to validate the pay raise. So an email will be sent to you and the time frame to complete them will be included. If you have any questions related to anything, please let me know." Monica was extremely curious as to her new pay raise. She currently was earning $60,000 yearly. Monica clicked on the email titled "new position". She read the job description and then she saw the pay grade and salary. Wow!!!! Only Jesus could have done this miracle. Senior Human Resource Personnel - Grade 14 = Salary $75, 000. Monica went from Grade 12 - Grade 14 in less than two months. The body of the letter advised 4 courses for completion in order for her pay grade to take effect. Monica knew she could come in early for the following week and finish those courses by Wednesday and that would qualify her update for the next pay period. Monica went from Human Resource Coordinator at $60,000 to $75,000, just because of her obedience to the Holy Spirit. Her salary more than doubled, going from $35,000 to $75,000. Monica knew that the blessings of the Lord added riches and no sorrow. This would help with their wedding and reception plans. Monica couldn't wait to tell Shawn! She took her cell phone into the restroom. Monica walked by each stall making sure she was alone before dialing Shawn. Shawn saw his cell phone light up, and then it vibrated on his desk.

"Hello," Shawn answered.

"Hi Sweetheart, I hope I'm not disturbing you." Monica normally waited until after work hours.

"No Baby. I'm available to you always." Shawn knew it must be important for her to call at this time.

"You'll never guess what happened. When I came in I pulled up an email that described a new policy as the result of something that happened over the weekend." Monica said barely taking a breath.

"Really," Shawn listened.

"Yes and Mr. Clemons had a meeting with me today, asking for me to take over her position temporarily and offering me a bonus as well!!!" Monica was ecstatic.

"Baby, that's great!" Shawn waited for her to continue.

"Now, that's confirmation of the word that you gave me, not to go to that out of town business opportunity. God had other plans for me!" Monica was hyper.

"We need to celebrate, honey," Shawn stated.

"The only thing I want to celebrate is my love for you," Monica said with a slight sensual tone.

"Baby, you are really changing my temperature and I'm going to have to get something cool to drink." They both laughed simultaneously.

"Well, baby. I'm going to let you get back to work, but thank you for taking a moment to speak with me. Love you," Monica expressed.

"Love you too, Darling." Shawn and Monica hung up.

Lunch Time at Make Me Over

Keiki was still in shock over the fact that Shawn asked Monica to marry him. It was kind of odd that he had not even mentioned that she would be there. She had not heard from Monica and guessed that she was just in another zone. Seated not too far from her table at the cafe, Keiki spotted Brian. He had just walked in and picked up a vitamin water and soup from what she could see. As Brian was paying for his items, he caught Keiki in his peripheral vision. Brian smiled as he walked over to her.

"Hey You! What's going on?" Brian asked.

"What's going on? I don't know, you tell me," Keiki said with disgust

"Whoa, what's the matter with you?" Brian face changed.

"Are you serious? I tried to hook you back up with my girl and you just dumped her-just like that; and then you sit here, like nothing!" Keiki was so perturbed.

"Oh I see. You think you know me. First of all, I haven't heard from your friend since ummmmm, let me guess, since about 2 or more weeks ago. What am I supposed to do become a priest??"

"Brian you are so full of yourself. I'm glad that she moved on with her life. Thanks be to God."

"Well Keiki, I had hoped that things could rekindle, but I guess time took its toll."

"I guess Selena had absolutely nothing to do with anything," Keiki challenged. As Keiki finished her statement, she saw Shawn as he walked into the cafe area and proceeded to get an orange juice and what looked like a fruit assortment.

"Maybe you know something I don't, Keiki. So you tell me," Brian said.

"All I can tell you Brian is that at least God sent Monica everything she needed and "He" just walked out of the cafe." Monica watched as Shawn paid and walked down the corridor on his way back to his office. Brian quickly turned to see Shawn as he was walking into the elevator.

"What are you talking about?" Brian was confused.

"I'm sure you will hear it sooner or later, might as well be sooner. Monica is engaged to be married to Shawn." Monica saw Brian's jaw drop. He was truly, unmistakably shocked.

"Well, Brian, I didn't know you cared. Close your mouth before a fly gets into it." Keiki stood up from the small table and proceeded to the elevator back to her office. Brian just sat there perplexed, not knowing how to accept what he just heard. He knew he had no right to feel any kind of way, but still it was like an unexpected blow. Brian felt a tinge of envy and even though he had a pretty good deal with Selena, he didn't like the fact that Shawn seemed to beat him out. True he wasn't totally upfront with Monica, but that didn't mean that he didn't care.

As Shawn sat in Selena's office, his mind was consumed with many thoughts and he knew that he had to put some things in order for the wedding to go as planned.

"The proposal that you did for the credit repair company, "Born Again", was accepted. So congrats and I would like your team to pick that up and get that rolling. Anything else, before we wrap things up?" Selena asked, as she looked over her list on her calendar.

"Yes, I will be taking some vacation for the month of November and December, so I'll put my request in by the end of the week."

Shawn did not want anything to prevent him from what he needed to do. He knew that his role as a manager necessitated him to put in his time as early as possible.

"I see. Selena now looked up from her calendar. How much time will you be taking?" Selena was curious now. Shawn barely took any sick days and usually carried over most of his vacation days.

"I'll probably use 4 to 6 weeks," He said casually.

"Wow, that's unusual for a man that barely takes days off, but I guess you work pretty hard for your time. You've been here what 10 years?" Selena pried.

"It's been 11 years," Shawn said as he stood from his chair. Now Shawn wanted to cut things short, as he did not like to indulge in his personal business, especially with a shark like Selena.

"Well, I know that you have to get back to work, so I'll let you go." Selena watched as Shawn moved with no hesitation.

Monica was about to wrap things up with work day. She had received a few emails and had spoken to Jamie and Myra from the Chicago office. Monica advised that she would have a phone conference with them, when they were ready to put the new policy into works. Monica hears her cell phone vibrate in her purse. She sees the number of the missed call and dials it from her office phone.

"Hey, how are you?" Monica asked.

"I'm good. I was calling to see what's going on with you. I wanted to give you some space, because I know that you had a lot on your plate with the whole engagement," Keiki said.

"Yes, I have been really just busy with my mom and stepdad and yesterday was spent with my Sweetie." Monica's face was lit up.

"I was truly surprised, since I didn't even know you guys were back together," Keiki said.

"I thought that Shawn would have told you when he invited you to the barbeque." Monica was confused.

"Well, he invited me, but I guess he wanted to surprise us both," Keiki said wishing she hadn't brought that up. Monica felt that something still was funny, but her wedding plans were more important than this oddity.

"And what a surprise it was to us all. Girl I have just been running ragged and wanted to ask you something."

"Sure, go ahead." Keiki was glad Monica didn't get into the details about them getting back together.

"I've always looked forward to this day and you and I have talked about going to each other weddings, so - would you be my Maid of Honor?" Monica was now getting sentimental.

"Wow Girl, of course I would. I'm so excited for you." Keiki was relieved that Monica dismissed the whole barbeque issue.

"So when will we get together?" Keiki asked.

"I'm going to speak to a couple of others, who will be in the wedding party and then we can set up a date. Hopefully, this weekend," Monica replied.

"Oh, alright. So how big will the wedding be?"

"It will be moderate, something that will be elegant and memorable." "So, I'm about to leave work and I'll call to let you know when we will be meeting, ok?"

"Ok, later." Keiki hung up. Keiki packed up her things and headed for her jacket. The temperature was a bit cooler now that September was here. Keiki headed for her car in the parking lot and there Shawn stood, only a few parking spaces away from her SUV.

"Hi, how are you?" Keiki said.

"I'm doing well and yourself," Shawn answered cordially. "Congratulations on your engagement." Keiki smiled wide.

"Thank you."

"I was pleasantly surprised that you guys got back together," Keiki stated. Shawn knew that this was leading up to something, but he didn't have the patience to indulge her.

"Maybe we can have lunch again and you can share how you guys got back together." Keiki had the look a woman who was feigning to hear a good love story.

"It would probably be better that you speak with Monica about that. I'll see you later." Shawn jumped into his car while still talking. He pulled off after he finished. He did not wait for Keiki to respond. Keiki felt mortified and wondered why he was so dag-gone rude. How would she be able to put up with this arrogant dude, she thought, as she stood in the parking lot staring watching him speed off?!! If he didn't see it with his own eyes, he may have not believed it.

"That was kind of rude," Brian said. Keiki swung around startled to hear Brian's voice.

"What are you doing here? And why are you sneaking up on me?" Keiki felt embarrassed that he may have heard their conversation.

"I work here, remember?" Brian was so sarcastic. He had a smug attitude and he was going to milk this for all he could.

"So, you like him?" Brian teased.

"What, what are you talking about? Like who, Shawn? Of course not. He's definitely not my style." Keiki was nervous.

"C'mon Keiki. I know women, but more importantly, I know you." Brian came a bit closer giving her more eye contact.

"I don't know what you are talking about and I don't have time to debate this foolishness with you. I have better things to do and talk about," Keiki spewed out.

"Alright, you might be able to fool your girl, but I see you. I see you more than you know." Brian laughed while tormenting her. Keiki drove home in disgust. She was just demeaned by two men and now she was being accused by a scum bag that had no right to even judge her.

Monica was told by Roy Clemons that Carolyn would not be able to come back to work until the investigation was complete. So she would be coming in earlier to work on the classes and doing just about any project that he needed. Monica was still curious about what Keiki said earlier. Her intuitiveness was leading her to get to the bottom of her uneasiness.

Shawn was sitting in his driveway thinking about this Keiki character. Although he did not care for her, it was up to Monica to see her for who she really was. Shawn saw his phone vibrating in the console of the car.

"Hello," he answered.

"Hi, are you home yet?" Monica asked.

"I was just about to get out of the car. How are you?" Shawn sensed immediately that something was bothering Monica.

"I'm just perplexed about something."

"Is it something I can help you with?" Shawn was now walking with his cell in his hand, opening his front door.

Monica was already in her bedroom and lying across her bed sideways. Sitting up, she prepared herself to share what she was feeling.

"I spoke with Keiki today and she said something odd. She said you invited her to the party, but she was unaware that we had gotten back together. How is that so?" Monica was curious as to his explanation.

"I invited Keiki like I promised I would. I never volunteered that we were back together, should I have?" Shawn discerned Monica's response.

"But why wouldn't you tell her that I was going to be there? Because then it seems that you were asking her out on a date." Saying it aloud, Monica realized the implication that it was making on Keiki.

"You're right Monica. So why did she accept, if she thought for one moment that you may not be there?" Monica felt a sickening feeling rise in her belly. He was right, but what was his motive to even do that.

"I see your point, Shawn, but it still does not answer as to why you would ask her. Was it your intent to prove that Keiki was interested in you?" Monica felt so small to think that her friend would do such a thing.

"Monica, I know I have a bad habit with testing people, but I've never lied or misrepresented myself to you. Your friend Keiki accepted an invitation to my family barbeque, not knowing me; my family or that you would be there. I can only say that she agreed with no questions about you." Shawn hated that he was having this discussion over the phone. He preferred the advantage of communicating face to face, especially with something of this nature. He knew this type of news could send anyone into a state of depression or anger.

"I don't know what to think now Shawn. It's all so incredible to believe. This is a woman that I've known for over ten years

"And you've known me for just two months at best," Shawn interrupted.

"I didn't invite Keiki to the barbeque to prove that she was attracted to me, I wanted to show Keiki what You really mean to Me."

"While we are on the subject, did she tell you that we had a talk at work together on her break, right after we broke up? Or did she forget to mention that too?" Shawn knew he had to make Monica see what she wanted to dismiss.

"No, she didn't. I still can't understand why you are telling me this now instead of when it transpired." Monica's head was spinning and her fingers were running through her hair as she paced.

"Would you really have accepted it?" Shawn had to break things down to her more gently. "Baby, at the time, I was upset at the Brian thing and my head was not in the right place. There were multiple things going on. I took advantage of the fact that Keiki likes attention and she was willing to give me the information that I desired about you." Shawn did a full disclosure to prevent Keiki from distorting facts.

"Did Keiki tell you about Brian?"

"She didn't have to."

"I need to think Shawn. I'll talk to you later."

"I'm going to come by."

"That's not necessary."

"I will see you in a little while." Shawn ignored her and hung up without waiting for her response. Monica was confused, hurt and didn't know who or what to believe. Her emotions were all over the place. She took a quick shower and put on a pink sweat suit. Her door bell buzzer went off. She buzzed him in and left the door cracked, while she went back to her room to spray a quick shot of Chloe on her body. She could hear Shawn come into her condo. Monica went into her living room and almost fainted when she saw Brian sitting on her sofa.

CHAPTER 16 ½
TWO HEADS ARE BETTER THAN ONE

"What the?!?!" What on earth are you doing here Brian?" Monica was nearly floored.

"I'm sorry I didn't call, but I knew that you probably would not give me the time of day, which is understandable; but I just had to see you," He said with sincerity.

"See me for what Brian?" Monica's anger was full to the brink.

"Number one, to say that I'm sorry that I wasn't totally honest with you, you deserved better," Brian said.

"You came all the way over here and wasted my time to tell me that you're sorry. Sorry is an understatement of Who and What you are!! Secondly, I already know what and who I deserve and I have Him. Thirdly, I don't need you coming up here assuming that I need closure, because I don't." Monica was seething now and her hands were pointing and shouting while her body was moving profusely.

"You have every right to say and feel whatever comes to your mind, but please let me finish and then I won't bother you again," Brian pleaded. Monica wanted to get rid of Brian, because she knew that any minute Shawn could show up.

"Look, I'm expecting "My Fiancé" any minute so you need to disappear." Monica walked to the door and opened it, so he could leave. Brian stood up moving close to the door but stopping short.

"Monica please, listen to me. I only want you to know just one thing"....Brian was interrupted.

"What's that Bro?" Shawn slips through the door (that Brian never closed). Monica and Brian were both stunned.

"Hey man, I'm just here to let Monica know that Keiki is someone you really need to watch. Listen I hope you take heed. I'm out."

Brian wanted to exit as fast as possible seeing that Shawn was in no mood to talk. Brian could see that Shawn came in ready for anything. Monica watched as Brian stepped down from Shawn and he slid through the small opening leading out the front door. Shawn did not budge and it's almost like he wanted to rip something apart. Monica carefully studied Shawn, as he stood there with his fists clenched.

"Did you come here to fight?" Monica asked in a non-confrontational manner. Shawn's face was hard and stern. Monica wondered what was going through his mind. Shawn realized that his body was extremely tight and tried to release his rage. He still didn't move or speak.

"Could you come here please?" Monica was treading lightly. She had never seen Shawn act this way. He still stood there like a statue. Monica walked past him and closed her door. She then carefully took his left hand unraveled his fist and led him to sit. Neither of them spoke for an eternal minute and Shawn continued to be a dark mood.

"Why are you acting this way?" Monica probed.

"I'm not acting." Shawn looked down into Monica's eyes and she saw fire in his eyes, but not in a romantic way.

"Did I do something wrong?" Monica asked.

"Why was he here?" Shawn asked gritting his teeth.

"I didn't invite him. I thought it was you buzzing my door and I let him in. I went to my room to get something, came back and there he was," Monica explained. Then it hit her that her beautiful fiancé wasn't so flawless after all. All this time she had not taken notice that he was jealous. Shawn looked away and his thoughts ran in all directions. Monica used her small hand to guide his face back towards her.

"Please don't be upset Baby." Monica spoke sweet and tenderly. Shawn moved his body, indepthly staring into her eyes - he searched her soul. Monica knew that if she could make an emotional connection to Shawn- it could soothe him.

"Can I have a kiss at least?" Monica was determined to reach him. Shawn looked at Monica's face and began to calm himself. She was finally seeing him in a jealous squabble. Monica reached up and kissed him while he remained partially stiff.

"I guess that's all I can get, huh?" Monica was now getting discouraged. She went to get up, but Shawn pulled her back.

"What, I can't move either?" Monica looked at him confused.

"I don't want to see him in this place again." Shawn was now a bit more tempered.

"Ok." Monica knew that he was serious. She only wanted to comfort him.

"I love you Shawn." Shawn studied Monica's eyes, as if examining the fullness of her being.

"We'll see." Shawn acted as if to challenge her heart. Then he couldn't hold back anymore. He grabbed her and kissed her deeply; but this kiss was different from the others - it was more desperate, more intentional. This kiss was sweeping Monica away; it was like Shawn was claiming her. Monica wanted to break away not because it didn't feel good, but because she sensed a losing of self and a joining or an oneness with him and it frightened her. Shawn held her chest to his chest and she could feel his heart beating against hers. Shawn felt Monica's reluctance and he pulled her in even more. A part of him wanted her to know just what she was getting herself into. At a turning point, he perceived that her body was ready to give in to him completely and he knew he had to release her.

"I love you more Monica, but please don't play with me." Shawn spoke in her right ear with such intensity. He stood and left Monica literally shaken. After Shawn was gone, she could still feel the impression (like a tattoo) branded on her lips. She was convinced that not only was he jealous, but possessive as well.

Shawn lay on his back; arms folded behind his neck and contemplated how close he was coming to taking Monica to a place where only married people should go. He acknowledged he had to repent for his vivid imaginations of Monica. His love and passion were mounting up in him like a fiery volcano. He pulled out his calendar and decided to make a date. Today's date was September 6, and November 6, would be a short eight weeks. He didn't care if it was an unrealistic goal, their days were numbered. He refused to keep tempting Monica or himself. Shawn prayed before falling into slumber.

Monica was sleeping and awoken by the urge to go to the bathroom. The clock on her cable box read 3:11 am and she opened her window slightly, as she was warm. Monica thought about how she would handle Keiki. A pain arose in her stomach, as she recalled the words that Shawn and Brian stated. She wouldn't discuss anything on the phone with Keiki, as she wanted to confront her face to face.

Monica noticed the indicator light shining from her cell phone. She saw a text message that Shawn had sent:

"Shawn: Here are Leah & Rachael's contact number(s). I went thro ugh the calendar and chose the date of November 6, 2011 as our wedding date. Tell me what you think."

Monica saw that the text came through at 12:00 am. She thought that Shawn was absolutely crazy, if he thought that 8 weeks would give them enough time to plan their wedding. She decided to speak to him sometime in the am. In the meantime, she began to fantasize about the special day that was soon to come. The following days in the week were brutal for Monica, as she had to take courses from 7:00 - 9:00 AM prior to her regular duties and then with the additional administrative work that was added, she was spent. Monica had spoken to Shawn on Wednesday regarding the wedding date and he told her that "all things were possible to them that believe". She thought how amazing it was that people, especially Shawn, knew how to appoint scripture at just the right time. Still, she was able to get Leah and Rachael to agree to meet her on Saturday. She also spoke to Keiki and she advised that she would be there too. Now it was Friday and she knew that she had better call her mentor, Leslie. She had been so busy that she did not give her the news yet. Monica called Leslie on her speakerphone as she drove home.

"Hello," she answered.

"Hi, Mighty Woman of God, how are you and your Husband doing?" Monica asked.

"Oh it's Mighty Woman of God, there must be something going on in the heavenlies today" Leslie teased Monica.

"Actually, I have been so busy and I want to apologize that I have not filled you in with the news." Monica was waiting to get blasted by Leslie.

"Go on" Leslie said.

"Shawn and I are engaged," Monica said smoothly.

"Engaged!!!!! What??? When did this take place? Oh my goodness!" Leslie was ecstatic.

"Les, it has been such a roller coaster ride and I have only had a small space to breathe. I don't even think I had the opportunity to tell you that my mother and stepdad came for the Labor day holiday, but we were all invited to Shawn's parents labor day barbeque; which just happens to be their anniversary and they celebrate it with style, I must say," Monica noted.

"Wow, so you must have known that something was about to transpire, as he brought you and your family to meet his. That was a defining moment all in of itself." Leslie waited to hear the rest.

"You said a mouthful. Well, Shawn and his twin sisters took turns to congratulate and honor their parents during the barbeque. The next thing you know, he calls me up to the platform that he was speaking from and introduced me. He requested for the band to play a dedicated song, then he cut them off and asked me to marry him right there in the middle of the barbeque." Monica's heart beat faster every time she thought about the proposal.

"My God! What a romantic and loving man. I can respect the fact that he did not care who liked it or who didn't - he claimed you in front of his family, with no hesitation. He also let your parents know where he stood. That is a Mighty Man of Valor, trust me. God sent you his finest," Leslie commented.

"I know. I'm just so blessed, that I find it hard to even fathom." Monica was now parked in front of her building and tears welled up in her eyes.

"Baby, I want to meet him. When can that be arranged? Perhaps, we can do a dinner here," Leslie said.

"Sure that sounds good. You've really been so instrumental in getting me where I am spiritually; I would love for you to be my Matron of Honor," Monica asked humbly.

"Of course, I will. I'm just so absolutely happy for you dear. You deserve it - God has done such a work in you in the last 3 years. You are not the same woman that I met years ago. This is one event that I would not miss, with the help of my Lord." Monica and Leslie prayed before hanging up from one another. Monica advised that she wanted Leslie to come to meet with the wedding party meeting on Saturday.

Shawn was clearing off his office desk, as he completed the video concept for the "Born Again" client. The commercials would have a recurring comedic tone. Shawn sent it over to the media team for them to do their part coming up with the characters that would bring light to his concept. Shawn also changed his vacation request to accommodate his tentative November wedding date. Shawn picked up his brief case and cell. He saw that he had a missed call from Jalek. At that moment, he realized he needed to talk to him about all the things that were happening so quickly in his life. Shawn dialed Jalek.

"Hey Bro. Haven't heard from you in a minute, what's going on with you," Jalek inquired.

"Wow man, you have perfect timing. I really need to speak to you, but I don't really want to talk over the cell," Shawn said.

"So I'm just getting off right now, are you still in the building?" Jalek was walking towards the elevator.

"Yea, why don't we meet downstairs in the cafe area, maybe we can grab something quick." Shawn and Jalek agreed and they hung up.

Shawn could see that Selena was still in her office and she was speaking to Brian. Shawn saw Jalek sitting in the second row at a table to the far left hand side. He seemed to be looking at some kind of magazine.

Jalek stood as Shawn approached the table and they did their normal brotherly hug slash hand slappy thing.

"So what's happening, you look different? Talk to me," Jalek said as he sat down.

"I'm engaged," Shawn revealed.

"What?? You gotta be kidding me. Congratulations!!!! Jalek got up again and hugged Shawn and they sat down again.

"Oh c'mon man you have to divulge some details. Now Jalek's teeth were all showing, as he could not contain his happiness for Shawn.

Jalek had just turned 53 years old and he fared well with time. Jalek wore a bald head and was a handsome man. He stood at 5' 10" and had a slight belly bulge, but he did workout two to three times a week.

"Man, that night that you prayed for me, I went to Monica's house and confronted her on some issues. After that I invited her, her mom and stepdad to my family's yearly anniversary barbeque, I had already bought the ring and was just looking for the right time to spring it on her. Then I thought, what better time than right after my family had the opportunity to meet her." Shawn's face glowed.

"Shawn, this is the real thing. I feel it in my spirit and I can't wait to meet this woman who has you so open." They both laughed as he made that comment.

"But for real man, I just look at your growth. I remember how anxious you were for the right woman and how methodical you were. I used to tell Jackie (his wife) that we need to pray this one in. I was afraid that you would settle or slip (they both laughed). Look at you - you are really glowing, my man. Isn't God good?!?!" Jalek said.

"God is better than good - he's Magnificent," Shawn replied.

"None of this would be complete if you couldn't be a part of it. Will you be my best man?" Shawn became more serious then. Jalek's eyes changed and he looked at Shawn as he responded.

"I would have been hurt, if I didn't play some role in this special event. You already know that I am your best man; always will be." Shawn and Jalek continued their conversation, as they walked out to the parking lot and said their goodbyes.

CHAPTER 17 - WEDDING PARTY

Monica scheduled everyone to meet for lunch in Bay Shore, New York. She had found a great place to view some wedding gowns and hoped that they could sit, eat and discuss the eight ridiculous weeks that they would have to pull this off. Monica called everyone to give them the address to the restaurant. Keiki tried to suggest for them (her and Monica) to ride together, but Monica told her that she had another appointment right after their meeting. Monica's cell phone was vibrating, but she saw that it was a text so she continued to drive. Only minutes away from the restaurant, She thought about the fact that she was about to make plans for her wedding. It was really happening, she thought. The lot was semi full and she parked and picked up her cell to the view the text recently received.

Leah - We're here. We already are seated, ask for Edwards' party.

While reading the text, Keiki rang her cell.

"Hello," Monica answered.

"Hey, just pulled into the parking lot. I think I see your car," Keiki said. As she pulled her SUV up to park right next to her, they both hung up. Monica came out of her vehicle and Keiki hugged her. Monica returned the embrace, but something was still not quite right. She resolved to just let things take its course. As they walked in together, Monica quickly recognized Leah and Rachael seated at a table close to a wall where it was more secluded. Monica walked over and greeted them and introduced Keiki as well.

"Hi Ladies, I want to introduce you to my best friend and Maid of Honor," Monica said.

"Hello," Rachael said. "Hi," Leah spoke dryly.

"Hi, nice to meet you," Keiki said, before they took their seats.

"I heard that this was a really exceptional steak house," Monica said.

"Yes, it seems fairly decent," Rachael agreed. The waiter came over to greet them.

"Good Afternoon Ladies. My name is Charlie; I'll be your server today. Would anyone like to order drinks and appetizers?"

"Can you bring me a glass of ...?" Rachel interrupts Leah.

"We'll have two orders of raspberry lemonades." Leah looked at Rachael with an attitude.

"I'll have a cup of water with lime or lemon," Monica said. "I'll take a cup of coffee, light and sweet," Keiki said.

"Appetizers?" Charlie inquired.

"You can't stop me from eating," Leah said to Rachael.

"I'll have calamari, please." Leah looked at Rachael defiantly. Everyone else wanted more time to view the menu.

"So ladies, we are waiting for one more person, which is my Godmother. I don't know if you guys may want to order appetizers, if she's not here in the next five minutes," Monica said.

"Maybe we should just wait, in case your God-mom may want an appetizer," Keiki threw in. Leah sat proudly, thinking hers was already on its way.

"While we are waiting, I wanted to fill you guys in with some of the specifics of the wedding. Shawn and I have agreed to the date of November 6, 2011," Monica said knowing what the response would be. Everyone at the table's response was similar; disbelief.

"I see my brother must be in a rush for some reason," Leah said, with a smirk on her face.

"That's really cutting it close girl. I don't see how it could be elegant or memorable with that timeline," Keiki added.

Rachael and Leah shot Keiki a look and Monica could feel the tension building at the table. The waiter came by and dropped off the drinks and Leah's calamari.

"Listen, I know it's soon and for a good reason, but let's get beyond that, since that has already been established. I know that this can be done and it will by all means be beautiful, elegant, but most of all memorable." Monica turned to Keiki, as she made the last comments.

"What type of wedding are you guys planning to have as far as budget goes?" Keiki was thinking that this wedding must be low budget at best.

"What are you some kind of wedding planner?" Leah asked. She was getting hot under the collar now. Keiki's face turned a shade of red, as she started to respond.

"You don't have to have a certificate to know that an 8-week wedding with a low budget, will take a lot of ingenuity and miracle working power." Keiki shot with sarcasm.

"Wait a minute! Who said that this would be low budget!!! You need to stopping assuming things and making an A!!!" Monica was interrupted...

"Good afternoon Ladies," Leslie chimed in. Monica looked up and saw Leslie and her whole countenance relaxed. She stood up to hug and greet her.

"Hi Woman of God; I'm so glad that you are here, please have a seat." Monica sat Leslie between her and Leah. She introduced everyone to Leslie as she sat.

"So it looks like you all have started talking about the wedding plans. I apologize for my tardiness. I have a baby at home in the form of a man," Leslie said lightheartedly. Just then the waiter, Charlie, popped back in to take their orders. The ladies all ordered and he left.

"I need to use the ladies room, will you join me Keiki?" Monica asked, but her eyes made more of an urgent request.

"Sure, why not." Keiki followed with an attitude.

Bathroom

"What is your problem? First you insult Shawn and his judgment of the timeline. Then if that wasn't bad enough, you insinuate that this is going to be a ghetto wedding. Let me tell you something, Shawn is anything but low-budget or ghetto. Truly you must be mixing him up with somebody else you know. If you have a problem with me or being the maid of honor, then speak your peace, because I'm too blessed to be stressed right now." Monica gave Keiki an ultimatum.

"I can't understand why you are speaking to me like this. I'm trying to be here for you and you are treating me like the enemy; and this Leah is really a witch. I don't know how you expect me to work with these women. Keiki acted hurt."

"Keiki this is not about you right now. Those ladies are soon to be my sisters in law. I will have a good relationship with them, in Jesus Name," Monica said. Leslie, her mentor, came in as she completed her sentence.

"Everything ok in here? The waiter brought our food. Ladies, let's finish this meeting." Leslie could sense the tension at the table and more so in the ladies' room. Everyone continued to discuss the wedding plans, but now things were much smoother. Leslie added a different element to the atmosphere. Monica told them of a lovely bridal shop in Carle Place, on Long Island and that she had an appointment to view dresses.

"I think it's a great idea that you have a scheduled appointment to try on dresses today. Who knows if you may find the perfect one and then that will be one less thing on the list that you'd have to be concerned with," Leslie said.

"That's so true," Rachael commented. The women made their way to the Bridal Shop and parked. Monica was greeted by her hostess, Renee, for the day.

"I'm glad to be of service to you and I have a wonderful selection of various designers that I want you to view. Here are some of the styles that you may be interested in..." Renee showed the ladies quick samples for them to get an idea. Monica was impressed with the designers Mori Lee, Allure Bridals, Pronovias (Barcelona) and Angelina Faccenda. Each of the women held a gown that Monica picked out and would bring it into the dressing room to assist her in putting it on. Rachael was the first one to accompany Monica into the dressing room. She stripped down to her bare essentials.

"This is quite lovely and the color is unique," Rachael stated.

"Yes, I wanted to try something other than white, just to see how it would fair my skin tone. I like the tones, but the fit is just so-so. What do you think?" Monica asked.

"I think if you don't love it, then you must try on one that you can't bear to part with," Rachael said, while she smiled.

"Thank you for your honesty. Can you send in Leah for me?" Monica gave Rachael the gown that she removed.

"I'm so glad to get out of your maid of honor's space. I don't mean any harm, but she is a b-witch and I would use the other word, but I'm respectful of your Godliness," Leah said, helping her try on the next gown. "I know you guys got off on the wrong shoe today, but I pray that things will be different the next time," Monica responded.

"I just don't like her, honestly; from the time I laid eyes on her at the barbeque. She was just sitting there trying to look cute. Even though I like women, I thought she was just fake. I don't trust her." Leah was just straight from the hip. Her hair was in corn rolls braided to the back and she wore sweats.

"I appreciate your directness and trust me, I value your opinion." Monica looked at Leah with tenderness. Leah felt a certain kindredness towards Monica too. It wasn't an attraction like with other women, but it was more like a real sister affection that was uncanny.

"Thank you. So what do you think about the dress?" she asked.

"This one is gorgeous and it makes me look like a Barbie doll." They both laughed. "It's definitely a contender. Could you hold on to this one and send in my maid of honor?" Monica gave her a motherly look like be nice. Leah came out to the main area and saw Keiki searching for more gowns and she had two in her arms.

"Your girl is looking for you," Leah said simply giving her a no nonsense look. Keiki walked away thinking, how could Monica have chosen such a classless female to be in her wedding party. She thought oh well it's not her wedding, so why should she worry.

"I brought two gowns that way you can try on another one before your Godmother brings in the last one." Keiki had nervous energy. Monica looked at the other gown that Keiki had picked out and it was thoughtful for her to bring it, but it was definitely not her style. Monica tried on the one that she picked first.

"What do you think?" Monica asked as she studied herself in the full length mirror.

"It's nice," Keiki said.

"But???" Monica saw her hesitancy.

"I just think it would be more for a younger bride." Keiki was actually about 5 years junior to Monica. Monica gave her such a look, that even Keiki flinched.

"So you're saying I look too old to wear this gown?" Monica stood there waiting for her reply.

"No, that's not the way I meant it. I was saying that this style reminds me of someone that..... oh never mind. I can't say anything to you, without it getting twisted around." Keiki was frustrated.

"I didn't mean to twist the words that you said." Monica was hot! "I have a question for you," Monica said.

"Why didn't you mention that you and Shawn had a conversation about me?" Monica waited for Keiki's response. Keiki was taken off guard and her mind struggled for the right response.

"I didn't think that Shawn would make such a big deal of us speaking in the parking lot," Keiki said.

"No dear, I wasn't referring to that time. Although it seems you had quite a few conversations that went unmentioned." Monica knew that Keiki was burying herself.

"Am I being accused of something? I mean what, is Shawn off limits to say hi?!! I do work in the same location. I would think that was pretty normal!" Keiki was embarrassed and flustered.

"I asked you a simple question, Keiki, and you have yet to answer it. How about you just explain to me how you accepted an invitation to come to his family's barbeque, not even knowing if I would be there?" Monica stood there with a telling eye at Keiki.

"You know what, I do not have to stand here and be interrogated. Why don't you ask your fiancé some of these questions instead of me? I guess he's too squeaky clean to have an ulterior motive." Keiki was exasperated and she took the other gown and hung it on the hook, as if preparing to leave.

"My goodness, Keiki, you really are evading the issue. I'll tell you what; I will relieve you of your duties as my Maid of Honor, because you have no honor. As far as our friendship goes, a wise woman once told me that there are some who will be friends, others enemies, but there are an elite crew who mock them both by being frien(d)enemies. Now you, my dear, are a frien(d)emy in every sense of the word," Monica spoke to her without raising her voice.

"How dare you? I've done nothing but support you"...Monica interrupted Keiki.

"You've done nothing but manipulate me, so your assignment is over," Monica said, while looking at herself backwards in the mirror, while viewing the gown.

"Good, I'm out of here!" Keiki stormed out. Leslie saw her leave and she went into the dressing room with the final gown.

"What happened, Monica?" Leslie asked.

"I just let Judas hang himself," Monica said nonchalantly and proceeded to try on the last gown.

"Finally, this is divinely suited." Monica smiled, looking at the fit and beauty of this gown. They took the gown made by Designer Pronovias (Barcelona) named Babel, as Monica's choice and she made an appointment to have it altered to fit. Leah and Rachael kissed and hugged Monica, before they left the parking lot. Leslie stayed a few minutes after they left to talk to Monica.

"You know, it's okay to mourn your friendship Monica. You have known Keiki for over 7 years. I know that what you discovered was painful," Leslie stated.

"I hear what you're saying, but I'm just not in the mode to concentrate on her. I have 8 weeks to plan for this wedding and now I'm one person short of helping me meet that goal. I'm just glad that you wouldn't abandon me," Monica resolved.

"Alright, Dear. I'm here for you and I will do my best to make this a royal wedding (smiling); but I want you to call me, if you need to just talk okay? Love you much." Leslie squeezed Monica's hand through her car door window. Monica walked to her car that was one space away. She put on some praise and worship music, buckled her seatbelt and was on her way back to Connecticut.

CHAPTER 18 - PANIC SETS IN

Shawn had just gotten the girls ready for their baths. They spent the day at his parents and had eaten all the goodies and favorite dishes that only a grandmother would indulge them in. Now it was 8 PM they were about to read their bible and say their prayers. Shawn normally read to them before they fell asleep, but he was still upset at the conversation that he had at his parent's home. Shawn did some light housework while the girls bathed. He wanted to make a phone call to Jalek for prayer, but he realized his phone was missing. He knew that it must have been left at his parents' home. It's a shame that the technology of a cell phone carries all of your contacts and now he couldn't call anyone, not even Monica.

Monica just took a long bath and checked her cell for any missed calls, but nothing was there. She wanted to talk with Shawn and express what happened at the Bridal Shop. Monica decided to call Shawn. The call just went to voice mail. Monica left a brief message. She was a bit unsettled and turned on her television to see if anything interesting came on. She heard her alert ringer as she had drifted off to sleep. A text message came through her phone.

Leah: I know it's late but I'm a night owl. I just saw some nice girlie dresses on the website of the shop we went to. Here's the link. A smile went across Monica's face and she knew that Shawn's sisters were real and she looked forward to getting to know them better. Monica typed back: You're the best. I'll check them out. Later Honey, enjoy your evening. Monica looked at the time and noticed it was well beyond evening, it was 11:48 and she saw that Shawn had not called her back or texted her. Monica was so desperate to hear his voice and she just wanted to know that he was okay. It was not normal for him to not call or respond. She tried calling again and no answer. Monica lay in her bed contemplating worse case scenarios and couldn't go back to sleep. She asked herself "what would Shawn do".

Monica put on her sweats, a jacket and sneakers, grabbed her purse and was on her way. She felt a bit nervous, but after all this was no longer a boyfriend - girlfriend situation, she was his fiancée. Her carnal mind told her he was sick, he was perhaps entertaining someone else and various similar types of situations. Monica thought, just for her own peace of mind - she needed to know. Parked in front of his townhouse, she looked at his car parked in front of hers. Monica's stomach had knots in it. She now was afraid to knock on the door, as it was so late- 12:12. Monica mustered the courage to knock on the door lightly. It was dark and nothing seemed to be moving. She knocked again, just a tad bit harder. Monica saw a light maybe from the hallway come on. She heard him coming closer to the door. The door opened and a voice spoke.

"Monica?" Shawn questioned.

"Yes. I'm sorry to come by so late." Monica hoped he wouldn't be upset.

"Come in. Are you okay?" Shawn was shocked to see her.

"I'm fine. I just didn't hear from you and I got concerned and wanted to make sure you were alright." Monica said.

"I'm okay. Come have a seat over on the sofa." Shawn closed the front door, as Monica sat on the couch. Shawn went to check on the girls and they were snuggled up in their beds asleep. Monica then realized the girls were there. Then Shawn came and sat down on the seat opposite of Monica. Monica was mesmerized by Shawn. He was wearing pajama bottoms only and his chest was massive, muscular and abs - fabulous.

"So talk to me. I know you went to your first meeting today, how did things go?" Shawn asked.

"Maybe we should talk tomorrow honey, it's late. I just remembered that your girls were here and I don't want to disturb them," Monica replied.

"It's too late, you're here now." Shawn stated.

"I tried to call you." Monica changed the subject.

"I actually left my phone at my parents; but none of that matters, so you might as well get comfortable, because you will be hanging with me now."

"Shawn, I have to get home before I get too sleepy."

"You should have thought about that before you came. You're not leaving. It's too late and I will not have you roaming at this hour of the night." Shawn was being very stern and Monica saw his demeanor change.

"What about your daughters? I don't want to set a bad example in front of them." Monica was torn, as she wanted nothing to get in the way of her relationship with her future daughters.

"We'll work that out - but in the meantime, let's go to the den, so we won't have to whisper anymore (he chuckled)." Monica watched Shawn from the den. He went towards the bedrooms and came back with blankets and plenty of pillows. Monica shared with Shawn all that transpired at the lunch and bridal shop and He listened attentively.

"Wow Baby, I know that wasn't easy for you; but I applaud your ability to handle it the way you did. Plenty of other women that I know would have either gotten physical, or it would have been a real drama filled event," Shawn said.

"I'm just glad that it didn't have to get to that point."

"It's getting late, aren't you going to get some rest? Monica advised.

"I'm not sleepy yet." Shawn was rubbing Monica's hair and massaging her head. They both were lying on the carpet with blankets and pillows spread out. Shawn was lying on his side facing Monica and he wanted to kiss her, but he felt apprehensive.

"What are you thinking about?" Monica said.

"Honestly, I was thinking how I could kiss you without going too far," Shawn said.

"Hmmmm. I see." Monica didn't know what to say. She knew that the last time her body wanted to betray her and have "it's" will be done-instead of "The Father's". Shawn turned on his back to try to alleviate the heat between them. He was at war with his members literally. Now he just closed his eyes. Monica could tell that Shawn was struggling and she wished she could help somehow, but she was battling herself.

"Baby, why don't I just lie on the sofa and get ready for bed," Monica said. Shawn didn't respond right away, but paused slightly.

"Ok Babes. I will stay down here. I don't want to leave you right now." Shawn's eyes were still closed as he spoke.

"Shawn come, I want you close to me," She said. Shawn sat up and turned to look at Monica. She was lying down on a pillow with a blanket wrapped around her. She must be tired he thought. Shawn went over to her and kissed her lips softly. Monica's eyes opened and she kissed him back and proceeded to massage his bald head. Shawn pulled his face up and turned with his back towards her and motioned her hands to keep massaging his head.

"Your tiny hands are magic to me. Don't stop it feels so good." Shawn was enjoying her hand therapy and fell asleep with his head on her chest as did Monica.

Morning at Shawn's

Shawn looked at the clock and it read 9:02, he could hear one of the girls' footsteps in the hallway. He looked at Monica as she slept with her arm covering her face. Shawn got up and walked towards the hallway and his girls greeted him. He put his finger to his mouth to shish them. He motioned them to go back to their bedroom.

"Good Morning, ladies. I have a guest sleeping in the den and I don't want you to wake her up. So I want you to be very quiet, until she gets up okay?" Shawn said.

"Who's in there, daddy?" Shantell asked.

"Monica is in there." Shawn replied. The girls had a surprised look on their face.

"Can we see her daddy?" Sharde asked. Shawn thought about it for a moment.

"I'll tell you what. If you promise to be extra quiet, you can look only for a second; then I want you both to go in your room, while I make breakfast, okay," Shawn said. The girls shook their heads excitedly. The girls and Shawn tiptoed and peeked in to see Monica turned toward the inside of the couch, as her hair was now spread across her face. Shawn hurried them silently to their rooms. Then he went to the kitchen and commenced cooking. Shantell and Sharde whispered in their rooms about Monica.

"I wonder why daddy let Monica stay overnight," Sharde said.

"Maybe she got sleepy?" Shantell said.

"But daddy never let anybody else stay here before," Sharde said.

"Yea, but Monica is Daddy's wife - almost," Shantell added. Shawn smiled to himself, because the girls' wall was close to the kitchen and their whispers were not as quiet as they thought. Monica felt warm and turned over to see the time. It was 9:32, she wondered if Shawn was getting ready for church. She could smell food, but no sounds from the girls. Monica looked for her footies, as they must have come off during her sleep. Monica folded up the blankets and stacked up the pillows neatly. She found her footies and tried to comb her hair with her hand. She reached for her purse to go to the restroom to freshen up. As she was walking by the kitchen, she saw Shawn.

"Good Morning," She said to Shawn.

"Good Morning Sweetie." Shawn looked at Monica with her pocketbook.

"Come Baby." Shawn walked Monica to his bedroom and suite.

"I'm going to run out to the store and I'm taking the girls with me. I want to get a few things. Take a shower and I'll bring you back some fresh undies, okay," Shawn said.

"Alright Baby," Monica smiled. Shawn put the breakfast in the oven on the lowest degree, warm. He gathered Shantell and Sharde and he drove them to the same shopping area that he took Monica to before. "Alright Girls, I have to go shopping for Monica. Will you help me?" Shawn asked.

"Yes. I wanna help," Shantell said.

"What store are we going to?" Sharde asked.

"We can go to Marshalls," Shawn said.

Shawn and the girls went to Marshalls and WalMart too. Monica took a long bath instead of a shower. She found some bath salts that Shawn must use from time to time. Monica lay in the tub for about twenty minutes and commenced to washing and then rinsing off. Monica came out and scrubbed the tub with Shawn's soft scrub cleanser and sponge he had under the sink. Monica put on his robe, as she wanted to wait for her undies to finish dressing. Monica always carried deodorant, small vial of perfume oil and lotion. After layering her body with some scents, she heard them coming through the front door. The girls were bursting with energy and Shawn attempted to calm them, advising that would be eating breakfast momentarily. Monica could hear Shawn's footsteps were getting closer to the bedroom door. Shawn knocked and waited for a response.

"Come in," Monica said. Shawn came through the door with three shopping bags. Two were from Marshalls and the other from Wal-Mart.

"What did you buy Honey?" Monica's eyes lit up.

"I bought something for you to wear and something for you to keep here," Shawn said. He put the bags on the bed, where she could reach them. Shawn leaned over to get his morning kiss. Monica kissed Shawn back and she could tell that Shawn was enjoying her freshly mouth washed teeth. Shawn was giving "ummm" sounds and he started moving his hands on her waist, pulling her close to him. Monica began talking in between their kisses.

"Baby, you know the girls could come in at any moment." Monica protested, mainly because she had no clothes on under his robe. Monica's shoulder blade was exposed and if Shawn kept tugging, he may have a glimpse of other parts of her body.

"They know better than coming into my room unannounced," Shawn said still kissing her and now going for her neckline. "Baby, you smell so good. I could just imagine how you ..... " Monica interrupted.

"Honey, I need to get dressed." Monica was almost panting.

"Hurry up and put some clothes on. I have breakfast ready. I just have to make the plates." Shawn stood up and had to shake off this love-jones that was trying to overtake him. Shawn left the room and Monica, like a little girl, went through every bag. Shawn had a mini wardrobe in these bags. The clothes that he purchased were as follows: a wrap- around black dress, sheer black stockings, eight pairs of a variety of panties, athletic suits (one grey, the other black), two pairs of dark blue jeans, two sweaters, and a pair of tall leather black wedge heeled boots. In the WalMart bag was an electric toothbrush, two night gowns, Calgon bath beads, Dove bath wash, a pink and white bath sponge, Secret deodorant, feminine sprays and other feminine cleansers, shower cap, a comb and a brush. Monica was flabbergasted, as she couldn't believe that this man literally thought of everything that any woman would need as a stay over factor. He even had panti-liners in there. "Geez, he wasn't kidding around." Monica looked at the detail of the panties; there was a color for each day of the week. Monica decided to put on her grey sweat suit that had pink and silver designs featured. Monica brushed her hair into a ponytail and prepared to greet her soon-to-be daughters and have breakfast with her super-man. Monica could hear the girls giggling, as she came down the hallway.

"Hi Ms. Monica," Shantell said.

"Hello Beautiful." Monica rubbed her head, as she walked by her.

"Hi." Sharde waved. Monica waved and flashed a wink to her.

"Awwwww daddy, you were right. Ms. Monica is wearing the outfit that you picked out," Shantell protested. Shawn just smiled as he was making the girls plates.

"Oh, you ladies helped your daddy pick out some outfits for me?" Monica had a surprised smile on her face.

"Yes and daddy let me pick out a sweater." Shantell was cut off by Sharde.

"Yep, can we show you what we picked out?" Sharde's face lit up.

"Girls we are going to eat first, then we will see if Monica wants to do that later." Shawn finished their plates and sat at the table. Monica sat waiting patiently.

"Can you please bless the food, Monica?"

"Sure. Heavenly Father, I just thank you for providing us with this nutritious food and bless the hands that prepared it. Please provide for those that do not have food and create miracles in their homes. In Jesus name, I pray. Amen." Everyone else said "Amen". Shawn, Monica and the twins ate their food and had seconds. The girls enjoyed helping their dad clean dishes after their meals. They finished and immediately looked for Monica. Monica and Shawn were relaxing in the den and talking about the wedding.

"Baby, do you know who you want to do our wedding ceremony?" Monica asked.

"I have thought about it, but I really need to pray about it." Shawn said.

"You didn't plan to go to church today?"

"I did, but when you came, I decided to make it a family day. The girl's mother will be picking them up early today. So, I figured we could just take a day to enjoy each other. I believe in balance. Besides, my Bishop and I talked; he knows that I will be taking time here and there for wedding preparation."

"What about your Pastor?" Shawn inquired.

"I minister with Regina and whenever I'm unable to come in, I send her and the pastor's wife a text." Monica was glad he cared to ask.
Shawn didn't realize that Regina had that type of consistent relationship with Monica. He had met her through Pastor Richards and they were very cool until she tried to cross the lines of friendship. Now they maintained a big brother, little sister role.

"What time will the girls be leaving?" Monica asked.

"They should be getting picked up by 2:30. Initially, she was to pick them up from church, but I told her we were staying in today," Shawn said.

"Oh, I see. Then that gives me some time to spend with them before they go," She noticed that it was 11:03AM. Just then the girls came into the den doorway.

"Ms. Monica, can you come to our room, so we can show you something?" Shantell asked.

"Sure, Sweetie." Monica rose up and followed the little ones to their bedroom. Sharde and Shantell took turns vying for Monica's attention. Shantell showed Monica her drawings and art work. Sharde pulled out puzzles and showed her ability to put them together. Shantell got frustrated at Sharde, when Monica spent what she perceived more time than with her. She went to complain to her dad. Shawn was taking advantage of having the girls spend time with Monica and he was pleasantly surprised that they were bonding with her so quickly and almost effortlessly.

"Daddy, Sharde is taking Ms. Monica and not letting me show her things." Shantell pouted with her little lips.

"Well, I'm sure you can both show her things honey. Didn't Daddy teach you that you have to share and have patience?" What does the bible say about patience?"

"Uhmmm. (Scratching her head) It says it's a virtue." Shantell looked at her daddy innocently, with her big beautiful brown eyes.

Shantell heard Monica calling for her and she scurried back to her room, not even looking back at her dad. Shawn chuckled to himself. He thanked his Lord Jesus that he had sent his Queen to him and she was everything he ever could ask for or even dream of. Monica was intelligent, loving, sexy, beautiful, loved the Lord and family oriented. He prayed that God would show him how to keep his family, business and ministry intact without anything suffering. Shawn decided to find out why it was so quiet in the girls room. Walking down the hallway, he heard the television and when he peeked in-he saw Monica lying on her side with Sharde on her right under Monica's shoulder and Shantell was to her left lying in front of Monica with a pillow. They were all watching "Tangled". This moment was video worthy and he wished he could have caught it on film. Shawn settled with the mental imagery and went back to the den area. Shawn fell asleep watching episodes of Law and Order -SVU. He was awakened by Sharde.

"Daddy, I see mommy's car," she said.

"Oh, ok. Get your sister and I'll take you outside," Shawn stated, but before he could get up good, the doorbell rang. Shawn went to the door and Lydia stood on the other side.

"The girls will be right out," Shawn said.

"Alright, can you make sure they wear their heavier jackets-it's getting cold out here," Lydia said. Shawn nodded and waved at Lydia's husband sitting in the car.

"Hurry girls, your mother is waiting for you." Shawn spoke.

"Ms. Monica, can you come meet my mommy?" Sharde asked in front of Shawn. Monica looked at Shawn and he looked outside and got Lydia's attention. Lydia walked back to the house and Shawn opened the door for her.

"Mommy, I wanted to show you Ms. Monica," Sharde said.

"Oh, ok." Lydia reached out to shake Monica's hand. "It's nice to meet you."

"It's nice to meet you also. You truly have beautiful girls," Monica expressed, as she released her hand shake. Shantell turned to hug Monica before they left.

"Your girls are so wonderful," Monica said to Shawn after he closed the door.

"So are you." Shawn gave Monica a look of pure love.

"Thank you darling. Looking at the time, I guess I better get myself ready for the road," Monica said.

"What do you mean? You're not leaving yet. We haven't even spent any time together." Shawn looked at Monica like she had two heads.

"Geez, I thought you might want to have some you know - alone time," Monica said sheepishly.

"I've been alone way too long," Shawn pulled Monica close then. "Unless, you want some alone space?" He looked into Monica's eyes and felt he could just live there. It was moments like that made Monica want to melt.

"No, it's not that I want to be alone. I just know that our chemistry is really.... "she just let her words fade." Shawn knew what she meant.

"I'm going to be good, I promise." Shawn said. Let's spend some time talking about the wedding and where we are. Shawn was getting hungry and noticed that Monica must have fed them something before they left. He saw the empty wrapper of wheat bread in the garbage.

"You fed the girls?" Shawn asked.

"They wanted a sandwich and I didn't want to disturb your nap." I wasn't sure if their mom wanted to give them something, so I tried to give them just enough to carry them over."

"That works. Thanks. Are you hungry, I'm starving?"

"What do you have in there to cook?"

"Why don't we look?" Shawn motioned them to the kitchen.

Monica saw turkey meat, pasta, sweet potatoes, chicken, frozen vegetables, hot dogs, beans, fries, chicken pot pies and other frozen type meals.

"Hmmmm, I know you're hungry so let me just get you something real quick okay." She said in a motherly way.

"Alright, I'm going in the den-the kitchen is all yours. Monica put together something really fast as she promised. She found a serving tray/stand. She put two plates and two cups with ginger ale as well.

"Don't laugh at my poor man's rendition of a quick afternoon snack." Monica held her breath to see Shawn's reaction. Shawn burst into a hearty laugh…

"You are so cute, my sisters and I used to make this only you did a little twist I see." Shawn took a bite and turned to Monica in surprise. "Wow, baby this really has good flavors." Monica was relieved. She had cooked hot dogs and beans but added spicy sausage with brown sugar and other spices. She also found a box of jiffy corn muffin and pan fried it.

"Baby, this is really good and what is this bread that you made?" He asked.

"It's pan fried cornbread." Monica was elated that he really liked it.

"I really appreciate the passion you put into everything you do." Shawn's face was more sober and he continued to eat his food till it was gone.

"So let's talk about our wedding." Shawn finished his last bite and used the napkin to wipe his mouth and hands.

"I prayed about who should do our ceremony and I believe God wants it to be Bishop Cunningham." He stated. Monica was concerned since the vibe in that church certainly wasn't exactly like the welcoming committee for them to get married.

"I remember you said that you wanted our wedding to be small, intimate just our loved ones. Then reception would include everyone else that we want." Shawn knew that Monica was not comfortable in his church.

"So then let's talk about our reception and honeymoon." Monica stated.

"Did you do your homework?" Shawn looked at Monica with his arms behind his head in a lazy position.

"Do you mean regarding research?" She asked modestly.

"You know what I mean." Shawn replied with a waiting in his tone.

"Well, I looked at having our wedding and reception at L'Escale Restaurant. These are some figures (approximately $2000 - $3000) that I was able to obtain yesterday when I met with the owner's assistant. I also thought about locations for our honeymoon and the place that I choose was the Hanalei Colony Resort, Hawaii. The package is called the Tropical Romance in Kauai and it's for 7 days in a premium oceanfront condo. The flight, hotel and rental car would total cost is $3594.34. My wedding gown came up to $2147.00, your tuxedo rental is $175.00 with accessories. I did not find the shoes that I would wear with the gown, yet. I'm also waiting for the quote from Rachael regarding the beauty salon for the wedding party: hair, nails, etc. My mentor, Leslie is getting the flower arrangement information. The limousine(s) one for the wedding party and the other for you and the best man, etc came out to $800 for one and $150 for the other. The marriage license is $38.00 and I guess you'll tell me what your pastor charges for the marriage ceremony. Shawn was totally amazed and impressed by Monica's ability to get so much down in the span of time given. He was also proud that she was still staying within the budget for a moderate wedding cost that they discussed. Shawn changed his position of laid back on his arms as she really captured his attention.

"My goodness you've been quite busy. Your attention to detail and research certainly explains why you've been promoted and so quickly, I'm impressed. Believe me that's not easy to do-not by my standards anyways. Come here and let me hug you." Shawn sat up and waited for Monica to come hither.

"No, you come to me." Shawn was surprised and leaned up and drew closer to Monica.

"I'll come to you any time of the day - you have me like that." Shawn whispered in her ear and left small kisses on her neck. Monica began to squirm under his lips and took small breaths while trying to be calm.

"Baby, you're not telling me what you think." Monica loved his tenderness but she needed his feedback.

"Ok, ok. Alright, here's the deal. You've done a fabulous job here and we are right on target as far as budget goes. Just need to find out about the limo rentals. Explain how you got those figures." Shawn went right into business mode.

"We will need two limos, one to pick up you and the groomsmen and the other has to fit about 10 of us. The one that will pick you and the guys up will be a Rolls Royce four seater. The one that will pick the wedding party including myself will be the Chrysler 300 Ultra and it seats 12 people. They each are ranging $150-160 an hour. Once the Chrysler drops us off it can go since the wedding party will have their own vehicles parked at the wedding/reception site. The Rolls Royce will remain here to wait for us to take us to the airport and that will probably be 4 hours tops. I figure we can do an early morning wedding from 9:00 to 11:30 and shoot for the airport. The flight that I found leaves at 1:00 and arrives in Hawaii about 11:00pm.

"Wow, you really have done your homework." Shawn looked at Monica in a new light. I'm looking at the figures that you gave me and it comes out to roughly $8800.00. So, we still have to calculate the flower arrangement, photography, salon fees and other wardrobe costs. Two things I am concerned about are the time we will get into Hawaii and that we only have a seven day trip." Shawn stated.

"Yes, I understand where but we can still continue our vacation here in the tri state area." There are also plenty of loose ends to take care of. We have to find out how we will handle my condo. I have to move my things, and you promised we could change something's here." Monica smiled thinking that she could add her touch to this bachelor space.

"True. We can spend the next weeks securing everything and I'll let you look around and see how your stuff can fit in this space." Shawn said.

"As a matter of fact, let's look at the dimensions, closet area and storage." Shawn stood and Monica followed him. They both spent the next hour discussing the possibilities of how things could be rearranged. Monica talked about how some of her furniture could be integrated into the home as well. Shawn's landline phone rang. He went to his bedroom to answer the phone. Monica was shocked as she never even knew that he had a landline phone.

"Thanks, Sis can you drop that off to my job tomorrow. I appreciate that. How's Kevin? I'm here with Monica getting ready to get something to eat." Shawn noted.

"Sure, I'll let her know. I'll see you tomorrow. Later." Shawn hung up.

"That was Rachael. She was over by my mom's and she found my cell phone. She said that she would drop it off to me at work." Shawn saw the confused look on Monica's face.

"What's the matter?" He asked.

"I never knew that you had a landline phone account." Monica looked at Shawn like Detective Columbo would look at a potential criminal.

"Oh I'm sorry Babes; it's just that I rarely even use that phone. Sometimes, I even forget it's here. I need to try to store some of my important numbers in there for times like this." Shawn dialed Monica's cell number from his house phone.

"There now you have this number too. I'm going to make sure that you have my office number as well." Shawn added.

"What are we going to eat?" Shawn rubbed his tummy like a kid. Monica looked at the time on her cell and it was 5:55pm.

"I don't know what you want but I want to get home before it gets too late in the evening." Monica hated driving as it is.

"Why are you in such a rush to leave? I bought you a few things, so you would not feel pressured to rush home. I don't need my space Monica." Shawn really wanted to understand why she had to go home. While Monica could see the irritation in Shawn's face, she just assumed that she had spent enough time there.

"I'm not rushing…I just." Monica didn't want to say what was in her heart. Shawn took Monica's hand.

"Baby, I need you to understand that my home is your home. You can stay here as long as you want. You will be my wife in about 7 weeks. There's no reason for you to try to get out of my way. Don't you see the effort that I make to keep you here?" Shawn had such a serious look on his face.

"Yes, I do." She said nothing more.

"Now go into that kitchen and find us something to eat." Shawn patted Monica on her bottom lovingly. Monica laughed as she realized Shawn was playing his position as the husband already. Monica found some cans of salmon in his cabinet. She decided to make them salmon patties with fried dumplings and a colorful salad with baby spinach, yellow/orange peppers, red onions, cucumbers, tomatoes and avocado. Monica also saw a peach orchard drink, seltzer, orange juice and lemons in the fridge. Monica mixed up a virgin cocktail with crushed ice with those flavors. She could tell that Shawn had a sweet tooth, so she opened the pound cake that he had and took some strawberries, whipped & heavy cream, raspberries and the vanilla ice cream he had and made them a dessert. Shawn's mouth couldn't wait to taste what his nose was experiencing. Monica was full of surprises and he was excited see what she came up with. He knew that there weren't that many choices but Monica did not ask him to go to the store and that meant that she was resourceful. Shawn could hear Monica calling him to the kitchen.

"Ready to eat?" Monica inquired. Please wash your hands as I put your plate out for you." Shawn went into the hallway bathroom and washed and dried his hands. He was anxious to see what she came up with. It smelled like fish but he knew he had no fish in the house. Shawn sat down at the table and Monica presented the food with such beauty. He anxiously waited for her to finish and sit so that he could bless the food. Monica washed and dried her hands as she was cleaning. Then she sat, knowing the Shawn was waiting for her.

"Father, I just want to thank you for this food, the hand that prepared it and the fellowship that comes so freely and untainted." Please bless your daughter in the way that she needs it the most. In Jesus name, I pray." They both said Amen. Shawn took a few bites and continued to eat and get more servings.

"Where did you learn how to cook like this?" Shawn was bewildered.

"I learned it from my mother and from other people along the way. I also love watching cooking shows and enjoy trying new ways to make dishes interesting." Sweetie, we really need to go food shopping for the next time I'm here." Monica was so pleased that Shawn liked her food.

"You are right, I'll take care of the shopping, but baby, you really are good." Shawn winked at her and continued to chow down. Shawn finished his food and Monica surprised him with the dessert.

After they completed everything, he cleaned the kitchen and Monica watched him briefly. She had a nagging feeling about something.

"Babes, what did you say that day to convince him Aaron to led you to my condo?"

"I told him that the truth, that a woman like you only comes once in a lifetime and I only have one life to live." Shawn admitted.

"Really, Shawn. No wonder he said it was an outlandish."

"To him it was but to me, it was my reality. Shawn got quiet, as he said a whole lot more that day but that was between him and Aaron and God.

"Alright." I'm headed for the shower." Monica said.

Shawn grabbed his exotic drink concoction that Monica made and headed back to the den. He thought about how they would spend their evening.

Monica was really enjoying herself and thanked and praised God while she showered. Tears of joy ran down her face and she washed her body. She thought that every woman deserved to be loved and treated in the way that as Shawn exhibited to her. Monica chose to wear an ankle length pink gown with matching slippers and robe. After putting her lotion, deodorant and brushing her teeth, Monica put a few drops of perfume oil on. She heard Shawn knocking on the bedroom door while she was still in the bathroom.

"Come in." She called to him.

"I picked out something for us to watch, are you almost done?" Shawn wanted to grab a quick shower too.

"Yes, I'm finished. She opened the door and Shawn caught her scent immediately.

"Jesus knows that you smell heavenly. Let me get in there real quick and you just get comfortable and I'll be there before you know it." He stated. Monica went to the den and saw the pillows and blankets. Monica took what she needed and laid on the couch. Shawn brushed his teeth before showering and quickly washed. Next he put on his deodorant and sprayed some of Usher's colognes on. He put on a sleeveless t-shirt and his gray pajamas. Shawn slid his slippers on and headed for the den. As he entered the doorway, he saw that Monica was asleep. He didn't want to awaken her but he just wanted to kiss her goodnight. He put his lips as gentle as he could on her forehead and said goodnight as her eyes flickered looking up at him. It was 8:25 PM. She arose.

"Honey let's watch a movie before we go to sleep." Shawn used the remote to press play for the movie lodged in the DVD player.

"I hope you like Hancock? I tried to watch it before but was too distracted, Shawn noted."

"Sure, why not?" Monica had only seen bits and pieces. The movie was an action packed, semi superhero, romantic themed drama. He liked it even though it was still a chick-flick. Shawn had a thing for superheroes. Monica and Shawn lay on the rug with pillows and covers. They were close enough to touch but their bodies were spaced out as not to tempt one another. Monica fell asleep five minutes prior to the end of the film and had rolled over facing Shawn. Shawn kissed her before covering her up.

Shawn went back into his bedroom wishing he had told her to take his bed. He thought about how much he enjoyed just being with her. In the weeks to come, he would have to find ways to deal with his increasing sexual frustration. He planned a vigorous schedule to compensate for his never ending energy. Even with other women that he dated it was not as intense and unbearable. Shawn lay in the bed wondering what their wedding day would be like. He contemplated their wedding night and how things would be up until he could take her as his wife. Shawn had never been celibate for so long and this is the first time that he did not take a bite of the forbidden fruit. Shawn prayed about the intimacy between Monica and him. God let him know that all would be well as long as he did it God's way and not his. In the morning everything went smooth. Neither Shawn nor Monica had any breakfast. They got dressed and kissed each other prior to departing. Monica now on her way to work with the black dress and new boots that Shawn had bought her. She felt a new pep in her step. Her peace came because of the sereneness in Shawn's place. She woke up about 6:15 and prayed for forty minutes before she cleaned the den area. Her job was about twenty five minutes away versus her normal ten to fifteen minutes from her condo. Shawn woke up with such a carnal desire for Monica that he was glad that she was in other room. He forced himself to his knees and stayed in communion with God for a half hour before he heard Monica moving around. Shawn wore a basic black suit with a crisp white shirt and tie that had white, silver and blue stripes. Shawn carried his all-weather black coat. Although, Shawn liked Monica's fashion sense but he wanted to go shopping with her to collaborate on outfits that they could wear together on their outings.

Monica walked into the office at 8:00 am and knew that today would be a fast paced endeavor. She said her good mornings, grabbed a cup of java and commenced her class to start her day.

CHAPTER 19 - WHO HAS COLD FEET?

Over the next few weeks things were like a blur to Shawn and Monica. Then it was only two weeks left till the wedding. The wedding rehearsal that they had on the previous weekend, October 24, 2011 was humorous; when you put Leah, Shawn and Rachael together it's a recipe for amusement. Leah played a practical joke on Rachael by pretending that she was dating some guy that came with her to the rehearsal. Rachael face turned a certain shade of red. Then the guy, named Junior, playing along said that he and Leah were expecting a baby. Rachael was so confused and conflicted that she grabbed Shawn when he came into the church for the rehearsal and told him everything that had transpired. Suddenly you heard a laughter that Monica had never witnessed before bellow out of the back room of the church. Rachael came out of the room with Shawn continued laughter. Rachael was so embarrassed when Shawn told her don't you remember that's Junior the guy we went to high school with and he is definitely not a ladies' man and you know what I mean. Leah, Shawn and Junior laughed until it was time to practice. Monica saw the bond that they all shared and she was happy that she would be a part of that love that they all seemed to exhibit to one another. Shawn went and hugged his sister Rachael in a protective manner - assuring her that he would help her to get Leah back. Shawn's way with his sister was almost resonate with his way with his daughter's. You could tell that he was very protective over them as well. Monica stood in front of her closet in the living room and started moving her coats, jackets and other outerwear into wardrobe bags. She had been packing every Friday to get prepared to make her final move this week and the following week is the wedding. Tomorrow Leah and Rachael were throwing her bridal shower at their parents' home in Greenwich, CT. Monica only met with her soon-to-be Mother in Law once but she felt no inhibitions to see her again. She could hear her cell phone vibrating but could not tell where it was coming from. The phone's light was blinking when she went to pick it up from one of the boxes that it fell into. She had one missed call. Monica dialed the number back.

"Hello Dear," came the welcoming voice,

"Hi Les. I saw that I missed your call. Monica said.

"So what are you up to tonight? Are you ready for your bridal shower?" Leslie asked.

"Yes, I'm thrilled to meet with you and my new family." Monica's eyes were excited.

"I'm so glad that this day is coming very near and close." Leslie said.

"It will be so special that you will witness it with me." Monica answered.

"The day that I'm referring to is your wedding day, not the shower." Leslie stated.

"Of course, I'm so ready to get married." Monica stated.

"I pray that you are Monica. I hope that you're not just excited about the wedding day but the pending "happily ever after" as well." Leslie spoke.

"But why would you say that? This was a Prophetic Word that you yourself spoke over me a year and half ago. God would not have sent him if I was not prepared, right?" Monica became a bit defensive and irritated by what she viewed as a lecture coming.

"You are right. God did speak it and now he's bringing it to pass but we still have responsibilities relating to the blessing." Leslie responded.

"What do you mean?" Monica felt a drop in her excitement and could tell that Leslie was about to give a word of wisdom.

"Did you talk to Shawn yet?" Leslie said in a tender motherly tone. Monica thought about the context of what Leslie meant and she felt anxious.

"I really haven't thought much about it really." Monica knew what Leslie was referring to.

"When are you going to tell him?" Leslie asked.

"I just need to find the right moment." Perhaps I'll tell him right after the event tomorrow." Monica said with a heavy heart.

"Alright. I know that you understand the magnitude of what's at stake. So, I'll keep you in prayer, ok?" Leslie stated.

"Thank you. I respectfully solicit your prayers." Leslie added. Leslie's husband, Charles spoke in the background. "Let me run the ole ball and chain is pulling at my ankle." Leslie joked.

"Love you and tell hubby hello for me." Monica and Leslie hung up. Monica meditated on the words that Leslie spoke and put on some praise and worship music to change the atmosphere. Monica ran across the little bag that her former supervisor, Carolyn had given her. She had never even opened the birthday gift that Mr. Clemons purchased for her. The box contained a female African-American angel that carried a green gift box (wrapped with a red ribbon) in one hand and a gray candle in the other. It was beautifully constructed and she placed it on her nightstand. What a thoughtful and unusual gift she said to herself. As the night was spent, Monica felt drained and took her shower and went to bed.

Shawn just hung up from his conversation with Jalek. Jalek and his wife wanted to set a date for them to have dinner. Shawn told them he would see if Monica would be available for Sunday or tomorrow after her bridal shower.

Saturday D-day

Monica had slept in longer than she thought. It was nearly 11:30 and it was strange that she did not feel rested after sleeping for nearly 10+ hours. She felt that maybe she was coming down with the flu. Monica had some Dayquil and decided to take some to keep from catching it full speed. The party would start at 1:30 and she would find out if Shawn wanted to help her move some of her things into his space today. Just then she heard a phone ringtone of "More of You" by Fred Hammond. It was her fiancé as she had hoped.

"Hi Baby." Monica answered.

"Hey Darling. How are you?" Shawn was excited each day as it came close to the wedding day.

"I'm ecstatic and can't wait to see you." Monica felt a bit better just hearing Shawn's voice.

"Ahhhh that's what I wanted to hear. Are you sure that you're okay? Sound like you have a cold or something?" Shawn picked up her tone.

"Yes, I'm about to take some Dayquil to ward off any bug or cold." Monica answered.

"I wanted to see if we could meet later for dinner or tomorrow at my best friend's home but if you're under the weather, I understand." Shawn was a bit disappointed.

"No No. I'm fine; please let them know we will be there. What time?" Monica asked.

"How does six o'clock sound?" I know that your shower will start at about 1:30 right?" Shawn stated.

"That's perfect Darling." Do you want me to come to you or just drive directly to their house?"

"I'll pick you up at your condo after you leave the bridal shower."

"Alright honey. Well I have to run and get ready for my party. Love you." Monica said and they both hung up. Monica's shower was invigorating but she still took the Dayquil to help her with her body aches. Monica had picked out cotton cashmere laced back tunic with black ribbed leggings. The raspberry colored sweater brought out her red tones in her skin and made her glow. She wore the knee high riding boots that her fiancé so cleverly purchased her. Since they were going for dinner later, she picked out a second outfit and left it on her bed, so she could quickly change when she got back. Monica loved how her hair flowed; as she paid for the look of loose curls by wearing rollers the night before. Her hair style was similar to when she first met Shawn. She put on minimal makeup and peeked to see the time was 1:15. Monica put the address in her vehicles built in navigation system even though it was an easy route and quite close to where she lived. Monica could see the house from the winding roads in the gorgeous Greenwich Neighborhoods that others only dreamed of living. She parked in the same area as she did before. Suddenly she felt a tinge of nervousness in her belly, but she rang the bell to the massive mansion like door. Rachael answered the door and hugged Monica.

"Hey, we were just about to call to make sure you were okay. Come on in." Rachael escorted her into the family room and there were about twenty ladies seated around the room. Monica felt self-conscious and wondered who all these people were.

"There she is…my new sister." Leah came over to greet and hug Monica. Leah began to introduce all of the nieces, aunts and sisters in the church. Patrice, Shawn's mother came out and served hors d'oeuvres, fruit punch and she saw dessert dishes placed on the dining table in the other room.

"Alright everybody, we are going to start this party with some cool music and Monica please open your first gift." Leah raised her arm to wave her to come get the gift. Leah put on a mix cd that she made. It had a little of everything including Latin sounds, Caribbean, gospel and R&B. It was a great compilation of upbeats and spiritual sounds that Monica was really feeling. She was almost overwhelmed with the support that she never expected. Leslie came in and was standing in the door way and Leah ran to get more chairs to accommodate people that came in after Monica started opening gifts. As the day went on Monica felt her temperature rising more and more and she began to feel hot flashes. Rachael noticed that Monica looked a little flushed. As each gift was opened, everyone clapped and gave ooohhh and ahhh sounds to the variety of gifts that Monica received. The last gift to be opened,

Rachael went up to Monica and whispered in her ear: "Are you alright honey?"

"I'm fine, just thirsty." Monica stated.

"I'll be right back; I'm going to get you some water." Rachael went in the kitchen and headed back to the family room. Everyone was adoring the last gift opened and Rachael went in to give her the bottled water and suddenly all Hell broke loose. Monica fainted and Leah standing beside her barely caught her. Screaming, Leah called for her mother Patrice. Leslie had stepped out moments before to go to the restroom. Hearing the ruckus in the main room, she rushed back and saw Monica passed out in Leah's arms.

"What happened? Leslie and Patrice said simultaneously!!!"

"I don't know, she just fainted," Leah was shaken. Leslie and Patrice went over trying to revive her and everyone else was in shock. Monica was barely able to adjust her eyes and was not able to speak without slurring her voice.

"Call 911, right now!" Leslie stated with alarm. Patrice grabbed the phone and called the ambulance. The ambulance in their region was efficient and in less than fifteen minutes they arrived. Leslie accompanied Monica in the ambulance and gathered her purse.

"Someone please call Shawn." Leslie called out as they closed the ambulance door. In the ambulance the attendants gave her oxygen and Leslie held her hand and prayed. Leah grabbed her cell phone and dialed Shawn's cell phone as she trembled.

"Hello." He answered.

"Shawn." Her voice was shaking.

"Leah." He barely recognized her voice but saw her number populate.

"Something has happened to Monica." Leah got out.

"What! What happened, tell me!!" Shawn's blood pumped through his heart and he was more alert than ever.

"I don't know, she just fainted," Leah said.

"Where is she?" Shawn was now putting on his shoes and looking for his jacket.

"The ambulance picked her up and she's on her way to Greenwich Hospital."

"Who's with her?"

"Leslie went in the ambulance with her."

"I want you and your sister to get there and call me, I'm on my way." Shawn was already in his vehicle when he hung up.

Greenwich Hospital

Leslie paced the floor and prayed in her "heavenly language." God moved miraculously as Leslie found all of Monica's insurance information in her purse and now they were setting her up in a room. The nurse advised Leslie they would be admitting her because her blood pressure was extremely low. Leslie saw Rachael and Leah coming down the hallway of the 3rd floor.

"How is she?" Rachael asked.

"All I know is that she is in and out of consciousness." Leslie said. Leslie saw the doctor come out of Monica's room. He looked around and the nurse pointed him to Leslie.

"Hello. My name is Doctor Rollins. I'm treating your daughter?" He asked.

"Yes, She's my God Daughter, Leslie stated."

"Were you there when she collapsed?" Dr. Collins asked.

"I was there but I wasn't in the room when it happened." Leslie stated.

"Who was with her?" He asked.

"I was and she looked a bit flushed so I went to get her some water. When I came back to give it to her, she fainted." Rachael spoke up.

Just then Shawn saw Leslie and his sisters and proceeded down the hallway to meet them.

"Oh here's my brother." Leah said. They all turned to view Shawn along with the doctor.

"Are you a relative Sir?" Dr. Collins asked.

"Yes, I'm her fiancé." Shawn said as he shook his hand. Shawn wasted no time on the courtesies and moved right into questions and answers.

"What happened?" Shawn wanted answers. Rachael gave him the quick and simple version as she knew her brother had no patience in settings as such of these. Shawn pulled the doctor to the side and accompanied him close enough to view Monica in her room. He spoke to him regarding her status and the possible reasons this happened.
Shawn walked back to the ladies after speaking to the doctor. They all looked at him hoping that he received more information.

"I'm going to look in on Monica." Shawn's face was stressed.
"What did the doctor say?" Leslie asked.
"He told me all her vital signs were low: heart beat, blood pressure, pulse. They are not sure what happened. They took blood and the test results should be back shortly." Shawn said. He walked away and into Monica's room. She did not have a roommate as of yet and he was glad that he was alone with her. Monica looked peaceful sleeping. Shawn held Monica's hand and began to pray. Leslie, Rachael and Leah went to the waiting room and began to console one another. After about an hour, Shawn came out of the room with glossy eyes that clearly had tears in them.

"I need to call Monica's Mom to let her know what is going on. Do you have her number?" He asked Leslie. Leslie gave Shawn Monica's cell phone and told him it should be in her contacts. Otherwise, she would look in her cell phone book. Shawn scrolled through Monica's phone and found the number listed as Mother Frances. He dialed the number.

"Hello." Frances recognized her daughter's number.

"Hello, Ms. Williams, this is Shawn - your daughter's fiancé." Shawn stated. Frances got quiet because she felt something had to be wrong for him to be calling from her cell instead of her.

"What happened, Shawn?" Frances stood up from her bed. Jeremiah watched his wife as she looked concerned.

"I'm not sure what happened, but Monica is here in the hospital. "Apparently, she fainted at her bridal shower and now the doctors are monitoring her vital signs, which are a bit low. We are now waiting for the blood work to come back to see what it shows." Shawn said in agony.

"Oh my God! Please keep me posted. I'm going to see if I can get a flight out tomorrow morning." Frances was nervous.

"I'll keep you posted, but I want you to promise me that you will not make any arrangements yet. I'm here, my family is here and Leslie is here too. We are going to believe God and get through whatever this is. Everything is in His hands not ours. Trust me Mrs. Williams; God did not bring us this far to let us down." Shawn expressed.

"Yes, you're right. God holds the keys, Son. Please call us when you get more news, no matter the time or hour - you hear me," Frances said.

"Yes Ma'am, I hear you loud and clear. Please don't worry and I'll be speaking to you shortly." Shawn and Frances hung up. Shawn's heart was hurting and he just remembered that Jalek and Jackie were probably waiting for them to come to their scheduled dinner. It was now 5:45 pm. He went to make the call to Jalek. The doctor came back in two hours and looked for Shawn. He saw him in the waiting room and Shawn stood to met with him as they walked down the hallway and stood by Monica's room.

"The test results came back and there is something there in the blood like a layer of film of some sort. Not sure if I've ever seen anything like it. I have one of my colleagues that will be here on staff in the morning. I want him to look at this data and we can see what we are dealing with. So far she is stable, but we can't seem to keep her conscious. We will continue to keep her on the IV and watch her throughout the night." Dr. Collins could see the pain in Shawn's eyes.

"Alright. Thank you for doing all that you can. I want to know something before you continue on with your rounds," Shawn asked.

"What is that Sir?" Dr. Collins asked.

"Do you know Jesus, Dr?" Shawn asked, as he looked boldly into his eyes. Dr. Collins was stunned at Shawn's serious unforeseen question. He saw that Shawn was a man that really was not asking, just for the asking.

"I've heard the name, Mr.?" Dr. Collins, now wanting to address him, with more of a more respectful tone.

"It's Edwards and I really appreciate your honesty. Have a blessed evening." Shawn laid his right hand over the doctor's shoulder and squeezed it in an endearing way and walked back to the waiting room. Dr. Collins had indeed heard many people talk about Jesus and on various occasions others would cry out to him during crisis or death in the hospital; but the question still remained, did he know Jesus? This would proceed to haunt Dr. Collins for quite some time. Shawn no longer wanted to chit chat, or have the sad faces staring at him not knowing what to say.

"I'm going to stay with Monica tonight and hopefully we can get more clarity on what is happening to her tomorrow. There is a specialist scheduled to examine the tests and then we'll know how to pray. For now, please go home and get some rest. If I need you, I will call you tomorrow," Shawn stated. Leslie determined that Shawn wanted some alone time with Monica. She looked at the girls and said her goodbyes.

"Shawn, I'm sorry for the circumstances that are bringing us together today; but I must say you are, without a shadow of doubt, all and everything that God said you would be. The Lord has given you the heart of David, the wisdom of Solomon and the anointing of Joseph.

I'm certain that Monica is in good hands with you." Leslie reached out to hug Shawn.

"Woman of God, thank you. We will see each other again at the wedding, I prophesy it," Shawn said. Leah and Rachael hugged Shawn and left. Shawn looked at his cell and saw that he had missed calls from his mother and he knew that his sisters would fill her in. Right now, he needed to focus on Monica. He went back in the room and no one bothered him as he stretched out on the chair next to Monica's bed. Near the window it was a little chilly, but he wrapped his jacket around him and prayed himself to sleep. Shawn was awakened by the noise of a fully staffed hospital. He looked at his watch and saw that it was 8:30 am. The nurse had come in throughout the night to check Monica's vitals. Shawn picked up his phone and saw missed calls and text messages. Shawn saw that Lydia called. He prayed before he left the room and then went to the waiting area to return some calls.

"Hello," Lydia answered.

"Hi. I just received your message," Shawn noted.

"Yes, I wanted to know if you were planning on seeing the girls, even though this is not your weekend. I know you'll be on your vacation for the next few weeks and I'm sure they will miss you sorely." Lydia said.

"I'm aware, Lydia. Right now I'm in the hospital and I'll need to talk to you about that later when I can better focus, alright." Shawn actually had planned to spend the day with them, until this emergency event came up.

"Oh, I'm sorry. Are you alright?" Lydia asked.

"Yes, it is Monica, she's here," Shawn said.

"Oh my God! I pray that everything will be okay," Lydia stated. Shawn could hear his girls in the background tugging at their mother to speak with him. Shawn's heart melted.

"Put them on the phone together, please," Shawn asked.

"Hi daddy," they both held the phone and said it in unison.

"I miss you both so much, but daddy is in the hospital right now taking care of Monica," Shawn said.

"What happened, Daddy?" Shantell asked.

"Ms. Monica wasn't feeling well and became weak. So now she needs to get some rest for a few days," Shawn explained.

"Oh," Shantell said. Sharde was in the background and she whispered: "That means we can't see Daddy today." Shawn was so torn, but he didn't want to bring the girls to hang out not knowing how long he would be, or the circumstances surrounding her condition. Lydia took the phone back.

"Alright, so let me know what's going on," she said.

"I will." He hung up with Lydia. Shawn called Jalek back, as he had left a message as well.

"Hey man, how are you holding up?" Jalek recognized his phone number.

"I'm casting my cares on Him, Bro," Shawn responded.

"That's the word; listen -Jackie and I were up late last night praying and in intercession for you and Monica. Jackie has a word from the Lord for you brother." Jalek called for his wife.

"Hello." Jackie came on the line.

"Hey Sis, how are you?" Shawn was feeling more strength, as he had started to get weak.

"Yes my Brother, God is working some things out. As we were interceding last night, the Lord was showing us that there has been an attack lodged out on Monica, this wedding and ultimately her life.
There's a woman that really is super jealous of Monica and she has put some type of witchcraft spell to cause this illness. The doctors will look, but it is spiritual more than physical. I wanted to ask if we can come and pray and lay hands on her," Jackie stated.

"Of course, you can. I would be so honored if you would," Shawn stated.

"Hey Man, Jackie and I will be there within the next hour, okay." Shawn agreed and they hung up. Shawn went to the nurse's station to see if they would give him some type of toiletries to wash his face and get his mouth presentable. He left his travel kit in the car and did not want to go outside until Monica was conscious. He sat in Monica's room near her bed and saw a shadow coming towards the room. His mother came in and behind her stood his father.

"Hi Mom, Dad. Thanks for coming." Shawn hugged his mother and his father rested his hand on his son's shoulder and squeezed it. They all took up the chairs in the room and talked for a bit. As promised, Dr. Collins and another doctor came in and he introduced the blood specialist as Dr. O'Conner and they left the room to allow them space. Shawn did not move far from the room, but his parents walked down to the waiting room. Shawn remembered Frances, but he really did not want to call her just yet. Twenty minutes went by and Jalek and Jackie were there. They walked over to Shawn and hugged him and Jalek patted his back.

"The doctors just left the room and they told me that they will be back in about an hour or so," Shawn said.

"Alright, let's get started." Jackie was ready to pray. They all stood in the room with Monica. Shawn held Monica's hand and they prayed and interceded for forty minutes without interruption. In the midst of their prayer, Leslie had come in and stood at the door as if guarding it. A few times, the nurse would come by and she would respectfully asked her to come back as they should be finished shortly. Shawn came out of the room and greeted Leslie and felt his phone vibrating. He excused himself, as he recognized the number.

"Hello," Shawn answered.

"Hi Shawn, I'm sorry to bother you, but we were out and Shantell started to cry and scream, saying she needed to talk with you," Lydia said.

"Put her on the line," Shawn said.

"Daddy, I feel funny and I tried to pray for Ms. Monica, but I keep seeing monsters." Shantell was crying in between her words.

"Where are you?" Shawn asked. Lydia heard the sternness in Shawn's voice.

"We're in the parking lot of the hospital, Shawn. I didn't know what to do. She was hysterical at one point. I thought maybe you could just come see her and that would be enough," Lydia explained.

"I'll be right there." Shawn began taking long strides to get to the parking lot. Lydia was located in the front of the main entrance and she was standing next to her vehicle, holding Shantell in her arms. Shantell ran to Shawn when she saw him. Sharde looked at him as he picked up Shantell. Shawn waved for Sharde to come to him as well.

"What's the matter?" Shawn looked up into Shantell's eyes.

"I want to pray for Ms. Monica, Daddy."

"But you said you see monsters when you pray," Shawn responded. Shawn quickly heard, "Suffer little children to come unto me, and forbid them not: for as such is the Kingdom of God".

"I'm going to take them upstairs to see her for a minute, can you wait?" Shawn asked Lydia.

"Sure." Lydia sat back in her vehicle. Shawn took his daughters up to Monica's room and they went inside. Shantell looked at Monica and grabbed her right hand near the window side of the bed.

"Sharde, we need to pray," Shantell said. The girls began to pray, using the scriptures of by his stripes was she made whole and two can chase 10,000 and ended with In Jesus Name. Shawn watched the intensity of how they prayed and he heard someone call his name and stepped out softly. Shawn saw that his father had called him. Shawn was still feeling estranged over their last conversation.

"Hey Shawn, I just wanted to tell you that I was wrong for the things that I said to you. You are a man of God and his wisdom is with you." Kenneth reached out to embrace his son. Shawn hugged him and released some of the pent up emotions with a few long sighs.

"I forgive you," Shawn said. With that he walked back into Monica's room, only to find the twins doing something strange. Shantell sat on the bed whispering something in Monica's ear, while Sharde continued to pray holding her hand. While Shawn tried to figure this out, he witnessed Monica's right hand moving. In amazement, he went into the hallway to advise everyone that Monica was responding. They all stood in awe as Shantell lifted her body from speaking in her ear, and the tears were rolling down her angelic face, as if watching for something. Next, Monica's eyes were stirring and they all witnessed Monica's eyes open.

"My God…" Jackie said. Shawn went over to the bed and sat on the side by Sharde. Monica looked at them and was barely audible. Shawn looked back and asked them to call for the nurse. The hospital scene was purely a miracle from Heaven. Shawn made sure that the doctors understood that Jesus was real and they had no medical evidence to document her recovery. Shawn stayed another night and was able to get Monica discharged early that morning, which was Halloween, Monday, October 31. Shawn was able to speak with Mr. Clemons, Monica's boss and they authorized FMLA for the remainder of the week, at which time her vacation would commence. Shawn, with the help of Jalek and the other groomsmen, moved Monica's things into his home. Shawn would not let Monica do any lifting or cooking during the remainder of the week. For the rest of the time, everyone took a shift to stay with Monica. Shawn would have loved to stay with her from Monday - Friday, but his physical desire was overbearing to say the least. He stayed with her Monday, Rachael - Tuesday, Leah - Wednesday and by Thursday she protested that she was fine and everyone was just being overprotective. Shawn wasn't feeling right about it, so he called Leslie to just see if she could stop in for an hour or so and he would take over after work. Leslie was more than okay to go. During her visit, Leslie felt uneasy and she couldn't understand why.

Suddenly she realized what it was. Leslie dialed Shawn, while Monica was napping.

"Hello." Shawn answered.

"Hi Shawn, I was wondering if you could meet me at Monica's right now and if you can bring your friend with you? We need to pray," Leslie stated.

"I'll be there shortly." Shawn contacted Jalek and Jackie and they agreed to meet them there. Monica woke up and felt a bit weak. She looked around and called for Leslie. Leslie was buzzing Shawn in from downstairs. Shawn had met Jalek and Jackie outside and they were on their way up. Monica tried to get out of bed, but her legs were like noodles.

"Oh Sweetie, it's okay just lay down. Shawn is here, we are going to pray for you," Leslie said. Monica was feeling like she was in a twilight or dream - like state. She listened to Leslie and layed down. Leslie went to open the door and led them into the bedroom. She explained that the Holy Spirit said there was something in the house that was set here to cause this witchcraft spell to linger. They all looked around the room and Jackie saw it first.

"There it is," Jackie cried out. They all looked in the direction that Jackie pointed. Right there on the nightstand was the Angel sitting adjacent to Monica's pillow.

"Get that thing out of here," Jalek advised.

"Be careful, don't touch it with your bare hands," Jackie said.

"This object has been dedicated and it was chanted over and covered with some kind of strange dust," Jackie advised.

"We need some anointed oil," Leslie said. Shawn knew where Monica kept hers. He went and obtained it. Shawn took a paper towel and removed the statue of the angel and put it in a paper bag. Leslie began smearing the oil on Monica and the nightstand and they all prayed in unison. Shawn took the idol outside and burned it before throwing its ashes away. He came back with Monica's keys and joined

in the warfare prayers. Monica did not seem to respond to the prayers. Shawn began to get angry and started to pray violently in the Spirit and he felt a wind in the atmosphere, but continued and pursued until there was a breeze of change and the room felt at peace. Monica asked for some water. Leslie went to get a bottle of water and gave it to her.
Monica drank the bottle in one sitting.

"Thank you," she said, feeling better, but still a little weak.

"Thank you all so very much;" Monica said.

"You are definitely of the Beloved My Dear," Jackie said. Monica looked at Shawn, as she had never met Jalek or Jackie. Shawn introduced them and they all left her bedroom, with the exception of Shawn.

"Wow honey! I feel like I could sleep the whole night. The clock read 8:00 pm," Monica stated.

"I want you to get some rest, Baby." Shawn went to the living room where everyone was chatting.

"I can't thank you all enough for being here and standing post, being true people of God." Shawn was tired and wanted to just rest himself.
"Well, we are going to go now and you need to get some rest." Jackie looked at Jalek and they were in agreement.

Leslie whispered to Shawn. "Will you be staying tonight?"

"I have no choice," Shawn said with a crooked smile. They all left and Shawn went back to the bedroom and saw Monica lying there peacefully. Shawn looked around and found the clothes that Monica had brought him before. He took a quick shower and then he lay at the bottom of Monica's queen size bed. He tried to get comfortable, but to no avail. Finally, he moved her pillow around and stacked them between his body and hers. He went right to sleep, like a baby.

Friday morning, Monica realized that she had very little clothes left in her condo. Almost everything was at Shawn's house. Shawn was still sleeping and Monica had loads of energy. She began to make sure all her wedding gear was in order. She went into the spare room, where she kept all of her honeymoon and wedding stuff. She was cautious to keep these things separate. Monica had her lingerie packed in one bag, casual/beach wear, evening wear, perfumes, oils, shoes and feminine items as well. Her gown(s) was in the heavy garment bag and she made sure Shawn's nosy self would not see it. Everything was ready packed and organized. Monica went to brush her teeth and wash her face. Next she went to prepare breakfast. Monica fixed some round turkey sausage, cream of wheat, Belgian waffles, scrambled cheesy eggs and home fries. She heard Shawn moving around and his footsteps went to the bathroom. The hot water was ready for tea and she bought a pitcher of orange juice and prepared to dress her table for the meal.

"Good Morning," Shawn said as he strolled into the room.

"Good Morning. I hope that you are hungry."

"Very Hungry." Shawn looked at the food and was ready to dive in. They sat and talked about the days that was about to come and Shawn told her he needed to go and let her prepare for tomorrow. Shawn and Monica kissed and said their goodbyes. Monica cleaned the dishes and went through her condo with a fine tooth comb; cleaning, dusting and vacuuming. Monica looked for her cell, as she was about to call Leslie. She saw that her mother called and she dialed her.

"Hello," Frances answered.

"Hi Mom."

"Hi, Darling, I spoke to your sweet fiancé over the last week and he has really made me feel so comfortable, knowing he is taking good care of you."

"Oh good, Mom, I'm glad that he puts you at ease."

"Yes, he's a gem. We'll be leaving tonight at 7:30 pm and arriving 10:00 pm tonight my dear. We're going to go straight to the hotel and will see you tomorrow. I hope you are ready for your big day," Frances said with a smile.

"I'm as ready as I will ever be Mom," Monica responded.

"Well, Jeremiah and I are on our way out, but we'll see you tomorrow morning," Frances said.

"Have a good time, Mom. Love you." Monica and Frances hung up. Monica had scheduled her appointments at the salon for 2:00 pm. The one that she selected was a Dominican shop and she found them to be reasonable and they worked fairly fast. The owner agreed to shut down the salon from 2:00 - 6:00 for her wedding party only. Monica met Leah, Rachael, Leslie, and her prayer partner Regina. Monica had to tell her Pastor Jones and his wife Marilyn that she needed time off and they understood. Monica had kept Katrina (the other intercessor) up to speed, because so many things had happened and she had to take up the bulk of ministry. Regina agreed to become a bridesmaid, to take the empty spot that Keiki left. Now, Monica still needed a Maid of Honor. Monica had thought hard and prayed. In the salon everyone had their own stylist and a person designated to do their pedicure and manicure. In the morning, Rachael would do everyone's make up, as she had that flair. Their day in the salon was so rich with girl bonding power and Monica thought that she had never felt so much encouragement from women in all her days. As they were winding down and they were all just about done, Leah was complaining about all this pampering stuff. Monica went over to her and told her to stop whining so much and they all burst into laughter. As they all paid for their beautiful transformations, Monica walked closer to Rachael and Leah.

"I have a question," Monica asked

"Yeah," they asked in unison.

"If it's not asking too much, would you be my maid of honor tomorrow?" Monica, now directing her question to Leah. Leah was so stunned, that she looked at Rachael as if to say, well answer her.

"She's talking to you," Rachael commented.

"You're asking me????" Leah face turned beet red.

"Yes. I'm asking you," Monica said.

Leah's eyes filled with tears and she had to catch her breath. Leah was a beautiful girl with her plump sized body.

"I…stammering guess so," Leah responded. Monica went and hugged Leah and she embraced her for a few moments.

"Thank you," Monica said. As they parted and went to their perspective cars, Monica saw Rachael approaching her vehicle. Monica rolled down her car window.

"Hey Lady, you have no idea what you have just done," Rachael said. "Leah is never going to be the same. Thank you for your love." Rachael embraced Monica and left. Monica went home and thought that tomorrow this time, she would be married and on her way to Hawaii. Monica spent some time reading the word and God showed her the scriptures pertaining to the Proverbs 31 Woman. She felt that God was about to put that anointing on her. Monica saw that the time was 8:00 pm. She decided to call Shawn before she went to bed.

"Hello," Shawn answered.

"Hi Baby," Monica said.

"Hi, Sweetheart, how did your salon day go?"

"It went very well. I asked Leah to be my maid of honor."

"Really? How did she respond?"

"She was shocked; to say the least, but I believe she was appreciative."

"Baby, that's wonderful. I miss you."

"I miss you too. After tonight, we shall not miss each other anymore."

"You are so right."

"Well Honey, I just had to hear your voice before I went to sleep. I look forward to seeing you in the am," Monica said.

"Alright, Beautiful, Love you. Goodnight." Shawn and Monica hung up. Monica snuggled up with her big scarf on her head to protect her hairstyle. She fell asleep trying to watch "Why did I get Married, part one".

CHAPTER 20 - RIVERS OF LIFE

Monica was up by 7:00 am. The wedding party was to meet her at her house by 7:45 and they would leave at 8:15. Monica took a bath with salts and scents. Her legs were freshly waxed and smooth as butter. Monica put Nivea all over her body, as it had a satin creamy finish to it and did not interfere with her perfume. Monica decided to wear Chanel 5 Premiere. She purchased three pairs of stockings, just in case there was an accident. She put on her shimmering sheer stockings and she heard her buzzer go off. It was exactly 7:45. She buzzed the girls in and waited for them to come up.

"Morning," Monica greeted everyone.

"The Limo is fabulous," Leah said as she embraced Monica.

"I saw Leslie coming, should I buzz her in?" Rachael inquired.

"Yes, please. I'm going back in the bedroom." Monica had a white satin short robe on with her heels and lingerie on.

"Come on back," she motioned to Leah. Leslie and Regina arrived at the same time and came up in the elevator. The women all helped one another to get dressed and to look their best. Leah was at Monica's beck and call and hardly let anyone beat her to serving Monica.

"Monie," Leah called her for short, "You are about to jump the broom Baby." Leah looked at Monica with loving eyes.

"Yes, I know. I hope I don't trip." They chuckled together. Frances, Jeremiah, Patrice, Kenneth, Leah, Regina, Leslie, Rachael and Monica were seated in the white Chrysler 300 T stretch limousine. The limousine took off and Monica's Pastor, Ronald Jones and wife Marilyn followed them and soon as they were traveling, they spotted the men in the White Rolls Royce, as they were headed to the restaurant. From Monica's condo, the restaurant was only twenty minutes and they arrived there promptly at 8:30 am. On arrival, Leah rushed Monica and the wedding party crowded around her to prevent Shawn and the others from viewing her. They had a private room for Monica and a separate room for Shawn. Leslie was again the guardian angel set at post. Leah and Rachael fussed over Monica and Rachael gave Monica a makeover that any Hollywood star would be envious of. They checked her dress and jewelry and then Leah called in Leslie.

"It's time," Leah said. Monica was confused and looked around, wondering what they meant. Monica could hear the shuffling around just outside the door and could tell that the restaurant was filling up with the guests scheduled to view her first wedding at 45 yrs old. Monica was filled with anxiety and on pins and needles. Leslie came up to Monica.

"Here is something old." Leslie took a ring off her index finger and put in Monica's index finger.

"Here is something new." Leah put on her a silver bracelet with various heart charms all around it.

"Something borrowed." Patrice, put a white mink stole around her arms. Monica's eyes were starting to tear. Rachael stood by with Kleenex's to dab her eyes.

"Something Blue." Rachael passed the Kleenex's to Leah, as she knelt down and held her gown up to put an ankle bracelet with marcasites baby blue stones on her leg. Monica breathed in and someone knocked on the door. Leslie peeked out and dipped back in.

"They are ready for you my dear." Leslie looked at Monica. Monica was shaking and Leah and Rachael had to support her as she walked.

"Baby, you are the most beautiful bride I have ever seen." Frances kissed her daughter on both cheeks right before they opened the side door, which lead to the outside balcony. Leslie went out first and got the attention of Pastor Cunningham and he alerted the organist to begin the ceremony. Leslie and Leah made sure that the groomsmen and bridesmaids were all lined up and the twins were ready for their parts. As the music began to play, everyone took their positions and started their march to the well-known music leading them down to the altar. The first person to go down the aisle was Reggie, the drummer from Shawn's church; next, Rachael went down in her very feminine lavender v-neck dress, that had rose petals on either side of her chest; the next groomsman was Prophet Paul from Shawn's church; then Leah came with her gorgeous rose petalled, single strapped dress that featured a satin slip and crisscross bodice; following her was Jalek, the best man; after that, Shantell and Sharde who had matching dresses that were white with lavender sashes across their tiny bodies; then the matron of honor, Leslie, came down with a roman style gown with slits across the arms, that brought a classic flow of femininity to her; lastly, as Shawn waited patiently, he was looking absolutely dapper dressed in a cutaway coat with striped trousers, a lavender-green vest and striped ascot tie. His groomsmen had similar wear with the exception of a green colored vests and dark trousers. As the family and other witnesses stood, the music changed to welcome the bride. Monica took each step and walked with her head held high and her train was effortlessly spread out evenly. Her Gown was off the shoulders (corset in design), revealing the beauty of her curves. The front bodice had the tiniest scallops of design pattern throughout to the waist. From the waist down were lacy medium scallops that blossomed into what appeared to be what clouds were made of. Monica swayed back and forth and she looked onward as Shawn was almost hypnotized by her very presence. Monica felt assured that this man that she kept her eyes fixed upon, was the King that God had promised her. Monica could hardly notice the music or anyone else around her. As she reached the front of the altar, she felt an ease. Pastor Cunningham came forth with the opening prayer and asked who gives this woman away. Pastor Jones stood as her Spiritual Father. Pastor Cunningham gave them the charge to remind them of the vows and covenant that they were embarking upon. Shawn and Monica turned for the reading of their vows:

"In the name of Jesus I, Shawn, take you, Monica, to be my wife, to have and to hold, from this day forward, for better, for worse, for richer, for poorer, in sickness and in health, to love and to cherish, for as long as we both shall live. This is my solemn vow."

"In the name of Jesus I, Monica, take you, Shawn, to be my husband, to have and to hold, from this day forward, for better, for worse, for richer, for poorer, in sickness and in health, to love and to cherish, for as long as we both shall live. This is my solemn vow." Frances and Patrice were dabbing their eyes, as the wedding was so touching and they were filled with joy for their children. The Pastor requested the rings. Jalek came forward and brought the rings to the Pastor. Pastor Cunningham handed them the rings. They both repeated "with this ring I thee wed…" Pastor Cunningham said the words that Shawn and Monica were anticipating to hear.

"I Pronounce thee Husband and Wife."

"You May Kiss the Bride." Shawn was not ashamed as he kissed Monica and they both held each other with passion and fire. The crowd whistled and cheered. Everyone stood and the wedding party began their march back, with the groomsmen escorting the bridesmaids and the music was already in motion, as Monica was whisked away by Leah and Rachael. "Sorry, Brother. You will see her soon." Monica waved at Shawn as she left him at the altar. Shawn was not lonesome, as many from his church, family and others came to shake his hand, embrace and congratulate him. Monica was escorted back to her dressing room. Leah helped Monica climb out of her wedding gown and Rachael picked up her reception dress. Leslie knocked on the door and came in.

"Rachael, dear, your Sweetheart is lonesome looking for you." Rachael looked up.

"Go Honey, I have this under wraps," Leah said.

"You've been so wonderful to me Leah. I could never repay you, or your sister for what you have done for me." They were both near the mirror and Leah looks at Monica through the mirror.

"You're the one that has brought love, passion and unity into our family and for that I really love you," Leah voiced. Monica became teary again.

"Alright, alright. Why don't you just meet me out there, I'm just going to say a quick prayer, before I come out with my next look." Monica smiled.

"Ok. I'll see you in a minute. Don't make me come looking for you. I'm too pretty to get ugly." Leah threatened. They both chuckled. Monica looked at herself sideways, front and back. This dress was form fitting and had a mermaid flair. The front had gathers that clung to her body to produce a feminine appeal. Monica felt glamorous in this dress. Monica saw one of her shoes, but couldn't find the other. She went around the room and started getting a bit flustered. The door came open.

"Leah honey, can you help me find my other…" she looked up and Shawn was standing there with a look that could melt wax.

"You're looking for that shoe." Shawn pointed in the corner right by the door that he came in through.

"Oh yes. That shoe," Monica said. Monica put both shoes on and she noticed that Shawn was just staring at her.

"What?" Monica finished and stopped.

"You're so beautiful," he said simply. Shawn moved in close to Monica and slid his hand around her waist.

"I wish I could just let all these people disappear and we were in Hawaii at this very moment." Shawn's eyes were glistening. Monica could feel such a deepness with Shawn that sometimes frightened her and she wondered how he could have such an effect on her.

"We'll be there baby, tonight." Monica reached up and kissed him tenderly and his lips were so soft. Shawn's eyes were still closed, when she leaned away. Monica took Shawn's hand and led him out to the reception area. The reception was beautiful and as the toast was made and the first dance was to Brian McKnight's/Vanessa Williams "Love Is", romance fluttered the restaurant and the food was supreme. The photographer went to each table to produce their wedding video. Monica did the money bag dance. Monica and Shawn greeted every table to thank everyone and to take pictures. It was definitely a top notch classy affair. Shawn and Monica were acutely aware of their tight time schedule to catch their flight at 1:30pm. Monica and Shawn were looking for one another as the time was 11:45. They let their parents and sisters know that they were leaving. Shawn and Monica were seated in the Rolls Royce and away they went. The airport ride was twenty minutes at best. They arrived at the Newark airport and their luggage was checked, as well as their tickets. Monica and Shawn changed their outfits just in the nick of time to be comfortable for their trip. They had an hour layover in Los Angeles, California. The first flight was from 1:30 to 5:45pm. Then they caught the second connection and it departed at 6:45 and arrived in Kauai at 10:00 pm. Shawn and Monica should have been exhausted. Shawn actually convinced Monica to take an herbal tea recommended to calm her. He had picked up these tea bags that were good when you couldn't sleep. He had used them on occasion and knew that they had no side effects and you did not wake up groggy. He asked God to forgive him, but he wanted her to be alive and energized by the time they landed. When they came off the plane, even at 10:00, it was a beautiful serene island. Monica was up and felt like it was 6:00 instead of 10:00pm. They were able to get a taxi to their hotel, which was a secluded secret hideaway. It was a cottage, which was right on the water. The lights were opulent and all your eyes could see was magical and heavenly. There was a brilliant waterfall and the greenery and landscape were just like in the movies - flawless. Monica was perplexed, as when she made the reservations it was an oceanfront condo and this was a villa - a cottage of sorts. Shawn tipped the taxi driver and everything was brought into the cottage and Monica just looked around in confusion.

"Shawn this is absolutely unbelievable; but I did not pick this. I reserved an oceanfront condo on a segregated island. I mean, don't get me wrong-this is far nicer for us as newlyweds and on a grander scale, I'm sure." Monica looked at Shawn and he was just taking everything in and finally he spoke.

"I changed our reservations. You did so well on the budget I gave you that I wanted to surprise you. I set this up for ten days and we will have a private chef, who should be here any minute." Shawn said as a matter of fact.

"Oh Man. Shawn you are unbelievable." Shawn came and they hugged each other sideways. Monica wanted to cry, but just didn't have the strength.

"Why don't you do get comfortable?" Shawn said. Monica took her lingerie bag and Shawn took the other luggage and put them in the room, while she visited the state of the art jetted bath. The marble floors and tiles were just amazing. Monica took a quick shower, as she did not want to keep him waiting. After she put her evening wear on, she lavished her skin in the creams that were supplied to her in her elaborate powder room. The ivory colored racy laced one-piece was a deep v-neck that accentuated her cleavage and fit her like a glove. She could hear Shawn's voice and figured the chef had come to fix their meal. Monica took her matching robe to wear, since the chef was there. He greeted her and Shawn patted the seat next to him for her to sit. The chef poured them champagne. There was an interesting miniature container of what looked like a - miniature barbeque grill - the scents emitted of a sweet and sour odor, but also a seafood essence was clearly seeping through. Inside this replica barbeque grill was a porcelain pot of a delectable soup and the other pot was filled with a seafood combination of crab, shrimp, lobster and creamy sauce. On the side was succulent bread, similar to corn bread in texture. The chef also had a dessert that looked like red velvet cake - which was her favorite in the whole wide world. Shawn tasted the food and was satisfied. He advised the chef that he was okay to go.

"I made sure our first meal would not be too heavy, as we are here late. Although we crossed the time zones, our bodies don't recognize that it's 10 pm here," Shawn said. Monica just stared at Shawn.

"Is everything ok honey?" Shawn asked.

"I couldn't ask for more," Monica said. She took off her robe and Shawn changed his position in the way that he was seated. Shawn made sure that he was seated so that he could view Monica's body.

"Hmmmm. You look amazing," Shawn observed and then blessed the food. Monica sipped on the soup and the flavors were dancing on her tongue. The bread was supreme. She was full, once she ate the soup. They had a full kitchen and she told Shawn that she would have one bite of dessert and then save the rest.

"I want to make a toast to you Honey," Monica said. Shawn nodded for her to speak.

"You are not like any man that I've ever known, read about or even could hope for. I toast you, Shawn, because you are the answer to my prayers." They clicked their glasses and took a sip.

"Why don't we take our drinks and finish in the other room," Shawn said. Monica knew which other room he meant. They took their glasses and Shawn collected the bottle of champagne with them.

"I'll be right back." Shawn went into the bathroom, took one of his bags and Monica could hear him taking a shower. Monica felt an overwhelming panic attack coming upon her and she tried to calm herself, by having another glass of champagne. It helped a bit, but the nagging butterflies in her stomach did not diminish completely. Monica heard the water stop and her heart began to race and she thought for sure that Shawn could hear her heart beating, as he came back into the bedroom. Shawn stepped out of the bathroom with a white striped sheer pajama pants. Shawn looked at Monica and her facial expression looked nervous.

"Are you okay, Baby?" Shawn inquired. Shawn came closer and sat on the bed with Monica. Monica didn't know where to begin, but she gathered herself and spoke.

"I've been waiting to share something very important with you since you asked me to marry you, but it never seemed to be the right moment." Monica paused watching Shawn's demeanor. Shawn turned his whole body to focus on Monica.

"I have a secret and I pray that you won't look at me differently after I reveal it to you." Monica paused again. This time she breathed slowly. Shawn would not dare interrupt or assist her. He could sense the hushing of the Holy Spirit.

"When I was a young girl about 10 or 11, I was molested by my uncle. I told a cousin, who then went and told all the rest of the family. I was ostracized and my dad never wanted to believe it, seeing it was his brother. I've never been able to have a real intimate relationship with anyone, because of my distrust." Monica finished and bit her lip, waiting for Shawn's response. Shawn was literally in shock -he didn't know whether to be mad, hurt or what. Anger was the first emotion that emerged, then hurt. Monica could see the range of emotions that was surfacing on Shawn's face and his body grew extremely tense. She knew she had to confess the truth, but this is the reaction she feared.

"Are you telling me that you are a virgin, Monica?" Shawn managed to speak.

"I believe, yes, you could say that." Monica was shaking now. Shawn sat quietly before he spoke again. Taking Monica's right hand.

"First, I am so sorry that you experienced something that was so painful, that it left you scars and held you in a limbo like state. Secondly, I'm hurt that you did not feel comfortable enough to share this with me before. Thirdly, I need you to understand that this and nothing else can change the way I feel about you." Shawn saw the fear of rejection all over her and could tell that she was emotionally distraught, but he had to find a way to manage his own pain, alone.

"I'm going to go for a walk and I'll be right back, ok?" Shawn was being as gentle as he could muster right now. It was like the Holy Spirit was containing him in a straight jacket.

"Ok," Monica said simply.

Shawn got up, went outside, looked out to the water and walked to the beautiful ocean then sat down at the bank. He needed to talk to his Father.

"God, why would you do this to me? You never once showed me this. You let me get blindsided." Shawn thought how Monica had been holding onto this all these years and he wished he could find this guy and ... he just decided that he needed to swim. Shawn shed tears of anger with hurt intermingled. Shawn swam out several feet and then came back to the bank and let the waves of water crash on his back, as he laid face down and cupped his eyes with his hands. That's when God spoke. The Holy Spirit told him that he has prepared him for the wife that he prayed for. This is the woman that was predestined for ministry, love, friendship and much more than he could ever imagine. God told him that he allowed him to go through the last few relationships to equip him to handle Monica mentally and emotionally. God let him know that he was mandated to love and protect her, as His daughter was entrusted to him. Shawn listened and his thoughts rushed to his sexual vigor and appetite. Then God spoke in a small voice, Monica is all that he would ever need and physically he knew what to do.

Monica layed on the bed for a few minutes, but her tears and sobs were drowning her. She didn't know when Shawn would come back. She thought that he may annul the marriage, after all no sex had happened yet. Monica was sick in her soul and started throwing up in the bathroom, because of the stress. Then God spoke.

"Why do you fret? I love you Daughter and so does your Husband that I gave you. Go outside and meet him." Monica looked at her face in the mirror and she was a mess. She washed her face and put eye drops in her eyes to get rid of the redness. She put on some lip gloss and went. She went to the open porch like area and could see Shawn lying down face first. Monica moved towards Shawn. As Monica came closer, Shawn sat up and could see her silhouette frame coming from the cottage. She looked like a dream walking to him. Shawn waited for her to come to him.

"Will you swim with me?" Monica asked boldly. Shawn nodded and they held hands and swam out together. Monica turned on her back to float a bit and Shawn pulled her and she stood up, her feet scarcely hitting the bottom of the ocean. Shawn was 6' 3 and was able to stand in that part of the water. Monica grabbed onto Shawn and began to kiss him. She held onto Shawn's neck and he molded his body to hers holding her waist. Monica felt an excitement running up her inner thighs. Monica's body flowed against his. Monica's dress was molded onto her figure eight body. Shawn lifted Monica up and carried her to the shore and continued until they reached the porch area. Their clothes were soaked and Shawn removed his sheer pajamas and Monica wanted to turn away, but couldn't. Monica lifted her dress to remove it over her head as Shawn watched. He looked at how beautiful and delicate her chest was as she lifted the dress off. Shawn was hungry for Monica, but he maintained himself. Shawn carried Monica into the bedroom, wearing his boxers. Monica was wearing a white lacey thong that contrasted her caramel toned skin. Monica took the liberty of removing Shawn's briefs. Shawn could barely contain himself and watched as she removed her thong. She moved her body up on the bed to make room for him. The lights in the room were made dimmer. Monica was filled with anticipation. Not wanting to put his full body weight on her, he rested on his left side while hovering over Monica. Monica reached up and touched Shawn's face.

"In our future, I promise to open up more to you," she said. Shawn was so deeply in love with Monica, that he just kissed her hand and held it.

"Monica, I love you more than you can probably understand. I want you to know I'm going to make you feel things that you have never felt. Don't be afraid or run from it," Shawn explained.

"Ok." Monica nodded. Monica kissed him and rubbed his chest tantalizingly. Their lips and tongues melted into one another, they entered a zone and Shawn could feel his members yearning for her. Monica felt Shawn's intensity, she wrapped her left leg around Shawn's hip. She didn't know if she could handle him, or even bring him any satisfaction, but she was willing to do whatever it took. Shawn could feel that Monica was framing her body to accept him. As he grazed her with his movements, her body followed his rhythm. Shawn wanted to push her to the point where she could no longer wait.

"Baby..." Monica panted.

"Yes." Shawn could see that she was almost to that pressure point, but in order for her body to be receptive, she would still have to endure pain initially.

"Please Shawn," was all Monica could say, under the fire that her body was enveloped by. Shawn placed his circumference there in her femininity. Monica was moving her body to receive him.

Shawn whispered. "I want you to relax as much as possible. The pleasure will override the pain later," Shawn said, as he began to go higher into her. Monica's head went back, once she felt a stinging like a knife breaking her skin as she cried out. Shawn held the curve of her back and roundness of her cheeks, while he made gentle explorations. Monica was holding her breath, and then tightened her muscles.

"Relax, Baby, you have to let me in," Shawn pleaded with her.

"Do you trust me?" Shawn looked into Monica's eyes.

"Yes." Monica's eyes were filled with big tears. Shawn continued, until he noticed an opening leading to more fluidity. Monica was squeezing him ever so tight. Shawn was after that perfect place that held a certain plateau for Monica. Monica began to give in more and more and Shawn was able to get into her at greater depths. Monica started taking short breaths and Shawn knew she was feeling the waves of ecstatic vibrations. He began riding the waves and seeking, reaching the next body of sensation. He studied Monica and she had finally allowed her body to fully receive and felt her beginning to have volcanic pleasures. Shawn was taking it as slow as possible and Monica wrapped her other leg around him, as if to keep from falling. Shawn began to feel Monica's inner body tighten its grip and he knew what was coming, as he himself was trying to hold back; but now, there was no reason to. Shawn let himself be at one with Monica and they both let out love sounds, as currents of pure passion boiled over onto them. Shawn lay partially on his side and on Monica. They lay silently for a few minutes, as their heart beats slowed down. Shawn used his hand to wipe Monica's hair from her face.

"Are you alright?" He kissed her forehead. Her warm brown eyes answered for her. "Yes, Baby," Monica said.

"I'll be right back." Shawn went into the bathroom and turned the tub faucet on. He called Monica into the bathroom and they took their first bath together. Shawn lay with his back resting on the jetted tub. Monica was facing his chest. Her hands massaged his body, while he meditated for a moment.

"Have you ever had a climax before?" Shawn asked purposefully.

"Not really," Monica stated. Monica felt a little embarrassed talking about it.

"Monica, you're my wife now. I want us to enjoy each other fully and be able to communicate freely," Shawn said. Monica turned sideways as Shawn spoke. Shawn had an undeniable sexy and sensual quality and she just wanted to explode every time she looked at him.

"Did you enjoy me, Shawn?" Monica's eyes resembled a wide eyed teenager. Shawn's dimples reappeared, as he looked like he was visualizing it.

"Very much," He said.

"Are you sure?" Monica said it with a girlish charm. Shawn leaned over now, peering into Monica's face.

"I can show you better than I can tell you," Shawn said to Monica.

"In fact, let's finish up here." Shawn took a bath sponge and washed Monica's body and could sense her body temperature rising for him. Monica joined Shawn when he stood up and washed him. She was amazed that he could fit himself into her inner frame, viewing his body. Shawn took a towel and dried off. He went back into the bedroom and removed the used covers from the bed and remade the bed. Monica put her lotion and oil on, while the water drained from the tub and then she cleaned it. Looking in the mirror, it was like she was looking at a different person. Monica came back in the room wearing her white baby doll lingerie, with matching thong. Shawn's eyes followed Monica's every move. Monica sat on the bed and gave him a come hither look. Shawn's excitement could not be hidden. Monica climbed on top of Shawn and he was pleasantly surprised that Monica felt comfortable with that. They kissed and caressed each other and Monica managed to accept a fraction of Shawn, while she was in that position. Shawn wanted more and took her by the hips and placed her on her backside. Now, he would show her what he meant by his reply in the bathroom. Shawn's lips went to places that brought tears to Monica. Now her body craved him.

"Shawn," Monica mumbled. He was enthralled in the moment. Shawn knew Monica was aching to come into contact with him and he wouldn't delay any longer. Entering the passageway to Monica was so blissful and Shawn took each second deliberately. Within a short time, Monica was bathed with tiny droplets of perspiration. The heat from her was like an oven. Shawn instinctively knew that her body was ready to release.

"Baby," Shawn spoke softly. Monica's eyes met Shawn's. So much pleasure flooded her body that she shuttered, weeping uncontrollably. Shawn seized the moment and he reaped every bit of pulsation that her body yielded him-while he gave of himself piece by piece. Monica was amazed that she had missed out on this all those years but she was grateful to have waited to share it with Shawn.

"I love you Shawn," Monica expressed.

"I love you more," Shawn affirmed. Shawn lay there holding Monica and he understood what God had promised was true. She was more than enough woman for him mentally, spiritually, emotionally and physically. Lying there, they wondered about what else was in store for them. Only time would tell in their happily ever after days.

ISBN:
ISBN-13:

ABOUT THE AUTHOR

Joyce Stewart is a freelance writer and poet, who is currently employed by Cablevision Systems in Long Island, New York. She at one time considered studying law but after she tried working as a paralegal realized that she was more interested in creative writing. During her short career choice as a legal assistant, it was then that she discovered her gift and love for writing poetry.

Joyce is passionate about relationships and marriage. She believes that God has ordained marriage and uses love to keep order and submission between the two. She considers God as the ultimate romantic because as she puts it, He rescued us by sending a ransom in the form of Jesus.